A
KILLER'S
WIFE

ALSO BY VICTOR METHOS

A
KILLER'S
WIFE

VICTOR METHOS

THOMAS & MERCER

Published by Thomas & Mercer, Seattle

www.apub.com

Amazon, the Amazon logo, and Thomas & Mercer are trademarks of Amazon.com, Inc., or its affiliates.

ISBN-13: 9781542003919 (hardcover)
ISBN-10: 1542003911 (hardcover)

ISBN-13: 9781542003896 (paperback)
ISBN-10: 154200389X (paperback)

Cover design by Christopher Lin

Printed in the United States of America

First edition

What is revealed to us as the conscious mind is no
more than a flicker in the flames of the subconscious.
Beneath our awareness lies a forest of terrors, of all
the darkness of nature. In rare individuals, these
ghostly drives break free, and monsters climb out of
the abyss.

—*The Psychopathology of the Subconscious Drives*,
by Dr. Nicolas H. Lagrand, as translated from
the French by Harold Martin

1

Jordan Russo swung the passenger door open and leapt from the moving car.

The first thing she felt was the hot sting of asphalt against her bare legs. It scraped the skin off her knees and thighs, pain flooding her body as though she had been set on fire.

She would've screamed, but the road had knocked the breath out of her. She tasted blood pooling in her mouth and tongued the jagged edges where teeth had broken with the impact.

When she tried to sit up, a blinding agony, like being stabbed with knives all over her body, made her wonder if she'd fractured ribs. But she forced herself to sit up anyway, wincing from the pain.

She looked around. This far into the Nevada desert, there was nothing but clear blue sky, red rocks, sand dunes, and cacti for miles.

A screeching noise from in front of her. The car had slammed on its brakes.

"No," she muttered, nearly sobbing.

She pushed herself to her feet, and instantly her right leg gave way. She braced herself against the pain, stood again, and hobbled toward the large rock formation across the nearest sand dune.

Jordan looked behind her as the driver got out of the car.

"No, no . . ."

She forced herself to run, stumbling twice. She was crying now, thinking of her mother. If she died here, her mother would be completely alone in that big house and would never find out what had happened to her.

Her leg gave out again just as she reached a boulder near the formation, and she collapsed against it, using it for balance as she scrambled behind it. There was a small nook between the rocks—the opening wasn't large, but maybe it was enough . . .

She got down on all fours and forced her body through the small opening, the boulders scraping her skin and squeezing her injured ribs. The pain was so overwhelming she had to cover her mouth to stifle a scream.

The nook was the size of a closet. She wedged herself against the rocks and looked up. A narrow space between the boulders let in a stream of sunlight. Her hands trembled as she reached into her pocket and took out her cell phone. The screen was shattered, but it was on.

"Please," she whispered, "please please please . . ."

No bars were showing. She dialed 911, and it wouldn't go through. Every bit of strength left her with the silence on the other end of the phone.

Footsteps crunched on the sand outside.

She gasped and covered her mouth, her eyes wet with tears as urine soaked through her shorts and dripped down her torn and bleeding legs.

A hand lunged through the opening and grabbed her ankle.

"No! Help me! Please, somebody help me!"

She felt a violent tug that nearly ripped her leg from the hip socket. Her fingers clawed at the ground, grasping nothing but loose sand. With one powerful yank, she was pulled out into the hot sun, screaming as the shadow fell over her.

2

A scream pierced the silence of the courtroom.

Jessica Yardley leaned back against the witness box as the defendant, Donald Burrow, surged across the defense table. Yardley could see the rage in him, the pure hatred. For a moment, everyone, even the defense attorney, froze. No one was stopping him.

All at once, the normal speed of the courtroom resumed. A bailiff tackled Burrow at the waist. Another jumped on him and slammed a knee into the man's back, yanking his arms up behind him at a sharp angle as the pen he'd grabbed as a weapon fell from his hand.

Yardley exhaled, though she hadn't realized she'd been holding her breath.

The judge rapped his gavel, calling for calm. Yardley turned to the young woman on the stand, a high school student Burrow had locked in his cellar for two days before she'd managed to escape and call the police. She was trembling, used tissues wadded up in her palms. Yardley took her hand and said, "He can't hurt you anymore."

The judge bellowed, "Counselors, approach."

Yardley and Martin Salinger approached the judge. The judge turned the microphone off and said, "I'm sure you have a motion, Mr. Salinger."

"Obviously we need a mistrial, Judge. There is no way this jury is going to be impartial after seeing that."

Yardley's brows rose. "I disagree," she said. "In *Oregon v. Kennedy*, the Supreme Court made clear mistrials are there to protect defendants against prejudicial behavior by the prosecution or the bench, not from their own behavior. Otherwise, whenever a trial is going poorly, a defendant could just attack somebody with a pen and get a new trial."

The judge nodded. "Ms. Yardley is correct. Let's get back on the record and make it official."

"Your Honor," Salinger pleaded, "you might as well just string up my client now, because there is no way that jury is going to be impartial."

Yardley said, "Then maybe tell him not to attack people in front of them next time."

"I've made my ruling, Mr. Salinger, and you will be free to appeal it. Please step back."

The moment court adjourned for the day, Salinger leaned across the aisle. "The plea offer still on the table?" he said. "Thirty years?"

"It is."

"Gimme half an hour, then. Thanks for keeping it open. A lotta prosecutors wouldn't."

"I'm not vindictive, Martin. Believe it or not, I'm here to protect his rights, too."

Her phone vibrated just then. She raised a hand to signal to Salinger that she'd wait to hear from him. When she glanced at the caller ID, her stomach dropped harder than it had when Burrow had come at her: it was her daughter's school.

She answered and said, "What did Tara do now?"

"I really think it best you speak with Mr. Jackson." Denise, the high school secretary, had a voice that managed to sound simultaneously compassionate and angry. "Tara is in his office right now. Can you come down?"

"All right, give me half an hour."

She lifted her leather satchel and stood to leave when she saw two men in dark suits lingering at the back of the courtroom. One wore the laminated ID badge of an agent with the Federal Bureau of Investigation clipped to a loop on the front of his slacks, to make getting in and out of court with his firearm easier. He had shoulder-length hair and scruff, something she knew his SAC in Las Vegas had criticized him for several times but which he wore as a badge of honor now. Cason Baldwin had on more than one occasion said to her, "Screw J. Edgar Hoover and his yuppies."

The man standing with Baldwin was short and squat, Hispanic, with the faded blemish of an old, partially removed tattoo jutting out from his right sleeve.

"Thirty years for luring that girl into his car outside a church and doing what he did after?" Baldwin said as she approached. "That seems like a life sentence if I ever saw it."

She grinned. He still looked the same as when they'd briefly dated, long ago as that had been. "Justice applies equally to everyone, or it doesn't apply to anyone. That was the time the sentencing matrix determined, so that's what I gave him."

"It calculated that because he's a first-time offender, but he's still scum."

"He has rights, too, just like everyone else. I won't take that away from him."

Baldwin chuckled. "You always did have that soft heart." He glanced at the other man and said, "This is Oscar Ortiz. Oscar, Jessica."

Ortiz got a text message just then and looked down to the phone in his hand as he said, "Hey."

Yardley stepped to the side as the family of Donald Burrow brushed past her to get through the double doors. Most of them didn't look at her, but his mother stared directly at her with red, wet eyes and said, "I hope you have a son and the same thing happens to him so you feel what it's like to know your boy is gonna die in a cage."

Yardley waited quietly as they filed out.

"Pff, whatever," Ortiz said when they'd left. "Tell your son to quit pissing off God, and won't nothin' happen to him."

Baldwin looked at him a moment and then turned to Yardley and said, "Can we talk?"

"I can't. Tara's school just called and I need to be down there."

"It'll just be a second."

"My car's parked underground. I suppose we can talk on the way."

"No. I'd like to talk in private. If we can. I promise it won't take long."

Ortiz's expression was intense, too. Yardley glanced from one to the other. Anything mundane could've been handled with a phone call. Being here in person—Baldwin had something to ask her that he knew she wouldn't like.

"All right. I've only got a few minutes, though."

———

The Second Street federal courthouse in Las Vegas was a square steel-and-glass building of four stories referred to by some of the staff as the Borg Cube, a reference Yardley didn't understand.

The attorney/client rooms were large, with brown oak tables and windows that looked out to the palm tree–lined streets. Yardley sat down and placed her satchel on the floor. Ortiz shut the door.

"So you nailed the Green Street Kidnapper," Baldwin said. "That's a pretty big case to settle. That neighborhood is lucky Burrow hadn't moved on to killing anyone."

"That girl deserves the credit for finding a way to escape. Just ask me, Cason."

"Ask what?"

"You want to ask me something you're nervous I'll say no to. That's why you're here in person, in the afternoon, when you know I'm most eager to go home and just might say yes for convenience. So let's not waste time. Just ask."

He cleared his throat and glanced at Ortiz, who looked amused that she could so easily read him. Baldwin unlocked his iPad and slid it over to her.

A photo of a couple in a bedroom, taken from the foot of the bed. A female with long brunette hair in a black tank top and green panties, the male next to her in black boxer shorts. Both of them were facedown. The white duvet was soaked with dark blood. The wall above their heads had arterial spray that looked like something a hyper child would do with a can of paint, and Yardley knew their throats had been slit.

A shot of ice went through her, and she gasped quietly, though she couldn't be sure the men hadn't heard. She had seen this scene before. Seen it multiple times. The memories had, over time, turned amazingly thin and indistinct, but now, in a flash, many of them filled her. The most prominent was that of her ex-husband, Eddie Cal, standing in front of her in the kitchen of their one-bedroom apartment. Sirens wailing outside as the boots of a SWAT team stormed up the cement stairs to the second floor, her stomach swollen with their child, and him gently placing his hands on her shoulders and saying, "I'm so sorry. I tried to stop."

Those were the last words they had ever spoken to each other, and they surfaced in her mind from almost sixteen years ago as if she had just heard them.

"Sophia and Adrian Dean," Baldwin said. "They were found about a month ago in their home in North Las Vegas." He paused. "They have two children, three and seven. They're the ones that discovered them in the morning. They slept through what happened to their parents, which means—"

"Why are you showing me this, Cason?" she said.

He glanced at Ortiz again and then swiped to the next photo on the iPad. If not for the clothing, it could've almost been the same photo. A brunette with long hair facedown in a bed, gray sheets this time instead of white, and a man wearing basketball shorts and what had once been a white T-shirt.

"Ryan and Aubrey Olsen. They were found two days ago in their home in St. George, Utah. You'll notice the blood patterns are—"

"Much worse," she said coolly as she slid the iPad back to him.

"Yeah."

"I still don't understand why you're showing these to me."

Baldwin and Ortiz glanced at each other, Ortiz as though he were embarrassed to be there.

"We think it's a copycat of Eddie, Jess. And we need your help."

3

Yardley looked down again at the photograph of the Olsens. They were caked in blood, from their throats and shoulders to their arms and backs. Aubrey's hair was matted and dark with it. Ryan's head was tilted slightly to the side, and she could see one glassy eye staring at nothing. Like the eyes of fish in the summer open-air markets they sometimes had in Santa Monica, where she'd grown up.

"Not my division. You got a collar, you take it to screening and—"

"No, no collar. In fact . . . we don't have much to go on."

"We don't have shit," Ortiz interjected.

Baldwin looked down at the photo.

He's not taking back his iPad or letting it sleep, she thought. *He wants me to keep looking at it. He's desperate.*

"Oscar's not wrong," Baldwin said. "We have nothing. And when I say nothing, I mean nothing. There was no sexual assault here, no break-in, nothing missing that we could tell. With the first one, North Las Vegas PD thought it could be anything. Business partner pissed off about money, revenge, lover one of them was having an affair with . . . but when someone with St. George PD recognized the scene and called them, they knew. And they called us. I didn't even recognize the kill signature at first, and then last night I was pinning some photos of the Deans up on the board at the federal building, and I remembered where

I had seen it. I pulled up photos of Eddie's scenes, and they're almost identical."

"Almost?"

"The females aren't nude here, obviously, because there's no sexual assault. And he closes the bedroom doors when he leaves. Eddie never did that." He put his hands on the table and interlaced his fingers. "Jessica, I need your help with this. Nobody knows Eddie's case better than you."

Yardley remembered that Eddie Cal's last appeal would be decided soon and then his execution scheduled. She wished it had already happened.

"I'm assuming you're joking," she said, staring at Baldwin. "I am the last person that knows anything about Eddie Cal. And this is not my department, Cason. You're the investigators. When you got something, bring it to screening, and if they assign me the case, I'll take a look and we'll work it. Until you get a collar or at least a person of interest, there's nothing I can do. Why do you even have this case? Without rape there's no federal crime. Let the local police departments handle it."

"Adrian Dean was a systems information officer for the DEA. He sat at a desk and did coding and programing, training other people, things like that, but he was technically federal law enforcement, so I picked up the case myself. I figured we can add the Olsens to the same case and . . ." He paused a moment. "And anyone who comes after."

She kept calm and tried to remain motionless, but her stomach was twisting into knots, and she had begun sweating. Law enforcement was a machismo patriarchy; she had fought her entire career as a federal prosecutor to make sure none of them ever saw a hint of weakness. One of her supervisors, a woman who had retired at fifty and owned a restaurant now, had advised her: "Show your feelings, and you're just an emotional woman that can't be trusted. Don't show them, and you're an icy bitch that can't be trusted. Take your pick."

"There's something else, Jess," Baldwin said. "I've never even read about a scene so completely clean. I had the evidence response team go through that place for twelve hours. Nothing. We can't even tell what kind of blade he used because he ripped the wounds open wider to hide it."

Ortiz added, "They're three weeks apart. So we got about two and a half weeks until the next one, if he's not speeding it up or anything. I mean, he could just stop, I guess, but we don't think so. Right? I mean, you know this type of thing."

"I *know* it?"

Baldwin glanced between them. "He didn't mean it like that. He just meant with your education and experience, you have some insights that could be helpful."

She chuckled mirthlessly now. "You have crowds of PhDs and psychiatrists to help you. You don't need me."

"Yeah, they wanna help. They wanna help so they can get their faces in the news. Not to catch *him.*"

Yardley picked up her satchel and stood. "Sorry. I'm not an investigator. I'm a prosecutor. Find a person of interest, and let me know when you need warrants. Other than that, I can't help."

She left the room and waited until she heard the click of the door closing before she pressed her hand to the wall and leaned against it, sucking in air as though she were breathing through sand.

Eddie Cal.

He had been a painter and sculptor by trade. The type of man that always wore jeans and T-shirts spattered with different-colored paints. She had loved that about him—his indifference to what other people thought of him. She'd found it alluring.

Only later, after his murders had come to light, did she realize it wasn't something he did consciously. He was, in a very real sense, unable to believe that other human beings existed separate from his experience of them. That they had their own opinions and emotions separate from his. *They're just longer pigs,* Eddie had once joked about art critics. Now she knew he'd meant it to apply to the whole human race. Had she, too, just appeared like a longer pig to the man she'd allowed into her heart?

She closed her eyes and took two large breaths, and when she opened her eyes, the calm veneer had returned. On her way out of the courthouse, one of the marshals wished her a good night, and she kept her gaze straight ahead, pretending not to hear him.

4

White Sands High School was a newer building made of glass and steel. The county wanted to appear modern and had taken out a bond to build a school with all the amenities, including several computer labs with the latest Apple computers as well as a library that put the public library to shame. In the hall that led to the front office, posters hung on the walls. Announcements for musicals and plays, artwork by the graphic design students, a notice about an upcoming dance.

Yardley remembered her high school years vividly. Her father had abandoned her and her mother when she was thirteen, and her mother had gotten drunk most days to cope. Her income went from full time to part time and eventually to unemployment and welfare disbursements. Yardley began working at fourteen, bagging groceries and selling fruit on the side of the road. High school was her only reprieve from real life, and the chance to read Chaucer or study anatomy excited her. She had few friends and even fewer boys interested in her, but she was content where she was: studying nights after a shift at the grocery store and taking care of her mother when she came home from the bars after blowing her unemployment check.

Her mother had drunk herself to death when Yardley was eighteen. She remembered the cold rain at the funeral, that it had cost Yardley her entire savings to even have one, and that no one had shown up but her. She had an aunt somewhere that had sent a card, and one of the neighbors had asked Yardley if she needed anything, but other than that, it was as if her mother had never existed. The thought that you could live a long life and have no one remember you had terrified Yardley to her core.

At the front office, she asked for the vice-principal, and a receptionist led her back to where Tara sat in the hall, her eyes calmly taking everything in. Nothing slipping past their notice. Every once in a while, those deep sapphire eyes sent a small shock through Yardley. She had only seen eyes that blue in one other person: Tara's father.

Cody Jackson, a slim man with wire-frame glasses and a bow tie, rose from his desk and shook her hand. He asked them both to step inside his office. Yardley noticed the sway when Tara stood, a slow drifting in circles of the body caused by the unbalancing effects of alcohol, indicating her daughter would fail the Romberg test, a test commonly employed by police to determine if someone had been drinking.

"I don't know what to say," Yardley said when they were seated.

Jackson nodded and kept his eyes on Tara. "Her chemistry teacher noticed the odor of alcohol. When she was confronted, she grew quite agitated. At one point we thought she might turn violent, but instead she vomited in the hallway. I've had her at the nurse's office since. The nurse determined an ambulance wasn't necessary, though I was close to calling one."

Yardley stared at her daughter, who wouldn't look at her. "It's the middle of the afternoon, Tara."

She shrugged.

"Where did you get the alcohol?"

"A friend."

"What friend?"

She shrugged again.

Yardley lifted Tara's chin and made her daughter look at her. "What. Friend."

She pulled her face away.

14

Yardley turned to Jackson and said, "This will never, ever happen again, I can assure you. She won't have the means for it to happen again because she is grounded the rest of the semester, and her phone is going to be shut off."

Tara shouted, "What! You can't do that."

"Watch me," Yardley said calmly.

Tara folded her arms and shook her head. "You're such a bitch."

Yardley felt the anger flare in her stomach. It rose hot into her face, but if not for the clench of her jaw muscles, no one would have been able to tell she had any reaction.

"What's her punishment, Cody?"

"She nearly struck a teacher in anger. I think a three-week suspension is appropriate. As well as cleaning the halls one day with the staff after school to make up for the time it took for them to clean up her mess. I'll have to put a letter in her file as well, and she'll be on probation when she returns to school. By rights, I could expel her, but because of her excellent academics, I'm willing to cut her a break."

Yardley knew Tara didn't study; she could listen to a few lectures and ace her exams. Her intelligence was both astonishing and unsettling. At the age of five, she'd explained Heisenberg's uncertainty principle to Yardley at the dinner table. At seven, Yardley had caught her reading Nietzsche on the balcony of their home.

Several teachers had urged Yardley to let her skip a few grades or put her in a gifted school, but she had refused.

Occasionally, thinking about Tara's intelligence sent a chill down Yardley's back. School for Yardley, though enjoyable, had been a colossal amount of work. Tara had inherited her father's intelligence: Eddie Cal had an IQ of 175.

"Tara," Jackson said, "will you please wait outside?" When she'd left, he said, "She doesn't belong here, Jessica. Ms. McCombs caught her doodling in her class the other day. She thought it was drawings, but Tara was working out mathematics problems in vector spaces and scalars. I had to google what those were, and I still don't understand them. And she's already gone through all the AP classes we offer and taken all the college credit we can give. We simply cannot challenge someone like her here. She's bored and acting out. She needs to be in a gifted school or test directly into a university. Probably a graduate program at a university."

Yardley shook her head. "You know our background. It took me so long, Cody, *so* long, just to give her a semblance of a normal life. I don't want her feeling like an outcast in any way; that's why I've never pursued that for her. Besides, for the first time in her life, she has friends. She doesn't want to go anywhere else."

Jackson sighed and folded his hands on the desk. "There's two paths someone with her caliber of intellect can go. If they receive love and support and the correct amount of intellectual challenge, they can become an Albert Einstein or a Steve Jobs. If they're bored and their mind is left to find its own amusement, they will become a—"

"If you say Eddie Cal—"

"No," he said, shaking his head. "I was going to say Billy Mackerus. He's a gentleman I sometimes see begging for change outside a restaurant near my home. He was a professor of philosophy, working on theories I can't even pronounce, and now he's in and out of drug rehabilitation centers and jail. His mind went toward the second path. Tara needs to be challenged, and I can't give her that challenge with the resources I have."

Yardley nodded. "Thank you for calling me, Cody. I'll make sure this doesn't happen again." She rose, and once outside the office, she said to Tara, "Let's go."

When they were in the car, Yardley held out her hand. "Phone."

"Mom, I'm sorry I said that. It was just—"

"Phone."

Tara hesitated and then took the phone out of her pocket and handed it to Yardley, who put it into her purse. She drove them home in complete silence. Tara kept her arms folded across her chest the entire time.

When they parked in the driveway, Yardley finally asked, "Was it Kevin?"

"It doesn't matter."

"It matters to me. Who was it?"

"I told him to get it. It wasn't his idea."

"How did he get it?"

Tara didn't say anything.

"I swear to you, Tara, I will call one of my friends at the FBI and have Kevin investigated today. They can have a talk with him about supplying alcohol to minors."

Tara stared at her in silence.

Yardley pulled out her phone and began dialing.

"Wait, Mom. Don't. I don't want to get him in trouble."

"He's already in trouble. Who?"

"His . . . his dad."

"His dad?"

She nodded. "His dad is laid back like that."

Yardley shook her head. She exhaled and said, "I have to go back to work. I want you in the house. No friends over and no going out without my permission. If you go out without asking me first, I'm increasing your grounding to two semesters, and I'll just throw your phone in the garbage. Are we clear?"

Tara nodded and went to open her door.

"And Tara? If you *ever* call me a bitch again, I will pull you out of school and homeschool you myself. You won't see your friends again until you turn eighteen and move out. Do you understand me?" Tara nodded. "I need to hear it. Do you understand?"

"Yes, I understand." She got out and slammed the door. Yardley rubbed her temples for a minute, a headache pushing its way forward from behind her eyes.

She had to remind herself sometimes that Tara might share traits with Eddie Cal, but she was nothing like him. Not in any of the important ways, not in the ways that made her Yardley's daughter.

Once Tara was inside, Yardley took a deep breath and pulled out of the driveway.

5

Yardley attempted to focus on her existing cases, but her mind kept drifting to a couple lying in a bed, blood-soaked clothing sticking to pale flesh. Yardley wondered if the Olsens had watched each other die or if one of them had passed too quickly for that.

The sun was going down by the time she headed home.

White Sands, Nevada, was forty minutes from the downtown courthouse and federal building in Las Vegas where she worked. Yardley had wanted someplace far enough away that work and home couldn't meld into each other.

Her home sat on a hill overlooking the valley, with thick glass for walls to allow in the most sunlight possible. A vast expanse of empty desert surrounded the neighborhood, and farther out, on clear nights, she could see the iridescent glow of the Las Vegas Strip.

When she walked into the one-story home, she heard music blaring from Tara's room. Yardley tried her bedroom door, and it was locked.

Yardley reached up to knock but then dropped her hand. What would be the point? Tara was both more intelligent and more stubborn than her. She could hold a grudge seemingly forever. Yardley wondered if sons were as difficult to raise as daughters.

Wesley stood over two plates of crab with mashed potatoes and a bottle of wine in the kitchen. He wore a polo shirt, and his gold watch gleamed in the setting sun. In his unobtrusive Tennessee accent, he said, "Rough day?"

She put her satchel down and sat on one of the barstools at the island in the kitchen. Since Wesley had moved in a few months ago, she'd been spoiled with homemade dinners every night. "Yes, and they seem to be getting more frequent." She sighed. "I don't like that boy she hangs out with. I don't trust him."

He shrugged as he put some garnish on the mashed potatoes. "Did your mother ever trust your boyfriends at that age?"

"My mother couldn't be pulled away from the bars long enough to notice I had boyfriends." She dipped a finger in the gravy and licked it off. "Tara has no idea what's out there. What men see when they look at her. She doesn't understand what people are really like."

He took her hand and kissed it. "*You* are a great mother. And *she*, despite the rough edges, is a great kid. Don't sweat it. Plus we choose who to become, don't we? She'll choose right. Just give her time. Now let's eat before this crab gets cold."

———

They sat at the table on the balcony, overlooking the desert. The sun had set, and the stars took its place, a sparkling blanket in the vast blackness above them.

They drank good white wine and ate crab as Wesley told her about his day. A law professor at the University of Nevada, he spent the day teaching classes and a couple of hours afterward as a volunteer mentor, supervising interns and young attorneys at the Guardian ad Litem's Office, an office set up to protect children in the court system.

Most guardian ad litems dealt with divorce cases, representing the children during nasty custody disputes, but Wesley worked on only those cases where neither parent was fit to take the child. If both parents were deemed unfit for custody, he became the de facto guardian and helped the courts determine what would be best for the child: to live with a relative or to be placed into foster care. His passion for the helpless and underprivileged was one of the reasons Yardley had fallen in love with him.

They'd met at the law school when Wesley had taught her second-year legal research class. She'd found him exciting. He was handsome—all the girls in class thought so—but his mind was what attracted her. He had an ability to break complex problems into simple components and explain them in ways anybody could understand. To Yardley, simplicity was the highest form of elegance. From then on, any course Professor Wesley Paul taught, she took. Whether she needed the credits or not.

What followed was the typical cliché: she became his teaching assistant and slowly got to know him. After she graduated, they stayed close, having occasional lunches and dinners as well as drinks on stressful days. There was even one weekend together in Yellowstone when Yardley's date—Cason Baldwin, ironically—fell through. Wesley insisted on sleeping on the couch.

But after years of friendship, Wesley finally told her that despite her reverting to her maiden name, cutting her hair short, and never speaking about her past, he knew who she was, knew her background with Eddie Cal, and had waited for her to reach a place where she could begin thinking about a relationship again. That patience spoke volumes to her.

After Cal, she had resolved to never be in a relationship again. To never hand her heart over to someone that could laugh while crushing it. But Wesley had been kind to her from the moment they'd met. He was intellectual, but intellectual about practical matters like law and politics rather than art or architecture like Cal. Where Eddie Cal was tall and muscular, Wesley was shorter and more rotund. In many ways, he was Cal's polar opposite. They'd begun dating a year ago, and he'd moved in with her and Tara nine months later.

"You haven't heard a word I've said, have you?" Wesley asked.

She touched his hand in apology. "That obvious?"

"What are you thinking about?"

She sighed, then sipped her wine and watched the headlights of a car winding down the canyon road ahead. "Do you remember Cason Baldwin? That agent that worked the Boulevard Rapist case with me?"

He nodded as he kicked his shoes off and leaned back in the seat. "The gentleman you dated before me?"

She grinned. "That's the one."

"Nice guy. Looks more like he should be smoking pot in a band than a federal agent, though. He should look the part if he wants to be taken seriously. What about him?"

"He came and saw me today." She hesitated. "He wants help with something."

"Yeah? Exciting case?"

"He thinks there's a copycat of Eddie Cal."

Wesley stayed silent a long time. So long that she looked at him to make sure he had actually heard her.

"What does he want with you?" he finally said.

"He wants my help. There've been two couples, one in North Vegas and one down in St. George. Three weeks apart. He thinks there'll be more."

"You're a prosecutor. What do you have to do with it?"

"That's what I told him. He says I have insight into it because of Eddie."

He snorted. "That's ridiculous. You told him to shove it, right?"

"Yes, I turned him down." She hesitated longer than she meant to and knew he had picked up on it.

"But you're thinking about it."

"I'm not."

"Yes you are. You can't lie to me, Jessica."

She exhaled loudly and watched the way the moonlight reflected in her wineglass. "Something about it . . . just . . . I don't know. I don't *have* to think about it anymore. It's a choice if I want to or not. I feel like I have power over it after almost sixteen years. Maybe I could contribute something."

"I know you deny how much Eddie influenced you. You think your choices have always been your own, but it's difficult for a person to look at themselves objectively. You were a photographer before Eddie, and then a year after his arrest you're in a master's program for forensic psychology, and then law school, and now, you're not only a prosecutor but a prosecutor that specializes in domestic violence and sex crimes. Do you really believe that episode of your life doesn't have power over you? And I'm not saying your life is a reaction—it's not. I'm proud of everything you've done; what you've accomplished is amazing. But this is not where your mind needs to go. After so long, why would you want to risk going backward?"

She swallowed a sip of wine. "I know you've told me a million times I'm not responsible, my therapist told me a million times I'm not responsible, the victims' families told me I'm not responsible . . . but I feel responsible. I was his wife, Wesley. I was his *wife*. There were signs everywhere, and I was blind."

"Yeah, there were signs. All of them after. Hindsight is like that. It tricks your brain into thinking life is predictable. It's not. Eddie Cal was one of those rare freaks of nature that are born every few years that look and act human. You can kiss them and feel their lips or talk to them and think they're sympathizing with you, but they're blank inside. A black hole. They simply are not there. No one in your position would've done anything different than you."

"You can tell me that all you want, I can even force myself to believe it sometimes, but the feelings don't go away. Feeling is a type of intelligence, too. I feel like I could've stopped it."

"And what, helping Baldwin with this is some type of redemption? It won't work. It won't change how you feel . . . and I'm scared of what it will do to you." He glanced out over the desert. "You had another nightmare last night. You started thrashing around like you were fighting someone. It only lasted a few seconds, but it was there. Do you really not believe those episodes are your mind telling you something? Do you think this will alleviate what you feel?"

She said nothing.

"Will you do me one favor? Will you talk to your therapist about it? I think she'll say the same thing as me: Don't do it. Don't go backward."

She sipped her wine and got the distinct impression that Wesley already knew she had made up her mind to at least look at the case.

After dinner, she called Baldwin's private cell phone.

6

Baldwin emailed her the files and let the detectives at the St. George PD know that she would be heading down there tonight. An officer would meet her at the Olsens' home.

"You sure, Jess?" Baldwin said over the phone as she was driving. "I don't want you to do something you don't want to do."

"You brought it to me hoping that's exactly what would happen, Cason. Don't hide behind fake sympathy now. Besides, I'm just looking. I haven't decided to help you yet."

The highway was empty, with the exception of a few cars and semis speeding up through the canyons from Nevada into Utah. During the day, the drive could be lovely for someone fond of deserts, which she was, but at night there was only empty blackness. Blackness and the shadowy monstrosities where mountains stood in daylight.

St. George wasn't far, and Yardley found the Olsens' home quickly. The city sat in a flat valley encircled by red rock mountains and sand dunes. Yardley thought it looked like a massive bowl.

The home was perched on a cliff overlooking the city. From this angle she could see the white eastern facade of the Mormon temple in the center of the city.

She parked at the curb behind the patrol car. A plump man in a tight police uniform approached her as she exited her car.

"Been waiting twenty minutes," he said.

As a federal prosecutor, she technically had jurisdiction over all territory in the United States, and federal court trumped state court. It created an unspoken tension with local law enforcement that a federal prosecutor, a female federal prosecutor, could come into their cases and decide to take them if she wanted to.

She smiled. "Sorry. Don't live in the state. I appreciate your help in this, Officer."

He frowned and handed her a key. "Drop it back off at the station when you're done. Or I can wait here if you're not going to be too long."

"Probably not long."

The truth was she had no idea how long she would be, but she liked the idea of him out here while she was in the home: she didn't know how she would react.

"All right, I'll wait."

Yardley turned to the home. Most prosecutors never visited the scenes of crimes they prosecuted, and many didn't even speak to the victims, leaving that to the social workers and victim advocates. Yardley gave her cell phone number out to every victim of every case she prosecuted and visited every scene at least once.

The home itself was a tan, flat pueblo style with cacti near the doorway. Gravel instead of grass, a common trait in the desert, and a long driveway that led to a two-car garage. Yardley peeled off the yellow police tape across the front door and set it down on the porch.

Inside, the air was warm and stale. No windows had been opened in three days. Soon, the family would hire crime scene cleanup crews and ready it for sale. Realtors in Utah were not required to reveal that murders or suicides had occurred in a home unless they were directly asked, and Yardley felt a twinge of sadness for the family that would move in and learn from the neighbors afterward what had happened here.

She flicked on the light. The furniture was modern and the living room sparsely decorated. The carpets had the familiar pressed-down patterns of an electrostatic dust-print machine. The forensic techs with the FBI's evidence response team would lay down sheets of Mylar and then turn the machine on, sending waves of electrostatic power through the material. Then they would take soft rollers and push them down over the sheets. Anything loose in the carpets—hair, fiber, sand, even shoe impressions made from dust or dirt—would get sucked onto the sheet. Whatever they found would then be sent to the FBI's Trace Evidence Laboratory in Washington, DC, for analysis.

Dozens of homicide and kidnapping cases had been solved because of matches made using the machine. People didn't consider that the carpet fibers in their cars and homes were uniquely identifiable—and so easily transmitted from place to place. Once a person of interest was found, the laboratory could match any fibers located at the scene with the carpet from a suspect's car or home.

The techs usually only laid the sheets down in areas the unsub, the unknown subject, would have likely walked. Here, the carpet pattern extended to every corner. Baldwin had told the truth: he'd worked the scene as much as possible and found nothing.

Yardley pulled out her phone and opened the files he'd sent: the initial St. George police reports; the FBI's murder book on the case, including grid-search and blood-spatter-analysis results; and the toxicology and autopsy reports. The autopsy reports, though only preliminary, were over fifty pages.

The pathologist's initial conclusion was that both victims had died from exsanguination—they'd bled out. There were multiple lacerations on Ryan Olsen's hands, running across palms and fingers. He had tried to fight, probably even after his throat had been cut.

The direction of the knife wounds and type of blade used were unknown. Like Baldwin had said, there were indications the unsub had tampered with the wounds to make determining the type of blade impossible. Yardley wondered if he'd worn gloves to do that or if he'd wanted to feel the slickness of the injuries on his bare skin.

The Olsens' neighbors had been the ones to call the police after Isaac, the Olsens' only child, had opened his parents' bedroom door the next morning and seen what must've been his worst nightmare come to life.

Yardley put her phone in her purse and walked into the kitchen. Hanging over the oven was a thick wooden plaque that read, THE KITCHEN IS THE HEART OF THE HOME. She opened the refrigerator, recognizing items that had filled her fridge when Tara was young: small pizzas, hot dogs, blueberry waffles, juice. She closed the door. She didn't want to go into the bedroom yet, so she entered the family room at the end of the hall. There was a large television with a sound system and DVD rack. On the bottom of the rack, she noticed an electronic tablet. She took it out. It was unlocked, no password. Sticky with what she guessed was candy or chocolate. Isaac's tablet. She clicked into the photos and videos. She opened the first video and watched.

It was recorded from the height of a child as his parents prepared dinner. Ryan was telling Aubrey about an article he'd read in a magazine, and Isaac snuck around the corner. Ryan pretended not to notice him and said, "And I think we should give Isaac up to Grandma and Grandpa. He doesn't clean up his messes, so he'll be better living there."

"I agree," Aubrey said with a grin.

"Dad!" Isaac shouted.

"What! Isaac, you've been there this whole time?"

Yardley smiled.

Ryan grabbed Isaac and started tickling him. Isaac laughed and dropped the tablet, and the recording stopped.

Yardley put the tablet back. She knew she would've liked the Olsens. She inhaled deeply, then walked to the bedroom.

7

Yardley stood outside the bedroom doors. Double doors, white with copper trim. She pictured Isaac in the morning opening both doors and what he must've seen. She took both knobs and pushed the doors open, the way a child might.

Inside, the room seemed to scream to her.

The duvet had been taken for analysis, but the mattress had been left behind. Blood, after it had dried, turned a dull gray.

The yellow numbered placeholders documenting various angles of blood trajectory had been removed, but the carpets were crusted dry with blood around the bed. Spatters of blood clung to the ceiling, to three of the four walls, and to the windows looking out over the valley.

The first time Yardley had seen blood jet from a major artery being cut quickly was at a crime scene of Eddie Cal's. After the numbness of his arrest had worn off, she'd forced herself to look at the crime scene photos. To visit the grave sites of the families and watch the interviews with surviving victims. It was, her therapist later told her, self-punishment. Yardley had punished herself so thoroughly that it had caused a schism in her psyche. One that had required years to heal from.

Baldwin's report indicated they'd been thorough. Beneath the copper scent of blood, she picked up traces of magnetic fingerprint powder.

She had no doubt Baldwin had also asked for fluorescent powder just to be sure there were no prints. But if he was truly a copycat, the unsub wouldn't have come in without gloves. He'd probably shaved his entire body and worn a cap to prevent leaving hair at the scene. Eddie Cal had done those things.

Forensic investigation wasn't the way they would catch someone like that.

Inside the closet, the Olsens' clothing looked as if it belonged in a morgue. The harsh fluorescent light cast a green tinge that gave the impression that the clothes were rotting, that they would decompose and disappear along with the Olsens' bodies.

Yardley had to tell herself that was impossible and that her perception was skewing. It was probably time to go.

On the top shelf were packages of unopened toys.

She left the room and turned off the light. Heading back to the kitchen, she spotted Isaac's bedroom. It wasn't more than ten feet from his parents' room. Yardley pulled up a transcript of his interview at the Children's Justice Center. He'd said he hadn't heard anything that night. Yardley wondered if Ryan Olsen had thought the unsub would kill Isaac next and that was why he'd fought even while bleeding to death.

Yardley sighed quietly as she stared into the child's room.

She learned from the caption above the transcript that Isaac's birthday was next week. She went back to his parents' room and took the toys down, all three, then turned off the lights in the home.

Once she'd returned the key to the officer and he'd left, she sat down on the front steps and looked out over the city. A football game was going on at the local high school, and she could hear the bellowing of the announcer and the occasional cheer from the crowd. She dialed Baldwin.

"Yeah," he said.

"I'll let Roy know tomorrow that I'd like to be the screening prosecutor for this. I don't have any other trials coming up, only a few pending cases that are going to settle."

"I can't tell you how much I appreciate this, Jess."

"I'm assuming Isaac is staying with a foster family. I'd like their address. I have some birthday presents for him."

8

The next morning, Yardley let her supervisor, Roy Lieu, know that she wanted to be the screening prosecutor for the Dean and Olsen cases. He agreed.

Yardley knew she was lucky to be a federal prosecutor. The state prosecutors were overworked and had little time to help in any investigations or interviews. Federal prosecutors could pick and choose their cases and take all the time they needed. Whereas a state prosecutor might interview a victim once before a trial, Yardley could interview a victim ten times if she wanted. She could send the FBI to collect evidence she required and turn down cases she felt didn't need to be prosecuted. As a state prosecutor, she wouldn't have had the time to help Baldwin.

Yardley checked her watch. The St. George Police Department would be holding a briefing on the Olsens in an hour, and Baldwin had asked if she would be there with him.

She waited outside the building for him.

The black Mustang came to a stop in front of her. Ortiz was in the passenger seat, so she got into the back. The car smelled of warm leather and a cherry air freshener that hung from the rearview mirror.

Baldwin reached back and handed her a coffee. They merged onto the freeway and sped toward Utah.

"I owe him twenty bucks," Ortiz said.

"For what?"

"I bet him you wouldn't do it. Most prosecutors don't take extra work when they don't need to."

———

The St. George Police Department was in a square brick building up on a hill surrounded by office buildings.

The interior was clean, without the raucous shouting from arrestees in holding cells that many police stations in more populated cities had. In a large room sat about twenty police officers in the half desks used in school classrooms. The watch commander and a sergeant stood at the front of the room and shook hands with Baldwin and Ortiz. Yardley leaned against the wall, trying to remain inconspicuous.

"All right, everyone, settle down," the watch commander, a large man with a potbelly, said. "We got Agent Ortiz and Agent Baldwin here with us today to talk about the Olsens. And before they get into it, I want to say something: I heard some of you referring to this as the work of a serial killer. I do not want that said anywhere near this case, you hear? The last thing we need is for people to panic that we have a serial killer loose. This is not a Dark Casanova killing. As far as the media knows, and as far as our reports are concerned, as of right now, this is an unsolved murder—that's all." He nodded to Baldwin. "What d'ya got, Agent Baldwin?"

Dark Casanova. Yardley hadn't heard that term in a long time. It was Eddie Cal's nickname. A reporter for the *Los Angeles Times* had come up with it, because of Eddie's good looks. The reporter had said Eddie looked like James Dean, had he lived past the age of twenty-four.

She remembered a headline from after his arrest that said, "Dark Casanova and His Blonde Bombshell Are the Modern Bonnie and Clyde." It showed a photo of her and Cal from years earlier, relaxing on a beach. She remembered having to take a shower after seeing it; she had scrubbed herself so raw her skin had burned.

Baldwin stepped forward, his hands on his hips, spreading his suit coat apart and revealing the .45 in its holster. He had done it purposely: Law enforcement was a gun culture, and the type of gun you carried spoke about you. A large .45 was his way of telling them, *Mine is bigger than yours.*

"As of right now we don't have much to go on. I agree with Lieutenant Ubanks that we can't have this labeled as a Dark Casanova case. I've heard rumblings of the name Dark Casanova Junior, which is probably even worse because it's demeaning and might piss this guy off and spur him to act sooner rather than later. While it's true that these have most of the hallmarks of a Dark Casanova slaying, and we are working under the assumption that this in fact is a copycat, we don't want that released to the public yet. Sometimes a copycat doesn't realize they're a copycat, and when they see something like that on the news, they change their tactics and methods. We need him to think we know nothing about him for right now."

One of the officers in the front raised his hand.

"Yes, Officer Clark."

"I saw that we don't know how he got into the house. Do you got anything on that?"

"We have a guess. Granted, it's a good guess, but a guess nonetheless. No locks or windows were damaged; no neighbors saw anyone hanging around the property that day or night. At this point we think he may have had a key, or more likely a universal lockpick. There are ones you can buy from novelty websites that open nine out of ten locks in the world."

"What about the alarm?" another officer said.

"We checked with the alarm company, and they had a false alarm at eight twenty-seven in the p.m. Aubrey Olsen answered the alarm company's welfare check call and said it had just gone off but that they were home and nothing had been opened. The alarm company told her to check the front door since that was where the alarm had been set off, but she said she was within twenty feet of the door the whole time and didn't see anything. Our theory is that the unsub broke the connection on the front door just enough that it would set off the alarm—maybe by inserting a credit card or blade between the sensors or using a lockpick to open it a couple inches—to distract the Olsens, and then ran around the home and entered through the door on the side of the garage, which didn't have a sensor. Most people don't put sensors on doors in the garage. The time of death is around midnight, so he would've hid somewhere in the garage or home for about four hours. We don't know the significance of this chain of events yet. It would've been far less work for him to just wait until they were asleep and enter through the garage door then. So that's my long-winded way, Officer, of saying we're still working up theories as to why the alarm was set off, because as of right now we're not certain."

Another officer said, "You sure there was no rape? I mean, people can hide that sort of thing."

"No, there is no indication in either Mrs. Olsen or Mrs. Dean that there was any sexual assault, which is the major difference between this copycat and Eddie Cal."

"I mean, why do it, then? Aren't all these guys just crazy perverts?"

Baldwin said, "I think maybe Ms. Yardley from the US Attorney's Office can better answer that question and give us an outline of what we're probably looking for. Her advanced degrees in forensic and clinical psychology and experience prosecuting sex crimes make her a valuable asset in this investigation."

Yardley knew he had thrown in the line about her education and experience to establish her authority for the male officers. Still, she wished he hadn't asked her to address them. She could tell them nothing about who did this.

She stepped forward. "We used to believe that the murder itself was the sexual act. In this case, a profiler, even from just ten years ago, would say this unknown subject is likely impotent. Either it's purely psychosomatic, or he's suffered some sort of injury that prevents him from attaining an erection. The knife was a surrogate for his sexual function. He's probably Caucasian and in his early to late thirties, and an alcoholic or drug abuser with extremely high intelligence."

She glanced at the officer who'd asked the question. "That type of profiling, through massive data accumulation by everyone from the CDC to the WHO, has been proven false. The fact is we don't really know why these men do what they do. The latest research suggests an organic origin: for example, a malformation in the amygdala—the region of the brain responsible for regulation of emotions—that leads to a misfiring of the sexual and violent impulse. According to one theory, these men quite literally believe that sex and violence are the same thing."

She glanced to Baldwin, who was watching her.

"On the other end of the spectrum, you have Dr. Daniel Sarte, a professor of psychiatry at Harvard Medical School and probably the world's most respected authority on violent psychopathology. He believes the origins are not organic, that these men very willingly choose to do what they do, and that they are adept at separating themselves from their actions. That they—again, quite literally—believe they are passengers watching the suffering they inflict, that they're not the ones doing it. Many serial sexual murderers have reported a 'dark voice' that whispers to them and tells them what to do. In both theories, the offenders are typically, though not always, of high intelligence. Which is why they're so difficult to catch."

"What?" another officer, a man with a buzz cut, said. "You think he's smart?"

"The crime scene is spotless in terms of forensics, and the clever way he distracted them with the alarm, whether to ensure no one was near the garage when he entered or for some other purpose, shows logical, systematic thinking. I wouldn't be surprised if he was in one of the technical or medical professions, like an engineer or medical doctor. Many serial murderers that display this type of complex thinking come from those backgrounds."

The watch commander said, "Do you think we have a couple weeks to find him before the next one?"

"While these two sets of murders were three weeks apart, the cycle typically accelerates."

"What d'ya mean?"

"Serial murderers of this type kill in cycles. There're six phases. The first is the aura phase, where the killer loses his connection to reality and begins living purely in the fantasy world in his mind. The fantasy leads him to the trolling phase, where he begins to actively search for victims, and then into the luring phase, where he plans how to entice the victim into a vulnerable position. Then the capture phase, which in this instance is his invasion into the home. Followed by the actual murder phase, and finally a severe depression phase after the high of the murder fades. There are many instances of serial murderers committing suicide in the depression phase."

"Shit yeah, let's hope," one of the officers said to chuckling.

Yardley grinned. How relieved she would be to have this case resolve in such a clean way. It wouldn't be, though. Monsters like this could cling to their diseased lives with manic desperation. What Eddie Cal had done after being caught was proof of that.

As though her thoughts were transparent, another officer raised a hand. "You're the ex-wife of Eddie Cal, aren't you?"

The officers went completely silent, all eyes glued to her.

Every so often, freelance paparazzi selling photographs to the highest bidder would show up in her life, and her photo would circulate again. She recalled one headline—"Bride of Frankenstein"—above a photo of her going into a grocery store. She had caught Tara reading that particular article on her laptop.

Yardley could feel their stares on her skin and had to resist the urge to turn away.

"I am."

"So is that why you're on this? Because you know so much about it?"

"I'm here," she said, "because this is the type of case I handle at the US Attorney's Office."

"But you've gotta have some thoughts on why this guy is doing it, right? You were married to it."

Baldwin tried to say something, but Yardley spoke first.

"The psychopathology of copycats is massively different from that of the perpetrators they copy. The copycat is more similar to a stalker than what we would consider a serial sexual predator. The killing, for them, is a means to an end, whereas for a true sexual sadist, the killing itself is the end. So I'm afraid my . . . past doesn't come to bear on this. We'll have to catch him with just good old-fashioned police work."

Baldwin said, "That's why it's so important for us to make sure we share everything we have. I know all about the pissing contests we could get into and the who did what when. I don't care about credit for this. I don't need or want my name in the papers. I want one of you to catch him, or for him to kill himself or, shit, get struck by lightning. I don't care. I just want to stop him. So please, please, please, don't hog any leads. Let's get this bastard and watch him fry for this."

Several of the officers nodded along. The watch commander took over from there and fielded a few questions. They would canvass the Olsens' neighborhood again, going a few blocks farther this time, hoping a neighbor had seen someone they didn't recognize.

Yardley knew it was pointless. Cal had only gone out at night. He would kiss her before he left and tell her he felt inspired and had to go to his studio to paint. Once, his mother had called late at night, and they'd had a conversation about what a hard worker Eddie was. She still took Tara every year to the Cals' ranch to see her grandparents. She wondered if the memory of that conversation made his mother feel a dim nausea as well.

How many times did he crawl into bed with me after butchering a family? Did he shower first in our bathroom, the blood washing away in the same tub I took baths in?

An image forced itself into her mind: her nude body in a bathtub overflowing with dark blood.

Yardley noticed her hands trembling, and she pressed them together and held them low so no one would see.

The briefing ended, and the watch commander shook Ortiz's and Baldwin's hands and nodded to Yardley as the officers filed out.

"Have you checked the sex offenders?" Yardley asked Baldwin.

"Interviewed everyone in North Las Vegas and was going to start today in Washington County."

In serial murder investigations, registered sex offenders were a treasure trove of potential suspects. The man power needed to question everyone in an area was enormous, but with the FBI's resources and the incentive for local law enforcement to avoid causing public panic by labeling this the work of a serial predator, she had no doubt it was a priority.

"I want to help," she said.

He watched her a moment. "You sure?"

"Yes."

"Jess, you don't have—"

"I'm fine, Cason."

He watched her a second longer and said, "Oscar is going out in a couple hours after he checks with some parole officers. I have a meeting with the SAC to give him some updates, and I'll meet up with you guys after." He paused and glanced to the officers filing out. "If it ever gets to the point where you can't take it, there's no shame in that. No case is worth your mental well-being."

"If he is a copycat, then Eddie is as responsible for these murders as he is for his own. There was nothing I could do before, but I can now."

Baldwin put his hands in his pockets, his lower lip tucking behind his top lip, an expression he made whenever he was mulling something over. "Okay, but just don't forget that this isn't Eddie Cal, and you don't owe these victims anything."

"Explain that to Isaac Olsen."

9

By evening, she and Ortiz had conducted eight interviews. Yardley's back ached, and she was starving. Most of the offenders had decent alibis, and the few that had said they'd been home alone didn't fit the picture Yardley had in her head. They would be cleared, too, once their internet usage and cell data on the nights of the killings had been verified.

She liked Ortiz. During their drive, he'd talked a lot about his new baby daughter and about how he'd come into law enforcement. It made her curious if he knew more about Baldwin's childhood, about his mother's murder, than she did, but he said Baldwin never spoke about it.

In the car on the way to their last interview of the day, Ortiz said, "There's been somethin' I been dyin' to ask you and I don't know if it's appropriate or not."

"Really? This should be good. Go ahead."

"Eddie Cal. Did you ever feel like somethin' was off? You talk to neighbors of guys like that, and they all say the same thing, that somethin' just never felt right about him but they could never say what. I just wonder 'cause I think we all got instinct to help us survive. You ever read *The Gift of Fear*? See, fear is a gift to us—it helps us stay away from danger even when we don't know danger is there. I'm just curious if you ever had that."

Yardley stared out the window at the passing stores in a strip mall. Liquor stores, smoke shops, and now a marijuana dispensary. A relatively new addition to Las Vegas.

After a good ten seconds, she finally said, "No, never."

"Not ever?" he said. "The entire marriage?"

"Not even once. He was, objectively, the sweetest, most charming man I have ever met. There wasn't a person that Eddie ever said a harsh word to."

He nodded thoughtfully. "Let's finish with this fool and then grab a burger. There's this awesome burger place like three blocks from his house."

They pulled up to an apartment complex on the outskirts of town. One-story buildings with flat roofs. Yardley thought they looked more like storage units than apartments. Behind the complex a hill led up into the sand dunes.

"Dilbert Morgan," Ortiz said as they parked. "You believe that? *Dilbert?* That just sounds like a sex offender name. It's like a hundred bucks to change it."

Ortiz knocked on the door as Yardley glanced around. The apartments had small patios and yards in back, most of them filled with old patio furniture and dying plants.

"Dilbert, open the door. This is Oscar Ortiz with the FBI. I need to talk to you. You're not in any trouble, but we gotta talk."

He pounded again.

"Not home, and he don't work. His PO said he didn't answer when he called him yesterday and today, too."

"Might've gone out camping or something."

Ortiz shook his head. "He's new on the registry. He's not allowed to leave the city without his PO's approval."

Yardley heard something from the back patio. She stepped around the corner of the building and saw a man opening the gate in the patio's fence. He looked at her for a second and then sprinted down the alley behind the buildings.

"He's running."

"Shit," Ortiz said, booking it after him.

Yardley phoned Baldwin, who told her he'd have police down there ASAP. He told her to get in the car and stay put.

Yardley walked to the back patio. She couldn't see the man or Ortiz, and she didn't hear them either. The gate was still open. She pushed it wider and peeked inside. Sliding glass doors led into the apartment. She glanced around and then went in.

The apartment was quiet and smelled like sweat. She felt her pulse pounding in her throat. Maybe it was best to wait outside like Baldwin had suggested. There was no good reason for her to be in here; she wasn't an investigator. Still, the curiosity was too much. Most sex offenders had been conditioned to cooperate with law enforcement fully. For one to run meant that potentially getting shot struck him as a better prospect than what would happen if he were caught. Whoever had killed the Olsens and Deans wouldn't let himself be taken alive.

On the coffee table in front of a worn brown couch were piles of marijuana and an ashtray filled with used cigarette butts. The kitchen light was on. Bottles of whiskey and vodka lined the area behind the sink. Yardley leaned around into the hall that led to the bedroom and said, "Hello? Anyone here?"

A bathroom was to the right, dirty and smelling of urine. The sink was filled with old shavings and crusted toothpaste. Several amber pill bottles lined the sink, and she took a quick look. Some of them were antipsychotics.

A text arrived from Baldwin that said, They're on their way. Talked to Oscar. He lost him up a hill.

A noise came from the bedroom.

Yardley froze.

She tiptoed to the doorway. The bed wasn't made, and the sheets were filthy with cigarette ash and stains. The closet doors were closed. She was about to turn away when she heard it again.

A slight shuffling. Like shoes on carpet.

"Hello?"

Yardley reached into her purse and took out her canister of Mace. She didn't hear any sirens outside.

Yardley swallowed and stepped closer to the closet. "Is someone there?"

Slowly, her heartbeat deafening in her ears, she held the Mace up with one hand and opened the closet door.

A young woman lay on the floor, her hands and feet bound. Duct tape covered her mouth. Makeup mixed with tears ran down her cheeks.

Hysteria overtook the woman. She started sobbing and thrashing, and her shoulder hit Yardley in the cheek as she tried to help her to her feet. Yardley wrapped her arms around her, using all her strength to keep the woman from striking her. She felt the woman's heartbeat against her chest: it felt like the hammering of a fist.

"It's okay, it's okay, you're okay . . . I'm not going to hurt you."

The woman wept uncontrollably, and Yardley felt her body give up and collapse. The woman tossed her head back against the wall, unable even to breathe. Yardley pulled the duct tape from her mouth.

"Please . . . please get me out of here. Please!"

"I know. I know," Yardley said, trying to calm her. She removed the rest of the duct tape and called 911, requesting an ambulance.

"We can wait outside. Come on. The police and ambulance are on their way."

They exited onto the patio and turned toward the parking lot just as Ortiz came back. His eyes went wide, and he said, "Holy shit."

Yardley leaned against Ortiz's Cadillac and watched the paramedics evaluate the woman in the back of the ambulance. Several uniforms were there along with Ortiz and Baldwin, who were interviewing neighbors and going through Dilbert Morgan's apartment. Baldwin came up to her and said, "I shouldn't have let you come out. This was really stupid of me."

"I'm fine, Cason."

"Yeah, but you might not have been. What if he decided to circle back? I put you at risk, and I'm sorry."

"You didn't do anything. I chose to go into that apartment. I could've sat out in the car. It wasn't your choice." She motioned toward the woman with her head. "Who is she?"

"Rachel Miller. Dilbert's girlfriend. She said he lost it last night. She came over and he was pacing the apartment, mumbling to himself. He said something about her being in on it and tied her up and stuck her in the closet."

"I found antipsychotics in the bathroom. He might have had a psychotic break. Any luck finding him?"

Baldwin shook his head. "He ran into the sand dunes. I'm sure it won't be long."

"Did you find anything in his apartment?"

He exhaled and glanced back at Rachel. "Nothing yet. No weapons, not even kitchen knives. Probably doesn't keep them around because of his condition. He left his phone and I'm having the tech with the St. George PD unlock it so we can see what's there. What do you think, though? He fits your profile pretty well."

"It's not a profile. Just some broad guesses I gave to the police because you put me on the spot. I have little idea what the man we're looking for is like. You should consult with Daniel."

Dr. Daniel Sarte, who Yardley had briefly mentioned to the St. George PD, had written the definitive personality inventory for determining psychopathic traits. The FBI frequently used him for drawing up profiles and then helping with interrogation tactics once the suspects were caught. He had helped Yardley understand the way psychopaths and sociopaths interpreted the world, and she had helped him understand how to better handle cross-examination in court after a particularly poor performance in a trial involving a defendant accused of bombing his former employers.

Baldwin nodded. "I gave him a call last week, after I knew what it was. He's reviewing the files and said he would get back to me." He watched her a second. "What do *you* think, though? Just a guess?"

"I think the unsub that killed the Olsens and the Deans was extraordinarily organized and thoughtful. Not someone with paranoid delusions and psychotic breaks. He would appear, on the outside, normal to everyone else."

His gaze drifted toward the apartment. "That's what I thought. But you never know. Maybe we got lucky?"

10

By the time Yardley got home, she felt fatigue climbing its way up her legs and into her muscles like a fast-moving disease. She and Ortiz had never gotten that burger, but the last thing she wanted to do now was eat.

A note on the counter from Wesley told her he had to be at a free clinic for the Guardian ad Litem's Office and would be back around nine. Tara's bedroom door was shut—and probably locked. Yardley listened for a moment and heard her on the phone with Kevin. She softly touched the door and then went to the kitchen.

She forced herself to take some vegetables out of the fridge and made a salad, eating alone at the kitchen table. Tara came out of her room but didn't say anything as she got a soda out of the fridge.

"Tara?"

"What?"

"I think we need to discuss Kevin."

She took a few steps toward her mother and leaned against the kitchen island. "What about him?"

"I spoke with the school officer after the drinking incident the other day. Last year, Kevin was suspected of impregnating a girlfriend, who then transferred schools. I'm guessing he's never told you that. And did you know he was nearly arrested last week for breaking into cars in the school parking lot?"

"It wasn't him."

"The officer believes it was."

"Innocent until proven guilty. Right, Mom?"

She stayed silent a second, watching her daughter's cold blue eyes. "I don't think he's appropriate for you."

"It's not your choice."

"I don't want to fight. I really don't. I'm just telling you that he's the type of boy that uses girls. And when he's done using them, he discards them. I don't want to see that happen to you."

She rolled her eyes. "Yeah, you're one to talk about picking men, right?"

"What did you just say to me?"

Tara folded her arms. "I think you heard me. It must be difficult to find out that the man you shared your bed with was sharing it with the dead, too. Do you ever wonder, Mom, what attracted you to a monster like that? Do you think there's maybe something inside you that knew who he really was the whole time?"

Yardley's jaw muscles contracted, but otherwise she remained motionless. Tara had an ability to see a person's most vulnerable spot and cut it with a razor. It was a trait that had, on more than one occasion, made Yardley wonder what type of person her daughter would turn out to be.

"I don't regret my time with Eddie Cal for one reason and one reason only: because it gave me you."

Tara blinked softly but said only, "I'm going to my room now."

Yardley watched her brilliant, troubled daughter shut the door to her bedroom. Did Tara understand she had a choice in who she became? Eddie Cal's parents were good people and loving parents, and they'd created something less than human. It was proof that environment and genetics couldn't determine who you chose to become, and some days it seemed like all Yardley could do was hope that Tara chose well.

———

Wesley came home a little before nine. She was in bed with her glasses on, which she only wore around him, reading a book on the history of the Byzantine Empire. He crawled onto the bed and kissed her.

"I missed you," he said, his face a few inches from hers, staring down at her lips.

"I missed you. How was the clinic?"

He rolled his eyes and sat on the edge of the mattress, sliding off his shoes and suit coat. "One awful case after another. You can't believe the things people do to their children during a divorce. How was your day?"

"Interviewed eight sex offenders and found a young woman tied up in a closet."

He stared at her. "Are you serious?"

"Yes."

He raised his eyebrows as he stood. "Wow. Here I was feeling sorry for myself. You okay?"

"I'm fine. Just haven't been in screening for years, so I forgot what it's like to actually interview people as part of an investigation."

"Do you miss it? Seems like being in court every day is more your thing."

"It is. But I have to admit there was something about it. The excitement. I saw him run, the man that held her. It was exhilarating."

She wouldn't tell him about going into Dilbert Morgan's apartment by herself. He had already mentioned several times during the past year that he had contacts at every large law firm in the state and that she could easily make three times what she made as a prosecutor if she went into private practice. She figured he was uncomfortable with the type of cases she prosecuted. If a serial rapist got acquitted or released on bail, it wasn't impossible that he'd target her. Career criminals blamed the prosecutors and police for their misfortunes. And violent sex offenders were typically unable to take any responsibility for their actions, sometimes even believing the victims secretly wanted the assault. A female prosecutor trying to send them to prison became an easy scapegoat for their problems.

"Well, don't get used to that exhilaration. You know, once we hit thirty-five, it's a fact of life that our bodies begin to deteriorate. You're thirty-eight now and starting to feel it. I did, too, at that age. You start looking for things that make you feel young, and they're rarely the things that are good for you."

She laughed. "I'm not racing motorcycles, Wesley. I just enjoyed being out of an office or courtroom for once."

He slipped off his shirt and threw it in a hamper in the closet before undoing his belt and pants and walking into the bathroom. "I'm just saying," he said as he turned on the shower, "be cognizant of how you feel. If you think you're fighting evil, your brain can trick you into doing things you never thought you could."

She listened to the soothing sound of the water until a text message pinged on her phone. It was from Baldwin. They'd caught Dilbert Morgan.

11

The interview room at the St. George police station was little more than a table, a few chairs, and a window looking out over some trees between the building and the offices next door, all dark at this time of night. Television shows depicting police work had the two-way mirrors and sophisticated recording equipment, but that was rarely reality. Reality was that every time a city hit a budget deficit, they cut funding to their police force and told them to do more with less. People rarely understood that technology, not sleuthing, was responsible for most arrests, so when an officer had a laptop in his cruiser that was fifteen years out of date, he was not going to make the kind of connections he could with a new one linked to every law enforcement agency database in the country. Serial sexual predators were masters at slipping through the knowledge gaps that formed between law enforcement agencies.

Yardley watched Dilbert Morgan through the square window on the door of the interview room. He had several tics, and his hands trembled to the point that he had difficulty keeping them on the table because his fingers would tap against it. The man who'd killed the Olsens and Deans would likely be calm and collected. Even in a police station, his pulse would stay low, and he would smile and answer questions with courtesy, deflecting accusations softly and expertly. Dilbert Morgan appeared like a man about to have a heart attack.

Baldwin stood outside the room with her and had Dr. Sarte on the phone from Boston. Yardley could hear what he was saying.

"I'm not sure he fits the profile I'm drawing for you," Sarte said. "Many predators are proud of their accomplishments and can't wait to brag, but this particular person has taken great pains to remain undetected. He does not want the attention. At least not yet. Keeping a woman bound in his closet and then running from you, when he likely could've spoken with you and diverted your attention away, isn't what your subject would do. At least not the man that killed the Olsens and Deans."

The fact that Sarte had said "accomplishments" to refer to murders sent a jolt of revulsion through Yardley.

"Well, take a look at the psychiatric files I'm sending over," Baldwin said. "He was diagnosed with paranoid schizophrenia at twenty-one and has spent most of his life in institutions of one kind or another. We checked his meds, and it looks like he stopped taking them two months ago."

"He might be too unstable to interview right now, Cason. You may want to commit him and then approach him when he's calm and medicated. He may even have remorse for his actions and be willing to discuss them."

Ortiz approached with an unopened soda in his hand.

"He might lawyer up when he's more with it and I'll have missed my shot." Baldwin paused. "Is there anything I can do to maybe set him off? If he loses it, maybe we'll—"

"You know I would never help with that, don't you?"

Baldwin sighed. "Yeah, I do. Worth a shot. Thanks, Doc."

Yardley watched him a moment. There had been a case once where Baldwin had contacted a witness who was set to testify against a serial rapist. The defense argued that Baldwin had shown her photographs of the defendant before the lineup. Baldwin had denied it, as had the witness, but Yardley had always wondered if it could be true. His motives were pure, she didn't doubt that, but there was a thin line between pushing hard for a justified conviction and convicting an innocent person. As a prosecutor, she couldn't allow that line to be crossed.

He hung up and said, "You ready?"

"After you," Ortiz said.

They entered the room as Yardley watched through the glass. Dilbert Morgan rocked back and forth, his arms across his chest. He wore glasses that had fallen halfway down his nose. His thin frame gave him the appearance of a stick figure come to life, and Yardley noticed that his lips were so chapped they were bleeding in several places.

"I n-n-need t-to go h-home."

He spoke with a thick stutter and avoided their eyes. Ortiz opened the soda and set it in front of him. "Thirsty, Dilbert? You were out in them sand dunes a bit."

Morgan picked up the soda and took a long drink, some of it dribbling down his chin and onto his shirt. He belched, put the soda down, and then folded his arms again, resuming his rocking. Baldwin and Ortiz sat down across from him.

"Rachel's okay," Baldwin said. "She wanted you to know she's okay." He paused. "Do you remember what happened, Dilbert?"

"Sh-sh-she was j-just going t-to t-t-turn me in."

"Turn you in for what?"

He shook his head. "I w-want to g-go home."

"I know, Dilbert, but we can't have you go home until we know what's going on. You could have really hurt Rachel. Now, I know you didn't want to hurt her, right?"

He shook his head vigorously.

Ortiz said, "Dilbert, have you ever hurt anyone else like you did Rachel? I mean, I know you don't mean to hurt them, but was there anyone else?"

"I w-want t-t-to go h-home."

"I know, but we can't have you—"

Yardley opened the door. "Cason, can I see you a moment, please?" Baldwin leaned back in the chair. "Can it wait?"

"No."

He glanced at Ortiz, who shrugged. The two men rose and joined her.

"What is it?" Baldwin asked once the door to the interview room had closed.

"It's clearly not him."

Baldwin glanced back to Morgan. "We don't know that yet."

"Cason, it's not him."

"Well, let me finish with him, and we'll determine that."

"Fine. But I'm not comfortable with you two ganging up on a mentally ill suspect without him having a lawyer." She took out her phone and dialed the federal public defender's office's after-hours line. "This is Jessica Yardley of the US Attorney's Office. I need an attorney down at the St. George police station for a Dilbert Morgan under investigation for homicide." She looked to Baldwin. "The FBI has two agents here, Agent Baldwin and Agent Ortiz, and I would like to have Mr. Morgan represented if he decides to speak with them."

The operator let her know that someone would be down within the hour.

"He didn't ask for a lawyer," Baldwin said, scowling.

Yardley put her phone away. "Someone will be here in an hour. Call me afterward and let me know if they decide to let their client speak to you."

She turned to leave the station without waiting for a response.

"I like her," she heard Ortiz say to Baldwin. "She keeps your dumb ass in check."

12

Yardley heard from office chatter that Dilbert Morgan had been cleared as a suspect in the Dean and Olsen murders. Rachel, the girlfriend, had been with him both nights, and they were even on camera at an all-night pharmacy around eleven on the night the Olsens had been killed. The fact that Baldwin hadn't called her made her wonder if he regretted asking her to help on the case.

It was past one, and she was about to go to lunch when Baldwin appeared at her door.

"Hey," he said.

She sat back down in her chair. "Hi."

He leaned against the door, his hands in his pockets. "How'd you sleep?"

"Well. How about you?"

He grinned. "I hate awkward small talk."

"Who says it's awkward?"

He sat across from her. "I'm sorry. You were a hundred percent right. Anything I got out of him would've been tossed. I don't know what came over me."

"When a hunter is closest to his prey is when he makes the most mistakes. Or so I'm told."

"My dad used to take me up. After my mom died, he thought it was a way for us to bond. And you're absolutely right. The excitement of the hunt ending clouds your thinking. So you forgive me?"

He had said "died" and not "was killed" or "was murdered." Yardley wondered if there was something that had made him reconsider her death being a murder or if it was just easier to not use that word.

"Nothing to forgive. What's the plan now?"

"The plan is to sit around and wait because we can't do shit, Jess. We got nothing on the second canvass through the Olsens' neighborhood, and he very well may be planning to kill again in less than two weeks."

"It's not your fault, Cason. I can tell by those dark circles under your eyes you're giving up sleep for this. You're doing everything you can. Don't blame yourself."

He shook his head. "I keep seeing the next house. You didn't go in when it was fresh. I got called the night the Olsens were killed. Pictures don't do it justice. I'd forgotten the human body could even hold that much blood. It reminded me, actually, of the hunts with my dad. Sometimes he'd hang the buck from a tree and cut its throat to drain it. Seems like that's what he's doing to them." He rubbed his face with both hands. "Guess I'll just have another scene to go into fresh."

"I'm sorry. I know it's not easy."

"Yeah, well, that's why all us federal agents are rich, right? This is what they pay us for." He swallowed. "Jess, I don't have anything, and he's going to kill again very soon." He inhaled deeply. "I want to ask you to do something for me, and it's not pretty."

"What is it?"

"I'd like you to visit Eddie Cal and ask him to help us."

Yardley was so stunned she couldn't speak. She stared at Baldwin, who held her gaze and wouldn't look away. The only thing that indicated he'd said something shocking was a slight blush in his cheeks.

"Cason—"

"You can't imagine how impossibly difficult it is for me to ask you that. I'm so sorry. I thought we'd find something to at least give us the hope that we could catch this guy before the cycle was up, but there's nothing. I've torn those people's lives apart, interviewed every friend and family member they have, every neighbor, everything. We even found people that had registered drones in the vicinity and viewed any videos they had from that day, hoping we'd catch someone driving slowly by the homes. Nothing. I don't ask for favors lightly, but I need this."

Baldwin had previously had cases like this, even worse—the Beltway Butcher had been his most notorious. What was it about these murders that struck such a deep chord in him?

"I can't do it, Cason. I hope you understand."

"I know what I'm asking. I'm asking you to tear open a wound you just barely got to heal." He rose. "I'm not going to beg, and I'm not going to sit here for an hour and try to convince you. All I know is if I didn't ask, I'd feel like shit when I got the call from the police that they've found another couple. And I think if you say no, you will, too."

———

When Yardley was alone again, she sat quietly and stared out her window. A large electronic sign across the street advertised a burlesque show with scantily clad girls dancing, smiles on their faces. The image flipped to a sizzling steak, and then a few seconds later to cold beer, and then to a crowded dance club. The words **WE WON'T TELL IF YOU WON'T** flashed across the sign. Then the image returned to the dancing girls.

She went outside. It was abnormally hot today, and she remembered an article she'd read in a criminology journal about how crime, across cultures, tended to increase on hot days.

At a nearby café that some of the lawyers and judges from the federal courts went to, she sat in a corner by herself and ordered a diet soda with a tuna sandwich. She took out her phone and called Wesley.

"Hey, gorgeous," he answered.

"Hey. How's class?"

"Just got done with an interesting discussion on the *Old Chief* case. How about you?"

"I, um . . . I'm debating doing something I'm not sure is a good idea."

"Oh yeah? What?"

She almost told him, and then she stopped. He would talk her out of it, and even though she told herself she hadn't decided and was just mulling it over, she knew that was a lie. Baldwin was right. When that call came in, or when it was eventually on the news and she saw the faces of the couple, or the weeping children being taken out of the home and put into a police cruiser, it would slash at her. Maybe even ruin the prosecutor's office for her. What, after all, was she in this for if not to protect people like the Olsens and Deans? Any line prosecutor in the office could get convictions. That wasn't what this job was about to her. It was about something much deeper, and she had never really explained to herself what that was.

"I'm debating getting a cheeseburger with fries for lunch."

A pause, and then Wesley burst out laughing. "That is a conundrum. Your figure is amazing, and you have nothing to worry about. YOLO."

"I really just wanted to hear your voice. I'll talk to you later."

"All right. I'll see you at home. Love you."

She leaned her head back against the booth and watched the way the sunlight refracted off the glass in splinters of light. Then she rose and paid for her order but told them to cancel it.

"You sure you don't want it boxed up?" the cashier said.

"No, thank you. I'm not hungry anymore."

13

The Low Desert Plains Correctional Institution sat in an empty valley forty miles outside of Las Vegas. The surrounding deserts gave it a postapocalyptic feel, almost like it didn't belong in this time but instead three centuries from now, when laws no longer applied and the mass of men simply had to be locked up to keep them from destroying society. Maybe it was already starting to get that way now. She didn't know.

Yardley had called ahead and spoken to the warden, Sofie Gledhill, who'd brought several cases to Yardley. They had a mutual trust for each other. Yardley agreed that she would expedite any case Gledhill brought, and Gledhill agreed that she would never bring a case that wasn't warranted. Over the years, she had given Yardley several sex crimes related to murders committed in the prison. Yardley had prosecuted every one, gotten convictions on two through jury trials, and cut deals on the rest.

Gledhill met her at reception dressed in a suit, her Nevada Department of Corrections badge hanging by a lanyard around her neck. African American and with glimmering green eyes, Gledhill had always looked to Yardley as though she could be on the cover of any fitness magazine, and she had told Yardley that she in fact had been headed for the Olympics for track when a knee injury had derailed her athletic career at nineteen.

"Love the shoes," Gledhill said as she gave Yardley a hug.

"A gift. Wesley's always saying I don't treat myself enough, so he got me a gift card."

"Well, he's right. This business we're in will eat us up if we don't take some time to do things for ourselves. I meditate twenty minutes twice a day, rain or shine, and run an hour at lunch on a trail near here. You should come with if you're looking for ways to stay fit."

"I take boxing classes."

Gledhill grinned. "Yeah, that does seem more your style." She glanced at the corrections officer behind the front desk. "You sure about this? I can't talk you out of it?"

"There's a reason I'm here that isn't really public yet. The FBI is keeping it close to the chest to prevent any panic. But I promise I wouldn't be here if it wasn't necessary."

"FBI? Cason Baldwin?"

"Yeah, how'd you know?"

"He came in a month or two ago and saw Cal."

Yardley felt a pulse of anger, small and sharp, in her belly. "Did he."

"I assumed it was just a standard interview. You know how the field agents are. Superstitious like crazy. They think they need to pick up the scent like a bloodhound or whatever. I figured he wanted to meet Cal to get in the mind-set of catching someone like him. Is that not what it was?"

She shook her head, trying not to show the anger she was feeling. "No, I don't think so." She cleared her throat, attempting to push Baldwin out of her mind so she could focus on what she had to do. She would deal with him later.

"Well," Gledhill said, "if you're sure you're sure, I won't stand in your way. He'll be cuffed and chained even with the partition, and I'll have a guard posted behind you."

"No, I need privacy with him. He won't talk with someone else there . . . and I need the camera turned off."

"No way. I need everything recorded."

Yardley glanced at the corrections officer, who was listening to them. She looked away when she noticed Yardley watching her. "Let's talk on the way."

They were buzzed through metal doors and into another waiting room with a locked metal door at both ends. There was no camera here, and it was where Yardley said, "There's a copycat. He's killed two couples so far—that we know of. I'm here because Cason and I think that Eddie can help."

The door at the far end buzzed to be opened, but Gledhill didn't open it. "Wow."

"If he's being recorded, he won't be honest with me."

She blew out a deep breath. "Okay. I'll shut it off. You have my word."

"Thanks."

She led Yardley through a long corridor before they turned down another one. The general visitation rooms were on either side of them, and at the end of the corridor were the visitation rooms for the prisoners in protective custody. Cal had committed—in addition to torture and murder—rape, and in prison, sex offenders had bull's-eyes on their backs. Cal was in protective custody twenty-three hours a day and only allowed outside in the yard for one hour.

The visitation room was split by a glass wall bordered by cement. Three layers of glass with an intercom on either side separated the visitor from the inmate. Yardley sat down on the steel chair. Gledhill stood behind her and spoke into the camera. "Shut it off, Tommy."

The red light on the camera turned dark.

"Take as long as you need, hon."

"Thanks, Sofie."

She nodded and left the room. The metal door on the other side of the glass buzzed and slid open, and Yardley's ex-husband walked in.

14

Baldwin's office was small and cramped. He sat at his desk with his suit coat off and his sleeves rolled up, his tie undone. The small desk fan blew warm air over his face, and sweat rolled down his neck and dampened his collar. He checked the temperature: 110.

A bottle of hydrocodone was open in front of him on the desk, and Baldwin popped two of the pills. He counted the pills he had left: only a dozen. He would need more soon. The pills had been in his medicine cabinet from knee surgery last year. He'd started taking them again three weeks ago, telling himself it was just to relax the muscle spasms he was having in his back. But it was more than that. It was an all-consuming stress he hadn't felt since he'd been hunting Henry Lucado, a.k.a. the Beltway Butcher.

Most of the Butcher's victims had been strangled, but there was one who'd had her throat slit in a manner similar to Aubrey Olsen: ear to ear. From that entire case, the only image that had stuck with him was that young girl on the side of the road with her throat torn open, her mother hysterically fighting relatives to get to her little girl's body. A crowd had gathered, and Baldwin had seen nothing but a sea of cell phones recording when he'd arrived on scene. As if they were witnessing some interesting stunt at a carnival.

It bothered him that he couldn't remember the girl's name.

Ortiz came in just as Baldwin was slipping the pill bottle into a drawer and said, "Hey, got some funky stuff."

"What's up?"

"I told Detective Marsh over there with the St. George PD to call us on any reports filed for stalking or suspicious people in the area. He sent a few things over this morning. First one is some guy that said someone from the alarm company came up checking all his doors and windows, but when he called the company, they said his alarm was fine and they didn't send anyone out."

"Huh. Where was this at?"

"Gardner Avenue in St. George. I don't know, though, 'cause it seems weird for him to hit the same city. It was North Vegas and then SG, so he should hit somewhere else, right? He'd be tryin' to get a buncha different agencies involved and hopin' we don't work together."

"That's true, but these guys get obsessed quickly. If he happened to see some couple that caught his eye, he might risk it for them. What else?"

"Some lady said she saw a dude standing in front of her house at like midnight just staring in the windows, and a family said someone came to the front door and tried to get in but took off when the father came out of another room and saw him."

"Well, it all sounds like bullshit, but I don't have anything else to do the rest of the day. Let's go."

Baldwin parked in front of the Miles family home. An affluent area, just like the Deans' and Olsens' neighborhoods. A large home with several windows in front; a second story of almost all glass overlooking the valley.

He knocked, and a woman with brunette hair answered; she was fit and trim.

"Hi, is Jay here?"

"Yeah, can I ask what this is about?"

"I'm Agent Cason Baldwin with the Federal Bureau of Investigation. We're following up on a report he filed a week ago with the local police department."

"Oh yeah, hang on. We were just having dinner."

The woman disappeared into the house, and a man came to the door wearing sweats. He was chewing something and looked from Baldwin to Ortiz and said, "Hi, guys."

"Jay Miles?"

"Yeah," he said, holding out his hand. Baldwin and Ortiz both shook, and Jay said, "Did you guys find him? The guy that was checking my doors and windows?"

"No," Baldwin said. "We just had some questions about that, if it's all right."

Miles stepped outside and shut the door behind him. "Shoot."

"We read your statement and were wondering if you've seen anything since you filed the report. Maybe the same van driving around up here."

"No, nothing."

"And your neighbor's positive it was the alarm company he saw?"

"I showed him a picture of the logo and van for the company, and he said that was definitely what he saw. My neighbor across the street saw it, too."

"This ever happened before?" Ortiz asked.

"No. The officer at the police station said they make mistakes sometimes and go to the wrong house, but my neighbor talked to him. Seems like he might've figured out then he was at the wrong house."

"Which neighbor was it?"

"Right there. Bill Cox. And Colleen Boyle across the street right there."

Baldwin took out a card and handed it to him. "If you see him again, or if anybody comes by your house that seems off, give me a call, would you?"

"Sure. Um, can I ask why the FBI is involved in this?"

"Just being careful. There've been some break-ins in the city and people were attacked. We need to investigate claims like this. I would probably have the alarm company come out and check everything. You may want to get a good dog as well."

He looked from one to the other. "Guys, you're kinda spooking me here. What's going on?"

Ortiz started to say something, but Baldwin interjected. "Like I said, just being careful."

He nodded. "Okay. Well, yeah, I'll have them come and check everything."

The two agents walked across the lawn to the neighbor on the south side. When they were far enough away, Ortiz said, "You don't think we should tell him?"

"What will that do? Other than get him to maybe shoot his teenager coming home late at night."

"I'd wanna know."

"Know what? Some guy in an alarm company uniform came out and checked the alarm. It's probably nothing. They'll hear about the murders soon enough anyway. And I told him there've been break-ins and attacks. He doesn't need to know the details."

An elderly man wearing a robe answered the door, his hair wet like he had just stepped out of the shower.

Baldwin showed his badge and said, "Bill Cox?"

"Yeah. You guys finally here about them damn cars that come speeding up here? There's this one boy right over there that has a Camaro, and he comes—"

"Mr. Cox, we're here about the alarm company representative you saw at Jay and Rosalyn's home next door."

Cox lowered the hand that was pointing across the street. "Oh. Yeah? When was that?"

Baldwin and Ortiz exchanged a glance. "Couple of days ago. Can you give a description of who you saw?"

Cox thought a moment, and Baldwin saw the glazed-over look in his eyes, a look his grandmother had had much of the time later in life, just before she'd started talking about the World Series game her father was planning to take her to for her twelfth birthday.

"I don't remember," Cox finally said. "He was white, I think."

Ortiz said, "Do you remember his hair color? Did he have any tattoos or anything like that? Something we could use to identify him?"

Cox waved a dismissive hand. "I don't know. Who remembers stuff like that?"

Baldwin said, "If you see him again, will you do me a favor? Will you take a picture of him? If you do that, I'll have a talk with the teenage boy across the street about his speeding."

Cox looked at him suspiciously and said, "All right."

The men left and crossed the street to talk to Colleen Boyle, the neighbor who'd also seen the alarm company serviceman, but a teenage girl answered the door and said her mother would be home later tonight. Baldwin left his card.

The two men got back in the car. Ortiz said, "I'll get a sketch artist out here for Cox."

"He's gone, Oscar. Dementia. I've seen it before. He can't help us. Maybe call Marsh over at the PD and ask if he's got the manpower to have some extra patrols up here, but that's all we can do. The officer was right: servicemen get the wrong address all the time. We chase these down over the city, that's all we're going to be doing." He rubbed his hands across his face. "Besides, our guy wouldn't be so stupid to come out during the day. He'd be here in the middle of the night when everyone's asleep."

Ortiz looked at the Mileses' home. "Hope you're right, man."

"Well, if I'm not, we're going to feel like shit for a really long time."

15

Yardley's heart seemed to miss a beat. She glanced down at her arms and saw gooseflesh, though the room was warm.

Eddie Cal looked different. His once-long hair had been cropped short and was now speckled with gray. The scruff on his face was white, though he was only a few years older than her thirty-eight. His forearms, the only part of him other than his face and neck not covered by the white prison jumpsuit, were pale and muscular.

The last time she had seen him, he'd dazzled her. Even as he'd said goodbye. That same irresistible charm he'd possessed from the first moment she had met him.

He told her he'd tried to stop. He kissed her. And then he ran for the window in the bathroom of their apartment and jumped onto the carport below. He must have prepared for that moment, because he went straight to a manhole in the parking lot, climbed in, and disappeared. Leaving her to be thrown on the floor by the SWAT team while she screamed that she was pregnant.

Cal then went on a crime spree across two states lasting three weeks. First he killed an elderly couple at a gas station. He struck the husband so viciously with a large rock that it shattered his skull. He stole the car, and the wife was found on the side of the road later that night, strangled to death. A few days later he broke into a home and drowned a single twentysomething woman in her bathtub before taking her cash and jewelry. The one that really got to Yardley was the family whose minivan he ran off the road. He robbed them, killing the father and causing injuries to the mother and children inside.

Yardley could only read about the crimes months after his capture, unable to face the fact that she had shared the deepest parts of herself with him. In addition to his prearrest spree, he was convicted of the murders of three couples—of breaking into their homes at night, binding and gagging them, sexually assaulting the wives, and then slitting the couples' throats.

A month after his conviction, a jury had recommended the death sentence, and he had been on death row ever since.

Cal sat down. His eyes were the color of dark-blue rose petals—Tara's eyes—and his lips had a thin red sheen to them. The guard turned the intercom on and then left the two of them alone.

She swallowed. "The camera is turned off. I know you still have appeals pending, so you don't need to worry about this being recorded."

"You're even more beautiful than I remember."

His voice had a raspy quality to it now, a grainy harshness from disuse.

She felt faint, like the ground had been ripped from underneath her. She closed her eyes and counted backward from three. At one, she opened her eyes and looked at him.

"You look healthy," she said.

"I am healthy. And I plan on staying that way. At least for a while. My final appeal will be resolved in four months. Once it's over, I'll be executed. I'm choosing hanging. I won't be put down like some dog. I'll die like a man."

"Real men aren't executed for murdering helpless people."

The venom in her voice was too obvious. She'd tried desperately to mask it—she was only here to get whatever information she could out of him, and she'd never have to come back—but she'd underestimated how powerful a reaction she would have. She felt physically sick.

"Did you ever remarry?"

"I'm not here to talk about myself."

He watched her in silence for a while. "I never stopped loving you, you know. I realize everything changed for you when you found out, but nothing changed for me."

"Are you even capable of love? Do you know what it is, or is it some type of interesting abstraction for you?"

He grinned. "Did you get the paintings I sent you?"

Cal had been a popular painter and sculptor even before all this, and after his arrest and very public trial, the dozens of works he had created skyrocketed in value. The first painting Yardley had received came with a note that she should sell the paintings to provide for her and Tara.

"Yes, I got them. Thank you."

"But you didn't sell them, did you? Did you throw them in the trash?"

"No."

"You're lying."

"I'm not. I burned them."

He smiled. "How many?"

"All of them. And everything at your studio."

He chuckled. "That's really too bad. They took away my paints about five years ago after a . . . misunderstanding in here. Those paintings would be worth a small fortune now."

"I didn't want your money."

He nodded, and Yardley wondered how long she could last here. She felt like she was spinning in a gyroscope and a sudden halt could stop her heart.

"My father says you spend a couple weeks up at the ranch every year for Christmas. I'm glad you're still connected with them."

"Your parents are good people."

A slight pause.

"How is she?" he said softly.

Yardley couldn't speak for a moment. The idea of him thinking about *her* daughter revolted her. "She's well."

"Does she ever ask about me?"

"No. She did for a few days when she was ten. She was curious who her father was. I didn't think it'd be fair to lie to her, so I let her read about you online. She had a few questions and then never brought you up again."

He looked out a small window on Yardley's side of the room. "Will you do one thing for me? I know I have no right to ask, but will you bring her to see me? Just once."

"No."

His eyes turned to her, the eyes she had fallen in love with in a different life, which she saw nothing but hate in now. "Whatever else I am, I am still her father."

"You lost that right the second you decided raping and killing were more important to you. Do you have any idea what she went through? Everyone at her elementary school found out who she was and they started calling her Bloody Tara. Even the teachers didn't want to spend time with her . . . I had to move her to a new school. We had to do that twice. She's been an outcast her entire life because of you."

"I'm sorry."

"No you're not. You're not capable of knowing what that means."

He leaned back and exhaled. "You've read too many textbooks. The trifecta of serial murder, right? Animal torture, wetting the bed, and starting fires in youth. Did I do any of those things? You know I didn't have a terrible childhood. You know my parents loved me more than anything. I'm supposed to be incapable of empathy. How many movies did you see me cry at? How many sunsets? Do you remember when I saw a real Jackson Pollock for the first time? I wept like a child. Does that fit the traits of what they've termed a psychopath? Or is human behavior maybe on a spectrum, and we're all just somewhere on that spectrum? Some of us more one way and some more the other, none of us actually choosing where we fall but just being given our traits at birth?"

"You are a psychopath. Most psychopaths don't realize they are because they have no insight into themselves."

"I felt love for you. I felt empathy. I would've given you my life in a second if you asked for it. You can't reduce me to one term and say that's what I am. I'm not psychotic and I'm not dissociative. I did what I did because"—he blinked slowly—"*I liked it*," he hissed.

She swallowed and rose to leave. "Goodbye, Eddie."

"You didn't even ask for my help yet," he said as she turned away.

Yardley stopped. She turned toward him. He had a smirk on his face. She sat back down.

"I'm guessing Agent Baldwin has already asked you for help and you refused," she said coolly.

He nodded. "Pretty odd to have a copycat. Don't know if I should be offended or flattered."

"I don't think you can help. I just came here as a favor to him."

"That's a pretty weak appeal, Jessica. You think I'm really going to help just because you told me I can't?"

"Why would you want to? Clearly all you care about is yourself. In fact I think it thrills you that someone is out there doing what you did."

"Not what I did. Not from what Baldwin told me. There're subtle differences even beyond those your boy sees."

"What differences?"

He shrugged, a grin on his face. "That's what we're going to bargain for."

16

Baldwin's home in Las Vegas, like all his homes, was temporary. He never bought, as he moved around constantly with the Bureau. The longest he'd lived in any one location had been five years, and that was in his first post. After that, it was a rotation every three years.

Later in their careers, many special agents were given the option of which posts they preferred and slowly began to wind down and establish themselves so they could have families and some stability. That had never been his experience. He wasn't a pencil pusher, and he wasn't the guy the Bureau wanted in front of the cameras or testifying at congressional hearings, so he was the guy they used to fill holes in places that needed filling.

That was how he'd ended up catching the Beltway Butcher.

The Butcher had been killing high schoolers, both boys and girls, along a stretch of highway in Texas when Baldwin was stationed at the Austin Bureau offices. Catching him had been difficult because he committed the murders in his van and then dumped the bodies on the side of the road in different locations. Because the highway stretched for hundreds of miles, they could never find enough commonalities between the victims' lives to determine how he was choosing them.

The Bureau's theory had been that the Butcher was a trucker or other type of long-haul driver, but Baldwin didn't think so. He thought it was the killer's attempt to cover his tracks and that there had to be a pattern in the dumping sites. Humans, he had always believed, only thought in patterns. Whether they were conscious of it or not.

He traced all the dumping sites to within roughly equal distance of one city: Austin itself.

From there, Baldwin honed in on registered sex offenders, particularly those with convictions for kidnapping. He found Henry Lucado because he had attempted to kidnap a twelve-year-old girl waiting at a school bus stop. Something the girl had said in her statement to the police piqued his interest. She'd told them that Lucado had offered her a ride and said he gave rides to kids her age all the time and the kids enjoyed it.

Baldwin pictured a man with a malicious grin and rotting teeth, like some evil sorcerer in a fairy tale. When he looked at a DMV photo of Henry Lucado, he just *knew* he'd found the man he'd been looking for.

Lucado surrendered without a fight. When he opened the door to his apartment and saw Baldwin standing there, he just said, "Took you long enough."

When Baldwin had slapped handcuffs on him, the first thought he'd had was of his mother's funeral, something he hadn't thought about in fifteen years.

Had he told Yardley about what had happened to his mother? He didn't think so, but he was sure she knew. He wondered if it was one of the reasons they hadn't worked out, why he'd pulled away from her, eventually standing her up and leaving the door open for Wesley. Because if anyone would understand the motivation he had to catch the monsters, it was her, and he wasn't sure he could stand seeing that understanding reflected back at him every day.

He sat on his couch, sipping beer and watching a baseball game, but the television might as well have been off, since he couldn't pay attention. The only thing he could focus on was the next house. The next bedroom bathed in blood, the next child he would have to tell that their parents were dead.

He remembered the moment he'd found out his mother had died. The detective at the station where he'd waited for his father to pick him up had said it was an accident. That her boyfriend, Felix, saw her trip and fall down the stairs to the basement because she was too drunk. The detective said sorry and then left Baldwin alone in a room with no windows.

It wasn't an accident. Baldwin, though only seven at the time, recalled Felix shouting at his mother that he would kill her if she didn't shut her mouth and treat him with respect. Baldwin didn't remember what the argument was about, but he thought it had to do with the fact that Felix didn't work and relied on his mother for food and a place to live.

Before his father picked him up, Baldwin saw Felix as he was leaving the station. They stared at each other, and an understanding passed between them: Felix had killed her, and Baldwin knew it.

He joined the San Francisco PD right out of the navy and made detective only three years later. His first act as detective would be to pull his mother's case out of the archives and work it on nights and weekends. But before he had a chance to do anything, Felix died in a drunk driving incident. He ran his car off the road and crashed into a ravine. Baldwin had visited him in the morgue, his skin white as marble, lips the color of blue chalk. He'd bent down to Felix's ear and whispered, "Burn in hell, you piece of shit."

From the coffee table, he grabbed the bottle of hydrocodone and popped two pills.

Someone knocked on his front door. He shoved the bottle of pills underneath a pillow and answered the door. Yardley was standing there. She rarely revealed what she was thinking through body language or facial expressions, something Baldwin was trained to look for. He wondered if she'd always been like that or if it was a protective mechanism she'd only developed after Eddie Cal. It threw him off to not be able to read her like he could most people.

"Hey," he said.

"You're a liar, and I can't trust you anymore," she said. "I don't want to work this case with you. Find another screening prosecutor."

She turned and started down the driveway.

"Jess, wait. Wait."

He ran in front of her. "Would you please just wait."

She stopped. "I visited him, Cason."

"Oh."

"Oh? That's all you have to say to me? *Oh?*" She shook her head. "I'm so stupid. When you showed up at the courthouse, I actually thought you wanted my help. You just wanted his help, and he'd already turned you down flat. So you thought maybe the ex-wife could sweeten the deal and get him to open up. No matter how painful you knew this would be for me, you used me to get him to help you."

"Jess, that's not what happened."

"You can seriously stand there and lie to me again?"

"I'm not lying. He didn't turn me down. He agreed to help, but he said he would only do it if you were involved."

She shook her head, looking toward the passing traffic. "Why didn't you just tell me?"

"I knew you'd say no."

"So our relationship, all the future cases we would've worked, you burned that all for this one case? Just so maybe you could get Eddie Cal to help you? And by the way, he's not helping anyone. He's doing this because it amuses him. He's going to play with you until he gets bored or until they execute him, and you won't be any closer to catching who murdered those people."

"I have to try."

"Why? You've worked cases worse than this without batting an eye."

They were standing next to her car. A bit of dirt had caked onto the side-view mirror, and he rubbed it off with his thumb. "I talked to the Deans' children. I've told parents before that their children were dead, but it's never been the other way around. Ever. They had this look in their eyes I've never seen. It broke them in such a permanent way. They're just starting their lives, and they're already broken because of one prick that couldn't control himself." He was silent a moment. "Someone had to tell me the same thing once."

"I'm sorry you had to go through that, Cason. I really am. But if I see your name on a future case, I'm going to conflict myself out and give it to another prosecutor."

"I understand."

"When did you know this was a copycat?"

"I, um . . . right away. With the Deans. I went and visited Eddie a few nights after."

She took her keys out of her purse. "I'd like to go home now. Please move."

"There're going to be more, Jess. Eddie can help us. He hasn't talked to anyone about what he did or why, not even his lawyers. We have no idea how he chose his victims. What if he has insight into that? What if he knows how this guy is choosing them? Shit, what if he knows who the copycat is? I don't want to see another couple in a bed like that and know I didn't do everything I could to stop him. You want our relationship to end, fine. I get it. But help me this one last time. Help me catch him. I can't do it without you. Not until he screws up, and who knows when that's going to be. Will it be couple three or couple eight or nine or twenty? How many people will have to be murdered for you to pick up the phone and call me and say, *I was wrong, I'll help.* Just help me now, Jess." He stood close to her. "I don't want to tell any more kids their parents are gone."

She let out a long breath, and when she spoke, he knew he had her. That was the one benefit to how well they understood each other. "He wants a deal in exchange for his help. He wouldn't tell me what it was. But I'm sure neither of us is going to like it."

17

Tara resisted family dinners lately, but Yardley had insisted the three of them eat together tonight. She knew she'd need it after the visit to Eddie Cal today. She wanted desperately to give her and her daughter a sense of a normal family life, when they had anything but.

As she came inside, Wesley, standing in the kitchen, raised his brows, about to say something, warn her, but just then Tara's bedroom door opened and Kevin came out. A slim boy with skin so pale it had a greenish hue, he constantly wore a gray beanie on his head no matter the temperature outside. He had the distinct odor of marijuana and the bloodshot eyes of recent use.

Tara said, "Hi, Mom," and giggled.

Rage circumvented any rational thought. "In my house?" She stepped close to Kevin. "You come into my house high, and into my daughter's bedroom without me home?"

"Whoa, Jessica, chill. I just—"

"Get out."

"Mom!"

"Get out, Kevin. Or I'll call the police and have you escorted out."

He smirked and waved a peace sign at Tara before brushing past Yardley and leaving.

"Mom, how could you embarrass me like that?"

"You're never seeing him again, Tara. Ever. You're breaking up with him."

"You can't make me do that!"

"You were grounded and disobeyed me, and then you brought him into my home while he's high. By the way, how did he even know to come over? You don't have a phone."

She shook her head. "This is bullshit."

Yardley stepped closer to her daughter and stared her in the pupils. "You will never see him again. Is that clear? Or my next step is to withdraw you from school and homeschool you."

She chuckled. "Yeah, right. When are you ever home to spend time with me?"

The words cut.

"I don't want to fight, Tara. You're not seeing him again. End of story."

Tara tried to push past her. Yardley pushed her back.

Wesley came over. "Ladies, let's—"

"This is none of your business, shithead," Tara said.

"Tara!" Yardley shouted.

Anger rose in Tara's face. A helpless anger. The anger of a child who knew, ultimately, they didn't have the power to fight the parent yet, and so they had to destroy as much as they could in impotent rage instead.

"I'm moving in with him. His father said I could."

"I'll have him arrested for kidnapping."

Wesley said softly, "Jess, this isn't—"

"You can't stop me!"

Tara stormed out, pushing Wesley aside. She ran out the front door. Yardley chased after her and saw her running into the night.

"Tara! You get back here right now. Right now!"

She covered her eyes with her hand, trying to calm her heart. Wesley came up behind her.

"Have a glass of wine on the balcony and try to relax. I'll go get her."

"No, I should go."

"It'll be worse, trust me. I'll go. Just try to relax."

She watched him put on some slippers and pull his car out of the garage.

———

It was an hour later when Wesley and Tara got home. Yardley had been sitting on the balcony, staring at the stars and sipping a Long Island iced tea, with a bit too much gin. She'd been thinking back to when Tara was a little girl. Yardley had thought it would be the most difficult time of being a parent, the time when Tara was helpless and required her for everything. By the end of each day, especially when she'd been working full time to support them and going to law school, Yardley had felt like she could collapse and never get back up again.

She'd had no idea those were the times she would look back on and realize were the best times, and she wondered how they had slipped away so easily, like sand through an hourglass.

Wesley sat next to her. "Is she okay?" Yardley asked.

"She'll be fine. It's just normal teenage angst, Jessica. I see it all the time at the office. Except in this case, Tara is lucky enough to have a parent who cares as much as you do." He took a sip of her drink and said, "Is this pure gin?"

"Wanted something stronger than wine."

"Well, you got it." He took one more sip and gave it back. "You okay?"

"When did I lose her, Wesley? It feels like just a second ago she was throwing her arms around me and telling me she loves me, and now she can't stand the sight of me."

"All daughters have a complicated relationship with their mothers." He was quiet a moment. "What were you like as a teenager? You never talk about your past."

Yardley felt the heat in her face and stomach from the alcohol. She was just drunk enough to not change the subject, something she was expert at doing whenever Wesley asked about her past.

"I didn't have the time to rebel or hate my mother. I was working two jobs by the time I was fourteen and going to school. I'd work from two in the afternoon to six at one job and then seven to eleven at another. I'd study for a few hours after and then do the same thing over again the next day."

"Why so much?"

She sipped her drink. "We would've been on the street if I didn't work. My mother spent her unemployment checks on liquor, and then when those checks stopped, she started on the welfare checks. She would sell the food stamps to people for half their value to buy vodka and beer because you can't spend food stamps on alcohol. There was no money left for rent or food, so that was up to me. I wouldn't have enough for the gas bill or clothes or anything like that, but I was proud I was able to keep a roof over our heads and some food in the fridge."

He watched her in silence. "Where was your father?"

"He left us when I was thirteen. Probably dead somewhere by now."

He turned his head to look at the stars. "Do you remember the first time I asked about your parents? All you said was you didn't want to talk about them. I'm glad you told me all this, Jessica. We're in this together now."

Yardley enjoyed the warmth of the alcohol in her stomach, and she was suddenly grateful for having Wesley here. He treated Tara with respect and protected her as much as he could without being overly critical, something she wondered how to do. How to strike that balance between making sure your child didn't hurt themselves and turning them into a neurotic mess by micromanaging their life. It seemed to come naturally to Wesley. He would have made a good father to young children.

"She turns eighteen in a little over two years. What am I going to do when she leaves? She's going to run to the worst men. It's her father. She's been looking for her father since she was young. I was hoping to spare her that, but I can't." When she went to take a drink, she was surprised to find her glass empty. "I visited him today."

"You're kidding."

She shook her head. "Cason didn't want my help; he wanted Eddie's. But Eddie turned him down and said he would only help if I was involved in the case. That's why Cason came to me."

"What does he want you involved for?"

"Who knows? His amusement, probably. Maybe he thinks it's funny." She exhaled. "I wish he would just hurry up and die."

Wesley tapped his thigh with his fingers, a subconscious habit he had when he was deeply considering something. "Did he ask to see Tara?"

"Yes. How'd you guess?"

"Because if I was going to hurt you, really hurt you, that's the way I would do it. Through your daughter. You're not considering—"

"Never. He will *never* see her. I won't even take her to the funeral or tell her he's died. Maybe she'll see it online, or somebody else will and let her know, but she's not going to hear it from me."

"Well, I mean, I guess it's good that it's resolved, right? You don't have to screen these murders or help in the investigation anymore."

She didn't reply.

"Jessica, you can't seriously be considering—"

"What am I supposed to do, Wesley? He has to be caught," she said more angrily than she would've liked. The alcohol caused her natural composure to weaken, and she remembered why she didn't like to drink.

"Sure, he has to be caught, and he will be. But not with you involved. Don't put yourself through this. You barely survived it the first time."

She set her glass down and stood up. Her hands felt the grainy wood of the railing as a warm breeze blew through her hair. Darkness for miles and then the soft glow behind the mountain coming from the Las Vegas Strip. It cast shadows across the sands and canyons, and somehow, with the light, they appeared even darker.

"When I find out the copycat has killed again, it'll ruin my job for me. I'll still be able to prosecute for a while, but I'll know that when it really counted, I didn't do what I could. I'll realize it was just a job, and eventually, I'll quit. Probably leave the law altogether."

"So? That's not a bad thing. There're a million other things you can do. I've always told you to go back to your photography anyway."

Photography. *How?* she thought. How could she go back to taking photographs of trees and open fields, knowing that families were being slaughtered and she did nothing to help them? When she took a family portrait, would she only see them facedown on a bed in a room from nightmares? Photography had been her passion since she was a teenager, yet from the moment she'd found out about Eddie Cal's crimes, she'd known she couldn't go back.

She stared out at the glow behind the mountain and the monstrous shadows surrounding the city, as though they were coming to devour it.

He has to be caught.

18

Yardley got a booth at the café while she waited for Ortiz and Baldwin. A young couple sat near her, arguing about budgets and who spent what. She remembered when she and Cal were that young. Cal the artist, barely able to feed himself. But he'd seemed happy the first time Yardley met him at a gallery.

One of his pieces, a series of a man standing by a fence, his face gradually disappearing over the course of six squares until there was nothing left but the fence and the farmhouse behind it, had sparked her curiosity.

Cal came up and stood behind her as she stared at the painting and said, "Do you like it?"

"I do. There's something haunting about it. The artist needs some more training, though. He's too obvious. It's the cardinal sin of art to be obvious."

He smiled and said, "I'll be sure to let him know."

It was only later that night, when her friend introduced her to the artist whose work was on display, that she saw it was Cal.

"Sorry," she said, her cheeks flushing hot.

"No, you were right," he said with a handsome smile. When Cal smiled, his eyes seemed to sparkle.

Yardley was just out of college then and barely making ends meet as a photographer. She dreamed of making enough money to have the fancy car and the large house she'd never had in childhood, but Cal didn't seem to care a bit about money. He told her he would occasionally sleep outside his apartment on the sidewalk, just to show himself that if he lost everything, it wouldn't be as terrible as he imagined. "Nothing's ever as good, or as bad, as you think it's going to be," he said to her.

They'd slept that way together once—in sleeping bags, right on the sidewalk, listening to the traffic at the intersection up the street, smelling the exhaust from semis. Yardley knew then that everything they'd been taught was important in life was a lie. She'd never worried about money again after that night.

Baldwin walked into the café just then, and Yardley leaned back in the seat. Ortiz came in a second later and said, "What up, Jess?"

"How are you?"

"Hangin' in there with this fool. You know, I invited him out with some of the boys from the St. George PD, just to go bowling and have some beers, and he said he was gonna stay home and watch a documentary on autopsies instead. He's sick."

Yardley looked at Baldwin, and they held each other's gaze. "I don't disagree." She inhaled deeply and let it out. "I've decided I'm going to help you. But there's some ground rules."

"Anything," Baldwin said.

"Whatever happens with Eddie has to be approved by me. Anything at all, Cason. Even if it's just him getting an extra dessert. I have to know what's going on with him at all times."

"You got it, not a problem."

"We can't have two running dialogues with him. He'll turn us against each other. So only one of us can speak with him and present him with anything. Be his handler, I guess you could say. I'd prefer it to be you, but I think we both know it'll have to be me."

"I agree."

She glanced at the young couple as they rose to leave. "When you first met with him, what did he tell you he wants from me?"

"Just said he wants you involved. If he were a normal person, I would say he misses you, but who the hell knows what he really wants."

"All right. Next steps. I was thinking of taking him the case files and then interviewing him after."

Baldwin grimaced. "He did make one request that I guess we should fulfill before all that."

"What?"

"He wants to see where they were killed."

19

Yardley stood outside Judge Madison Aggbi's chambers. She knocked and waited until she heard the judge's voice say, "Come in."

Yardley entered the chambers and shut the door behind her. Aggbi was close to retirement, a woman of Moroccan descent who had once been a Rhodes Scholar. They had developed a mutual respect for each other over the years. She had told Yardley she appreciated that she never filed a frivolous motion or made unwarranted arguments in her court. If the case wasn't strong enough, Aggbi knew it would be dismissed as soon as it hit Yardley's desk. Both of them had an understanding that time was ultimately the only thing of value in the world, and they had a passionate affinity for not wasting any of it.

"Counselor, how are you?" she said without looking up from her computer.

Yardley sat down across from her. "I'm well, Judge. You look tan."

"Barbados. You ever been?"

"No, never been out of the country, actually."

Aggbi turned, removing her fingers from the keyboard. "You need to have some fun, too. Work can't be your entire life."

Yardley shrugged, a shy grin on her face. "Maybe later. When my daughter is grown."

"Ah yes, I know that siren call. You always think there's going to be a *later*. How old is she now?"

"Fifteen."

Aggbi shook her head. "I remember once when you had to bring her to court with you because you couldn't find a sitter. I think she was nine or ten. I swear I've never seen a courtroom more lit up with joy than when you have a happy child in it. Children have that power, don't they?"

"Yes, they certainly do."

Aggbi leaned the seat back, relaxing into it softly. "So what can I do for you today? You said this was a matter of some urgency."

"It is. I need an order signed." Yardley took the single page out of her satchel and laid it on the judge's desk.

Aggbi read it quickly. "You can't be serious."

"I am."

She placed the document down and put her hand underneath her chin. "You want me to authorize the release of a mass murderer so he can look at a crime scene?"

"Not release. He'll be shackled, with two FBI agents and a guard from the prison with us at all times. He will have a GPS monitor on his ankle and—"

"Why on earth would you think I would do this?"

"We tried to offer him photos, but he won't have it. He has information we need, and this is one of his conditions. He wants to see the homes in person."

"Jessica, I am not authorizing this. Can you imagine if he got loose and hurt somebody? I'm the judge that signed off on it, and you're the prosecutor that asked for it."

She nodded. "I know. But I also know you understand that I wouldn't ask unless I didn't have a choice."

Aggbi glanced through the document again and said, "Have you seen him since his arrest?"

"I saw him yesterday, for the first time since . . . well, since then."

"I'm sorry you had to go through that at such a young age, and while pregnant on top of it. I can't even imagine what that was like."

"It was like having your heart ripped out of your chest by the person you love most in the world," she said, embarrassed that the words had come out of her without her meaning them to. "But I need him now."

"For what?"

"I'm screening a quadruple homicide. We think he has relevant information that could help the investigation."

Aggbi thought a moment. "You're right. I do trust you. And I know you wouldn't abuse that relationship by having me sign something you couldn't handle. That's why I'm not going to question you in depth about this. All I will ask you is, Are you certain?"

Yardley hesitated. "Yes, I'm certain," she lied.

She didn't lie, ever. It felt like acid on her tongue.

"No, I'm not certain . . . but I think it's necessary."

Aggbi nodded. She took a pen and signed the document and slid it back to Yardley. "Be careful, Jessica."

———

Yardley stood outside the prison, pacing in front of Ortiz's car. The crime scene cleanup crews were scheduled at the Olsens' home tomorrow morning, so the visit had to be done tonight.

The sun had set an hour ago, and the bright lights of the prison guard towers illuminated everything around them in a harsh fluorescence. Yardley thought it resembled the light someone would see if they were being cooked inside a microwave.

"This is a terrible idea," Yardley said.

Ortiz, leaning against his car and scrolling through social media, said, "We done it before with inmates. He ain't gettin' outa his shackles. And I'ma bust a cap in his ass if he tries. Serial killers make my trigger finger itch." He looked up at her. "Sorry, shouldn't have said that to a prosecutor."

She kept pacing, her arms crossed as she stared at the ground. A few minutes later the gate slid open and Baldwin came out. Behind him, between him and a massive prison guard in a beige uniform, was Cal in his white prison jumpsuit. Chains ran from the steel cuffs around his wrists and ankles, underneath his groin, over each shoulder, and down to the cuffs again. It looked like some contraption Houdini would attempt to get loose from.

A prison van waited near Ortiz's car. Baldwin said, "I'll ride with them."

Cal smiled and winked at her. It sent a jolt of numbness through her, like drinking scorching-hot coffee too fast on a cold day. The van couldn't pull away fast enough for her.

When they were gone, Ortiz said, "I'll give him one thing: *Dark Casanova* fits that prick. He's a good-lookin' dude. The kind that could probably walk in someplace and everybody looks at him, right?"

It's the beauty of a spider's web, she thought, staring at the taillights until they disappeared in the darkness.

20

Baldwin hit the wall of the van with the back of his fist, letting the guard know they were ready to leave. A steel-grated window separated the prisoner area from the driver and passenger seats, with two openings about the size of golf balls so the guards could spray Mace if they needed to. Baldwin sat facing Cal.

Baldwin had always thought that Henry Lucado had been the most evil person he had ever met. A murderer of teenagers without an ounce of remorse. And yet here sat a man that had murdered more people than Lucado and not only didn't feel remorse but seemed to be joyful about it. An image of this *thing* making love to Yardley flashed in his thoughts, and it sickened him.

Baldwin withdrew a small amber bottle from his pocket and took out a white pill. Hydrocodone. He swallowed it without water. Cal just watched him quietly for a long time, until they were on the freeway.

"It must kill you to have to turn to me for help," Cal said, leaning his head back against the side of the van as though they were just taking a leisurely drive.

"Not my favorite thing I've ever done."

Cal grinned and tipped his chin toward the beefy guard. "He broke an inmate's back once. The inmate struck him on the side of the head with a tray of food. He lifted him like a doll and brought him down on his knee. He never walked again."

Baldwin didn't reply.

"Oh," Cal said with a chuckle. "That's why you chose him, isn't it? Well, don't worry. I have no plans of escape. But we haven't really worked out a deal yet."

"You haven't given me anything yet."

He shrugged. "And maybe I won't be able to, but I think I will."

Baldwin felt his teeth bite down, and he had to force himself to relax. "You know who it is, don't you?"

"How could I? I'm sure you checked my mail and visitors over the years."

"We did. How many marriage proposals did you get? I counted over forty."

"Yeah . . . odd phenomenon, isn't it? They sought me out knowing exactly what I was."

"They're disturbed women that need help."

"No, they're not. They want to die, at least subconsciously. They think they're doing it because it's thrilling: the ultimate bad boy. But what their mind really wants is to die. We never actually know why we do the things we do."

"I think you know exactly why you did the things you did."

"And why is that?"

"Because you're a lunatic."

He chuckled. "That isn't why."

"Then why?"

He smiled. "If I tell you that, you'll be able to find *him*, and what kind of bargain would I get then?"

The van rattled as it hit a speed bump in a quiet neighborhood. Baldwin felt the weight of his gun against his hip, and it took a small effort not to picture shooting Cal in the head.

"If you really know who it is, you could save us all a lot of time."

He shrugged. "I've got all the time in the world."

Now Baldwin grinned. "Well, for four months, anyway."

The two men didn't speak again until the van stopped in front of the Olsens' home. Cal had asked to see both homes, but Baldwin knew there was nothing at the Deans' anymore. The relatives had repainted it and put in new carpet and furniture, and it was under contract for a sale. On the off chance the new family that had bought it came by, Baldwin refused to let Cal go there. The family didn't need to see him in their new home, which was supposed to be the beginning of a new life.

"She's quite something, isn't she?" Cal said as the guard got out on the driver's side.

Baldwin didn't respond. He thought back to the invitation, the last one he had received from Yardley while they were dating, to come to Yellowstone with her and Tara. Something Yardley had been looking forward to for months. Baldwin had agreed, but then he'd had a case fall to him a week before they were supposed to leave: a young mother sexually assaulted and strangled in a park while pushing her baby son in a stroller. He'd told Yardley he didn't want to have the case reassigned and wouldn't be going on the trip, and he couldn't understand why it made her upset. It had seemed like such an obvious choice to him. The case had to come first. Only later did he realize what he had lost with his choice. But if he had it to do again, he wasn't certain he would choose any differently.

The guard opened the van doors and motioned to Cal, who rose and went over. The guard gripped his arm and helped him down. Baldwin hopped out as the guard checked Cal's shackles. Ortiz and Yardley pulled up a few minutes later.

Cal gazed up at the moon. "I only get an hour outside, and it's in the afternoon. It's something else to see the moon after so many years. I watched blood gush from the opening in a woman's throat in the moonlight. They had a skylight in the ceiling of their bedroom. It didn't appear like blood . . . more like a deep, thick paint. Do you know I never thought to mix their blood with my paints until I was already incarcerated? How wonderful that would've been to have those paintings in the world. Of course, Jessica would have burned those, too, I suppose."

Yardley and Ortiz approached them. Cal stared at her.

"You seem cold," Cal said. "Agent Baldwin, would you please give my wife your jacket?"

"I'm not your wife. Let's just get this over with."

21

They made their way up the driveway and to the front door, which Baldwin unlocked. Yardley hated the fact that Cal would be inside the Olsens' home. It seemed disrespectful somehow, like they hadn't asked permission and wouldn't have gotten it if they had.

Baldwin went in first, followed by Ortiz, Cal, and the guard. Yardley waited a moment and then joined them.

Cal stood in the living room and looked around. Above the fireplace was a photograph that had been blown up and put on canvas: the Olsens and a six-month-old Isaac. He sat between his smiling parents, his eyes sparkling with wonder. Cal stared at it, then said, "I'd like to see the backyard, please."

They went down the hallway and out the back door. Yardley hadn't been to the backyard. It was large, artificial grass with a small play set in the corner. Palm trees pressed against the fence, their deep-green fronds overhanging the neighbor's property.

"You're wrong, Agent Baldwin," Cal said.

"About what?"

"He didn't wait in the garage or the laundry room. He would want to watch them. Watch them as they really are. It would be thrilling, wouldn't it? To know they were about to die and they have no idea? It probably amused him to see them laughing and eating, not knowing it was the last meal they would share together." He lifted his shackled hands and pointed to the play set. "If he hid under there—it's perfectly blocked from view on three sides. Unless someone came out here, bent down, and looked, they wouldn't see him. And even then, he could sprint away over the fence. If he happened to get arrested, all he'd committed was trespassing, and he could make up some excuse about missing his medication that day and getting confused and then pick another family."

Baldwin stared at the play set. "Why would you think that's more plausible than him waiting inside?"

Yardley said, "Because that's what he would do."

Cal glanced back at her, a grin on his face that told her she was right.

"How'd he get inside the home from the garage?" Baldwin said.

"That I don't know. Alarms weren't as prevalent in my day. He must have some technical knowledge that allows him to bypass them."

"But he set off the alarm to the front door. Why do that when it's unnecessary?"

"Maybe he liked watching her scared. An alarm going off and the chaos that ensued afterward would be fun to watch, wouldn't it? See the fear in Aubrey Olsen's eyes. It probably sexually aroused him."

Yardley didn't like Aubrey's name coming from his mouth.

"I'd like to see the bedroom, please."

They went back into the home. The guard held Cal's arm as they opened the bedroom door, and Baldwin flipped on the lights. Cal stood a moment, perfectly still. He stared at the bloodstains as though he were looking at a piece of sculpture that had caught his eye at a museum. Taking a few steps forward to the foot of the bed, he reached down and touched the mattress.

"Don't touch anything," Baldwin said.

Cal removed his hand, then closed his eyes and breathed for a few moments. Yardley wondered if he could smell the blood; the scent had still hung in the air like a thin fog when she had been here before.

"You didn't include the autopsy reports in the documents you gave me," Cal said. "Did the husband try to fight? Have cuts over his arms and hands?"

"Yes."

Cal nodded. "He slit his throat first and then woke her up to watch him die."

The pathologist had speculated as much. "We already knew that," Yardley said. "You're not giving us anything useful."

"How about this: he had something around her mouth so she wouldn't wake up the child."

"We didn't find any ligature marks," Ortiz said.

"No, you wouldn't if something soft was used. Women's silk underwear, say."

Baldwin and Ortiz glanced at each other, and Yardley knew they hadn't tested all of Aubrey's underwear for trace evidence.

Cal looked at Baldwin. "You're not going to catch him. He has too much experience. Probably a detective or even former FBI. Someone that might've been fired for psychological problems."

Yardley had thought the same thing but hadn't told anyone, and it made her uncomfortable that she and Cal might think in a similar way. When they were married, sometimes they would finish each other's sentences, and the memory almost made her shiver.

Baldwin said, "You'd like that, wouldn't you? Have us turning on each other while you laugh your ass off."

"Check her underwear and any silk scarves, stockings, things of that sort. And go out into that play set and search the nook. Let me know what you find."

Baldwin motioned to the guard with his head. The guard and Ortiz took Cal out, and Yardley and Baldwin stayed in the bedroom.

Baldwin stared at the now deeply brown stains on the bed.

"You didn't test the underwear, did you?" Yardley said.

"We had forensics search the drawers, but we didn't test for DNA. There was no reason to think she'd been gagged, and if she was, killers usually bring their own. But he's wrong about this. If the unsub did use something to gag her, he would be smart enough to take it with him."

Baldwin opened the drawer to the dresser and looked inside at Aubrey Olsen's underwear and bras. "I think he knows who did this, Jess. Nothing suspicious in his prison visitor logs, nothing in his correspondence . . . but I think he knows. I can *feel* it. A copycat wouldn't just copy his crimes; he'd want to reach out and get Eddie's approval. And this must be a blast for Eddie. Getting to leave the prison, seeing this . . . spending time with you. I don't know how long he's going to play with us before he gives up the name."

"If he really does know, he won't give it up. Not without something in return."

"What does he want?"

"He wants to not be executed."

Baldwin scoffed as he closed the drawer and looked back at her. "We have no power over that."

"He knows that. But he's hoping for more killings. Right now, no judge or politician would allow his death sentence to be stayed, but a couple more killings, and it'll put pressure on just the right people to do something about it or catch the blame from the public. Eddie's hoping people in power will see that letting him live in exchange for helping in this investigation is the lesser of two evils."

22

Yardley was in her office, drafting a warrant on an unrelated case, when she got the text from Baldwin. Expedited testing on all of Aubrey Olsen's underwear. One pair of black panties tested positive for her saliva and some of Ryan Olsen's blood. Preliminary field test, so twenty percent chance of false positive, but I think Eddie was right.

Yardley leaned back in her chair and thought about how to respond. The main question was, Why hadn't the unsub just taken the panties with him? Most sexual predators, whether a sexual act actually took place or not, needed some memento to relive the experience later, and that seemed like a perfect item to take. It made Yardley question whether this was a sexual predator at all.

I'll call you later, she texted.

She left her office and went across the street to a small diner, where she ordered an egg white omelet with wheat toast to make up for the breakfast she hadn't eaten.

She took out her phone and dialed a number she hadn't dialed in a long time.

"This is Dr. Sarte," a male voice said.

"Daniel, it's Jessica Yardley with the US Attorney's Office."

"Jessica, how are you? So good to hear from you."

"You as well. I hope it's not a bad time."

"Not at all. I'm in between lectures at the moment. How is everything with you?"

Though Sarte had a special interest in sexual deviance, particularly having to do with violence, he had never once asked her about Cal or her time with him, and she admired him for it.

"I'm doing fine. Raising a teenage daughter, so you can imagine how that is."

"Raised three myself. I promise once they move out and realize how difficult life is on their own, they tend to appreciate you more."

"Well, we'll see. She's much more intelligent than me. She might be able to succeed without much effort and look down on why I had to work so hard all the time. Anyway, the reason I'm calling—I assume you know I'm involved in this case with Agent Baldwin?"

"I do, yes."

"Cason is convinced Eddie Cal knows who the copycat is. I went through his visitor logs for the past fourteen years. He's had nothing but academics and journalists visit him, and his mail is primarily from the disturbed reaching out to him as a kindred soul."

"Perfectly common with serial murderers of his type, particularly the more physically attractive ones such as Cal or Ted Bundy."

"I don't doubt that. But what I need is some insight on why he's said the only way he'll help is if I'm involved. I need to figure out what he wants with me and whether he actually knows who the copycat is."

"What's your intuition telling you?"

Yardley lowered the phone as her food came, and she thanked the waitress. "My intuition is saying he wants to hurt me and doesn't know anything."

"Are you certain you wish to discuss this, Jessica?"

"I know you've been curious and you've purposely not asked me anything about it, and I really appreciate that. But I think I'm to the point I need help. I'm feeling . . . I don't know. Lost around him, I suppose. If that's the right word. I don't know what he wants, and I'm afraid it's just to harm me or my daughter."

"It's certainly possible that would be his motivation. According to his history, he's been a sexual sadist since his late teens. As far as it pertains to you, however, I'm not sure that fits."

"How so?"

"Was he psychologically manipulative during the marriage? Physically or sexually abusive?"

"No."

"Not once?"

"Not once. I don't even remember him raising his voice at me. That was part of what made his arrest so surreal."

"Well, if you're asking my opinion, my opinion is that he's being manipulative for gain since his execution is on the horizon. He likely knows nothing about these new crimes and is hoping he can strike a bargain before you realize that."

"He seems to have some insight into it. He said that the females were gagged so that they wouldn't wake up the children. Cason had some expedited field tests performed and found a pair of Aubrey Olsen's underwear with her saliva and her husband's blood on it. Why do you think the copycat didn't take that with him? Seems like a perfect memento."

"Perhaps he took something else. Some offenders, particularly when they're in the home at night and there is no fear of anyone discovering them, like to video record their assaults."

A chill went down Yardley's back. The thought of having to watch those videos as part of this case made her nauseated.

She said, "Let's just assume, for the sake of argument, that Eddie does have some information that can help us apprehend this man. How would you go about getting this information from him?"

"There's only one choice in the matter. Eddie Cal is about to be executed. He would rather die than give the information freely, so you can ignore him and assume he's being untruthful, or . . ."

"Or what?"

"Or you can give him what he wants."

"Which is?"

"You."

23

Yardley signaled to the prison guard that she was ready for Cal to be brought in. She sat on the metal chair with her back straight. Sunlight from the single window in the room illuminated the handprints on the glass from visitors. Several of them were from children.

She had thought all day about what Dr. Sarte had said. Give herself to Eddie Cal to get what they needed from him. It was a long shot that he even knew anything. For him to know who the copycat was, they would have had to correspond, and there was nothing in Cal's logs to indicate he'd spoken to anyone but academics and journalists. Still, it was an angle that needed to be explored. If next week came around and another family was killed, she would constantly wonder what would've happened if she had played Eddie Cal's game.

One irritating thought kept pounding away at her, though: What had Sarte meant when he'd suggested she "give herself" to him?

Cal was led in and sat down. He grinned at her but didn't say anything until the guard had left.

"It was nice spending that time with you the other night," he said.

"Do you know who it is, Eddie?" she said, ignoring his comment.

"Maybe."

"No, no more games. I'm tired of them. You're going to tell me what you really want, and I'm going to see if I can get it for you. If you want to play games, I will leave and cut you out of this case completely."

"Will you now? And I wonder how you'll feel when that next couple is shown on the news, drained of blood? I can't imagine that would sit well with you. You always had a soft heart."

She sat quietly a moment. There was no use lying to him; out of everyone in her life, only two people had ever been able to see completely through her, to know her inside and out: Tara and Eddie Cal.

"If another couple dies and I didn't do everything I could to stop it, it'll hurt, but it'll hurt less than continuing to play games with you. I'll leave and never come back, Eddie. Tell me what you want."

He leaned back, his arms resting on his thighs. "Two things, both simple, really. I want to not die, obviously. I want my execution stayed and my sentence commuted to life."

"You know I can't promise that, but I'll see what can be done. What's the second thing?"

"That one's much easier. I want to see Tara."

"No."

"It's nonnegotiable."

"Then we're done here."

She rose, and Cal quickly said, "I know who it is."

Yardley held her breath, though she hadn't meant to, and she had to force herself to exhale as she sat back down.

"You're lying."

"I'm not."

"We've already gone through your mail and visitor logs. He couldn't have communicated with you."

He shrugged. "Maybe he's in here with me? Maybe he's a guard?"

Yardley felt an icy excitement, tempered with disappointment in herself. How had she not thought of that?

"Or maybe he's one of the janitors, or one of the contract employees that comes in to repair the air conditioner or replace light fixtures? Or maybe he handles our laundry? The thing is, Jess, you'll have to check every single employee in this place and then the hundreds of contractors they get bids from for the maintenance and construction and everything else. It'll take weeks, if not months. And the clock is ticking on that next adorable family." He leaned forward. "I don't want to die, and I want to see my daughter. Those aren't unreasonable requests."

Yardley swallowed. "I'll see what I can do."

———

When Yardley got home, she stood in the afternoon sun on her balcony. It had rained briefly, and a rainbow appeared farther out over the red rock mountains. She was sipping wine when Tara came out and sat at the table.

She'd been suspended now for four days, and as far as Yardley could tell, she spent most of the day reading texts on advanced scientific topics or painting. It was as though she'd been liberated to study the things she was really interested in.

Tara's paintings always made Yardley uneasy. Most of them got thrown in the trash, but she kept a few of them and hung them in her room. Yardley couldn't tell why some were thrown away and some were kept.

So far, none of them resembled Eddie Cal's works, but her fear was that one day she would come home and see Tara working on something that Cal had also painted. She couldn't remember now when it was exactly that Tara had started painting, and it bothered her that she'd forgotten.

They hadn't exchanged more than basic words since the fight about Kevin, but Yardley took her presence now as a good sign.

"The other day, Mr. Jackson mentioned again that you should test into a university or go to a gifted school. That they can't challenge you anymore and you're acting out." Yardley turned and looked at her daughter while leaning back against the wood railing. "Is that what all this is, Tara? Are you bored and acting out?"

Those blue eyes stared unblinkingly at her. "I won't go to a gifted school, but maybe it is time to transfer to UNLV. I'm interested in some topics that I'll need researchers in those subjects to help me understand. I'm not sure I want to leave Kevin, though. He graduates next year, so I might wait."

Yardley didn't show the disgust she felt at the thought of her daughter changing her path in life for someone like Kevin. "UNLV is a good school. You'll have fun and make a lot of new friends."

Tara answered while staring at the rainbow. "I'm a fifteen-year-old daughter of a murderer that's going to test directly into a doctorate program and get better grades than everyone there, Mom. I'm not going to be making any friends." She paused a moment, her eyes never leaving the rainbow. "You left your iPad unlocked the other day with the case files open. There's a copycat?"

Yardley felt anger rise in her, and she had to breathe a moment to let it subside. "Tell me you didn't look at the files?"

"I saw Eddie's name on the open page. I think if anyone has a right to know what's going on with him, it's me."

"Tara, that is not—"

"I heard you talking to Wesley about it, too. That you've gotten Eddie involved. What does he want in exchange for his help?"

"That's none of your concern. This isn't for you to worry about."

"We're past that, Mom. You can't protect me from him. He's my father, and nothing is going to change that."

Yardley felt weak. She sat down at the table next to her daughter and finished her wine before setting the glass down. "What he wants is irrelevant."

"Does he want to see me?"

There was a slight tinge of hope in her voice that broke Yardley's heart. She took Tara's hand. "Sweetheart, he will hurt you. That's what he does. Family, friends, wife, daughter—none of that matters to him."

Tara nodded. "I sent him a Father's Day card once. I was eight. I remember you sat me down when I was ten to tell me everything about him, but I knew long before that. I found an old driver's license of yours in a drawer with the last name Cal, and it didn't take long to figure it out. I waited for weeks to see if he would send something back, but he never did." She exhaled loudly. "It's a shame. I'd be curious to see what traits we share. Does he have an aptitude for mathematics, too? Is his favorite color purple? Does he hate the texture of raisins or the smell of rain on pavement?" She paused. "Is his darkness inside me, too? Dormant and waiting for its chance to get out?"

"Tara—"

She pulled away and stuffed her hands into her pockets. "Are you going to find the man that's copying his crimes?"

Yardley watched her in silence a moment. "Yes, we will."

"If he's really emulating Eddie, the ultimate prize might be for him to get to us. To kill the family of Eddie Cal," she said solemnly, looking down to her shoes.

"Tara, look at me . . . I will never, *never* allow anyone to hurt you. Nothing is going to happen to us. We will catch this man, and he will never hurt anyone again."

She watched the rainbow a moment in silence. "Better go. Need to look into a graduate program, it looks like."

She left Yardley alone on the balcony, watching gray clouds drift back toward the mountains. Making the rainbow fade to nothing.

24

Tara was in her room, Wesley was working in his home office, and Yardley was doing yoga in the living room when her cell phone rang. She intended to ignore it, but after it went to voice mail, it started ringing again.

"This is Jessica," she said, trying to keep the annoyance out of her voice.

"Jessica, it's Sofie Gledhill from the prison. Sorry for bothering you on your personal cell, but there's something you need to know right away."

"What is it?"

"Eddie Cal received an email about half an hour ago. We screen them before he receives them. Jessica . . . it's from the man that killed those two couples."

She felt a surge of adrenaline. "I'm on my way."

She quickly texted Baldwin and then changed into a black skirt and white blouse, running her fingers through her hair before going to Wesley's office. She knocked first, as he hated his concentration to be broken abruptly, and he said, "Come in."

He was seated at the desk with his bifocals on, staring at the blue light glittering from the monitor in the darkened room. The sun was nearly set, and only a faint orange glow came through the windows.

"I have to leave. I'll be back in a few hours."

"Where you heading?"

"The prison."

He stopped what he was doing and looked at her. He took his bifocals off and placed them on the desk.

"To visit him?"

"He may have received an email from the person we're looking for."

"What does that have to do with the screening prosecutor?"

"They may need a warrant. I can get an e-warrant within minutes if I'm actually there."

He considered her. "I'm not some first-year law student, Jessica. You don't need a warrant to check prison email."

"No, but you might to get records from the internet service provider." She went up and kissed him on the cheek. "Few hours, promise."

———

Baldwin wore a suit coat but no tie when he picked Yardley up. She noticed he hadn't shaved in a few days, and the dark circles under his eyes had gotten worse. His car smelled of Polo cologne and freshly cleaned leather. Ortiz sat in the passenger seat, wearing a Detroit Lions T-shirt underneath a suit coat.

Baldwin handed her his phone when she sat down in the back seat. An email was up on the screen. It read:

Mr. Cal,

I hope all is well with you. I know a little something about existing behind walls myself. I learned rather quickly that you must live inside your mind. That's something they can never take away from you.

I assume you haven't read anything of my work. Such a shame, I truly feel you would be proud of the continuation of your work I've taken upon myself.

You must receive voluminous amounts of mail, and perhaps even boasts such as these from potential admirers. To show you the veracity of my claims, I've attached a photo you may enjoy.

Will be in touch soon if I hear back from you.

With warm regards,

Your Admirer

Yardley scrolled down and saw the attached photo. A quiet gasp left her.

Aubrey Olsen. The photo had been taken from no more than two feet away. The black panties they had found were wrapped around her mouth, her eyes wide with terror, blood caked over her face and in her hair. Lying next to her, facedown in the bed, was her husband. The lighting of the photograph indicated it had been taken at night.

"We'll need to have OTD verify it," Baldwin said. "I sent it to them as soon as I got it with a request for expedition. I also called Greg down here."

OTD, the Operational Technology Division, was the technological wing of the Bureau that helped with forensic examination of technology. Greg Newhall was the OTD liaison for the Las Vegas Bureau office.

Yardley had relied on him heavily in the identification and apprehension of several rapists that had recorded their crimes on cell phones and uploaded them to the internet. Something that occurred much more frequently than the general public knew.

"It's her," she said softly.

When they arrived at the prison, Newhall was waiting for them outside. He wore a short-sleeve button-up shirt and had the thick glasses that a seventh grader would wear. His bald head shone in the harsh lighting of the prison parking lot, and he held an aluminum briefcase.

"Took you long enough," he said. The only one he smiled at was Yardley. "How are ya, Ms. Yardley?"

"Fine, Greg. Thank you for asking."

He had only ever called her Ms. Yardley, and she had noticed him looking at her whenever it seemed she wasn't paying attention. Once, at the gym across the street from the federal building, she had caught him watching her bend over to lift some weights off the floor. He'd blushed and wandered away. When she'd been leaving, he had made an awkward attempt to ask her to dinner, but she had told him she was already dating someone and it wouldn't be appropriate. He'd blushed again and apologized.

The four of them entered the prison and met Gledhill at the check-in desk. She waved them through the metal detectors and scanned her ID badge on the elevator.

The second floor housed the computer room, where most inmates were granted minutes based on good behavior. Because of their constant communication with their attorneys and a Supreme Court decision that granted them access to legal research, news, and archives, death row inmates were given unlimited access, but it had to be monitored.

Inside the computer room, a young guard and an older man in a sweat suit stood by. The guard looked nervous and had his thumbs tucked into the utility belt on his waist. The older man just looked annoyed.

Gledhill said, "It was that computer station there."

Newhall put down his briefcase next to the computer. He opened the case, revealing a microcosm of wires, motherboards, polished steel tubes and connectors, a monitor, and a host of other items Yardley couldn't identify.

Cal's email was already up on the prison's computer. Newhall clicked a few areas on the email, and a string of densely packed letters and numbers popped up in a new window. The code of the email. Newhall's normally anxious demeanor and body language instantly changed as he leaned forward, his fingers on his chin, and read the code on the screen like a medieval monk translating a lost document.

"See, you read these headers chronologically," he said. "Every new server it goes through adds its own snippet of code. So what you want to do is go to the top. That's the first gateway. That's the one you want."

Newhall opened a program on the monitor in his aluminum box; the window was labeled *MyCoolToolBox*. He connected the prison computer to the box, then cut and pasted the code from the computer into the toolbox, and another page of code popped up on the monitor. Newhall then connected a small device to the USB port of the computer. The code moved on both screens, with new code scrolling up from the bottom. He let it run for about thirty seconds before saying, "It's right there."

A string of numbers separated by periods appeared on-screen. A pop-up on the toolbox said, *IP not listed on blacklist.*

"That means it wasn't sent from an IP that's been used before by scammers. See, he tried to throw us off by sending it through different servers, probably used some program he downloaded for free from the web. Really simple stuff. He might as well have written it on a rock and thrown it through a window."

Newhall mumbled to himself and then hummed as he typed into the toolbox. Yardley recognized the tune as "She Blinded Me with Science" by Thomas Dolby.

"Okay," Newhall said after a minute. "Easy peasy. This is the gateway of origin and the IP it was sent from. They tried to create a false trail but, like I said, really amateurish stuff. They probably just researched it online and used what was there. Your guy isn't someone with any technical knowledge."

Gledhill said, "Why now? The murders started weeks ago. Why contact him now?"

Yardley and Baldwin glanced at each other. Baldwin looked down at the photo of Aubrey, which came up as Newhall scrolled through the email code.

"Because he knows Eddie's involved in the investigation now. And there's only one group of people that know about that. Law enforcement." He looked back to Yardley. "He's one of us."

25

When Baldwin dropped Yardley off at home, he said he would inform her of any updates and then added, "And Jess, I'm really sorry about lying to you. I shouldn't have done that. I hope you can forgive me for it."

She didn't respond as she got out of the car and went inside.

No sounds came from Tara's room. She opened her daughter's door. Tara slept on her side, her face turned toward Yardley. It was the face of the baby Yardley remembered. Only in sleep did she see that child anymore. When Tara was awake, Yardley became painfully aware that she was becoming her own woman, a person separate from her. It felt like a piece of Yardley being pulled out of her and drifting off into the world by itself.

Tara's paintings hung around the room, and Yardley purposely didn't look at them.

She shut Tara's door and went into her own bedroom. Wesley was already asleep. Yardley changed and slipped into bed, lying quietly and staring out into the night. The moon was a silver-white crescent glowing dimly pale through the glass doors leading to the home's second, smaller balcony.

Wesley's hand came up to hers, and their fingers interlaced. His eyes opened, and he watched her a moment before kissing the back of her hand.

"I hope you know what you're doing," he whispered.

He closed his eyes again, and she fell asleep that way, holding his hand with the moonlight streaming into the room and casting shadows in the corners.

———

OTD traced the IP address to an apartment in Primm about an hour outside of Las Vegas. It belonged to an Austin Ketner. The name sounded familiar to Yardley, and before she could think to look up why, another text came through. Baldwin had run his name, and the search revealed dozens of news stories: he was one of Eddie Cal's victims.

Yardley sat at her desk and read the story in the *Las Vegas Sun*. His parents had been Cal's third and fourth victims.

The investigators thought Cal had seen the family somewhere, possibly at a Mexican restaurant the Ketners had eaten at the night before their deaths. It was purely conjecture, Yardley knew. Since Cal had never spoken a word to anyone about his crimes, they had no idea how or when he chose his victims. The convictions were based primarily on DNA evidence typed from semen. Cal was what was known as a secretor and left semen at every residence. There was also a witness who Cal had missed when he'd been climbing through a window of one of the victims' homes. The witness had seen his car parked around the block and taken down the license plate. A subsequent search of his private art studio had found several items from victims as well as a kill kit with duct tape, rope, knives, and blade sharpeners.

Austin Ketner's older brother had found their parents dead.

A photo of Austin was embedded in the article she read. He couldn't have been older than ten or eleven. His eyes dull and vacant as he glanced at the camera. He'd be in his midtwenties now.

Yardley closed the windows on her computer and leaned back in her chair. A single thought wouldn't leave her: *What was I doing that night?*

Where had she been on the Tuesday night the Ketners had been killed? She had likely kissed Cal and told him she loved him as he left to murder Austin's parents.

She let out a long breath and then texted Baldwin back: I want to meet with him as soon as he's in custody.

26

Primm was an unincorporated area with only about two thousand people, so the Las Vegas Police Department handled their police calls. Baldwin had gotten them to provide a strike force of five officers. He and Ortiz drove their own car while the officers drove unmarked sedans to Ketner's address.

Ortiz drove while Baldwin read about Ketner. White male, midtwenties, loner, several alcohol-related convictions for DUI or public drunkenness, one ex-wife and a child he owed several years of back child support to. He wasn't law enforcement, and that had bothered Baldwin, but it turned out Ketner worked for a commercial cleaning company with contracts for the government buildings in Las Vegas—including the federal building. Ketner could very well have been inside Baldwin's office after hours, gained access to his files, and learned that Eddie Cal was helping them in the investigation.

"I thought I was done with this shit," Ortiz said.

"With what?" Baldwin replied, not looking up from his phone.

"Wearing vests and kicking down doors, man. I did it for five years with the narcs unit in Detroit. I just wanted a nice office job where I wouldn't have to pull my weapon every other day. It's not that I don't like it, but I need to stay safe, for Rebecca and my little girl."

"They put you where they need you. Besides, you're up for transfer in a year, right? Maybe you'll get lucky and they'll put you in bank fraud or something."

Ortiz took a sip out of a Big Gulp. "You think he's really our boy?"

"Email came from his apartment, and he's potentially got access to our files, and North LVPD's files. And he meets the rough outline Dr. Sarte provided."

"What about Jessica?"

"What about her?"

"What does she think?"

Baldwin looked at him now. "What does it matter what she thinks?"

He shrugged. "I dunno. Seems like she understands these types of men."

Baldwin turned back to his phone. "No one understands these types of men."

The apartment complex was near a casino that had a roller coaster in front and boasted on a sign that it was family friendly. The officers pulled around back behind the complex, and Ortiz and Baldwin parked in front. The CO of the strike force called Baldwin and let him know they were in position. Ketner's employer had told them he had Fridays off. The manager of the complex told them Ketner was home.

"Let me talk to him first," Baldwin said.

"Still think that's a bad idea. We should go in hot."

"Just give me five minutes."

An officer who'd been posted nearby informed them that no one had come in or out of the apartment. Ortiz was strapping on his vest when he said, "If this is the dude, he's outa his head."

"Just five minutes," Baldwin said as he got out of the car. "Could save us someone getting hurt."

"Or get your ass shot."

Baldwin wore a T-shirt and jeans. He slipped on an oversized Jersey Devils hoodie to cover the Kevlar vest. As he took the stairs to the second level, he pretended to be looking down at his phone. No one was out in the complex, though a garbage truck rolled in and headed to the dumpsters in back.

Baldwin knocked on Ketner's door.

A short man with cropped brown hair and glasses opened it. Acne dotted his face, and he had the burst capillaries in his nose of full-blown alcoholism. The effect was odd on his face, since he didn't look that much older than a teenager.

"Hi, hey, I'm hoping you can help me. I'm looking for Rachel Madrid? She lives a few doors down, and I can't get ahold of her."

"Don't know her. Sorry," Ketner said.

"Yeah, well, would it be okay if I left a package with you for her? I tried your neighbor, and they're not home."

He looked annoyed.

"Sorry," Baldwin said. "I know it's a pain, but I'm driving out to Colorado today and it'd cost me like thirty bucks if I have it sent."

"Yeah, fine."

"Cool. Thanks. It's a little heavy, though. Can you help me grab it from the trunk?"

Ketner sighed, clearly irritated, but said, "Let me get my shoes."

He left the door open while he went down a hallway in his apartment. Baldwin stepped inside. The place wasn't dirty or cluttered, but it held the permanent stench of pot and cigarette smoke. A computer sat on a small desk in the corner.

Baldwin glanced down the hallway. Then he clicked open the photos app on the desktop and scanned them.

"Hey!"

He turned to see Ketner standing there.

"What the hell do you think you're doing?" Ketner came forward and pushed Baldwin aside as he closed the windows on his computer.

"Sorry, just checking email," Baldwin said.

"Get the hell outa here! I ain't keeping a package for you now."

"Get down on the ground, Austin," he said calmly.

"What?"

Baldwin took the badge out of his pocket and brought it up a few inches. "Get down on the ground quietly, and this will go very smoothly. If you don't, in about three minutes, the officers that have surrounded your building are going to rush in here, and I can't predict what's going to happen. Though I'm sure it's going to hurt a lot more than you just listening to me."

Ketner's eyes went wide as he stood there motionless. In a flash, he swung at Baldwin. Baldwin ducked, came up behind him, and wrapped his arm around the man's throat. He swept Ketner's legs out from under him, landing on top of him as they hit the ground. Baldwin squeezed. He felt the gasp of air as Ketner tried to breathe.

"Easy, easy . . . just relax."

Ketner fought, arms flailing, trying to claw at Baldwin's face. Baldwin had his other arm pushing on the back of Ketner's head, completely cutting off the man's air. As soon as he felt him losing strength, Baldwin eased his hold. "That's right, just take it easy . . . take it easy."

Baldwin rolled off him, pulled out his phone, and texted Ortiz that he had him.

27

Once Ketner was secured in the car, with Ortiz in the driver's seat, Baldwin joined the officers in the search of the apartment.

They gathered the computer and a laptop to take to the station. Baldwin would rather Newhall go through it than whoever they used, so he quickly texted Newhall and told him he might need him later tonight.

Great, he replied. Can't wait. You're buying me dinner.

The officers were looking for weapons, notes, anything indicating Ketner had murdered two couples. That wasn't what Baldwin looked for. He looked for any indication that Ketner was the type of man that *could* murder two couples.

The small bookshelf in the living room held mostly spy novels. The fridge, nothing but deli meats and frozen dinners.

The bathroom cabinet contained several medications, including Percocet. Baldwin glanced around to make sure no one was looking and slipped the bottle into his pocket. Then he stood there, staring at himself in the mirror, before putting it back in the cabinet and leaving the bathroom.

In the bedroom, he put on latex gloves and ran his hands underneath the mattress, checking under the bed. The nightstand had three drawers: there were papers and a few photographs of Ketner with a young woman, probably his ex-wife. One photograph showed a little girl with curly blonde hair smiling widely as she sat on Ketner's shoulders.

The closet held few clothes and only two pairs of shoes. On the top shelf were several boxes. These were the documents Ketner had thought important: his divorce decree, receipts for large-item purchases like the couch and the television, and some old, empty wallets.

Toward the middle of the shelf sat a white shoebox. Baldwin brought it down and took off the lid. A necklace. He turned it over. There was an inscription near the clasp on the back. He read it, and his stomach dropped.

———

The LVPD brought Ketner to a station near downtown Las Vegas. A thoroughly modern building that would've made any police department in the country jealous. Baldwin gave strict instructions to the detectives assigned the case to not speak with Ketner until he arrived.

When he got there, Ketner was being interviewed by two detectives. Baldwin sighed and opened the door. He smiled at the detectives, who he'd never seen before, and said, "Agent Cason Baldwin, nice to meet you guys. You mind if I speak to you outside for a minute?"

They glanced at each other and then rose. Baldwin followed them outside.

"Look, guys, this is a federal matter. Our office has taken this investigation over. I know I'm not your boss and who gives a shit what I say, right? But the DA's Office and the US Attorney's Office have worked it out and agreed this should stay federal. I appreciate all the help you've given, but I need to speak to him alone."

"If he lives in the—"

"He's accused of crimes in North Las Vegas and St. George. He only lives in your jurisdiction. So please, just let me do my job and get him talking, and we can all go home."

One of the detectives scowled at him, but neither said anything. This case would attract massive media attention, and Baldwin had no doubt the detectives had gone in to question Ketner on orders from higher up. A chance to show the cameras they had beaten the Bureau to the punch.

Baldwin left the detectives standing there and entered the interview room. He took out his iPad as he sat down and looked at Ketner quietly for a while. Ketner nervously played with his fingers, then said, "Can I go?"

"Why would you think you could go?"

"Because I didn't do anything. Those detectives were asking me about some families that were killed. I have no idea what they were talking about."

"No idea at all?"

He shook his head. "There's been some sort of mix-up. I mean, you guys clearly don't have the right person. This is crazy. I would never hurt anybody."

Baldwin remained motionless for a good ten seconds before he unlocked his iPad. On the screen was a photo of a sapphire necklace.

"What's that?" Ketner said.

"Oh, come on, Austin. Give me some credit."

"What're you talking about? I've never seen that in my life."

"It belongs to a woman named Aubrey Olsen. She was killed about a week ago in St. George, Utah."

"Yeah, but what does that have to do with me?"

"I found this necklace in your closet in a shoebox."

His eyes went wide. "What?" He jumped to his feet, and Baldwin did, too, touching his firearm with his fingertips.

"This is nuts!"

"I need you to sit down, Austin."

"I've never seen that before in my life!"

"We can talk about that, but first I need you to sit down."

Ketner trembled. Baldwin removed his hand from his weapon and sat down first. Ketner followed.

"I'm telling the truth. I found that in your house, in a shoebox in the closet. The inscription is from Ryan Olsen to his wife. It's apparently worth quite a bit. You made a good choice in mementos. I haven't found anything from the Deans, but I have a feeling that I will as we go through your things." He leaned forward, his hands on the table. "I'm so sorry for what Eddie Cal did to you, Austin. I know he's the cause of all this. As far as I'm concerned, the Deans and Olsens are his victims, not yours. But we also need to protect other people that you might do this to. So I need you to be honest with me, and I promise I'll be honest with you. How many others are there?"

"Other what?"

"Other families you've done this to."

"Holy shit, are you not listening to me? I didn't do anything. I've never seen that necklace before in my life."

In his sixteen years of law enforcement, Baldwin had dealt extensively with men that could lie so well they probably fooled even themselves. Though Ketner's reaction seemed genuine, there was no plausible explanation for his having Aubrey Olsen's necklace at his apartment other than that he'd killed her. A pure psychopath was expert at manipulation, and Baldwin knew he had to tread carefully. If Ketner felt he couldn't control the situation, he would shut down and ask for a lawyer.

Baldwin took off his jacket. "I guess we're going to be here awhile."

28

Yardley had waited late into the night, but Baldwin's text never came, and he didn't reply to her messages.

When she arrived at the office in the morning, several prosecutors, including her boss, Roy Lieu, were gathered in the general office area past the metal detectors, sipping coffee and chatting. They saw her and started clapping.

Her face grew hot with embarrassment. "Something happen?"

Lieu handed her the *Las Vegas Sun*. The first-page story was about the apprehension of Dark Casanova Junior.

"Great work on this, Jess. The attorney general called to congratulate us. It's national news."

"How? This wasn't public yet."

"Agent Baldwin's ASAC called me to tell me they've made an arrest, and I got ahead of the story. There would be a lot of questions about why we put people at risk by not releasing information about a serial murderer in the community, so I gave an exclusive to the *Sun* last night in exchange for them spinning it a certain way. Basically explaining we couldn't release anything to the public because we believed the DCJ was following his press."

Yardley gritted her teeth. "Did Austin Ketner confess?"

"No, he denies it, but he has no alibi for the dates of both the Deans' and Olsens' murders, and they found a necklace of Aubrey

Olsen's in his closet and a pair of underwear from Sophia Dean tucked underneath his socks."

Yardley dodged the people coming up to congratulate her, went to her office, shut the door, and read the story. It painted a picture of a victim of Eddie Cal's who'd lost his way after the death of his parents. A young child scarred and broken who'd turned into the monster that had so deeply affected him. Toward the end, the story mentioned that they were running a search for crimes with similar elements to see if Ketner had claimed any other victims.

Yardley put the paper down and leaned back in her chair, staring blankly at the frosted glass walls of her office. The next killings could happen as early as next week if the unsub stuck to the cycle.

She texted Baldwin.

I want to meet with him right now.

———

The Clark County Detention Center looked more like a futuristic office building than a jail. Stone and plenty of glass to allow in as much light as possible. The architect had clearly meant to make a place where the staff would get sunlight during the day and be able to see the streetlights at night. Jail staff had high rates of depression, alcoholism, and suicide.

The all-white corridors echoed with her footsteps as she showed her badge and identification to two sets of guards. The badge allowed her to go through without being searched.

Another guard waited for her outside the visitation room and scanned an ID badge that turned the light above the door from red to green. The room had several windows and no glass partitions to separate the visitor and the inmate.

Ketner came in wearing a dark-blue shirt and blue pants with slippers on his feet. He sat down across from her, and Yardley looked at the guard that had brought him in and said, "Thank you. I'll call you when we're finished."

"You sure? I can stay."

"I'm fine, thank you."

She waited until he'd left before looking at Ketner.

"Who are you?"

"My name is Jessica Yardley. I'm the assistant US attorney assigned to your case."

"You have to help me," he said, his voice high with desperation. His eyes became wet with tears. "I didn't do anything. They think I killed four people."

"Did you?"

"No! I would never hurt anybody. I don't know how those things got into my apartment. That FBI agent doesn't believe me. He says he's going to investigate the case but that I may want to think about a plea deal to avoid the . . ." His voice cracked. "To avoid the death penalty."

Ketner's head fell low, and he sobbed.

"Where do you think those items came from?" Yardley asked. The majority of murderers she'd dealt with would not take an ounce of responsibility until they had absolutely no choice. And many of them had learned somewhere in life how to cry on command.

"I don't know. I don't have an alarm, and I'm gone from six to six five days a week. Someone must've snuck in and left them there and sent that email from my computer."

"Why would someone want to do that?"

"I have no idea." He looked down to the table. "My parents were killed. In exactly the same way they're saying I killed those people." His eyes met hers. "I would never in a million years do that to someone else."

Yardley swallowed down the guilt she felt. What would Ketner say to her if he knew she'd been married to the man that had murdered his parents? If Cal had said he was staying late at his studio that night, she likely would've been eating ice cream while watching a movie.

What movie was I watching while my husband killed your parents?

The thought sent cold revulsion through her. Whatever Ketner was now, wherever his life had brought him, she was responsible, too.

"We need to establish where you were on the two nights in question. April eighteenth and March twenty-second."

He shook his head. "How am I supposed to remember where I was on some random night a month ago?"

"I don't know. That's up to you."

He swallowed. "I eat out most nights. Yeah, I eat out most nights. I don't have dinner at home. What days are those on?"

"April eighteenth was a Friday; March twenty-second was a Wednesday."

"Um . . . Friday. Okay, I pretty much never eat at home on a Friday. I go out with some friends sometimes or just by myself and eat out. Look into that."

"Your attorney should be doing that."

"I don't have an attorney."

"You need to get one."

"I didn't do anything. Just check. *Please* . . . I don't want to die."

Yardley watched him for a few more seconds and then rose. Lying to yourself was the worst type of lie, and though she didn't want to admit it, she put into words what her instincts had already told her: she believed him.

29

Yardley waited across the street from the jail at a coffee shop. She'd texted Baldwin, asking him to upload Ketner's credit card statements to the US attorney case management site. Sipping coffee, she stared absently out the windows as clouds rolled in and blocked the sun, and a slight drizzle started. The Las Vegas streets weren't meant to handle rain, even small amounts, and puddles instantly formed. People ran from buildings to cars and vice versa, as though acid were falling from the sky.

"Hi."

She looked up to see a man in a sports coat with a turtleneck. Handsome with a strong chin and green eyes.

"Mind if I join you? I hate to see a pretty lady by herself staring at the rain."

"I'm fine, thank you."

"You sure? Pastry on me and an open ear to listen to what's bothering you. You look sad, so I thought maybe you'd want some company."

"That's considerate of you. But no, thank you. I'm fine."

"How about if—"

"I don't know what type of women this aggression works on, but I'm not one of them. Please leave."

He lost his smile and mumbled something inaudible before leaving. Yardley turned back to the rain pattering the streets outside.

Baldwin texted that the statements were ready. She logged on and quickly scanned them.

Ketner had no charges on March twenty-second, but he had two on April eighteenth, one at a drive-through coffee stand and one at a hamburger restaurant called Fat Blue Burgers. Yardley knew it. It was a fast-food place not far from Ketner's home.

The droplets of rain felt warm against her skin as she walked to her car.

The early lunch crowd had packed Fat Blue Burgers. Yardley cut the line and leaned over to the cashier. "I need to speak with your manager, please."

A woman in a black T-shirt and jeans came over. "I'm the manager. What can I do for you?"

"May we speak in private?"

She stepped to the side, and Yardley followed. She showed her the badge and said, "I'm with the US Attorney's Office. Someone we're investigating ate here one night. I'd be very curious to know what time. I saw the video cameras you have. How long do you keep the video?"

"It's just uploaded to our security people. We don't keep them here."

"Can you please contact them for me?" The woman didn't move. "I'm happy to get a warrant from a judge to make sure you're covered. It'll take a little time to process. In the meantime, can you get the video so I can have a look?"

She nodded. "Let me call the district manager and make sure it's okay."

———

Baldwin was waiting in his car at the curb when she arrived at Iron Fortress Security. He joined her on the sidewalk and said, "You work quick."

She wondered why he hadn't already run Ketner's credit cards before arresting him. She hoped he wasn't so wrapped up in wanting this case closed that bias affected him. When law enforcement officers looked to prove the guilt of a suspect, it never worked out well: it was how innocent people ended up in prison. When Yardley taught training seminars to federal agents or local police, she always told them that once they had a suspect, they should think in reverse: try to prove they didn't commit the crime. If they couldn't, it meant they likely had the right person, and then and only then should they gather more evidence for the court process.

The thought came to her again of Baldwin showing photos to a witness before a lineup. She watched as he put some gum in his mouth. He looked fatigued, and his normally pressed suit had wrinkles and looked like it'd been worn one day too many.

"Did you have anyone run his cards before?" Yardley asked as casually as possible.

"Didn't get around to it yet. Probably would've happened in the next day or two."

"Probably?"

He stopped and looked at her. "Yeah, probably. I have other cases still, you know. Is there something you want to say to me, Jess?"

"No. Just want to make sure we're on the same page."

"Well, we are. Now let's get this done. I got a briefing with my ASAC in an hour."

The security company occupied a small office on the first floor. Baldwin showed his FBI identification and said he needed to speak with whoever was in charge. Yardley saw a painting on the wall. A river ending in a waterfall that fell into a large pool. She stared at it awhile: Cal had painted something similar, but in his the pool had reflected an empty blackness. The water falling and disappearing into nothingness, and on the edge stood a young boy, looking down into the abyss.

By the time she turned back around, Baldwin had gotten a regional manager to approve their viewing the Fat Blue Burgers video. He led them to a room filled with monitors and other electronic equipment.

The manager booted up the videos while they stood in the back of the room. The videos were in color, and the quality was excellent. Most security companies had switched to digital.

"Okay, okay, okay," the manager mumbled to himself. "We got April fifteen, sixteen, seventeen . . . here's the eighteenth. You want the whole day?"

"Just probably after four," Yardley said.

"Well, I can't just sit in here with y'all. This is how you fast-forward, and this is how you rewind, these circular knobs right here. I'll pop in to check on you every now and then."

Baldwin sat down and began fast-forwarding. He got to double and then triple speed and took it a little further.

"Drive-through?" he said.

"He said he sat down."

They watched in silence awhile before he said, "It's him, Jess."

"Then you have nothing to worry about."

He looked back to her. "What is that supposed to mean?"

"Just that some fishermen get so wrapped up in the catch they don't notice they have the wrong fish. I know you're too even tempered for that. Stop. Right there."

Baldwin stopped and rewound the video. It was clearly Ketner. He ordered at the counter. When his food was ready, he took it and sat down at a table and ate.

"Seventeen minutes to eat," Baldwin said. "At around seven thirty."

"That doesn't fit the timeline."

"Sure it does, if he went to the Olsens' right after he ate. He knew he'd be hiding at the house for hours and wanted something to eat first."

"You talked to him. Did he really strike you as someone sophisticated enough to pull this off?"

"Why not? You can learn anything you need to online. And he has access to law enforcement files and forensic laboratories. Who knows how much he's learned over the years?" He swiveled the chair around to look at her. "You're right about the blinders law enforcement put on, but lawyers can have the same blinders. They believe so strongly in someone's guilt or innocence they ignore any evidence that doesn't fit their belief."

She looked at Ketner's face on the screen. Was that who she was looking for? The monster that had made Aubrey Olsen watch her husband bleed to death in their bed, knowing she was going to die next?

"Who we're looking for is so careful," she said. "Keeping the mementos at his home is about the sloppiest thing he could've done. Especially in locations so easily searched. He could've tucked them in a vent or kept them in a waterproof case in the toilet tank."

"Offenders like this lose their grip as time goes on—you said so yourself. They get sloppy as the fantasy and reality lines blur. Eddie did it, too. That's how he got caught."

"Eddie was thinking clearly. He was caught for other reasons."

"What other reasons?"

Before she'd met Dr. Sarte, he'd written a piece in a psychological journal stating he thought Cal had been subconsciously trying to get caught after he'd found out his wife was pregnant. That he had in fact been trying to stop.

Before she could answer, Baldwin said, "We think it was just two couples, but what if this was couple number six or seven for Ketner? By then, his thinking is completely skewed. Ketner's got the psychology, reliving the trauma from his youth; he's got the mementos in his home and the email sent from his computer; he doesn't have a solid alibi, and he had plenty of time to commit the offenses. I'm not seeing the problem."

"If I wanted to divert attention away from myself for these crimes, Ketner would be a perfect person to set up. People would think because he was a victim of Eddie's, he's gone insane and is doing what was done to him. From what I've seen, he's not sophisticated enough to be the person we're looking for."

"Do you know Ketner's IQ? Because I don't. A psychopath like him would be a master at manipulating others."

She shook her head. "I don't think it's him. I'm not saying let him go, but let's keep digging."

"He has Aubrey Olsen's damn necklace at his house!" Baldwin nearly shouted. "What the hell do you want to dig for?"

"Don't you dare yell at me, Cason. And I'm not filing this case against Ketner as it is."

He ran his tongue along his cheek, his face flushed with anger. "Maybe it was a mistake bringing you in on this. You're too . . ."

"What? Emotional? Too much of an emotional woman, Cason?"

"I wasn't going to say that."

She headed for the door. "Find me more, or I'm cutting him loose."

30

Despite her sharp tone with Baldwin, Yardley knew exactly what would happen with Ketner, and she had no power to stop it. The AG himself had called Lieu to congratulate the office on apprehending a killer that had gotten national press. There was no way they wouldn't file charges against him. If Yardley didn't do it, Lieu would simply take her off the case and assign it to another prosecutor that would.

The knowledge hung like a weight chained around Yardley's neck. She tried to shake it off by walking and got a call from Wesley as she made her second trip around the block.

"Hey," she said. "I feel like going out for dinner. Want to meet me somewhere?"

"Sure. But I was actually calling about Tara. She with you?"

"No. Why?"

"I know she's grounded, and I've been home all day and haven't seen her. Did you check her room this morning when you left?"

She stopped walking. "No."

"I took a peek around ten. She wasn't in there."

———

After trying everyone Tara knew and not finding her, Yardley figured there were only two possibilities left. Ice filled her chest as she parked in her driveway and raced to Tara's room.

Many of her preferred clothes and shoes were gone, as was a jewelry box she kept her favorite earrings and bracelets in. Tara kept her money in a jar in her closet, something she had done since the time she was seven years old. The jar wasn't there either.

Sharp panic threatened to overwhelm her. One possibility was that Tara had run off with Kevin after Yardley had made clear Tara wouldn't be seeing him anymore. The other was too horrific to even contemplate, but she forced herself to consider it: the copycat knew Yardley was involved and had taken Tara. But before putting herself through that, she had to make sure Tara wasn't with Kevin.

His home was in Las Vegas, about thirty minutes from the Strip. The neighborhood sat against small rocky hills, and the homes appeared dilapidated. She realized she'd been out here before: she'd come with a parole officer to search a defendant's house. He'd been convicted of a brutal domestic violence assault and was restricted from possessing firearms. His wife had called Yardley one night, terrified, and said that he had bought several firearms from a street dealer.

Luckily, the parole officer had found the weapons quickly, without incident. Yardley had agreed not to prosecute him for the new offenses if he moved out of the home and left the title to the wife.

She found Kevin Watson's home. His father, Dustin Watson, answered in a sleeveless shirt, smoking. His face pockmarked and greasy, he wore ripped jeans and dirty boots. Yardley caught a glimpse of a leather vest draped over a recliner. It had the patch of a motorcycle gang on the back—the Berserkers. She had dealt with them several times before.

"Is Kevin here?"

"Who are you?"

"I'm Tara's mother."

He looked her up and down. "What you want with Kevin?"

"My daughter left the house without permission, and I think she's with him."

He smirked. "Shit, well, that sounds like him. He got all sortsa ass comin' over here at all hours."

Yardley kept the anger out of her face. She forced a grin and said, "I would really appreciate if I could speak with him for a minute."

He shook his head. "Ain't here."

"I called the school and he never went today. Do you have any idea where he might be?"

"Nope," he said, staring down at her breasts.

She took out her card and handed it to him. His expression changed when he looked down at it: the look of someone that had served time. Ex-cons had two reactions to law enforcement: rebellion or subservience. Those that got out and rebelled against authority usually ended up back inside quickly. The smart ones, the ones not damaged beyond the hope of repair, realized that fighting all of society wasn't a winning battle.

Dustin Watson seemed like the type that rebelled.

"You a cop, then?"

"A prosecutor. Will you please have Kevin call me as soon as he gets in?"

He flicked the card into her face.

Her face steeled as she stared at him. "You're going to tell me where Kevin is, or I'm going to check if you're on parole and then tell your parole officer you assaulted me."

"Assaulted you? Bullshit. I ain't done nothin'."

"You threw an object and hit me in the face. That's assault. Now, do you know where Kevin is or not?"

He stared at her. Yardley took a quick step toward him, as though to hit him. He immediately backed up, a shot of fear in his face.

"Have him call me. Don't make me come back out here."

She was turning to leave when she glanced down to the chain hanging from his belt loop. It held a set of keys. With the keys was what looked like a flat pocketknife. It had the word *LOCKMASTERS* printed on it.

"What is that?" she said.

"What?"

She nodded to the keys. "It's a lockpick."

"Yeah, so? I get locked out of the house sometimes."

"Is it a universal lockpick?"

He spit onto the porch by her feet. "Unless you gonna arrest me, you need to get the hell outa here."

When she was back in her car, she went to the US attorney database on her phone and put in Dustin Watson's name and address. Then she called Baldwin. "I need your help, Cason."

31

When Baldwin arrived at Yardley's, she was standing out on the main balcony, a phone glued to her ear, on hold with an office supply store, waiting to speak to the mother of one of Tara's friends.

Baldwin said, "We have an Amber Alert out and an APB. I circulated her picture to the police departments north and south for fifty miles each way. Kids run away, Jess. It's just something that happens. But we'll find her."

"She's never done this before," she said, leaning against the railing. "That boy she's with . . ."

"I know." He hesitated. "The father admitted he left last night. Gathered some of his things and said he wouldn't be back."

"Left to where?"

He shrugged. "Father didn't know. Oscar says he didn't seem like the type that cared much about where Kevin went or with who."

A woman got on the phone, and Yardley explained the situation, but she said her daughter was at school and she didn't know anything about Tara, then ended the call abruptly.

Wesley came out, his phone in his hand, and said, "Had someone on the Las Vegas PD do me a favor and leave her photo at the more popular cheap hostels in town."

"Thank you," she said, and bit her thumbnail.

Wesley turned to Baldwin and said, "Agent Baldwin. It's been a bit."

They shook hands.

"I appreciate you helping us," Wesley said.

"Of course, anything you guys need. I'm going to head over to the high school and talk with some of the students that know Kevin. They had to drive wherever they're going, and since Kevin and Tara don't have cars, somebody drove them."

"Or they called an Uber," Yardley said.

"We'll check with all the cab and ride-sharing companies, too." He stepped closer to her and gently took her hands in his. "I'll find her," he said. "I promise."

"Thank you, Cason."

He nodded to her and to Wesley, who gave him an icy stare, and then he left.

She leaned over the railing and looked out at the empty desert. "I did this to her, Wesley."

"You did no such thing."

"She's trying to find where she fits in the world, and at every turn, instead of letting her figure it out, I punished her for it."

"What were you supposed to do? Let her run wild with this boy and act on whatever whim they happened to have at the time?"

"I don't know. Something. Something different."

He came up behind her and put his hands on her shoulders. The hot breath on her neck made her skin prickle, and he kissed her cheek and said, "You are a great mother and did everything you could. This was unavoidable, just something kids do because they don't know what else to do. I see it all the time at the Guardian ad Litem's Office. A lot of them return home within a day, a lot of them within a week—"

"And some of them never. And we can't tell which group she falls in."

He gently turned her around to look into her eyes. "We are going to find her and bring her home, and then the three of us are taking a vacation. Mexico, England, Scotland, wherever. Doesn't matter. We're going to spend some time together and work through this. Okay?"

"What if she's not with Kevin? What if that *thing* broke into our house and took my daughter? It's my fault, Wesley. I took this case. I brought him into our lives. If anything happens to her"—she turned back around and looked out over the desert—"I won't survive it."

32

The exposed brick walls of the cell were meant to convey some type of elegance, give it a modern feel, but Eddie Cal had always thought it resembled the inside of a wood-burning oven from centuries ago, where the bricks absorbed the essence of the food cooked inside. He wondered what essence these bricks had absorbed.

As he sat on his cot, his back against the wall, sliding a pencil across the smooth surface of a small canvas on his lap, he thought how ironic it would be if they had ovens here for the inmates to choose as a method of death. The veneer of civilization around the death penalty was a misguided salve. People, he thought, should take responsibility and see it for what it was: the murder of another person. Death row would run so much more smoothly if those in charge accepted that they were murderers, too.

The drawing, done freehand without a model, was as good as any professional artist on the outside could have made. Cal had been painting since the age of two. His uncle David, though a relatively decent man, had been a struggling businessman, always looking to make a quick buck if he couldn't borrow money from Cal's father, Steven. He had taken some of the paintings Cal had done when he was four and put his own name on them, claiming himself to be a Scandinavian impressionist. The paintings had sold well, until Cal had refused to make any more for him because he couldn't paint what he wanted.

His uncle had demanded he paint flowers and forests and rainbows, children by streams and families roasting marshmallows at campfires.

"Your paintings are getting . . . troubling, Eddie," he had told him at the age of five. "I think we should focus more on happy things. You like happy things, don't you?"

Happy things . . . happy things . . . Cal had wondered for thirty-four years what exactly his uncle had thought that phrase meant, and why he'd assumed it would be the same from one person to the next.

Cal had made a few more paintings, but the scam had ended when his father found out what Uncle David was doing, and he wasn't allowed to take Cal to his apartment anymore, where he'd been making the paintings for him. Cal had later heard David died of a drug overdose somewhere on the East Coast at the age of forty-one.

The drawing in his lap, sketched and without color, as the warden had only approved his access to a few supplies as a reward for helping the FBI's investigation, was a nearly exact rendering of his ex-wife. Nude and lying on the beach. Her hair wet with the incoming tide, a hand to her breast, her gaze lost in some distant memory. Her body had no skin, revealing the exposed sinew and muscle underneath.

On death row, the seventeen inmates that awaited execution knew each other, knew each guard, and understood that if they treated the staff well, they in turn would be treated well. In exchange for their good behavior, they were allowed to roam freely among the corridors. Cal had the additional security of protective custody, in case one of the other inmates tried to hurt him, but even he was allowed to roam if he desired.

None of the other inmates ever spoke a word to him or looked in his direction.

Cal rarely left his cell. There were no windows here, and one dark dungeon was as good as another, so he preferred to stay in his cell most of the time, though he liked having the cell door open. It reduced the sense of being trapped.

"That bitch was hot," a voice said from his cell door.

A guard stood there, a man with a scar running down the side of his bald head. He demanded the inmates call him Sergeant, though Cal was reasonably certain he had no prior service in a police force or military unit.

"I watched her on the cameras when she came. How the hell you lost a piece of ass like that I don't know. I woulda dug in and hung on like a monkey over a crocodile pit. Guess that's why your dumb ass is in here and I'm out there."

"You seem to be in here with me most days, Sergeant. You're as trapped as I am, but you're here willingly. Who's the dumb ass?"

The Sergeant approached Cal's cot and spit a green glob of phlegm onto his pillow. "Gimme the drawing."

"I'm not finished yet."

"You finished when I say you finished." He reached for the canvas.

In a flash, Cal leapt at him and swung. The fist connected like a steel bat and knocked the Sergeant back against the bars of the cell. Cal grabbed his television off the stand by the cot and slammed it into the Sergeant's head, knocking him unconscious and spattering blood over the walls. The television crashed onto the floor, a mess of broken glass and plastic.

Blood flowed out of the gaping wound in the guard's head and over the cement floor, drizzling toward the drain in the center of the cell. Cal stared at it. The darkness of it, the thickness, the way it slowly rolled and churned like a stream along the bumps and imperfections of the floor.

He soaked the tip of the pencil in the blood before putting it to the canvas, coloring in Yardley's face.

As an alarm sounded through death row and boots stomped heavily in the corridor outside, a smile crept to his lips.

He dipped the pencil into the blood again and continued his work.

33

Yardley had no sensation other than cold numbness, and the house felt like a cage. As Wesley watched the evening news from the couch, she went into Tara's room and sat on her bed, elbows on her knees, her head down as she stared at a pair of Tara's slippers. It felt like a limb had been cut off, and the shearing pain of the cut wouldn't get any better until Tara was home.

She'd spent the day obsessed with Dustin Watson, trying to find any sliver of evidence that could point to him being the copycat and wondering whether he'd gone so far as to plant his son in Tara's school just to get her to come to him willingly. His criminal history—from petty theft to attempted sexual assault—made him no saint, but was he smart enough to have killed the Deans and the Olsens? The only way to know for sure was to search his home.

Yardley had gone so far as to buy a lockpick and sit outside his house, intending to wait for him to leave and break in to make sure Tara wasn't locked up in the basement, but she'd lost her nerve when his biker gang had shown up, and she'd left a message for his parole officer instead.

Yardley looked at Tara's walls. Her paintings were up. Three of them. All were exquisite—the lines perfectly drawn, the paint smoothed and angled just right—and if someone didn't know it was a fifteen-year-old that had created them, Yardley was certain they would think it was a professional artist with decades of training and experience.

Yardley had once asked her why she painted, and all Tara had said was that everyone needed a creative outlet. They had never spoken about it since.

The parole officer had called her back and said she was out of town but would meet Yardley at Dustin Watson's home tomorrow morning.

Yardley had also explained everything to Baldwin when he had come to the house to check on her, and he had stationed two agents near Dustin Watson's home, keeping tabs on who was coming and going.

"If he leaves and there's no one home," Baldwin had said to her, "there might be a brief period where I could break into the home and search. But we don't have enough for a warrant."

They'd stared at each other, an unspoken resolve between them.

She had nodded, and he'd said nothing before he left.

Yardley couldn't be indoors anymore. After changing into yoga pants and a T-shirt, she said, "Heading out."

"Where to?" Wesley asked.

"Just going for a walk. I'm going to go insane if I just sit here in between walls."

"I'll come with you."

"No, I'd like to be alone."

Outside, even though the sun was setting, the temperature stayed hot, and she could feel the heat coming off the pavement of her driveway. The mailbox out front required a code, and she input the numbers and retrieved two envelopes. One was a statement from her health insurance provider about her therapy sessions. The other, a plain white envelope with no return address.

She took the letter out, and as she read the first few words, her mouth went dry and the hair stood straight on the nape of her neck.

The FBI's evidence response team had taken possession of the letter. Several of their forensic technicians were at Yardley's house right now. She stood outside on the front porch, watching them lift the envelope with small stainless steel forceps and place it into an evidence bag.

Baldwin paced the lawn, speaking with the Trace Evidence Laboratory in Washington. When he hung up, he came to her and said, "You okay?"

Her arms were folded across her chest, not because she was cold but because she couldn't be certain her hands weren't shaking, and she didn't want anyone else to see.

"He has . . ." The words wouldn't come. They were too terrible, and it was as if her body rejected them, refused to speak them for fear of making them true.

"He doesn't have her," Baldwin said. "Tara running away and you receiving this letter are two unrelated events that happened in close proximity to each other. You said Tara probably snuck out last night. That wouldn't have been enough time to send the letter."

"Unless he took her and dropped the letter off simultaneously. Made it appear as though it went through the mail."

"I doubt it, but I'm having Oscar check with the post office just in case. We'll know soon. And how would he get into your mailbox without a code anyway?"

As she watched a forensic tech with purple latex gloves put on thick black goggles and run a heat lamp over the mailbox, the words of the letter ran through her mind over and over:

> *So happy you've taken an interest in my work, Ms. Yardley. The Olsens seemed to particularly interest you, didn't they? Happy family. About as happy as a family could be. Imagine her shock as that first spatter of her*

husband's warm blood hit her face. I wish you could have
seen it with me.
   With warm regards.

It was the *With warm regards* that sent a shock like ice through her. No one but the guard at the prison who screened incoming emails, the warden, Baldwin, Ortiz, Newhall, and her had read the email to Cal. No one knew that the copycat had used that phrase in the closing of the email.

Wesley came out of the house and said, "We can stay at my condo until they catch him. I'll have to go clean it up first and get it ready, but it shouldn't be a problem. Plenty of room."

Yardley shook her head. "Tara might come back. I need to be here."

"Jessica—"

"No. I'm not leaving, Wesley. This is my home. You should go, though. This isn't your fight, and there's no reason for you to be put in danger."

He stared at her, and she could tell that she had hurt him. He said, "That's a helluva thing for you to say to me," before going back inside the house.

"You can't be here alone," Baldwin said. "It's good that Wesley's here."

"I know. I don't know why I said that. Just . . . reactionary, I guess."

"I think it might be best to have a patrolman up here at night. If the LVPD won't do it, I'll get someone from the Bureau."

"No. If you want to help, find Tara. Put every resource you have into finding her."

His hands on his hips, he glanced over his shoulder to two technicians chuckling about something. They saw him looking and stopped.

"Cason?"

"Yeah?"

"He called me Ms. Yardley in the letter. There's only one person in my life that calls me that."

Baldwin stared at her. She could tell he knew exactly who she was talking about.

And it fit. Someone who had the technical and forensics knowledge. Someone perfectly placed to set up Austin Ketner.

Baldwin dialed a number on his cell, his eyes never leaving Yardley. "Greg," he said, "this is Cason Baldwin. I owe you dinner for that help with Austin Ketner's laptop, and I'm free right now. Give me a call."

He hung up. "I'll head over to his house," he said. "If it's him, Jess, if it's been one of us this entire time, I don't know what I'll do."

"Text me immediately if—"

"Of course."

She watched him leave. While she waited, there was only one place she could think to go. One place that could give her answers.

———

Once at the prison, she sat in her car a long time. Staring at the dark clouds rolling past the moon. She had texted Warden Gledhill's private cell phone and asked for this arrangement, explaining that Tara was missing and she needed to see Cal right away. The warden hadn't asked any questions, just told her to give them twenty minutes to prepare the safety precautions and get Cal out of ad seg.

Yardley left her car. A guard, the massive hulk of a guard from the night Cal had been taken to the Olsens', waited for her by a side entrance to the prison. A young, short guard, Native American, stood with him. He smiled at her and said, "Hey, I'm Anthony."

"Hello."

Walking down the long corridor to get to the second building, which housed death row, she remembered suddenly that Austin Ketner was incarcerated still. That he was not the man that had sent that letter to her, since all his mail was monitored, and that he was likely not the man that had killed the Deans or the Olsens. Roy Lieu would fight cutting Ketner loose. He would say he had a partner on the outside, which was a theory he could move forward on. There were two of them, and that was why Ketner had the mementos but someone else had sent the letter. A conviction against him would play well with the cameras and therefore with her bosses, even if the public thought another killer still lurked out there somewhere.

"We had to put him in ad seg," Anthony said. "Sick shit busted open a guard's head real bad. Like, you could see skull and stuff," he said with obvious glee. "And then get this: used his blood to keep drawing with. He was drawing—"

"Shut up, Anthony," the other guard bellowed. His deep voice sounded like the growl of a large animal.

When they came to death row, they turned right toward some rooms Yardley had never been in before. *Administrative segregation* was the polite way of saying isolation. A barbaric practice, Yardley had always thought, but she didn't know what a viable alternative was. When an inmate could no longer be trusted around others, what was the government supposed to do with them?

The bare cement room had no windows or furniture, and Cal sat nude, leaning against the wall, his eyes closed in meditation. A bucket sat in the corner along with a roll of toilet paper. A thick, transparent plastic barrier separated inmate from visitor: transparent so that the guards could monitor inmates in ad seg around the clock for potential suicide attempts.

"Repugnant, isn't it?" Cal said, opening his eyes. "Seems like something they'd have done in the Tower of London five centuries ago, not today."

The steel bench in front of the barrier felt cool against her as she sat down. "They said you hurt a guard."

"Yeah, that will definitely leave a scar. It's his own fault. I only have four months to live, and they still think threats work on me. I have nothing they can take anymore, no threats they can make to motivate me." He stared at her, the darkness in his eyes piercing her. "What do you have to motivate me with, Jessica?"

She swallowed. "Tara's disappeared. And I got a letter today." She took out her phone and pulled up the photograph she had taken of the letter. She rose and pressed it against the barrier. Cal stood, tall and muscular, and white as an albino from lack of sun for over a decade. The steel restraints rattled as he approached the barrier. They stopped him two feet from the plastic.

"That's interesting," he said. "Is he right about your feelings toward the Olsens?"

"Yes."

"Any idea how he knew you felt that way about them?"

"I visited their home but not the Deans'. I didn't think anything would be there anymore."

He raised his eyebrows. "So it's someone that knows the case intimately enough to know you visited the Olsens' home but not the Deans'. Only one group can know that."

"Law enforcement. I know."

He nodded slowly, his eyes never leaving hers. "I think you have an apology to issue to that boy at the jail."

"Maybe you should give him an apology, Eddie. For murdering his family. He had nothing after his parents. No relatives old enough to look after him. He and his brother disappeared into the foster care system."

Cal sat down cross-legged on the floor. "You think the letter and Tara disappearing are connected? I don't think so."

"Why's that?"

"I never hurt children. If he truly is a copycat, he wouldn't either."

"Unless he's desperate and we're close."

"Possible, but why disturb you? There's no particular skill you can bring to the table that the FBI doesn't have. He should've antagonized the lead agent on the case, but instead he antagonized you. Why do you think that is?"

"I don't know." She leaned forward. "If you know who it is, Eddie, please tell me." The words tasted like foul rust in her mouth. "*Please.* He may have our daughter."

He inhaled deeply and closed his eyes. "You know what I'm going to miss most? The ocean breeze hitting my face while I'm on a boat. I haven't felt that for two decades. I remember the ocean has a scent, but I've forgotten what the scent is and replaced it with something else. It's a pleasant smell, like rain on freshly cut grass, but I know it isn't how the ocean smells. Isn't it funny the things your mind makes up when you don't have the real thing anymore?" He opened his eyes and watched her. "It's only with smell, though. Why do you think that is?"

"You have an eidetic memory. That's why you could always paint so perfectly with no models. Many people with eidetic memories report that smells actually impact them more than sights, even though the sights are what they can recall with perfect detail. Didn't you know that about yourself? Or did you just want to hear a compliment from me?"

He smiled, and the smile was awful.

"Are you enjoying my pain, Eddie? Do you hate me that much?"

"No. I don't hate you. I never have, not even for a second."

He had likely said it to show affection, but Yardley knew she would never feel affection for him again. The mask he had put on for her was off: the mask of a gentle artist who loved her, who loved the mountains and poetry and sunsets. With the mask off, it was hard to see him as even human.

"You hated me by virtue of what you did to me. All those years we were married, all the time I gave you, the pieces of my life, were based on a lie. You were playing a role, and I bet you just thought it was hilarious that I fell for it, didn't you? You must've thought I was the biggest fool in the world."

"No. I always told you your heart was too soft. You want to believe people are good so badly that it opens you up to be taken advantage of by people who are not."

"So it's my fault?" she scoffed. "You're no different than anyone else in here, Eddie. You're not special. You hurt others because you're weak, and you blame them for it."

"Not true, but I know it's difficult for you to look at me now as I am, rather than who you remember. It wasn't a role, Jessica. That person was me as well. Just a different part of me. And that part of me loved you."

"Then help me find our daughter. Do you know who this man is? If you don't, then tell me how he's choosing his victims."

"I have no idea."

"How did you choose them?"

There was silence while he thought, and then he said, "I told you what I want in exchange for my help. I want my reprieve."

"The only way to reprieve a federal death row inmate is through appellate courts or the president, and it's nearly impossible for someone that's killed as many people as you have."

He shrugged. "Those are my terms."

"Even to save your own daughter?" She shook her head. "I thought maybe there was something human left in you. Some flake of mercy. But I guess that died in this place, if it ever even existed."

She rose to leave, and he said, "If you had gone to the Deans' home, do you think he would have written you?"

"What do you mean?"

"Just what I said. If it had been reversed and you went to the Deans' and not the Olsens', would he have written you? If the answer is no, then there's something about the Olsens that worries him. Something he doesn't want you to see."

Yardley stared at him a long while. "If you change your mind and want to help me save our daughter, I'll tell the warden to get you a phone whenever you need, and you can call my private cell number. My own number, Eddie. I'm trusting you with that. That's how important this is to me."

He tilted his head. "A husband on death row and a daughter in a grave . . . that wouldn't speak very highly of you at the US Attorney's Office, would it?"

A slight curl to her lip was the only hint of emotion she allowed in front of him. "Help me find her," she said, "and I'll see about getting you a reprieve. Your life for hers."

34

Despite the late hour, Yardley drove straight to the Olsens' home. She called the St. George PD and got a lieutenant on the phone. The lieutenant said the keys had been given to the Realtors but that the Realtors had had some people go through it today and it might be open.

She parked out front and watched the house a long time before going to the front door. It was locked, but the windows had been left open. An attempt to get the smell of death out of the home, though she doubted the Realtor had thought of it quite that way.

The backyard fence was unlocked, and the large back window leading into the kitchen was open, so she removed the screen and crawled through.

The home was cool and smelled like lemon. On the kitchen table lay a stack of flyers with a description of the home and contact information for the Realtor. Decorations that hadn't been there last time Yardley had visited filled the home, and photos of some other family took up the rooms and hallways. This was no longer the Olsens' home, and nothing remained of them here.

Yardley did a walk-through and stopped before Isaac's bedroom door. She opened it and found new furniture and decorations like in the rest of the home. On the new nightstand was a copy of *Where the Sidewalk Ends*. It even had a bookmark placed in a random spot to give the appearance of life.

She sat on the bed and glanced around. The smell had left—the smell of Isaac she had experienced the first time she'd been here. It smelled of wood polish and air fresheners now. She thought it stank like a funeral home.

The entire home had become a deception. A temporary light over a horrific silhouette.

The master bedroom doors were open, as was the window. Though the sheets, blinds, carpets, and closet doors had all been replaced, the bed frame hadn't. It was the same dark-wood one the Olsens had lain on the night they'd died. Likely, it was an expensive bed and difficult to take apart and move, so the family had decided to leave it. Or maybe they didn't want it, and the Realtor didn't care.

The closets held clothes, but they were not the Olsens' clothes. The drawers in the bureau were empty. The mirror was new. Only one thing Yardley noticed spoke of what had happened here: the ceiling fan. On one of the blades, she saw a dark-brown splotch the size of a dime. She wondered if it would ever be cleaned or if it was just a scar on the house that would never be removed.

She sat on the bed and touched the pillow on the side where Aubrey Olsen had died. A shiver went up her arm and gave her gooseflesh: the pillow felt warm.

Yardley exhaled and rose, looking around one more time. If Cal was right and the copycat thought he had left something behind, it was gone now.

As she was leaving, she gripped the knobs on the double doors to close them and noticed a difference of pressure as she pulled the doors closed. Something she hadn't paid attention to the first time here.

One of the doors, the one on the right, was just a fraction harder to close. She opened them again and then peered at the hinges on that door. The hinge on the top looked newer than the ones in the middle and bottom. It had been replaced. It was surrounded by scratches in the paint. As though someone who had never replaced a hinge had grown frustrated and attempted to hurry, becoming sloppy with the haste.

Yardley leaned in close: the hinges had three screws each. The top screw on the upper hinge was a different color than the rest. The two screws underneath it were polished silver, but the top screw was a dull metallic color. She touched them and felt a difference between the top one and the bottom two. Could be that Ryan Olsen simply hadn't had a screw of the same type as the others and had used a different one.

Yardley took several pictures of the hinge and the screws with her phone. She'd show it to Baldwin. Ask if the evidence response team had cataloged it and found anything unusual about it.

Yardley looked at the bed one more time and then shut the doors.

35

"Bill was here again this afternoon," Rosalyn Miles said with a yawn, as she turned on her side in the bed. "He thought he'd borrowed our ladder, but I told him it was his. His memory is just getting worse and worse."

"I wonder if we should call someone," Jay said, not looking up from the paperback novel he was reading next to her. "Between that and the alarm company guy last week, he might be getting to the point he needs a nurse over there or something."

By the time Jay flipped to the next page, Rosalyn was already snoring. He envied her ability to drift off so easily. Depression had hit him hard last year when his mother passed from a stroke, and though for a time he hadn't had the energy to get out of bed, there were nights now when he was plagued with insomnia. Tonight, that meant he'd still been awake when his youngest, Abe, had had a bad dream. Jay spent a half hour with him, holding his hand while surfing some social media sites on his phone with his other hand.

Jay felt his eyelids grow heavy. He turned off the light and laid his book on the nightstand. Within minutes, he was fast asleep.

———

Jay felt a hand shaking him. A shot of adrenaline went through him. Fear was always the first thing he felt on being woken from a deep sleep. He saw Rosalyn's face near his, and it calmed him.

"What is it?" he groaned.

"I heard something."

"What?"

"I don't know. Something from the kitchen."

"It's probably Doug getting some water or something."

"Will you go check?"

"It's nothing, Ros. That's why we have an alarm."

"It was really loud. Please?"

He sighed and tossed the comforter off himself as he swung his legs over the side of the bed. Rubbing his eyes, he yawned and then rose and went out into the hallway.

The living room was still and quiet. It was far enough from the kids' rooms that they wouldn't see the light on. Jay flipped the wall switch. Nothing looked out of place. He went through the living room and saw several toys by the TV. He mumbled, "Damn it, Abe," as he picked up the toys.

The toy bin was in the playroom in the basement, and he headed there, turning on the light. He tossed the toys in the bin and turned to walk back upstairs when he saw that the bathroom door was closed. Two of his five kids slept down here, and Rosalyn always left the bathroom door open with a night-light on to ensure they didn't trip or pee all over the toilet.

Jay figured one of them was in the bathroom. He knocked softly, but no one answered. Inside, the bathroom was empty. Several more toys lay on the floor. He shook his head as he bent over to pick them up. When he rose, the knife swept down and slashed a fiery pain from his shoulder to his elbow.

Blood spattered against the wall as the figure jumped out from behind the shower curtain. A black stocking pulled over his head blocked any view of his face, and he wore a black shirt and pants. Jay screamed as the knife came down again. He stumbled backward. It missed his face and embedded into his collarbone.

Terror, agony, and adrenaline hit him like a bolt of lightning. Jay Miles fought.

He leapt at the figure and tackled him around the waist. They hit the side of the tub hard, the attacker's back slamming against it with Jay's full body weight on top of him. Jay was bigger, but the attacker was stronger.

He pushed Jay off, and they were on their feet again. The attacker swung in a wide arc with the knife, barely missing Jay's throat. The knife slashed across his chest, leaving a warm trail of blood that flowed down his shirt.

Jay knew he was going to die if he couldn't get the knife.

He tried to grab the handle, but his hands were too slippery with blood. The figure wore latex gloves, giving him a better grip. Jay pulled his hands up onto the blade. The steel cut into his flesh, causing him to howl in pain as he tried to pull the knife away.

Rosalyn came running down the stairs. She screamed.

"Set off the alarm!" Jay shouted, losing his grip on the knife.

Rosalyn ran to a window and opened it. The alarm beeped upstairs, a warning that allowed time to input the code. The boys came out of their rooms. Rosalyn grabbed them and sprinted up the stairs.

Jay put his full body weight onto the blade, pushing it back toward the attacker. The blade cut so deep Jay thought it had nicked the bones in his hands. He shrieked in pain but kept pushing until the blade's tip was near the attacker's throat.

The alarm finally set off after twenty seconds, and a deafening screech coursed through the house. So loud that Jay knew it would wake the neighbors.

The attacker let go of the knife. He bashed his fist into Jay's face. He got in three punches before Jay could readjust his position. He felt dizzy. One of the blows had cracked his jawbone.

The attacker ripped the knife out of Jay's hand. He bolted out of the bathroom and up the stairs.

"Rosalyn, run!" Jay shouted, before consciousness dimmed, and he saw nothing but black.

36

It was early morning when Yardley got the call. She hadn't even tried to sleep. Instead, she'd sat on her balcony and sipped wine and tried to distract herself by reading a novel. She'd now read the same paragraph three times.

Wesley hadn't been able to sleep either. He'd left earlier to drive the neighborhoods of Tara's friends, looking for her. She'd insisted he stay home, that he had classes to teach in the morning, but he'd said that he couldn't sit idly by while stress ate away at her. She'd worried that he was leaving because he was still upset about their exchange earlier, but he'd kissed her and told her he loved her.

The call was from Baldwin.

"Yes," she said, trying to suppress the excitement that swelled in her that Tara had been found.

"Jess, sorry to wake you. I thought you would want to know right away."

"What is it?" she said, her excitement turning to cold fear.

"There's been another attack."

Revulsion, and then nausea. A powerful wave of nausea that seemed to permeate even her skin. She saw blood dripping from ceilings, cold eyes like marbles, and the flesh surrounding them pale and drained. The scent of death filling rooms like poison gas.

She thought she might vomit.

"Jess, you there?"

"Yes. Tell me who the victims are."

"Jay and Rosalyn Miles. Oscar and I talked to them a few days ago. Jay reported someone from the alarm company at his home when no one was scheduled to be there. This one's different, Jess. They survived. His wife heard someone in the kitchen. Apparently some toys were left out there, and the killer must've tripped over them and rattled the pots and pans that hung over the island. He ran downstairs to hide in a bathroom and that's where Jay found him. They fought, but he got away. Jay's in the hospital. He's lost a lot of blood, but he's alive."

"I'm coming down."

"No, I just called to let you know. I know it's a terrible time to put this on you, but I thought you'd want me to loop you in. I have the ERT here, and some of my best people are flying down from Quantico today. One of them is an expert on lacerations from NYU medical school we've used before. The killer didn't have time to alter the wounds, so we'll know what type of blade he used. If our man can get it down to a specific type of knife, we might be able to trace knives like that purchased recently. It's a long shot, but it's something. And who knows what else he left behind that he didn't have time to clean up? Anyway, we're working it; there's no reason for you to be here. You just stay there in case Tara comes home, and I'll send you updates as I have them."

He paused. "I have someone following up with all of Kevin Watson's friends. If Tara's with him, they've got to sleep somewhere, and without much money I'm guessing that's a friend's couch. And my agents haven't taken their eyes off his father's home. He still has his motorcycle gang over. It's unlikely he would do anything with them there. Jess, I won't let up until she's back home."

"Thank you," she said. "And thank you for calling me."

"Try to get some sleep if you can."

She hung up and stared at her phone before placing it on the glass tabletop before her. She felt someone behind her and glanced back to see Wesley. He shook his head and said, "I didn't spot her anywhere. Anything from your end?"

"No."

He sighed and looked out over the desert. "Another attack?"

"Looks like it."

"And you were just ready to run over there?"

"I was."

He stood in front of her, leaning his back on the railing. "Why on earth would you think that was a good idea?"

"I'm the screening—"

"Do you think I don't know what a screening prosecutor does, Jessica? They sit in an office and go through paperwork. Sometimes, *sometimes*, they go out into the field and interview witnesses after the police to get in questions that were missed, or they maybe visit a crime scene, or something along those lines. Being this involved in the case, where you run to a fresh crime scene . . . it doesn't happen."

"That's an exaggeration. I've done it on other cases. They need warrants, they need advice . . . a prosecutor can make sure everything is covered constitutionally and can't be challenged later. Law enforcement gets sloppy when they think only of the capture and not the court process."

"Jessica, you interviewed a serial murderer on death row for information. That's not investigation; that's obsession." He squatted down in front of her and took her hands. "I can't watch this. I won't. I feel like my opinion means nothing to you."

"Of course it does. It—"

"No, it doesn't. Not really. You are putting yourself in danger when I asked you not to. That's not how this works. Not if we're trying to make this long term." He kissed her hands and rose. "I don't want you working this case anymore. I'm asking you as your partner to give it to someone else. If you don't . . ."

"If I don't, what, Wesley? You're not going to stay with me? Are you threatening me right now?"

"No, nobody is threatening anyone. I just want you to know that this is serious. If you were to ask something of me this seriously, I would do it in a heartbeat. And I expect the same from you. If you're unwilling, well, then maybe we need to consider the nature of our relationship going forward."

He went inside. Yardley decided she would be sleeping on the couch in the den tonight.

37

In the morning, Yardley woke in the den and went upstairs. Occasionally, Wesley would leave a little note for her, just letting her know he didn't want to wake her and that he loved her. No note here now.

Maybe he was right. Maybe it was time to end this case for her. To bury it like it should've stayed buried in the first place.

As she went to the fridge to make something for herself, her strength failed her. She slumped down against the fridge and put her face in her hands. Tears would have come if she'd let them, but a thought kept going through her head: *I'll be damned if I let them make me cry.*

Perhaps it was time to give up the case, and probably her career as a prosecutor, too. She knew, just *knew*, that when she abandoned this case, the work would lose meaning for her and become a slog every day. Better to cut her losses and do something else, maybe even move somewhere else. She'd made a mess of everything here, and starting fresh might be just what she needed. It had been a mistake to stay in Nevada, so close to where she and Cal had shared a life. She should've picked up and moved to Europe or Australia the second the divorce had finalized.

A deep sadness descended on her. There was a whole life she could've had. And if she'd left after, Tara wouldn't be in the danger she was in. Yardley had failed her daughter. And the pain of it stung like an ice pick in her heart.

When she finally rose, she realized she had left her phone down-stairs and went to retrieve it. She'd missed a text. All it said was an address and then a line that made her heart skip a beat: please help me mom.

———

The address led Yardley to an apartment complex in downtown Las Vegas. Three buildings with dead grass in between them and a swim-ming pool that looked like it had been emptied long ago, mounds of dirt and sand layered on the bottom.

The apartment number listed was on the second floor. The hall-ways, stained with graffiti, smelled of urine and mold. Many of the doors were cracked and broken, and the two windows on either side of the hall were smeared with substances she didn't even want to guess at.

Apartment 6. Yardley waited a moment. She was about to knock when she stopped. Instead, she pulled from her purse the .38 revolver she kept in a gun safe in her closet. Not once had she had to pull it out of the safe before, with the exception of having it cleaned a few years ago.

She closed her eyes, opened them, and then turned the knob and jammed her shoulder into the flimsy door. The wood was weakened with age and cheap to begin with. It cracked near the doorknob and swung open.

The apartment appeared as a mess of bodies, sleeping bags, fast-food wrappers, and old pizza boxes. Several stained mattresses filled the living room. Two people sat against the wall, a boy and a girl, probably no more than seventeen. A pipe was pressed between the boy's lips, and Yardley smelled the unmistakable scent of burning methamphetamine: a cross between melted plastic and burning hair.

"Where's Tara Yardley?"

The girl said, "Who are you, her mom?"

She said *mom* as though it were an insult. Yardley moved past them and down a hall. Two bedrooms and a bathroom. She opened the first bedroom door, and the shock of it took her breath away.

Tara sat on the floor, Kevin asleep next to her. Two other young men were asleep on the bed. Tara's eyes went wide, and she jumped up and ran to her mother and threw her arms around her.

One of the young men stirred and said, "Hey, what—"

Yardley lifted her gun. The man held up his hands.

"Whoa, easy, lady," he said.

With one arm wrapped around her daughter, Yardley backed out of the bedroom, and they left the apartment.

———

On the drive home, Yardley let her daughter cry. They didn't speak until the shine from the tears on her cheeks had faded. Tara was looking out her window when she said, "We were going to run away and live with his uncle in Los Angeles. He said he had some friends that had an apartment we could stay at for now. They were nice at first, and then they started telling us that we needed money to make it and the easiest way was . . . was for me to have sex with men for money. That they had other girls do it, and they were making a thousand dollars a week. I thought Kevin would hit them and scream his head off." She sobbed quietly. "But he said I should do it. He said it was a good idea and it was just sex and it didn't mean anything, and when I told him no, he got furious at me and said I couldn't leave."

She was crying again.

When she stopped, she looked at her mother and said, "You're not yelling. You're not mad at me?"

Yardley shook her head and softly said, "No."

"Why not?"

"Because I realized what losing you would feel like. I'm too relieved right now to be angry."

Tara turned her head toward the window and watched the passing casinos and shops. "I'm so stupid," she said. "I thought he was in love with me, but he didn't give a shit about me."

"You are not stupid. Look at me . . . you are *not* stupid. There's certain types of men, Tara, that look for the best in people and use it against them. Compassion, forgiveness, a willingness to help, pity, love—that's what they look for, and they use them against you. But those traits are not weaknesses. They're strengths, and don't ever let anyone convince you otherwise."

She shook her head. "Kevin's an idiot. He can barely read. All my intelligence, and someone like him completely fooled me."

"You see the best in people. You can't blame yourself for that."

She wiped the last of her tears away. "Then you can't either."

Yardley looked at Tara, and then she took her daughter's hand and held it as they drove.

38

Yardley called Lieu at work and said she was taking some time off, and she decided she was too angry with Wesley to let him know as well. Tara had eaten breakfast and then gone right to bed. Yardley lay with her awhile, then called a friend at the LVPD who was with the Missing Persons Division. She told him about the apartment and what Kevin had done, and the detective promised her he would be looking into it today.

Yardley made coffee in the kitchen, rehashing over and over the moment she'd opened the door and seen her daughter sitting among filth and squalor and three men that weren't letting her leave. The shock of it tasted putrid in her mouth.

Words hadn't even formed in her head when the horror had hit her. Opening the door, that fraction of a second to take the image in, had been enough. Enough to mentally destroy her if she had let it. The mind worked so quickly at times and so slowly at others.

The door.

Yardley stopped pouring the coffee and stared at the cup of dark fluid. The shock had been when she'd opened the door. It had been so painful because it was so sudden. A flash of terror absorbed in an instant. Activating the most primitive part of the human brain, the part that told an animal to run or fight or freeze.

Her heart pounding, she texted Baldwin:

I need you to do something for me. Right now, right away.

Shoot.

Go talk to Isaac Olsen. At the school if you have to. Ask him if his parents' bedroom door was broken the day before they were killed. If it wouldn't close all the way.

Because of the broken hinge photos you sent me?

Yes. Right away. Please.

Okay, you got it. Anything else?

Yes, Tara's home.

That's fantastic! I knew she'd be okay. Where was she?

Another time. Let me know about Isaac right away, Cason.

I will.

The next couple of hours were spent in anxious pacing. Tara slept the entire time, and Yardley pictured her leaning against that filthy wall in the apartment all night, unable to sleep, her eyes darting toward any sound in the dark.

The text came around ten in the morning.

Isaac says the door was broken. That he was hanging on it and broke it and it wouldn't close, so his dad was going to fix it that weekend.

Yardley could barely breathe. She called a neighbor, a pleasant retiree named Martha, and asked if she would come over and stay with Tara until Wesley got home.

Yardley threw on jeans and a blouse and rushed out of the house as Martha walked up the porch steps.

Baldwin sat in a chair across from her as Ortiz chatted with a secretary outside of Yardley's office. Baldwin had a rubber ball, something people with office jobs squeezed to strengthen their forearms and attempt to impede carpal tunnel syndrome. Yardley ran various searches on several different databases at once.

"It's unlikely," Baldwin said. "The female is nearly always the target in these types of attacks."

She shook her head. "There was no sexual assault. We assumed he was killing the husbands first to make the wives suffer while they watched them die, but I think it was a practical decision. The husbands were stronger. He was taking out the bigger threat first and gagged the wives so they wouldn't wake the children. The children are the targets. The rage is directed at them, and the violation is that moment they open the door and see their parents. It's important for him that they open the door to see the carnage in a single moment. It amplifies the pain. It wouldn't be the same if they walked down the hall and saw it from afar. They would have some time to process it, for the brain to dissociate to protect itself. It wouldn't inflict maximum trauma. The children are the link. That's how he's choosing them. The parents are just a tool to inflict the pain on them."

The database searches revealed little about the Deans', Olsens', or Mileses' children, so she went into the federal juvenile-records database. It was the most protected database in the entire court system, and only a select few agencies had access.

She searched for Isaac Olsen first, inputting the birth date from the case file. It took only a few seconds to bring up his court case history.

Suddenly her stomach felt like she'd swallowed molten steel. She had antacids in a drawer, but she couldn't take her eyes off the screen long enough to reach for them.

"It's adoption," she whispered to herself.

She couldn't sit. She rose and began pacing her office, biting her thumbnail.

"What?"

"Isaac Olsen was adopted."

"I would've seen that."

"It's a sealed adoption."

Sealed adoptions were heavily guarded, as most of the time they meant the adoptive parents didn't wish the children to know they were adopted, so the courts closed the files and didn't make them accessible to the public or even most law enforcement agencies. Before the widespread use of computers, they would destroy the physical files, but now records remained, buried, in the database.

She sat down again and searched for Emma and Eric Dean. Emma was the biological child of Sophia and Adrian Dean, but Eric was adopted. A sealed adoption. She searched for the five Miles children. Two were adopted, both sealed adoptions.

She leaned back in her chair as Baldwin came up behind her and read the computer screen over her shoulder.

"He's choosing them by whether they have adopted children," he said more to himself than to her.

"How, though?" Yardley asked. "Even local law enforcement doesn't have access to this database. He'd have to be FBI."

Baldwin shook his head. "No way. Not one of my guys. I can check, but there's no way. It'd be easy to spot someone logging in and accessing the database. It records any log-ins. What about someone from your office? An in-house investigator?"

"We only have two. One of them is female, and the other was sent to Florida for a case last week. He couldn't have attacked Jay Miles. And it's the same with the prosecutors: the log-ins are recorded. Too easy to check. Who else has access to this database?"

"The courts, so it could be a court employee. We'll have to run a check, obviously. Judges aren't exactly going to like getting interviewed in a homicide investigation, you know, so just be prepared."

"What about Greg?"

He shook his head. "He wouldn't have access. Besides, he was in Salt Lake City consulting on a case the night the Olsens were killed. I checked with the ASAC down there, and they had lunch together."

"Austin Ketner wouldn't have access either."

He glanced to her and then back at the screen. "No, I guess not."

"Anyone else?"

He shrugged. "Probably the adoption agencies, Guardian ad Litem's Office . . ."

All thought ceased in a flash of pain and realization. It was as if the words had pressed a button and a deep well in her stomach had sucked her down into herself. Yardley put her hands on the desk in case she fainted. When she lifted them, she rose and grabbed her purse.

"I have to go," she said as she hurried out the door.

39

"You can watch the videos in my office," Warden Gledhill said.

Yardley sat down at the warden's desk. "I appreciate it, Sofie, thank you."

"You're welcome. But like I told you before, he's only had a bunch of academics visiting him. An occasional reporter. No one interesting. We didn't let any of the crazies in."

"I'm sure it's nothing. Just need to make sure. How far do the videos go back?"

"It used to be tapes, and they'd reuse them, but since we went digital, we keep all of them. That was . . . I wanna say seven years ago? So that's as far back as you get."

"That'll be fine, thank you again."

"Mm-hmm. Let me know if you need anything. I'm going to lunch. I'll bring you back a sandwich."

Yardley began with the first visitor Cal had had seven years ago. A journalist with the *Las Vegas Sun*. The video camera in the visitation rooms for death row inmates hung in the corner. She could see Cal's hands, though not his face, but could see the upper half of the visitor's body clearly. The journalist was tall, black, and female. She skipped her and went to the next one, a professor of criminology at the University of Michigan. Another woman. Yardley skipped her, too.

She skipped eighteen male visitors after researching their identities. Only on the nineteenth did she stop. The visitation log said it was a man named Roger Kohi, a sociologist with the University of Nebraska. The visitor had blond hair sticking out from a baseball cap and wore glasses. He either had a thick beard or wore a fake one, but there was no mistaking it. She simply knew the face too well to be fooled.

Roger Kohi was Wesley Paul.

———

Yardley went through the rest of the videos. Roger Kohi had visited Cal thirteen times in the span of seven years.

The email sent to Cal with a photo of Aubrey Olsen attached had been a ruse to make her and Baldwin think Cal and the copycat had never met or corresponded before and to shift suspicion onto Austin Ketner. At least until the next murders.

The videos had no accompanying audio because of a Nevada Supreme Court case from the nineties where a jail had been found to be recording attorney-client conversations for information on new crimes. Yardley wished like hell she could hear what they were saying.

She had to be *absolutely* sure, one way or the other.

Yardley asked the warden's secretary to burn copies of the videos onto discs, then send her an email detailing the date and time and what actions she'd taken, so that she could establish chain of custody later if need be.

Wesley had kept his condominium when he'd moved in with her and Tara. Yardley had always assumed it was a way for him to keep his independence. He was forty-four and had never been married. According to him, never even been in a serious relationship, so moving in with someone, Yardley guessed, terrified him. She hadn't given a second thought to him wanting to keep the condo. Particularly since it was already paid off.

The condominium complex had the air of someplace exclusive. A gated community with an actual guard at the gate instead of an automatic arm. The guard asked who she was there to see, and she told him she was Wesley Paul's fiancée. He had her sign a visitor sheet and let her through.

The complex housed several buildings. The condo took up the top floor of a three-story building near the back, by the community swimming pool. Yardley stopped at the management office. Two women sat facing each other with large glass desks in front of them and paintings on the walls instead of posters.

Yardley smiled at the woman to the right of her. "I'm Jessica Yardley. I'm the fiancée of one of your tenants, Wesley Paul. I need to get into his condo and get a few things for the wedding coming up."

"Oh, okay. Is he with you?"

She kept her smile. "No, if he was with me, I wouldn't need to ask you to open the door, hon."

The woman raised her eyebrows. "Well, I'm sorry. I can't just let you in there. I don't know you from Eve, and if something goes missing, we would be liable."

She nodded and showed her badge. "I understand. But I'm also a US attorney, and this is part of an investigation."

"I'm sorry. I can't let you in without his permission."

Yardley took out her phone and dialed a number. Baldwin answered on the second ring.

"Where are you?" he said.

"I need you to do something for me, please."

A hesitation, and it didn't seem like the words would come, or maybe she didn't want them to. She didn't speak until Baldwin said, "Jess?"

"Please draft a warrant to search the condominium of Wesley Paul. I'll give you the details to state."

40

While Yardley waited for the warrant, she went out to the pool and watched some children playing. They played Marco Polo and then raced in the pool, one child upset that he had been cheated from victory because he didn't have goggles like the others.

A chill hit her when she realized that on the night the Miles family had been attacked, Wesley had been out until the sun was nearly up, allegedly searching for Tara.

She tried to read on her phone, tried to listen to music, to catch up on a few other cases, but nothing would distract her from the heaviness crushing her chest. She thought that this must be what the stirrings of a heart attack felt like.

An email notification dinged her phone. The e-warrant had been approved and filed.

Yardley showed it to the receptionist in the management office. The woman had apparently never seen a warrant and said, "Let me call our boss."

Yardley felt a simmering anger. It bubbled to the surface, though the only outward sign was her jaw muscles grinding her teeth together.

"I've wasted enough time. If you don't let me into that condo immediately, I'm calling the FBI agent I spoke with to come down here and arrest you both for obstruction of justice, and I'll have him kick that damn door down."

The woman's face paled. She attempted to say something, but no words came. The other woman rose and said, "Lemme just grab the keys."

———

Wesley's condo looked small. One bedroom, one bathroom, kitchen, home office, and living room. Only one closet in the bedroom and no pantry or linen closet. Yardley shut the front door behind her while the woman said something about signing a release.

The white carpets and simple furniture had an elegance to them, a simplicity appealing to the eye. No paintings, no photographs, no decorations at all. One television and DVD player and a bookcase filled to the brim with books. On the top shelf were about two dozen books on serial murder, abnormal psychology, and forensic investigation, along with biographies of Ted Bundy, Jeffrey Dahmer, Hitler, Stalin, and Eddie Cal.

The bedroom had a Japanese-style bed low to the ground with a thin mattress. A painting hung above the bed, and when she saw it, she knew she needed to sit because her legs might give out. It was one of Eddie Cal's paintings. One she had seen before. A black figure with a white face inside what looked like a box but what Yardley thought now was probably a grave.

She sat down on the bed and rested her hand on the pillow. It was cool to the touch and soft. Silk covers.

She pulled the pillows out of the cases and searched inside. Then under the bed, under the mattress, in all the clothing, in the drawers in the bathroom and kitchen. She searched the fridge, the freezer, and the cabinets. Wesley didn't have a toolbox anywhere, so she got a butter knife from the kitchen and unscrewed the vents and checked inside. Nothing.

Standing in front of the bookcase, she ran her fingertips over the spines. She skipped all the books except for the biography of Eddie Cal. The author had written letters to her, phoned her, texted her, emailed her, and shown up twice at her house. She'd finally had to file a stalking injunction against him to get him to stop. He was a blogger that had secured a six-figure deal for writing the book. Yardley had found out later he had been arrested for stalking and assaulting a neighbor and was currently serving a fifteen-year sentence.

The biography was long, probably about six hundred pages. Far more than Cal deserved, she thought. She pulled the book out and held it in her hands. It felt too . . . rigid. Opening it, she saw the first disc about a third of the way in. The second disc halfway in. Golden DVDs with no writing on them to indicate what they contained. She felt queasy.

It took a long while for her to build up the courage to put one in the DVD player and turn on the television. She inhaled deeply and closed her eyes. *Please . . . let me be wrong . . . let me be wrong.*

She hit play.

41

The video began with darkness, but Yardley could hear shuffling. Some metallic clanks, and then the lens cap came off.

She recognized the room immediately: the Olsens' bedroom. The image green but bright, and Ryan and Aubrey Olsen sleeping next to one another. The image stayed with them a long while, and nothing happened. Ryan Olsen snored.

More sounds coming from behind the camera. Yardley couldn't place them. Clothes maybe, or sheets. Something soft rubbing against something else. Ryan Olsen sniffled, and the snoring stopped for a brief period. Filling the silence was the unmistakable sound of breathing, but it wasn't coming from the Olsens.

Naked skin appeared to the right of the image. A man's buttocks and legs. A knife dangled in his fingertips. He stood at the foot of the bed with another handheld camera. Not a phone but a newer, sleek digital camera. He took several photos and then put the camera down onto what looked like a small plastic sheet he had laid on the carpet. The man's face was not visible, as he didn't turn toward the recorder.

The man tapped the blade of the knife against his thigh as he watched the Olsens sleep. The way Wesley would tap his fingers against his thigh when lost in thought.

The nausea Yardley felt sent a burning fluid up her esophagus, and she had to swallow to keep from vomiting. She put her hand to her mouth, as though physically pushing it down. The man slowly made his way around the bed.

The man glanced at the recorder, ensuring it was focused on him correctly. It was Wesley.

As quickly as the bite of a snake, he bent down and put the knife to Ryan Olsen's throat.

Yardley turned away. She couldn't hold it any longer. She ran to the bathroom and vomited.

———

When the retching stopped, Yardley flushed the toilet and pulled herself up to her feet using the sink. She stared at herself in the mirror. Though she knew men found her attractive and that she appeared younger than her thirty-eight years, she just thought she looked old now. Old and tired.

She splashed water on her face and rinsed her mouth. She let the water run over her hands for a long time afterward, long enough that her face almost dried. Her purse sat on the floor, and she lifted it and set it on the sink. She took out a disposable sanitary napkin and dried the spots on her face that were still wet. She didn't want to use one of Wesley's towels.

She avoided looking in the mirror. As she stepped out into the hall, she heard a voice.

"Hello, darling."

42

Time slowed. Yardley thought of a paper napkin falling to the ground from a table at a restaurant. She watched it shift and float and land silently on the floor. As though her limbs wouldn't respond to her brain's direction to move and stop the napkin.

Wesley had turned the DVD player off.

"You never asked to come here," he said, glancing around, his voice calm and even. "How do you like it?"

She didn't respond.

His hands thrust into his pockets, and he sat on the arm of the couch and exhaled loudly. "Imagine my surprise when the management office called me. I really thought this day wouldn't come. I thought, naively, I suppose, that I could keep this from you. I simply had no idea you would get involved in this case. I just wish you would've listened to me and left it alone. Ultimately, my dear, this really is your fault."

She almost said, *You need help, Wesley. I can get you help.* But from his eyes, she knew that would be useless. His eyes had, somehow, changed. Turned lifeless, like the eyes of a doll. Or perhaps it was just how she perceived them now.

"I'm leaving, Wesley. Get out of my way."

He held his arm out toward the door. "By all means, go."

The distance to the door came to about twenty feet if she went through the living room, maybe thirty if she went through the kitchen and around Wesley. Though slightly overweight, Wesley was strong and fast. If he wanted to grab her, she wasn't quick enough to get away.

"Back out of the condo and go down the stairs. And then I'll follow."

He smirked. "Do you think I'm stupid?"

"I think you love me," she lied. "And that you don't want to hurt me."

"Don't I? How do you know? You don't know the first thing about me. You don't even know my name."

The nausea was back as she pictured him in her bed, making love to her, his eyes locked to hers as he told her he loved her and she believed him. She had to strain to keep from retching again.

"You look absolutely pale, darling. Why don't you go lie down and have a nap in the bedroom? You'll find the bed quite agreeable. We can have a talk afterward."

She realized the reason he hadn't already attacked her was because of the neighbors. The units were compact: someone would hear.

"I'll scream."

"You could. And maybe someone will hear, and maybe someone won't. And even if they do hear, maybe they'll do something about it, and maybe they won't. Is that a risk you're really willing to take?"

"Are you? Do you want to join your idol on death row?"

He chuckled. "My idol. Interesting way to put it."

"What would you call him?"

He shrugged. "A dear friend and an influence. A mentor. But our work, see, our work was only similar, not identical. He helped me see the differences between us." A grimace came over him. "*Dark Casanova Junior.* I can't tell you how disgusted that made me. I had wanted to wait a little longer for this last one, the adorable Miles family, but I thought I should teach you all a little something about respect. I was going to use their blood to leave a note for you. I realized the media would have to call me something, so I might as well have chosen it. I was thinking *the Poisoned Braid*. Do you know where that comes from? Medieval Japan. Assassins would come in the night and cut a small hole in the thatched roofs of their targets. They would run a thin braided rope down the hole to the lips of their target and then drip poison down the braid. It would sometimes take hours to dribble down and touch the lips. That's the discipline these men, and sometimes women, had. The discipline and patience of death."

"You're no assassin, Wesley. You're a butcher that targets children."

He grinned. "The door hinge, I'm guessing?" He clicked his tongue against the roof of his mouth. "Such a shame. I meant to go back and replace that hinge later, but I was nervous Cason might have someone watching the house."

"I can't believe you took the time to fix a door. It's sloppy work."

He nodded. "Yes. I agree. It's not often I'm wrong, but I like to think I can openly admit it when I am. That was a poor decision. But thinking about the look on the child's face when he opened that door . . ." He chuckled. "Chance worth taking."

He closed his eyes and inhaled deeply through the nose as he lifted his head toward the ceiling. "You have no clue what it's like, Jessica. The muffled screams that bounce off the walls and seem to linger there, the eyes that pour the last of life out of them, and the smell." He inhaled again. "I can smell it at night sometimes. The smell of blood and empty bowels and sweat. It's disgusting and intoxicating at the same time. There's no other smell like the smell of a human being at the moment of death. Nothing even close. You lose yourself in it. You can't think clearly . . . it was . . . sublime." He opened his eyes. "How'd you know it was me?"

"When I realized the children were the actual targets, it wasn't hard to deduce that one of the only offices that would have a record of sealed adoptions was the guardian ad litem."

He nodded. "And then something just happened to click? Nothing just happens, Jessica. Your subconscious made the connections. Maybe you always knew and just didn't care?"

"No," she gasped softly.

He chuckled, sensing the cut. "Maybe you're just meant to be with someone like me or Eddie?"

She closed her eyes and imagined Tara. She had to survive this for her. Tara had no one else in the world.

As long as Wesley was talking, he wasn't hurting her.

Yardley glanced toward her purse on the sink. "How long did you follow me for?"

He beamed a little. "You wouldn't believe me if I told you."

"I think I'd believe anything about you right now."

He folded his arms. "I've been watching you for so long—I knew you before we even met. You actually saw me once. I was following you on a hot day in July and stopped for a drink at an ice cream store. You and Tara came in a few minutes later. We smiled at each other."

She thought back and couldn't recall any such moment.

"But you know what the most difficult part of all this was? It wasn't getting you to fall in love with me. That was actually easy. The most difficult part was getting a position at the law school. When I found out you had applied, I quickly applied there as well. I was teaching at a more, let's say, prestigious school, and UNLV only had adjunct positions open. They didn't understand why a tenured professor at such a high-ranking school would only want an adjunct position. So I earned pennies as an adjunct there while I waited. Luckily, a tenured position opened during your second year, and everything lined up." He paused. "Do miss where I lived, though. I hate Las Vegas. It's so . . . tasteless, isn't it?"

"Why now, Wesley? Why did you start the killings now?"

"That, I'm afraid, is better left a mystery."

He pushed off the couch toward her.

43

The clouds had rolled back, revealing a perfectly blue sky. Baldwin watched as Ortiz ate a double cheeseburger with chili and onions with the zeal of a man that had just been rescued from a desert island. The chili dripped down his chin, and he had to keep wiping at it with napkins between every bite.

"So my daughter," Ortiz said with a mouthful of burger, "her first word is *mommy*, right? And so I'm spending all my day off with her, like, all day. I make it seem like I'm doin' my wife a favor and taking the baby out so she can run errands, right? And I just work her all day. 'Daddy, daddy, daddy.' Just over and over again. By the end of the day, she's sayin' *daddy*. I didn't say nothin' to Rebecca, and she texts me and says she's sayin' *daddy* now and not *mommy*." He chuckled. "If Rebecca ever found out, she'd have my *cojones*."

"Huh," Baldwin said, staring off into space.

"That's all you gonna eat?" Ortiz said before taking another massive bite. "Justa buna bandwich?"

"Not hungry."

"Bhat's brong?"

"It's that warrant for Wesley Paul's place. If Jessica actually finds something . . . I mean . . . I don't know."

"You worried she's gonna toss anything she finds?"

"Well, I don't want to be that blunt, but yeah. She's in love, or thinks she is."

"Man, if it's him, if she had this happen to her again, you know how pissed she's gonna be? This psycho found her just because she was married to another psycho and then tricked her into falling in love with him? Get outa here. I'd be more worried about her killing him. She don't got a piece, do she?"

"I don't know." He tapped his finger against the table. "I can't just sit here. Let's go check on her."

"I'm not done."

He rose. "I'll get you another one after. Come on."

44

Yardley jumped into the bathroom and slammed the door shut. The lock spun just as the door bounced with Wesley's weight behind it. He kicked it, and Yardley leaned her back against it, pushing with her feet against the floor as hard as she could.

"Jessica, open the door. I just want to talk."

"I have my phone. I'm calling the police."

"Jessica!"

More kicks to the door. The edge nearest the doorknob cracked. It couldn't take many more kicks. She remembered she hadn't removed the gun from her purse after last night. She grabbed the purse and fumbled for the gun. It felt heavy in her hand as she gripped it. She pushed away from the door and moved into the tub, as far back as she could get. Two more kicks, and the door splintered and flew open.

Right then, she should've pulled the trigger. A hole should have appeared in Wesley's chest, and blood should have soaked his shirt. She could see it so clearly, like a vivid dream. For a moment she wondered if she had done it. Only when Wesley smiled did she realize she hadn't. An unsaid understanding bloomed between them now: they both knew she couldn't kill him.

He shook his head, the smirk never leaving his face. "I really thought you had it in you. You're the toughest woman I ever met. I thought if you ever found out, you really would kill me. But your parents were both chickenshits. Guess the apple doesn't fall far from the tree, eh?"

"I'll do it."

"No you won't," he said, stepping forward.

"Wesley," she said, panic in her voice, the gun shaking in her trembling fingers, "don't do this. Don't make me kill you."

"Hey, I just want to talk. You're not going to kill me for just wanting to talk, are you? I want to go out and make some coffee, sit on the couch, and talk about this."

"Don't come any closer. I'll do it. I swear to you I'll do it."

He took one large step, and the muzzle pressed against his heart. "Go ahead. Do it."

"Please don't," she begged, her voice cracking. "Please."

"Begging? Jessica, I have never seen you beg for anything. I have to say, it's quite pathetic. I really thought you were stronger than this. Or was that strength just a fun house–mirror version of you for everybody else to see?"

He reached up and grabbed the gun. As he did so, Wesley's head jolted forward with the amount of force Baldwin used to press the muzzle against the back of his skull.

"She won't, but I will. And I really don't want to ruin Jessica's clothes with your brains. How about we let go of the gun nice and slow and put our hands on the back of our head."

Wesley chuckled. His fingers slowly slipped off the gun and went to the back of his head, where Ortiz grabbed them and used them to twist him down to the floor, slapping on cuffs before banging Wesley's face into the tile.

"That's for ruining my lunch, *pendejo*."

45

The local LVPD detectives came quickly. Baldwin had decided to give them a courtesy call. Two of them arrived with several uniformed officers, who mostly hung around the door and chatted about a college game going on that night. One of the detectives, an obese man with a tacky blazer, wanted Yardley to give a statement right then, but Baldwin told him he would give her a ride home and take it there.

Yardley couldn't stay in the condo anymore. She waited outside for him.

"I don't even know what to say," Baldwin said as he walked up to her.

"You don't have to say anything."

"I'll give you a ride home."

"No, I have my car."

"You shouldn't drive right now. I'll drive your car and have Oscar follow us."

She nodded as she stared up at the condo. "I'm such a fool."

Baldwin stepped in front of her so she couldn't see the condo. "You are a human being who was the victim of a monster. You didn't find him—he found you. What he did, ultimately, had nothing to do with you."

She blinked slowly and looked at him. "If it was the first time, I might believe you." She looked back to the condo and said, "Let's go. I can't stomach this place anymore."

The drive wouldn't take long, but Baldwin thought he should ask her about how she'd found Tara, something positive that had happened, but then thought better of it. He was amazed she wasn't crying. He wondered if she would do that later when no one could see.

"Have you eaten?" he asked as they got off the freeway.

"I'm not hungry," she nearly whispered. Her eyes never leaving the passenger-side window.

"If you need someone to talk to, I'm here. I'm a good listener, and I'm your friend, Jess."

She didn't respond, her eyes glued to the passing city. For a moment he thought she was going to speak, but instead she leaned her head against the glass.

When they got to her house, she opened the car door and said, "Thanks," before stepping out. Baldwin had to roll down the window and call after her.

"I'll come back and check up on you. I'm going to get the ERT over to his condo. When you're ready, we'll take your statement. I'll let Lieu know you're going to be out the rest of the week."

"Thank you," she said as she turned away.

"Jessica?"

She looked at him.

"I can't even imagine what you're going to go through or what you're going to think about yourself, but I do know that what happened with Eddie would've broken almost anyone. But it didn't break you; it made you stronger. It made you stronger because you're a survivor. And it may not seem like it, but this will make you stronger, too. Because that's just the person you are."

Without a word, she turned away from him and went inside her house.

Baldwin took a deep breath and let it out slowly as he looked over the neighborhood. He wondered how the neighbors would treat her once they found out.

A headache had started at the back of his skull and drifted up to his forehead. The headaches were more frequent now. He figured it was a lack of sleep. A recurring dream woke him most nights.

He was a child in the dream and saw his mother in a grave looking up at him with vacant eyes. The eyes of the dead. The cemetery was wet from rain, gray clouds enveloping the headstones and the sky.

His mother's throat had been slit, her flesh pale from the loss of blood. Baldwin would reach for her, and she'd fade away to nothing.

Wesley Paul . . .

How could it possibly be true? Yardley felt like a fool, but so did he. He'd known Wesley for three years, even asked his advice once on a case involving a young child. He had recognized Henry Lucado as the Beltway Butcher from a photograph, but he hadn't suspected anything about a murderer of families he'd met half a dozen times.

He took a bottle of pills from the glove box. Something he'd picked up from a local doctor this morning after complaining about knee pain. He took two of them out and nearly popped them in his mouth but stopped.

How did I not see him?

His thinking had felt muddy lately, slow and arduous. Like he was constantly stuck in that moment after waking up from a long night's sleep and struggling to concentrate.

He tossed the pills on the floor of his car and pulled away. Wesley Paul was waiting in an interview room at the LVPD station.

46

The room seemed cool compared to outdoors. Wesley Paul sat stiff in his chair, handcuffed to a steel link that was bolted into the massive table in front of him. He tugged playfully at the cuffs, listening to the rattle of the metal on metal. He wondered if they would bring him a coffee if he asked.

The two detectives had tried to question him, and he had sat quietly without a word. Finally the fat one said, "To hell with him," and they'd left. They weren't who he wanted to speak with. This case would be handled in federal court, and the FBI was who he needed here.

Without having to wait too long, he was pleased to see Baldwin enter, along with Agent Ortiz in a disheveled suit, and pull up two chairs.

"Hello," Wesley said with a smile. "I don't think we've met. Oh, wait, you're the one that knocked me into the floor. Agent Ortiz, right?"

Ortiz rolled his eyes. "We got you, Wes, my man. We seen you in that bathroom attacking Jessica."

"You mean when she had a gun pressed against me? I had to kick down the door because she was threatening to kill herself, and then she turned the gun on me. So I seriously hope you have something better than that to come at me with."

Baldwin said, "What'd you do with the videos? Jessica said she saw some DVDs you had. We'll find them anyway. They're tearing your condo apart as we speak."

He grinned at him playfully. "I don't think I like you, Agent Baldwin. We have a history together. I would like to speak to Agent Ortiz, and only Agent Ortiz."

"No."

Wesley shrugged and leaned back in the seat. He made the motion of a key turning in a lock by his mouth.

Baldwin bit his lower lip, looked to Ortiz, and then left.

Wesley said, "Cameras make me nervous. Turn the camera off. You can record the audio if you like. I have no problem with that."

Ortiz watched him a moment.

"It's the only way I'll talk to you, Agent Ortiz."

Ortiz rose and unplugged the camera from the wall. The room was all walls, no two-way mirror. Ortiz left for a moment and came back with a digital recorder. He went to press play, and Wesley gently touched his finger, preventing him from doing it.

"Before we begin, I wanted to ask you something."

"What?" Ortiz said, withdrawing his finger from the recorder and leaning back in the seat.

"How's your daughter?"

The pain he tasted from Ortiz at that moment was tangible.

"What the hell you know 'bout my daughter, you piece'a shit?"

"I know she's not at home right now, Agent Ortiz."

"Bullshit."

"Call your wife and ask her to check the baby's room. I believe you'll find your wife rousing from a long nap she didn't mean to take. Almost as if someone had given her a sedative."

Ortiz hesitated and then took out his phone. He rose and turned his back to Wesley as the phone rang. Wesley turned on the digital recorder.

He listened while Ortiz spoke in Spanish. There was a pause, and while he waited, Ortiz glanced back over his shoulder. Seconds later, Wesley heard the high-pitched, panicked voice of a mother on the other end of the line. A smile broke over his lips.

Ortiz dropped the phone. "Where is she?" he shouted, rushing toward him.

"No," Wesley said, begging, "no, please. Stop, I'll tell you. Stop hitting me."

Ortiz swung with a right that knocked him out of the chair. Wesley's arm was still cuffed to the table, twisted now at an awkward angle that sent biting pain through wrist and shoulder.

"I killed the Olsens and the Deans. I said it—please stop!"

Ortiz kicked him in the ribs. "Where is she!"

"I have a storage unit in Las Vegas. It's right off the Boulevard, Castle Storage. I keep things there from the murders. Please," he cried, sobbing now, "please stop."

Ortiz kicked him again and again. Wesley shifted his body so that the blows would land on his face and head. One nearly sent him into unconsciousness, and he tasted the blood that popped out of his mouth like a burst balloon.

"I don't want to die!" Wesley screamed through his sobs.

The door swung open as Baldwin came in, the two detectives behind him.

"Oscar! Stop!"

Ortiz kept kicking him. Wesley felt one of his teeth chip before the other three men could pull him off.

He had a nearly uncontrollable urge to laugh, but he swallowed it down, along with a torrent of blood, and instead wept. Loud enough to ensure that the digital recorder would pick it up.

47

Yardley found Tara sitting on the balcony, reading a text on something called nanoparticle confinement.

Her heart broke all over again at the sight of her daughter. So much trauma in such a short life. How would her daughter trust anyone—even her—ever again?

And yet Tara, as she often did, surprised her. When Yardley told her, in halting tones, about Wesley, Tara said nothing, just quietly listened. They sat that way for a while until Tara finally said, "I talked to Mr. Jackson while you were gone. He called the dean of the math department at UNLV. They have tests I can take to skip as many courses as I need to."

And that was where they spent much of the day. Strolling across the UNLV campus. Though it was in the middle of the city, the campus had enough palm trees and green shrubbery to make it a pleasant enough area. Someplace that felt separate from Las Vegas.

It was where she'd first met Wesley. Or where she thought she'd met him for the first time.

She stopped on a patch of grass and sat down on a bench. Tara followed, and they watched a small fountain surrounded by palm trees.

"I feel like I've failed you," Yardley said. "I've exposed you to something I swore I would keep you away from."

"You shouldn't feel that way. You probably think something inside you attracts men like him, but it sounds like he's trying to follow in Eddie Cal's footsteps. He purposely found you. It wasn't anything inside you that attracted him; it was Eddie. Besides, someone really smart told me once that certain men look for the best traits in people to take advantage of."

Yardley stared at her a moment and lightly put her hand on Tara's knee, letting her know how grateful she was for what her daughter had just said to her.

"I thought you might scream at me. Blame me for all of it. I know you liked Wesley."

"I got along with him because I know you liked him. I thought he was creepy. He walked in when I was in the shower a couple times. I thought it was an accident, but now I'm thinking he did it on purpose." She looked at her and said, "Are you going to be okay, Mom?"

"Eventually, sweetheart, I will be."

They walked to the science and mathematics building and sat in on a lecture. Yardley guessed it was a graduate-level course in some advanced mathematics topic, and she had no idea what the professor was talking about, but Tara seemed interested, and her gaze never wavered. When the class was over, Tara said, "Be right back."

She went up to the professor and introduced herself. She asked questions about something called the Davenport-Schmidt theorem and continued fractions. The professor seemed more than happy to discuss it, and they spoke for several minutes. When they were through, Tara came back and sat next to her mother, a slight grin on her face.

"That was refreshing to talk to a teacher that actually knows more than me."

"So you like it here so far?"

"Yeah, I think I do."

They were silent for a bit as the students finished filing out of the classroom, and Tara said, "Mom, I don't want you to blame yourself for

Wesley. There was nothing you could've done differently. Just like there was nothing I could've done differently with Kevin. I realized it's not my fault. I wanted to believe he loved me, and there's nothing wrong with that. They're the monsters, not us."

Yardley watched the professor clean off the whiteboard with an eraser. "It still hurts. I thought after Eddie I would never get into a serious relationship again. Then Wesley came along, and I thought that maybe I was wrong. That Eddie was a fluke and that it was all right for me to have someone in my life."

Tara ran her finger over something a student had carved into the top of the desk. "What are they going to do with him?"

"*They're* not doing anything. This is my burden. I'm going to prosecute him, and I'm going to convict him. Then a jury will decide whether to impose a life sentence or the death penalty."

"Will they let you prosecute him since you lived with him?"

"I'll figure out a way. It's tough but not impossible."

After picking up an application packet and speaking with an academic advisor about the mathematics program, Yardley dropped Tara off at a friend's and then went to the gym.

She called Baldwin from the gym parking lot after an hour of boxing, including sparring with the instructor. Her arms felt like jelly, and her breath was like fire coming out of her lungs. Every ounce of strength had been sapped from her. She had punched the heavy bag the last ten minutes so fast her hands and wrists ached.

Yardley sat in her car for a long time and listened to Baldwin go through what had happened between Ortiz and Wesley and what they had been doing since.

A pang of agony went through her. Having just thought she'd lost Tara, she knew what Ortiz was going through. The dark thoughts that would swirl and wouldn't go away, the contingencies that played out over and over . . . the images of coffins and funerals you so desperately didn't want to think about but would anyway.

"How did he get Oscar's daughter?" Yardley said.

"We think he took her before coming to the condo. One of the receptionists interrupted a class he was teaching and said you had applied for a warrant. Oscar's house is maybe twenty minutes from the condo, so we think he probably stashed Emilia somewhere on the way over. I've got every agent we can spare looking for her now, and the sheriff's department and LVPD pulled officers from every patrol. We'll find her." He paused. "We're searching the storage unit he mentioned, Jess. It has everything. Photos of the Deans and Olsens before and after death, his kill kit with the masks and knives, different alarm company stickers for a van he's got somewhere so he can case their homes first, and . . . pictures of you."

"What do you mean?"

"He'd been following you and Tara for a long time. Some of these photos go back years." He paused. "There's some of you asleep in your bed. It looks like he'd been inside your house before."

She closed her eyes.

"He wouldn't just confess," she said.

"He got a pretty vicious beating."

"No, that's not what this was, Cason. He's had years to plan for his prosecution, and whatever he did was deliberate. I'm going to the office. Bring me everything you have."

———

Yardley walked into Roy Lieu's office in her gym clothes. She didn't want to waste any time, and this wasn't a conversation she wanted to have over the phone.

Yardley sat down across from him. The office's main decorations were photos of Lieu shaking hands with politicians from both major parties.

Lieu gave her a sad little grin. "I'm so sorry. We're all sorry, Jessica. We've put together a little GoFundMe for you. Just to help out."

"I appreciate that, thank you, but money's not an issue. Our finances were always separate."

He nodded. "Well, if you need anything . . ."

"What I need is to work."

"I understand. When my father died, work got me through it for a while. At least the hardest part. We have several cases I was going to give to Kendra since she's back from—"

"No. I just want Wesley's case."

Lieu's lips went rigid. She could tell he was thinking about how to reject her, because he thought he could hurt her feelings. It angered her; she didn't need protection any more than the men here, and in fact, she needed it less. But she swallowed her anger. Getting what she wanted was more important right now.

"I'm sorry, Jessica. I can't do that."

"It's not a conflict."

"It's clearly a conflict. You saw the videos, you were his girlfriend, and you better believe the defense will call you to testify. They'll grill you about the minutest detail of your lives."

"That just means I'd be a witness. There's no ethical rule that says I can't prosecute the case anyway, and there's plenty of precedent about prosecutors having to testify in trials they prosecute since we take part in investigations. It doesn't happen often, but it happens."

"Okay, even if you're right, how about the public perception? What if you lost? Do you know how that would look for our office? Everyone would think you lost the case on purpose because of your feelings for him. And Jessica, honestly, I don't know why you'd want to put yourself through this anyhow. I know you're emotional right now—"

"I am *not* emotional. This is my case. It has been from the beginning. I would've prosecuted it no matter who the defendant turned out to be. It shouldn't change now."

Lieu pushed his tongue against his cheek while he watched her. "I'm sorry, but the answer is no. I'm giving the case to Tim. You can be present in the courtroom. I don't have any problem with that. But I don't want you working this case."

"Who's representing him?"

Lieu gave a slight grin. "He's chosen to represent himself."

You're acting like a fool, Yardley thought. He was actually happy Wesley would be his own attorney.

"You're underestimating him."

"I'm not."

"He's a genius, Roy. Tim has never dealt with someone like this."

He put his elbows on the desk, a pen between his fingertips. "I think we can handle one defendant with a storage unit full of incriminating evidence, genius or not. We'll be fine." Turning toward the computer screen, indicating the conversation was over, he said, "Like I mentioned, feel free to sit in on any of the proceedings, though I personally wouldn't recommend that either. When you're ready to take other cases, let me know."

Yardley took a deep breath and said, "Roy, we both know you gave this case to Tim because his grandfather is the governor and you're currying favor with the biggest case this office has ever had. You've been doing it with him from the moment I saw you two working together. I'm not blaming you—I understand one day you want to enter politics; all men of ambition in government work do—but you can't do this. He will screw this case up, and . . . Wesley might come after me and Tara. I don't know what he has planned, but it's nothing good. And if he's released, he might think it'd be fun to kill us, or want to eliminate me as a threat, or maybe just tie up loose ends. I won't take that chance. I will *not* give him the opportunity to hurt my daughter."

"Who the hell do you think you are? You accuse me of giving Tim work to curry favor because of who his grandfather is? You don't know anything about it. Tim has double your experience and can remain objective about this, while you, clearly, can't. If you ever say something like that again, you can start looking for another job."

Yardley rose to leave and stopped at the door. "He's going to file a motion soon."

Lieu looked at her.

"A motion to suppress evidence," she said. "He's going to get everything he said during his beating suppressed, and then he's going to apply fruit of the poisonous tree to suppress anything else we ever would've found. He knew we'd eventually find the storage unit, and now he'll get everything in it and anything you dig up excluded."

"He kidnapped the child of a federal agent. No judge in their right mind—"

"No judge in their right mind would ever rule that beating a defendant during an interrogation is acceptable. And even if they did, the Ninth Circuit would overturn them in a second. What you have to go on is a broken door hinge and a video only I saw that they can't find now because Wesley hid it so well. He will paint me as a vengeful lover. He'll say we planned to get married but he called off the wedding because I became obsessed with this case. Oscar and Cason came into the bathroom when I had a gun pressed to his chest. He didn't have one pressed to mine. He's going to get away with this, and he's going to keep killing. Maybe starting with me."

48

The sun had already set, and there was no moon. The lighting in the death row meeting room was harsh fluorescence, giving everything a pale greenish-yellow glow. Yardley picked up her cell phone. The lock screen was still a photo of her, Wesley, and Tara hiking in the canyons. She deleted it, then deleted all the photos she had of him.

Cal was brought in and sat in front of her. He had cuffs on this time that ran down to his ankles, and Yardley wondered if he'd attacked somebody again.

"Did you know?" she said.

Cal watched her, a mischievous grin coming across his dry lips. "He's something else, isn't he? Like a lost puppy looking for his place in the world."

She leaned forward. "Did you know?"

Cal leaned forward as well so their faces were less than a foot apart. She could see her reflection in the glass barrier. "Who do you think sent him to you in the first place?"

Yardley leaned back, feeling a sudden chill, though there were no drafts possible in the room. "Why?"

"I wanted to keep tabs on you and Tara, and you would never respond to my letters. Wesley seemed like a good alternative. He would bring me photos and give me updates on what was happening in your lives. You should be flattered. He's quite fond of you, and he's a person incapable of real attachments. It speaks to your charm."

Yardley felt an agonizing disgust but made certain that her face remained passive.

"Why did he start killing? He went years without it and then suddenly began with the Deans. Why?"

"Did he start with the Deans? Hmm."

They held each other's gaze. "I'm going to convict him, and he's going to join you in here."

He shrugged. "I hope you do convict him. Rest assured, I've got more fans."

She glanced back to the door and saw the guard outside the square window speaking with somebody. "If I'm not able to convict him, is he going to come after me and Tara?"

"Why would you think that?"

"He might think it's fun or that it benefits him somehow."

Cal nodded. "It's certainly possible, mostly because he doesn't understand himself. He thinks he did this for the trauma it imposed on the children. But he doesn't enjoy killing; he's only convinced himself he does. He's a stalker, Jessica. And right now you're his obsession. Do you know much about stalkers?"

She nodded. She had prosecuted dozens of them. "Yes."

"What do you know?"

"They're one of the most dangerous types of offenders. They have a fantasy about the relationship with their victims, and when that fantasy is threatened, they feel it's better to kill the victim than have someone else take their imagined place."

He took two breaths before speaking. "I would say it's a good likelihood he will come after you and Tara if he is released. He won't let go of the fantasy just because you know who he is."

She shook her head, hardly able to stomach looking at Cal. "Do you even care if she dies, Eddie? I don't expect any sympathy for me, but is there any part of you that cares if your daughter is torn apart by a savage?"

He exhaled loudly and leaned back, his chains rattling. "You have to prosecute him. You can't let someone else do it."

"Why?"

"His legal acumen is impressive. Someone that knows him, knows his faults, has to be the one to go head-to-head with him. Besides, he'll want it to be you. He thinks you're naive. He'll assume you're too emotional to do a good job. And he'll want to spend time with you. Maybe he thinks he'll impress you in court with his skill. Regardless, his obsession with you will make him reckless. He won't be that way with anyone else."

She nodded, her eyes narrowing on him. "Goodbye, Eddie. I won't be back here again."

As she was leaving, Cal said, "Let me see Tara, and maybe I'll give you something that can help convict Wesley."

"What?"

"Bring her here, and I'll tell her directly."

Yardley stared at him. How, she wondered, had she ever loved *something* like that?

"Understand this, Eddie: I will die before I let you see her."

He smiled. "You might die anyway."

49

The day before Wesley's bail hearing, Yardley had every one of his items packed up in boxes and stored in a storage unit across town: from his toothbrush and slippers to his professional awards and pens. As soon as the case against him was completed, she would donate everything. His laptop she had handed over to the FBI.

The judge denied bail, and Wesley didn't put up a fuss. No one expected a judge to let him out to roam the streets.

Two days later, he filed one of the most insightful, persuasive motions and memorandums she had ever read. A motion and memorandum to suppress all the evidence in the storage unit, and any evidence that had arisen from it, as fruit of the poisonous tree. The motion was over 170 pages, citing case after case after case supporting his position. Two days wouldn't have been enough time to draft it. This motion had been drafted long ago for this very circumstance.

In addition, he challenged the warrant Yardley had gotten. Saying the warrant was so prima facie deficient, so obviously flawed, that no reasonable judge should have signed off on it. If granted, that would mean she hadn't had authority to be in his condominium and could be barred from testifying about what she'd seen on the video.

Ortiz had been put on leave from the Bureau. The officers, agents, and volunteers combing the neighborhoods and putting up flyers about his daughter had been unable to find any trace of her, though their efforts continued. No one had been in the room when Wesley had told Ortiz his daughter was missing, and Wesley denied it was said. Without physical evidence or witnesses, a kidnapping charge would never be brought.

Three days after that, Yardley picked up Steven and Betty Cal from the airport.

———

The Cals had always been fond of Yardley; she had known that from the moment they had met her. And throughout the years, they had been deeply involved in Tara's life. The fact that they lived in Las Cruces, New Mexico, made only twice-yearly visits possible: two weeks for Christmas in New Mexico and three days of them here for Tara's birthday. This was the first time they had come out because they were needed.

When Yardley met them at the airport, Steven pulled her close and held her. He smelled like leather and aftershave, and his big arms and barrel chest comforted her. She could've wept right there if she'd allowed herself.

They spoke little on the drive home, avoiding talk of Wesley entirely. She had told them enough on the phone, and she figured they had read about it. Martha, her neighbor, had told her she had seen a story in the *New York Times* about it.

Tara ran to her grandparents the moment they came through the door. The three of them held each other and cried.

When the crying was done, the joyful conversation and reminiscing began. Tara told them everything about UNLV and the mathematics program. About what she wanted to study and what industries she could change. Seeing her like that, surrounded by family, Yardley realized how isolated the two of them were and how deeply Tara longed for it to be otherwise.

"Let's go get a late lunch somewhere," Steven said.

"Why don't you guys go?" Yardley said. "I have something I have to do for work."

"You should take some time, Jessica. We'll stay as long as you need, but when you're done, you should come out to the ranch and stay there. We would love to have you both for as long as we can."

Yardley forced a grin and nodded. "Maybe. I'll be back this evening and bring dinner."

She showered and dressed in a blue suit with heels. Wesley Paul's hearing on his motion to suppress was at four.

50

Reporters and television crews crowded the hallway of the court and shouted questions at Yardley as she came in. One asked if she was still in love with Eddie Cal. Another if Tara was really his biological daughter.

Austin Ketner had been cleared of any involvement in the murders and released last night. One reporter asked if Yardley planned on apologizing to him.

The judge had, thankfully, closed the courtroom to the media.

The courtroom smelled of old wood and orange-scented floor polish. Yardley sat down in the back row of the audience pews. The only case on the calendar for this afternoon was Wesley's.

She was early, and only a marshal and the clerk were there. They nodded to her with sad grins, the way Lieu had. Baldwin and Ortiz came in a moment later. As did two men with LVPD badges on lanyards around their necks and guns in holsters underneath their blazers. The detectives that had been at Wesley's condominium.

Wesley came next.

Two federal marshals brought him out, one in front and one behind. He wore a white jumpsuit and white slippers, and his hands were cuffed in front of him. A neck brace clung to him as though it were glued to the skin. Both eyes had been blackened so deeply that dark blemishes still adorned them; his nose had a slight crookedness to it now. Even this long after Ortiz's beating, he looked like he'd been in a car accident just this morning.

A subtle sneer pinned his lips, as though he thought the entire system a joke. He turned around just once and winked at her.

The judge came out, and a bailiff bellowed, "All rise: Federal District Court for the District of Nevada is now in session. The Honorable Madison Aggbi presiding."

Judge Aggbi came out with glasses hanging low on her nose and eyed the courtroom over the frames before sitting down. "Be seated." She punched a few keys on her computer and said, "We are here today for the matter of Wesley John Paul versus the United States. Representing the government is Mr. Timothy Jeffries of the United States Attorney's Office. Mr. Paul has indicated he will be proceeding in this matter pro se." Aggbi looked directly at him. "Mr. Paul, you are barred here in Nevada as an attorney and have been a professor of law at various universities for over fifteen years, so I certainly do not need to remind you that representing yourself in any matter is a bad idea, much less with charges like this against you. Do you understand that I am advising you to be represented by counsel and that if you cannot afford counsel, this court will appoint counsel for you?"

He stood up. "I do, Your Honor. Thank you. I appreciate your concern for me. But I am fully of sound mind, not under the influence of any narcotic or alcohol, take no prescription medications, and am fully aware of my right to counsel and waive it knowingly. I have signed and filed a waiver of counsel document from the jail computers."

"Yes, and I have received your waiver of counsel and will now sign it and incorporate it into the record. If at any point in the proceeding you feel that you have changed your mind and would like representation, please let me know right away."

"I will, thank you."

The courtroom doors opened, and Tara slipped in with her grandfather.

Yardley rose and met them at the entrance. "You can't be here," she whispered.

"He slept ten feet from my room . . . I need to see this. Please."

Yardley looked to Steven, who said nothing, and then she moved out of their way as they sat down in the pews.

Judge Aggbi read through the charges. They ranged from burglary, breaking and entering, trespassing, and kidnapping, to aggravated assault and criminal mischief and mayhem, till she announced the most serious charges: four counts of first-degree murder. Sixty-three counts in all. Lieu had thrown in every single charge he could think of. She pictured Lieu and Tim and several of the other men in the office sitting around Lieu's office going through the federal criminal code, looking for anything and everything to charge Wesley with since the media was involved. There was a group of seven of them that spent time together, went for lunches and drinks. A few times a year they would ride four-wheelers in the sand dunes or take a trip to Catalina Island. None of the female prosecutors were ever invited.

Murders were usually handled in state courts, as the qualifications for the federal government to take over were so stringent, but because of Adrian Dean's background with the DEA, the judge had approved moving the entire case to the federal system. Defendants, whenever possible, preferred to be in state court. The federal system had far harsher sentencing guidelines.

"Okay, we are here on two motions filed by the defendant. The first is a motion to suppress the confession and exclude any evidence as per *United States v. Batane*. The second motion is a motion to suppress any evidence and witness testimony as obtained by a search warrant executed by this court and the Honorable Jacob Stein. The defendant has challenged the affidavit establishing probable cause that led to the granting of the search warrant by Judge Stein, stating that the affidavit is fatally flawed and deceptive." She looked at Tim. "Mr. Jeffries."

"Thank you, Your Honor. I'd first like to address the motion to suppress the confession and any subsequent evidence acquired and move to the motion as pertaining to the search warrant afterward."

"Sounds good."

"The prosecution would call Agent Cason Baldwin to the stand."

51

Baldwin strode up to the stand. A bailiff—who in the federal courts was required to be a federal marshal—swore him in, and he sat down and unbuttoned the top button on his suit coat. In court, he always wore a transparent elastic in his hair, pulling it back to appear more respectable. Yardley had once told him he looked like a shy accountant that way, and he'd laughed.

Tim went through the preliminary questions. A motion hearing was not a trial, and there was no jury to build a connection with or impress. The standard was to simply have the witness state who they were and their relation to the case before diving into the facts. Tim started by asking Baldwin his background—unnecessary and a massive time waster at a motion hearing. Then he said:

"What is your relation to this case, Agent Baldwin?"

"I am the primary investigator on this case."

"Please expound."

Baldwin described how the FBI had gotten involved with the murders of the Deans and Olsens and his grounds for making it a federal case rather than letting the local detectives maintain jurisdiction. He described the scenes and the investigation in brief sentences, knowing most of it was irrelevant to this hearing, but Tim kept asking him to continue. Finally Wesley stood up and said, "Your Honor, the defense, for the sake of time, would be happy to stipulate that the Deans and

Olsens were found dead and that the FBI conducted an investigation that led to my charges. Perhaps we could simply get to the meat of the matter?"

"Thank you, Mr. Paul. Mr. Jeffries, let's get to the relevant portion of the testimony, please."

Tim exhaled loudly, as he had to flip past several pages of questions. It was loud enough and so near the microphone that Judge Aggbi gave him a pointed glance.

"Please describe what you saw on the date in question, Agent Baldwin," Tim said.

"Certainly. Ms. Yardley had applied for a search warrant to be executed at the home of Mr. Paul and—"

"This search warrant right here?" Tim said, holding up the original warrant.

"If that's the one I brought with me, yes."

"Your Honor, the prosecution moves to introduce exhibit one into the record."

Wesley rose. "Your Honor, I believe decorum and rule twenty-two require Mr. Jeffries to let me examine the warrant before entry into the record."

"Certainly," Aggbi said.

Tim stood there a second and then showed the warrant to Wesley, who took the document and then looked it up and down before setting it onto the table. He tried to reach into the pocket over his heart. "Your Honor, I am sorry, but if I were simply the defendant, I would have no objection to these shackles. However, as my own attorney I will be required to examine certain things and be at the lectern and perhaps even approach witnesses. Mr. Baldwin will, I'm sure, be the first to tell you I surrendered peacefully without a fight and have no intention of going anywhere. I would ask that the shackles be removed."

"Marshal," Aggbi said, "please remove the shackles, but stay close by. If Mr. Paul approaches the witness stand or the bench without permission or attempts to go toward the audience pews, please restrain him for the remainder of the proceeding."

A marshal unlocked the shackles. Wesley sat down and slipped out the reading glasses from his pocket. He examined the warrant, something he'd probably read five times already, and his lips moved slightly as though reading along.

The warrant wasn't more than four hundred words, but Wesley took ten minutes to read it. Yardley didn't watch him, though. She watched Tim. He grew frustrated with every second, at one point asking, "Finished?"

"Not quite yet, Mr. Jeffries. Trials are marathons, not sprints," he said with a smirk.

The motion hearing had been going on for maybe thirty minutes, and he had already disturbed Tim's balance.

Wesley handed the warrant back and said, "No objection to the introduction."

"Thank you," Tim said briskly. He passed the warrant to the clerk. "Now, Agent Baldwin, please continue where you left off."

Baldwin glanced at Yardley, and an understanding passed between them as surely as if they had spoken it: Tim was going to lose this motion.

"As I said, Ms. Yardley had the warrant signed by this court, and she entered the home first. She was already there, so she went in with the warrant, as there was a likelihood evidence could be destroyed if she waited for Mr. Paul's permission. My partner, Oscar Ortiz, and myself arrived not long afterward. We heard voices coming from the bathroom."

"What did you do then?"

"I went in and saw Ms. Yardley standing in the bathtub with Mr. Paul standing in front of her."

"How did Ms. Yardley appear?"

"Terrified. She was trembling. She had her firearm, a weapon registered to her that she later informed me she had in her purse, out. It was pointed at Mr. Paul."

"What was Mr. Paul doing?"

"He was threatening her."

"Objection," Wesley said. "Your Honor, hearsay. Mr. Baldwin heard no threat and is quoting Ms. Yardley."

The judge looked at Tim, who said, "Did you hear a threat?"

"Did I personally hear it, no. But I could tell from Ms. Yardley's demeanor that she was terrified."

"What happened then?" Tim said.

"I drew my firearm and told Mr. Paul to release his grip on the weapon. His hand had come up on the muzzle of Ms. Yardley's weapon. He released the weapon and put his hands behind his head. Agent Ortiz then effectuated an arrest."

"Then what?"

"Mr. Paul was placed in a patrol car while a search of his condominium began. He was then transported down to the local Las Vegas Police Department station for interview."

"Explain what happened then."

Baldwin glanced once at Ortiz, who had his head down.

"We sat in an interview room with Mr. Paul. He informed me that he didn't like me and wished only to speak to Agent Ortiz. So I left the room. He then asked to have the video recorder turned off, which Agent Ortiz did. Agent Ortiz then left the room and borrowed a digital recording device from the LVPD and reentered the room."

"Could you see what was taking place in the room?"

"No. There were no windows."

"What happened next?"

"We heard shouting, loud shouting, and then the crash of a chair on the floor. I rushed in and saw . . . I saw Agent Ortiz standing over Mr. Paul. Mr. Paul was cuffed to the desk and on his back."

"What was Agent Ortiz doing?"

"He was striking him and shouting, 'Where is she?' Mr. Paul had informed him that—"

"Objection, Your Honor, hearsay."

"Sustained."

Baldwin cleared his throat and continued. "Mr. Paul had said something to upset Agent Ortiz, and Agent Ortiz assaulted him."

"Did Mr. Paul say anything during the assault?"

"Yes. He stated that he had committed the murders and that there was a storage unit that contained various pieces of evidence of the murders."

"Your Honor, I'd like to introduce the audio recording of Agent Ortiz and Mr. Paul's interaction as the prosecution's exhibit two."

Tim was about to walk toward the clerk but stopped and looked at Wesley. Wesley nodded once and grinned.

The clerk played the recording over the speakers of the court. The blows sounded vicious. Like someone punching the back of a frying pan. Wesley begged for Ortiz to stop with all the passion of a man holding onto the ledge of a cliff and pleading to be saved. It was difficult even for Yardley to pick up that he was disingenuous.

She glanced to Tara. She sat perfectly still as she listened to the recording, glaring at Wesley's back.

Tim then went into the specifics with Baldwin about how they would have found the storage unit even without the confession. It was a doctrine known as "inevitable discovery." Inevitable discovery said the evidence should be allowed in since the police were going to obtain it anyway.

Tim spent an hour going through the details of the investigation and attempting to make logical links to how the evidence would have been discovered even if Wesley hadn't confessed.

When he was through, he went into detail about the warrant. About the affidavit that Yardley had told, word for word, to Baldwin over the phone. Yardley knew how most warrants were deemed deceptive, and she knew how to exclude the language that would lead to that. Still, the evidence they'd had at the time was weak.

"Thank you, Agent Baldwin," Tim finally said. "I tender the witness to Mr. Paul."

52

Wesley strolled to the lectern. He had no notes with him. He simply watched Agent Baldwin awhile before saying, "How are we today, Agent Baldwin?"

"Fine. Thank you."

"Mm-hmm." He grinned at him and held his gaze. "I'd like to chat about inevitable discovery. A phrase Mr. Jeffries didn't actually use during his direct examination. Do you know what inevitable discovery is, Agent Baldwin?"

"Yes."

"And you gave the impression to this court that you would have eventually found the storage unit, correct? That it was inevitable?"

"Eventually we would have found it—yes."

"Yes," Wesley said, drawing out the *s*. "Could you please list the physical evidence pointing to a suspect that you had gathered in the—" He hesitated slightly, and Yardley was certain she was the only one in the courtroom that picked up on it. Wesley cleared his throat and continued. "In the Dark Casanova Junior slayings?"

"The physical evidence? We didn't have any physical evidence pointing to a suspect."

"No DNA from saliva or blood? Semen?"

"No."

"Hair?"

"No."

"Any fibers?"

"No."

"Dirt, sand, paint?"

"No."

"Any physical or trace evidence at all found at the Deans', Olsens', or Mileses' home that matched a suspect or pointed you in the direction of a suspect?"

Baldwin had to swallow before he said, "No."

"Well, then surely you must've had eyewitness evidence. Please list the witnesses to the Dean and Olsen murders and the Mileses' home invasion."

"We have Mr. Miles and his wife and children, of course. A neighbor, Mr. Cox, witnessed a man in an alarm company uniform inspecting the Mileses' home a couple days before the attack. The alarm company confirmed that no one was scheduled to be out there at that time."

"I see. And did you do a photographic lineup recently with this neighbor?"

"We did."

"Did he identify me as the man in the alarm company uniform?"

Baldwin slowly shook his head. "He did not. He was elderly and easily confused. After ten or so minutes, I felt it would be counterproductive to have him continue."

"Huh. Well, please list the other witnesses to these crimes."

Wesley picked up a pen and a legal pad off the defense table and readied them in front of him on the lectern, as though he were going to have to make an exhaustive list.

"There was another neighbor of Mr. Miles, a Mrs. Colleen Boyle, but she said she couldn't remember anything about the person other than that he was wearing an alarm company uniform."

"I see. Anyone else?"

"No. There are no other witnesses."

"The Mileses weren't able to identify anybody?"

"No, the attacker was wearing a mask of some sort."

Wesley cocked his head slightly to the side. "Why, Agent Baldwin, if I didn't know better, I would say you didn't have any physical or DNA evidence, you didn't have any trace evidence, and you had no witnesses indicating a single suspect in these attacks before you arrested me for them, correct?"

Baldwin said nothing.

"Your Honor, please direct the witness to answer."

"Agent Baldwin, please answer Counsel's question."

"No, we didn't have any of those things."

"Actually that's incorrect, is it not? Was there not a damaged hinge on a door at the Olsens' home with markings around it on the frame?"

"There was."

"Yes, I believe Ms. Yardley found that on a casual stroll through the home. You and the entirety of the FBI's evidence response team must've been tired or hungover that night, I suppose."

"Your Honor—" Tim said.

Wesley quickly said, "Would it be fair to say, then, the entirety of the case against me was built by Ms. Yardley?"

"She got the warrant that led to your condominium and the video, which led to your confession and the storage unit, so in a way, yes."

"So the entire case is built on the confession, the storage unit, and Ms. Yardley's eyewitness testimony of the video?"

"Yes."

"If those did not exist, please list the evidence you and the prosecution would present to this court to evince my guilt."

Baldwin bit down—Yardley could see his jaw muscles flex—and then he said, "There is none."

"Thank you," Wesley said with a smile. "Nothing further."

53

"The prosecution would call Agent Oscar Ortiz to the stand."

Ortiz rose and ambled to the stand. He was sworn in and sat down, taking a tissue and wiping his nose. His hair wasn't done, his tie loose on his neck. It didn't look like he had slept.

"Please tell us your background in law enforcement, Agent Ortiz."

Yardley nearly winced.

Wesley stood up and said, "Your Honor, as much as I would prefer to be in this courtroom than back in a cell, there is no reason for this. My understanding is that Mr. Ortiz is going through a family emergency right now. I would request we get to the point and release him. I will stipulate qualifications, location, offense, venue, and date of these attacks, only for the purpose of this hearing, to speed matters along."

"Mr. Jeffries, let's get to it."

Tim sighed and said, "What happened, Agent Ortiz?"

Ortiz glanced up at him and then back down to the floor. "We had . . . him, the defendant, in the interview room at the LVPD. He asked for Agent Baldwin to leave and said he wanted the camera turned off but that I could record it. Before I could start the audio recorder, he asked about my daughter, Emilia."

"What did he say?"

"He said she was gone. That I should call home and ask. That I would find my wife waking up from a sedative. I called, and my wife checked upstairs." He had to bite his lip. "Emilia was gone."

"Do we know what happened?"

He shook his head. "My wife said she was in the shower and came out and fell asleep on the couch. She thinks something was in a drink she'd left out on the counter. A soda she was drinking before her shower."

"What time was this?"

"Afternoon, around three."

"Does she often take naps around three?"

"No. Never. She doesn't like naps."

"What happened then?"

Ortiz shifted in his seat. "She said the phone woke her up, me calling. Then she went upstairs, and the baby was just gone. The windows weren't opened, the doors were locked . . . she was just gone."

Tim established the timeline, showing that Wesley would've had time to stop at Ortiz's house before going to his condominium to find Yardley. Ortiz wasn't doing well. Several times Yardley noticed him shaking, and when he would glance at Wesley, the venom in his stare seemed to fill the room.

"So what happened in the interview room?" Tim finally said, his hands thrust in his pockets.

"I just . . . I lost it. I lost my temper. He had my daughter." Tears came to his eyes. "My baby girl. She's gotta be so scared. She's all alone and doesn't know what's going on." He stared at Wesley. "Just tell me where she is."

The judge said, "Agent Ortiz, please dire—"

"Tell me where she is!"

Everyone in the courtroom focused on Ortiz because of his shouting, but Yardley watched Wesley. When he was certain no one else was looking, he winked at Ortiz.

Ortiz leapt over the witness box. He rushed Wesley like a line-backer. The marshals had been so focused on preventing Wesley from attacking anyone they weren't prepared for a witness on the stand to.

Wesley leaned back, anticipating the blows, and closed his eyes as the first one came. The fist crashed into his cheek and sent him to the floor. Ortiz grabbed him by the jumpsuit and managed to get two more blows in before being tackled by the marshals and Baldwin.

Ortiz wept and screamed, "Emilia! Baby, no!" as the marshals hauled him back to the holding cells. "Where is she? Where is she?"

54

Dinner consisted of steaks and mashed potatoes at a restaurant near the court. Yardley sat next to Tara, and her grandparents sat across from them. Steven sensed that Yardley wanted to speak with her daughter privately, and he announced halfway through the meal that he was exhausted and they would take a cab home and meet them there.

"Nonsense," Yardley said. "I'll drive you."

"No, it's fine," Steven said with a glance to Tara.

Yardley gave him a melancholic grin, letting him know she appreciated what he was doing. They hugged their granddaughter and left.

The restaurant was quiet, a place for retirees to come for early bird specials and lunch buffets. The lighting was dim, and there were few windows. A country song played quietly over hidden speakers.

Tara absently forked her mashed potatoes but hadn't taken a bite.

"Not hungry?" Yardley asked.

Tara set her fork down and looked up. "He's going to win, isn't he?"

Yardley was about to tell her no, that they would find a way to convict him, that she was safe, but Tara wasn't a child anymore. Not really. The most painful realization Yardley had to make was that she couldn't protect her little girl from the world any longer.

"Yes, he is."

"When he gets out, he's going to come after us. I can tell. I read about malignant narcissism last night. He thinks that other people aren't worthy to be around him. That we're all just here for him to play with."

"He's . . . unique. He has traits of malignant narcissism, but he also worships—" She almost said *your father* but managed to stop herself. "He worships Eddie Cal. I think he would do anything Eddie told him to. It's a difficult balance to be a narcissist and still know you're entirely under the sway of someone else."

"I want to see him. I want to see Eddie Cal."

It felt like Yardley's blood froze in an instant. "No."

"He's my father."

"So what? What does that word even mean? Just because you have a genetic link—"

"Mom," she said gently, her eyes gazing into Yardley's, "he's my father."

Yardley stayed quiet a long while. "Yes, he is."

"I want to see him. He might be able to help you if you give him what he wants."

"Tara, you don't have to do this. Whatever else is going on with all this, you will be safe. No matter what happens."

Tara picked up her fork and began playing with her mashed potatoes again. "I think that's the first time you've ever lied to me."

———

At home, Yardley made sure that Tara was settled in her bedroom and the Cals were comfortable. Then she changed into jeans and a sweatshirt and left.

The hospital was clean and lit well. It took a call to the supervisor of the two marshals guarding Wesley's room for her to be allowed inside by herself.

Wesley lay on a hospital bed, watching a symphony on television. He saw her, and a smile came to him before he clicked off the sound and motioned with his head toward a stool near the sink. Yardley sat a few feet away from him.

"I think he fractured my cheek. That gentleman can hit." He grinned at her and said, "Please remove the digital recorder and put your purse outside of the room."

Yardley hesitated a moment and then did as he asked.

"Pockets?" he said.

She showed him her pockets were empty.

"Bra and underwear."

"No."

He shrugged. "Then have a nice night."

A deep breath escaped her, and she showed him underneath her bra and lowered her jeans, running her hands along her underwear, showing she wasn't wearing a microphone or any other digital recorders.

"I'd get anything I said suppressed anyway. Would you like a soda? I can have the nurse bring you one."

"I'm fine. Thank you."

He watched her a long time. "Lord, you're beautiful. It stuns me every time. Almost like I forget."

Yardley had to swallow her revulsion. He reminded her now of a slick lizard, licking the air around him, and it seemed shocking that she would ever have let him into her home.

Hindsight has the power to make us feel like fools, she thought.

He turned back to the television. "You want to ask where Emilia is, correct? Beg for her life?" He looked at her again. "Well? Beg."

"I won't beg you for anything. You find it . . . amusing."

"Amusing is what I have now, Jessica."

"I'm assuming when you win this motion hearing, you'll be gone. Out of the country?"

He grinned but said nothing.

"Can I also assume that there won't be any retribution toward me or Tara before you leave?"

"Depends how nice to me you are during this whole proceeding."

She leaned forward. "Tell me where the girl is, Wesley. There's no reason to keep her anymore. You know you're going to win and we'll have to dismiss. Why keep her from her parents?" She swallowed. "Let them bury their child. The not knowing what happened, it'll eat them alive the rest of their lives."

"I know. Isn't it delicious? The gift that keeps on giving."

She looked away, pretending to wipe something from the corner of her mouth so he wouldn't see how much he disgusted her.

"You really should take over the case, you know. That Timothy is sloppy sloppy. Prosecuting too many simple drug possession and check fraud cases, I think. Made him soft. That's one thing I always admired about you: you never took the easy route. That's why you're so strong now. You become a good sailor in storms, not in calm seas."

Despite the fact that even the thought of it sickened her, she brought the stool close and put her hand on his. His cheek had swollen, and his lip was cut from Ortiz's blows. A hemorrhage had made the lower portion of the white of his eye black red. As though whatever filth was inside him bled out of his eyes.

"Tell me where she is, Wesley. If I ever meant anything to you, if in that dead heart you ever felt anything for me, please, let that family have some peace."

A gleeful mischief flashed in his eyes when he said, "Kiss me."

"No."

"Kiss me, and I'll think about it. Passionately, like you used to."

She had to squeeze her free hand so hard that she was certain her nails had drawn blood from her palm. Leaning over, she kissed him. His lips were cracked and tasted like dried blood. When she pulled away, she wiped her lips with the back of her hand, bile rising in her throat.

"Where is she?"

He grinned. "I don't think that was passionate enough."

"Wesley, where is she?"

He lifted the hand that was underneath hers and ran his fingertips up her arm. "Make love to me. Right here, with those marshals sitting outside. Make love to me, and I'll tell you."

The pain that shot into her almost made her fall off the stool. "I can't."

"Then no Emilia. Make your decision. You're a US attorney, too. You could get us a private room at the jail. That's my condition. You make love to me, let me do whatever I want to your body, and I'll tell you where the girl is. Your body in exchange for hers."

Yardley withdrew her hand. She stared at him, her eyes burning, her cheeks flushed with the anger she could barely keep contained.

"I swear to you, I'll make you pay for this."

She left the room and didn't look back at him.

55

Yardley pulled up to the prison early the next morning, the butterflies in her stomach making her jittery. She'd wanted to wait, to take time to set up a meeting between Tara and Eddie, but Tara insisted that it had to be now. Before Wesley was released.

"I'll be in there with you. If at any point you feel uncomfortable—"

"I need to meet him alone."

"Absolutely not. I'm doing this because he's your father and you have a right to meet him, but I will not leave you alone with him. And certainly not when there's no camera for me to see what's going on."

"He won't tell me anything if you're there. He's got some things he wants to say to me, and it's not for you to hear. It's between me and my father."

Yardley sighed and looked away. "Tara—"

"I'll be okay. I'm stronger than I look, Mom. I get it from you."

They held hands until a guard came out and said, "He's ready for you."

56

Eddie Cal sat on one side of a thick glass barrier. The barrier had holes in it near the top, large enough to carry sound but not large enough to pass anything substantial through.

His ex-wife stepped inside the room. "If you hurt her, I will make it my life's mission to ensure you pay for it. Do you understand me?"

Cal nodded but said nothing, his eyes never leaving Tara.

Yardley left, and the steel door slid closed with a metallic clang.

The young girl stood perfectly still.

"You can pull the wire out of that camera and make sure it's not recording."

He could tell his voice sent a small shock through her.

She turned toward the video camera in the corner of the ceiling. A black wire looped from it into the wall. She took the chair over and stood on it before yanking the wire out. Then she brought the chair close to the glass and sat down, watching him in silence. Her eyes were bright as sapphires.

He grinned and said, "You're the most beautiful thing I've ever seen. I wish our first meeting could've been somewhere more appropriate. This place desecrates you."

"I don't think there's anywhere more appropriate we could've met."

He shifted in his seat, and his metal restraints rattled. He recognized his voice in hers, like a distant echo he couldn't quite make out but knew was his own.

"I was told you're something of a math prodigy."

"Told by Wesley?"

He hesitated. "Yes."

Her eyes fascinated him. A blue so deep and bright they appeared otherworldly—he had never seen eyes the same hue as his until right now.

"I know you would've eventually killed my mother if you hadn't been caught," she said. "I don't know if she realizes that, but I do. I've studied your art. They have photographs of a lot of your paintings and sculptures online. Your art's an escalation. Each piece is more violent than the one you did before it. An article I read said you were working on performance pieces when you were arrested. With how quickly you were escalating, you eventually would've had nowhere else to go. You would've decided killing someone you love would be the highest form of expression. A sacrifice to your art. And that you were somehow making her immortal. Tell me I'm wrong."

He said nothing. Then he shook his head, a shy grin on his face. "All those years hoping to find just one person that understood what I was trying to do, and it turned out to be my daughter."

She looked down to her nails as she softly picked at dried skin on a cuticle. "I'm full of surprises, just like you."

"I can see the strength in you. It radiates off your body like fire on a phoenix. Your mother told me a little about the troubles you faced from your classmates in school. Everything that happened to you made you stronger. You shouldn't regret it. But if it helps at all, I *am* sorry."

She leaned forward. "You know, it felt like my entire life I had this missing piece. A large hole where my father should've been. We would go years without even mentioning you, but your absence was like this . . . ghost, always in the room with us. I thought if I met you, maybe that ghost would leave. Now I know it'll never leave, will it?" She sat back. "You can never be sorry enough, but there is something you can do. You owe me for what me and my mother had to go through, and I want payment."

He chuckled lightly. "It seems you have more of me in you than your mother let on. What payment?"

"First, I want some of your paintings. I can sell them, and they're worth a lot."

"Your mother burned them all."

"Bullshit. You're someone that loves secrets. There's no way you let any person, not even your wife, know where all your work is. Especially if you thought you might get caught one day. I want those paintings, and you're going to give them to me."

An unfamiliar warmth tingled his skin then, and he wondered if it was pride. Something another parent might feel watching their child hit a baseball or win a spelling bee.

"What else?" he said with a smile.

———

Yardley paced the corridor at death row for over two hours. Her thumbnail had been chewed down to nothing, ruining a manicure she had gotten a few weeks ago. The guard by the door watched something on his phone and would laugh every so often, and Yardley wanted to scream at him to shut up.

Finally, there was a knock on the steel door. The guard put his phone away and slid the door open. Tara stood there. Yardley looked at her eyes to see if they were puffy and red from crying, but there was nothing. She didn't appear shaken or nervous in any way. It was like she had just gotten done with a conversation that bored her.

"I'm ready to leave," she said.

"Do you want to talk about it?" Yardley said, putting her hand on her daughter's shoulder.

Tara waited until they were on the road.

"Wesley killed someone else," she said, not moving her gaze from the window.

"What?"

"He killed someone else that you don't know about. Eddie said it was the first person he killed. It was a woman he was obsessed with." She looked at her mother. "Like he's obsessed with you."

It felt like Yardley's heart skipped a beat. "Who?"

"Eddie said her name was Jordan Russo. It was nineteen years ago. Wesley lied about being born in Tennessee and living on the East Coast. He's from California. And his name's not Wesley Paul. Eddie didn't know what his real name was, but it's not that."

Yardley was quiet a moment. "Did he say anything else?"

57

Later that morning, Yardley, Baldwin, Tim, and Roy Lieu met in Lieu's office. It was the largest office on the US attorneys' floor, a corner office overlooking the Las Vegas Strip a few blocks away. Gray carpets and glass for walls on three sides. Yardley stood with her back toward the men, staring at the massive Ferris wheel on the Strip. The sun's glimmering rays broke against the steel spokes and fragmented over the valley.

The men were all sitting down. She could see their reflections in the glass.

"He had to be taken to the hospital," Tim said. "What the hell, Cason?"

"Me? I told you not to call Ortiz as a witness."

Yardley said, "It wouldn't have mattered. Wesley knew that would happen. He would've called him if we didn't."

Lieu exhaled and leaned back, his fingers forming a steeple under his chin. "Aggbi granted a continuance of two weeks this morning. We'll have to go back in there afterward. Mr. Paul will probably call Ortiz to the stand again. I want him in cuffs this time."

"Roy," Baldwin said, "he's a federal agent with—"

"He assaulted a defendant in open court."

"A defendant that kidnapped his daughter."

They sat in silence, those words hanging in the air like poison that stung with every breath.

"You're going to lose," Yardley said, not taking her eyes off the Ferris wheel.

"You don't know that," Tim said.

Lieu said, "She could be right. You might be able to beat the *Franks* motion and keep the warrant and Jessica's testimony in. The warrant affidavit is good. But the confession and storage unit and everything we found there might get suppressed."

"It's worse than that," Yardley said as she turned around and faced them. "Fruit of the poisonous tree is discretionary. Judges can apply it as far down the evidentiary chain as they feel fit. Wesley will challenge anything, *anything*, you find, saying it was found solely because of the excluded evidence discovered in his storage unit. You may win on some of the arguments with inevitable discovery, but you'll lose a lot more of them. He's going to win this case, Roy."

Tim said, "Jessica, save the drama. I've never lost a case in this office in over fifteen years."

"There's no cameras here, Tim. You can save it. I know how easy it is to say you're undefeated when you only prosecute cases you're practically guaranteed to win. Wesley is smarter than you, and he's been planning this for a long time. Years. You're going to lose, and we will never see him again once he's released. Unless he decides to kill me first, of course."

"That's bullshit," Tim said, his face now flushing red. "Roy, I can win this."

"Did you know he planned to call me to the stand if Ortiz hadn't attacked him and ended the hearing early?" Yardley said.

"What? He didn't give notice. He can't."

"He provided you with a list of witnesses, fifty-four of them. Did you go through each one?"

Tim shifted in his seat. "I went through them," he said, uncertainty in his voice.

"Then you would've seen my name in the middle. It was placed between two experts that have the same initials as me, *JY*, so that your eyes would glance over it. He buried me in the witness list, knowing you would miss it and hoping I would, too. That we'd be unprepared." She folded her arms and leaned against the glass behind her. It felt warm against her back. "Tim, you can't handle someone like this. He is going to get this case dismissed. And if not, a jury is going to acquit him."

Tim scoffed at her and said, "Roy, come on. I got this."

Lieu watched him and then turned to Yardley. "What do you suggest?"

"Once he wins these motions, he'll ask for an expedited preliminary hearing. The case will be dismissed then."

"Even if that happens, it means we have a few weeks, maybe even a couple of months, to dig up more evidence," Tim said.

"No," Yardley said with a hard stare. His pride had clouded his thinking, and it was beginning to aggravate her. "Anything we find has a taint to it now. The chance of it being excluded is too high."

"What do you suggest, then?" Lieu said.

Yardley rubbed her chin with her knuckle. "I've been looking into something. There was a young woman here that disappeared almost twenty years ago. Her body was found a few weeks later in the desert. She'd had her skull crushed."

"What does that have to do with Wesley?" Baldwin asked.

Yardley thought a second, unsure how much to reveal to them. "He told Eddie Cal it was his first victim."

The room went silent, until Lieu said, "Who is she?"

"Jordan Russo. She was seventeen. Left for the gym, and her mother says she never saw her again. The police determined she'd likely been kidnapped, but never had enough evidence to link any suspect. Then they thought maybe she ran away with someone . . . until they found her body twenty-two days later."

"Not his MO to kill someone in that way," Lieu said.

"It was his first. He hadn't developed his signature yet. He likely panicked and grabbed whatever was available, in this case a large rock, and hit her with it. It was, in a roundabout way, unintended."

Lieu leaned forward, his elbows on his desk, staring at a photograph of him and a senator on the wall across from him.

"So what do you want to do?"

58

The home was clean and quiet, only eight miles from her own. A little two-story house on a quiet street pushed back against the red rocks behind it. Isabella Russo answered the door in workout clothes, her brunette hair pulled back, peering through thick glasses. Without the glasses, Yardley thought, she would look just like Jordan Russo.

She gathered together the coupons that were out on the coffee table and put them in a plastic container with a lid before sitting down on the couch. Yardley sat across from her on a love seat. Above the fireplace were large framed photos. In the center of them was one of a stunningly beautiful girl. Jordan when she'd been perhaps fourteen or fifteen. Tara's age. Yardley remembered what she'd thought and felt the night Tara had run away. She wondered if Isabella Russo still felt that every day.

The other photos were not as prominent. Isabella and a large man with curly hair and two other kids. There were several photos of the children hung up as well, but Jordan's photos were always in the center between them.

The man she saw in the photos came out of the kitchen and said hello.

"Hello," Yardley replied.

He turned to Isabella and told her he would be back in a couple of hours. He kissed her on the cheek and left.

"That's not Jordan's father," Isabella said, anticipating her question. "Her father left us. With my best friend, of course. Isn't that how it always is? It's always the best friend." She was lost in thought a moment before she gave a mournful grin and said, "Jordan once told me that's why she made sure her best friends were always boys."

"She's beautiful," Yardley said, glancing up at the photo over the fireplace.

Isabella turned and looked at it. "She got her father's good looks. It's funny—I always thought I fell for her father's personality, but looking back on it, I don't think he had any. His looks just made me pretend all those terrible qualities didn't exist."

"I think maybe we're all capable of that."

She turned back around. "Luke's a good man. I met him five years after Jordan's death. I told him I didn't want any kids when we got married. Who the hell would want to bring kids into this world after something like that? But he finally convinced me that having brothers and sisters would be a way to honor her. That it would be like having a piece of her back."

Isabella had to stop a moment, and Yardley could tell she was fighting back tears. Even after two decades, the pain seemed as fresh as if Jordan had been killed yesterday.

"And it really is like having her back," she continued. "Her sister looks a lot like her. She would wake me up when she was younger, and it would shock me because, for a second, I would think it was Jordan. That maybe her death was just some nightmare I'd finally woken up from." She wiped a single tear away with the back of her finger. "I'm sorry. You must think I'm such a mess, crying after all this time."

"Never. Frankly, you have a strength I wish I had. To have children again after something like that."

She nodded and inhaled deeply. "I have a doctor's appointment soon. What was it you needed, Ms. Yardley?"

"Jessica. And I'm looking into Jordan's case. I'm so sorry to have to open this wound back up, but we have a man in custody, and there's some indication he might have been involved in her death."

Isabella's eyes went wide. Yardley had tried to temper the statement to not get her excited in case they decided not to file charges and nothing came of it, but the pain was too deep, and the hope that they would catch the man that had killed her little girl was too powerful.

"Who is it?"

"Have you been reading the news about the man they call Dark Casanova Junior?"

She nodded. "The one that killed those couples." She paused. "It's him?"

"We're not sure yet; that's why I'm here. I've read all the police reports in Jordan's case, and they mentioned no boyfriends, but a friend of hers from her work said she may have been dating someone. She never saw him, but Jordan told her about someone she was infatuated with."

Isabella nodded. "She had a journal. A little white one with the rings binding the pages. Tacky thing, but it was a gift from my sister. I tried to find it to give to the detective, but it wasn't in her room."

Yardley didn't say what she immediately thought: *He* had it. Either it mentioned Wesley and he'd destroyed it, or he got a thrill out of keeping it. Going back and reading Jordan Russo's most personal thoughts whenever he wanted to relive the killing.

"Something else was missing, too," Isabella said. "Her ring. Silver with a sapphire in the middle. On the back it said, 'To My Bumblebee.' It's the only gift she still had from her father. She never took it off, even to shower. When they found her, she wasn't wearing the ring."

Yardley nodded. The ring had been mentioned in the police reports. "Is her room still made up the way it was then?"

"No. I kept it that way until Luke. He finally said it was time for something new. It's my son's room now. All of Jordan's things are in the attic."

"Do you mind if I take a look?"

She led Yardley to a set of narrow stairs that climbed to the attic and said, "I need to get dressed. Just please don't take anything without telling me."

"I won't."

The attic was coated in dust and cobwebs. The stacks of boxes weren't labeled. Yardley opened the first one. It was filled with clothes, as was a second one. Mostly baby clothes and some from adolescence. Jordan's teenage clothes had likely been donated, or her sister had received them.

Another box held photographs of Jordan and her friends, makeup kits, perfumes, and lotions. Yardley lifted one of the perfumes and inhaled the scent. Earthy with a hint of amber. Something a young girl would pick out, thinking it made her seem older.

A claustrophobic sadness came over Yardley as she closed the boxes: The Olsens' lives had been put in boxes, too. Soon, they would be stored away somewhere with cobwebs to be forgotten.

Yardley rose and slapped the dust off her hands. The bitter anger she felt as she stared at those boxes, the only things left of a beautiful young life brutally taken before it had even really begun, took her breath away.

As she said goodbye to Isabella Russo, only one thought ran through her mind: *You will not get away with this, Wesley.*

———

Yardley stood in what had been Wesley's home office. Everything down to the last paper clip and pen, she had put in the storage unit until she could donate it, but now she realized she almost never came in here since Wesley had moved in. He'd told her that once his concentration was broken, it was difficult to get it back, so he should only be disturbed if absolutely necessary.

The office had a large bookshelf, now empty, a massive desk she'd bought for him as a birthday gift, a chair, and a monitor. There was a closet off to the side filled with things she'd had in here before he had moved in.

She went to the closet and opened the door. Her old office chair was stuffed in there, along with legal books, boxes of office supplies, a printer, and an old computer. Yardley began pulling everything out.

It took her a few minutes to go through everything, but nothing seemed strange or out of the ordinary. She looked in the closet again and noticed the shelf near the top. Two boxes were up there she hadn't searched. She took one down and opened it: nothing but reams of computer paper and a few wires and discs. She put it on the floor and took down the other one. Massive legal treatises, each thousands of pages in length. She remembered having to use these in law school, and even now, it gave her a twinge of anxiety as she remembered cramming for final exams that determined your entire grade for the course.

As she was about to put everything back, the thought suddenly hit her that Wesley had hidden the DVDs in a book.

She pulled out all the books and treatises and stacked them on the floor. She took off her shoes and sat down before flipping through them one by one. The smell of old wood-pulp paper brought back memories of late-night study sessions in high school, fueled by gallons of coffee because she was only getting a few hours' sleep working two jobs and attempting to get straight As so she could receive a scholarship to college. Without a scholarship, she wouldn't have been able to go.

She tried to remember if her mother had ever asked her how the bills got paid, since she'd spent all their money on alcohol, but she couldn't remember a time she ever had.

A thick brown legal tome of medieval English law felt far too light for how large it was.

She opened it.

It had been hollowed out. In the center was a small white journal. Written in faded red marker on the cover were the words *MY DIARY.*

59

It was during lunch when Baldwin went for a run. He hadn't had time today, but he preferred running in the mornings and sometimes even ran on the Strip. Las Vegas was a night town, and the early morning consisted of nothing but a few people drunkenly heading back to hotels after nights spent ravaging their bodies and wallets.

He hadn't gone for a run since going into the Deans' bedroom.

He grew winded within two miles and couldn't finish his run, so he headed home. The last bottle of pain pills sat on the counter in the kitchen; he'd been telling himself they were there "just in case."

As he drank down a glass of water, he took the amber bottle, emptied the pills into the garbage disposal, and tossed the bottle into the trash bin.

Yardley called his cell.

"Hey," he said.

"He knew her," she said.

"Who?"

"Wesley knew Jordan Russo. I spoke with her mother. She said Jordan kept a journal but the police never found it. I just went through the closet in the office I kept for Wesley. I found the journal in a hollowed-out treatise."

"Why would he keep it there?"

"It probably gave him a thrill to have it here in my house. To read it while I was just outside the door." A pause. "Anyway, the entries three weeks before she was killed talk about meeting a man older than her with a southern accent, who she called Wes. I called Isabella Russo about it, and she said the only times she had seen Jordan with an older man was when she went to pick up Jordan at her work. Jordan worked two jobs, one at a restaurant as a hostess and the other as a personal trainer at a gym. Isabella is certain it was at the restaurant she saw him. I didn't want to taint any lineup, so I haven't shown her a photo of Wesley. I sent you all the police reports and the autopsy results this morning. Go through them and give me a call back."

Baldwin puffed his cheeks and blew out a breath before hurrying to the shower.

———

The café bustled with activity as Baldwin sat in a corner and read through Jordan Russo's police reports. The homicide detectives, forensic investigators, and ME had done an excellent job with the investigation, but there just wasn't much to go on. They'd assumed sexual assault before her death since the body had been found nude, though the clothes had been on scene next to the corpse.

In the hot desert sun for twenty-two days, she had been completely drained of moisture, and there were plenty of signs of animals feeding on the body. The medical examiner couldn't make many determinations, and even the time of death was a rough guess. The only method of determining time of death after that long was body decomposition, but because of the heat, it had accelerated.

No journal was listed in the evidence logs.

They had no witnesses to the kidnapping or dumping of the body, and the case had been moved to the open-unsolved files of the LVPD eighteen years ago.

Baldwin texted Yardley.

The reports said she had a ring that was missing.

Yardley replied, Her father had given her a silver ring with a sapphire in the middle. It's her birthstone. The ring has an inscription on the back that says To My Bumblebee. It's what her father used to call her. I think Wesley kept the ring.

There wasn't a ring found in his storage unit.

I know. Come over to my house and pick me up.

60

Yardley watched as Baldwin pulled up in her driveway. She got into the passenger seat and said, "I put all of the things he had here into storage. I didn't go through them. I had movers do it."

"You think we're going to find the ring there? No way. He's too careful. If it's even him."

She bit her thumbnail. "It's him. And if it thrilled him to keep her journal in my home, I'm certain it would thrill him to keep other things as well."

He put the car in park. "Jess, you shouldn't be part of this. You have a conflict in this, and what if you're the one that finds something? How is that going to look?"

"No one else can do this, Cason. I wish to hell someone else could, but I'm the only one. We have to risk it."

He watched her a second. "You can come, but you're staying in the car while me and some other agents search. But even if we find it, he could just say she gave him that ring."

"I'm sure there's more if we start digging. The detectives at the time didn't know about Wesley."

He put the car in drive and pulled away. She watched him a second and then looked out the window. "I think Emilia's alive, too."

"Why?"

"An insurance policy, maybe. He would want to see if he could use her as leverage down the line. If he's somehow convicted, he'll try to bargain. She's more valuable alive than dead. So if he drove from Oscar's to his condo, he had to drop her off somewhere along the way. Someone is watching her."

"He could have locked her up somewhere and planned to go back himself to feed her."

She shook her head, though she didn't look at him. "No. He knew he was going to get arrested and that bail would be denied. Someone has her. I would get as many people as you can and go door to door."

"That would take months."

"Go to the media again. Get more volunteers from the public. The story's off the news. We need to get it back on. Wesley didn't have any friends that I knew of. He paid someone to watch her, and I'm guessing that person doesn't know who Emilia is."

At the storage facility, two men in dark suits were waiting for them by the gate.

Baldwin and his men sifted through everything quickly. The storage facility had been the remotest one Yardley could find. She'd wanted Wesley's things as far away from her house as she could get them.

From inside the car she could see the items they stacked on the ground as they emptied the boxes. Clothing, shoes, office supplies, trinkets he'd gathered on trips to Kenya or Cambodia. There was what looked like a replica of an ancient mask, faded and with water stains underneath the eyes that gave it the appearance of weeping. Beneath that was Wesley's orthodontic retainer, which he occasionally wore at night, a perfect replica of his teeth. It made her sick to think of her tongue ever being inside that mouth.

"Got something," Baldwin said.

He lifted a small wooden box with a lock on it. It appeared to be a cigar box from the eighteenth or nineteenth century and had silver trim.

"You seen this before?" he asked Yardley.

"He kept it in the office. I never asked him about it. I assumed it was cigars."

"The lock's really sturdy. More than cigars deserve."

Baldwin retrieved something from the trunk of his car. He laid the box down on the hood and lifted a collection of what looked like smooth keys and slipped them into the lock one by one.

"Stop," Yardley said.

"Why?"

"I'm getting a warrant," she said, lifting her phone to her ear.

"We don't need one. It's with his things that are in your possession, and we have probable cause anyway from the mother and the journal."

"I'm not taking any chances."

Yardley called in the warrant to her office, and her paralegal had it drafted and said she would run around until she found a judge that was off the bench and could sign it. While they waited, Baldwin lay on the hood of his car and stared at the sky. The other two agents leaned against the storage unit.

"You see your life this way when you were a kid?" Baldwin said.

"What way is that?" she said through the open window.

"Dealing with the people we deal with? I always wanted to be a fireman as a kid. Help people. No matter who it was in that fire, I would help them. Seems like you'd have a positive outlook on life, even seeing all the death and tragedy you would see. What we deal with is different. It changes your view of what people are. I just sometimes wonder where I'd be if I had pursued what I wanted to pursue."

"Impossible to know. You might be worse off than you are now."

"Or I might be married with a houseful of kids and working a job I love, rather than chasing freaks and eating fast food every night."

"Thinking that way serves no purpose."

He turned his head to look at her. "Let's make a deal. If you're single in five years, and I'm single in five years . . ."

She grinned. "You'd have to cut your hair first. I'm not marrying Bon Jovi."

Her phone buzzed: the warrant had been signed and emailed to her.

"We got it?" Baldwin asked.

She nodded. "Open the box."

It took Baldwin less than a minute to pop it open. He retrieved latex gloves from his trunk.

"Sapphire, right?"

"Yes."

He lifted first a lock of brunette hair, then a silver ring with a bright sapphire in the middle. Turning it over, he said, "There's an inscription. It says 'To My Bumblebee.'"

Got you, Yardley thought.

61

Tara was asleep in her room, and Yardley watched her from the doorway. She wondered if Ortiz was staring at an empty crib in his own daughter's room right now.

Steven Cal sat on the couch, his feet up on the coffee table, the volume low on the evening news. He smiled warmly as she kicked her shoes off and sat next to him, tucking her legs underneath herself.

"How was she?" Yardley asked.

"I think she had a lot of fun, but we didn't see her that much. She was out with her friends most of the day. She did tell us about that boy. She said she's nervous because he might try to call her."

"I'm having her number changed. I haven't told her this yet, but I'll probably have to take her out of school, too. She can't be near him again."

Steven's eyes never left the television, and she knew he'd already rehearsed whatever he was about to say. "We have excellent schools near the ranch. Fifteen kids per class, and everyone knows each other. There's a private school a few miles farther, too. I could easily provide that for her."

"She needs to be near her mother, Steven."

He nodded. "I know. But she's already starting life with disadvantages because of her father, so we have to give her as many advantages as we can." He looked at her. "This city is no place to raise a young woman. Maybe you've had enough of it, too."

Yardley rose. "Want a drink?"

She made two gin and tonics and handed him one. They sipped in silence as they watched television, though Yardley was certain neither of them paid attention to it.

"Are you going to visit him?" she said.

Steven took a long pull from the drink. "I haven't decided."

"He's still your son."

"I don't need to be reminded that he's my son. I know." Steven stared down into his drink, clinking the ice against the glass. "This is horrible to say, and it took me a long time to put it into words, but I wish he would've died when the police shot him. I prayed secretly that he wouldn't live. What kind of father am I to think that about my own son?"

"You're a father, but you're a human being first."

He shook his head. "I thought that if he was dead, maybe it'd bring those families of the people he killed some peace. Give his mother some peace. It took years for her to finally take down his pictures from around the house. Longer to get off the meds the therapist prescribed. If we went and saw him, it would dredge all of that back up. Everything we went through."

Yardley carefully crafted the words she wanted to say next. "You might regret seeing him, but you might regret it more if you didn't, because you're not going to get another chance."

She put her drink on the coffee table, kissed his cheek, and said, "Good night, Steven. And I'll talk to Tara about at least coming for a visit."

"Good night."

When she glanced back, she saw him wipe tears away on his wrist before covering his eyes with his hand and crying.

62

The charges for the murders of the Deans and Olsens and the attempted murder of the Mileses were dismissed for lack of evidence after Wesley's confession and everything in his storage unit was suppressed. The FBI arrested him for Jordan Russo's murder the moment the judge granted the dismissal.

Everything lined up over the next few days. Isabella Russo stood in a darkened room and identified Wesley from among six men in a lineup as the man she'd seen speaking with her daughter in front of the restaurant she'd worked at and the man in the driver's seat as he drove out of the parking lot. All the proper procedures were followed, and Isabella insisted she hadn't watched any of the recent news reports about Wesley's other crimes or seen his picture anywhere.

The ID would stand up in court, and if Yardley had any qualms about how quickly Isabella had identified Wesley, she kept them to herself. It was possible that the memory of Wesley's face had been burned so deeply in her mind that even twenty years couldn't diminish it. It was possible. Yardley decided she had only a finite amount of energy to worry about things, and this was one thing that didn't need to be high on that list.

Leaving the lineup, Wesley didn't have the confident swagger, the disdain and amusement exuding from his eyes, that he'd had at the motion hearing. Instead, he seemed furious. It almost made Yardley smile.

"What's the matter, Wesley?" Baldwin said, seeing it as well. "Didn't expect Jordan Russo to come back and bite you in the ass?"

As marshals led Wesley back to the jail, he sneered. "You must really be desperate to find a random homicide you think you can pin on me. When I am acquitted of this farce, and I will be, I will file suit against the US Attorney's Office, the FBI, and against you in particular for malicious prosecution and false imprisonment."

"We found the ring, Wes," Baldwin said. "And the hair, and everything else. You disgust me. And I'm going to laugh my ass off when that judge hands down a life sentence without parole."

Wesley's jaw clenched as the marshals dragged him away.

It was two in the afternoon when the message came in: the hair found in Wesley Paul's private lockbox was a match to hair taken from Jordan Russo's brush. Yardley had remembered seeing one in the boxes in her mother's attic.

Within seconds, she was standing in Lieu's office.

"The lab called me," he said before she could speak. "It's a solid case with the mother's testimony, the journal, the ring, and the hair. The mother said she would agree to an exhumation order on the body as well, so maybe we'll get lucky that something's still there."

"He's going to argue circumstantial evidence. That she gave him all of it and it's just a coincidence that she was murdered later and it had nothing to do with him. I don't think the jury will buy it, but we'll keep looking for someone that saw them together the day she went missing. In the meantime, I'll get the indictment drafted up and get everything submitted to the grand jury by—"

"I'm not having you prosecute the case, Jessica."

She let a beat of silence pass. "This is my case. I built it from the ground up. You wouldn't even know about this evidence if I—"

"I'm giving it to Tim."

"You can't be serious. Tim's part of the reason our original case fell apart."

"I stick by my original assessment. It would look improper to have you prosecute this."

When she started to argue, Lieu raised a hand and gave her a hard stare. "He is your senior in this office and was prosecuting homicides while you were still a first-year law student. You need to show him the respect he deserves."

"Tim is no match for Wesley. He—"

Lieu continued as though he hadn't even heard her. "I spoke to Tim about it, and he agreed that you could second chair. Help him out in trial, hand him evidence and other things he might need, take notes where appropriate, give him ideas for questions he may miss on direct and cross."

"*Hand* him things? Are you serious?" She folded her arms. "If I were a man, would you be telling me right now to second chair and hand him things?"

"Don't play that card with me. Sorry your feelings are hurt. But what can I say? You chose these men. You got yourself into this mess."

Yardley barely made it back to her office without screaming. She took a pencil out of her drawer, closed her eyes, breathed deeply, and snapped it in half, savoring the crunch in her hands. When she opened her eyes, she tossed the pencil in the trash and called Baldwin.

"Tim is going to be prosecuting this."

"You're shitting me."

"We have to make certain there's no chance this ends in acquittal."

He sighed. "Well, where should we start?"

63

The gray sky had hints of coming sunlight, and Baldwin wished he were lying on a beach somewhere. Weather affected his mood, and he didn't like the rainstorm that had clung to the city the past month.

He sat in his car outside of Yardley's house and texted her. She replied that she was finishing up a workout and would be out. She had, apparently, been working out two hours a day since Tara had left to stay with her grandparents in New Mexico a few days ago. She wouldn't discuss it, but Baldwin knew how worried she had to be about Tara's safety to send her so far across the country.

She came out in yoga pants and a zip-up hoodie and got into his car. She smelled like mint shampoo, her hair still wet from the shower. He could see the portion of her leg between the ankle and knee, stared a little too long at her muscular calf, and felt a twinge of guilt for doing so.

"I'm glad you came instead of Tim," Baldwin said as he pulled away from her house.

"He said to report back to him what the medical examiner says. He didn't want to miss his afternoon walk."

Baldwin glanced at her. "I'm so sorry you have to put up with this. It's bullshit. Everyone knows you're the one running this case, and no one's going to forget it."

She stared out the window. "Doesn't matter. I just want to make sure Wesley never gets out."

"If he ever tried to come after you—"

"There would be nothing you could do. You can't stay with me every minute. Remember that he followed me quietly for years. He's inhumanly patient. He would just wait until my guard's down and get at me then."

"I'm not going to let that happen, Jess."

"No," she said, looking at him. "*I'm* not going to let that happen."

———

The Clark County Office of the Coroner and Medical Examiner sat near a children's museum in an office park. Across the street was a barren field that the owners had been trying to develop as far back as Baldwin could remember.

They signed in and were led back to an all-white room with a metal gurney in the center and a green tarp over it. One of the assistant MEs came in, chomping on a donut, his face bent over his phone. He saw them and put the phone in his pocket. "Cason, been a bit."

"How are ya, Matt?"

"Hanging in there. Jessica, good to see you again."

She gave him half a grin but said nothing.

"So you found something?" Baldwin asked.

"Yup." He took a large bite before tossing the rest of the donut into a biohazard trash bin and washing his hands. He put on latex gloves and pulled back the tarp.

Baldwin had seen so many corpses in so many different conditions of decay that it meant almost nothing to him. It no longer shocked him, and if he wasn't mindful about his thoughts, it didn't even register as once having been a human being. So he could understand how Matt was still chewing on the remaining donut in his mouth as he stared down at the desiccated body. Yardley's eyes remained fixed on the corpse and revealed nothing to him.

"Right here," Matt said. "Take a look."

Baldwin stepped close to the body and bent over it. The muscle and flesh were gone, only the skeleton and some of the thicker sinew remaining. With all the teeth having fallen out, her head was nothing more than a skull with jagged cracks where the rock had crushed bone.

"Right here," Matt said, pointing to the right foot. "That's called the medial cuneiform bone. See those indentations right there? Hardly noticeable, but it's a bite mark."

Matt retrieved a plastic set of teeth from a cupboard and came back to the skeleton. He carefully lined up the teeth in the grooves on the bone. The mouth twisted to the right. "He had to have bitten down at an angle, like this."

"She kicked him," Yardley said. The two men looked at her. "She fought him and they ended up on the ground, or he was standing above her. She kicked him, and he grabbed her and bit down so hard he notched the bone."

Matt nodded and made the teeth snap shut before putting them back. "If her shoes were off or she had low-cut shoes, that's a pretty good theory. And would explain why there're no other bite marks. Your guy have a history of biting?"

"No," Baldwin said. "None of his victims displayed any."

"Then I think Jessica's explanation is probably best. She was crawling away or on her back and kicked him; he grabbed her and bit down into the first section he could. There's not much flesh on the medial cuneiform, so as long as that section isn't covered by a shoe, he pretty much just bit straight into the bone. That's why we have such good markings."

"How was this missed before?" Yardley asked.

Matt blew out a puff of air. "Well, she still had flesh on her, and with discoloration and being left out in the desert and all that, it could be easy to miss something like this. Plus, you know how you don't really wash your feet much in the shower but spend a bunch of time washing your chest and stomach, even though the feet are actually the part of your body with the most bacteria? It's kind of the same with autopsies. Something to do with an inherent bias. Even the most careful of us tend to glance over the feet and focus on the rest of the body. A newer resident at the time was the one that did the initial autopsy, and . . . I mean, honestly, I think they just plain missed it. It was probably hard to see, and they assessed the feet too quickly. I apologize for that, and I'll say as much in an updated report."

Baldwin said, "It happens. What's important is we have it now."

He nodded, staring down at the skeleton. "Get out your forensic odontologist and get to work and see if it's your guy. You need anything from me, let me know. I gotta run. Good seeing you both again." He covered the body back up with the tarp.

"What do you think?" Baldwin said when they were out in the hall. "We call our dentist to get out here with a cast?"

She shook her head, folding her arms as she leaned against the wall. "No. Wesley will file a motion to quash the order to allow a dental cast."

"Yeah, but he'll lose that for sure, right?"

"Maybe, maybe not. It's not worth the risk. I have a way, though. When we were at the storage unit, I saw his orthodontic retainer. Jury selection wraps up in the morning, so you need to get in touch with the dentist and see if he can make a cast just from the retainer." She watched him a moment. "Are you sleeping more?"

"Some. Why?"

"You look better. You seem . . . I don't know. Not as melancholy."

"Don't worry about me, I'm fine. You just focus on getting a conviction against that prick."

64

The first day of trial was a mess of emotions for most attorneys. Yardley kept her emotions in check as much as she could, pretending she was a mechanical device in court, there to perform a certain purpose and nothing else. Today, on the first day of Wesley Paul's trial, she had to take a beta-blocker in the morning because she couldn't stop trembling.

"Any preliminary matters to address before bringing out the jury?" Judge Aggbi asked.

"No, Judge," Tim said.

"Nothing, Your Honor, thank you," Wesley said.

"Then let's bring out the jury."

Yardley watched the men and women file in. Wesley smiled warmly at them. He held a pencil in his hand. He had purposely chosen a sports coat with patches on the elbows, and he'd taken spectacles out of his pocket and put them on. His appearance was that of a harmless schoolteacher. During jury selection, he had managed to make the jury panel laugh several times, annoying Tim so much his face had turned pink as he swore under his breath.

The judge went through the preliminary instructions, then said, "Opening remarks, please. Mr. Jeffries?"

"Thank you, Judge."

Tim adjusted his tie and took his notes with him to the lectern, which had been pushed up near the jury box. He cleared his throat and began reading the facts in the case like they were uninteresting musings on the side of a cereal box. No eye contact with the jury. Yardley thought the only effective thing he did was show a blown-up photo of Jordan Russo, point to Wesley, and say, "The beauty and potential of that young woman was snuffed out by this man here. Ladies and gentlemen, Wesley Paul was in a relationship with Jordan Russo, and a subsequent search of his personal belongings revealed Ms. Russo's ring and a lock of her hair. The hair, tested by the FBI's very efficient trace laboratory, triggered a DNA match to the hair taken from a brush of Jordan Russo loaned to us by her mother, who you'll also hear from in this trial."

"The ring could be explained away, but how would you explain to a jury why you had a lock of the victim's hair?" Tim had said to her yesterday, commenting that the case was a slam dunk.

"I don't know, but if anyone can, it's him," she had replied.

"Ladies and gentlemen," Tim continued, "this is a very simple case. Open and shut. Mr. Paul killed Jordan Russo. He caved her skull in with a rock. He bit so hard into her foot his teeth marked her bone. He—"

"Objection, Your Honor," Wesley said.

Everyone looked at him. It was customary to never object during opening or closing arguments, as it derailed thought, and opposing counsel would take retribution when it was their turn.

Tim looked over to him and then looked to the judge. Judge Aggbi said, "Grounds?"

"It's not clear those items will be introduced, Your Honor. My understanding is the teeth marks are not confirmed as of yet."

"They will be soon, Your Honor, and I plan on introducing them."

Damn it, Tim.

She had specifically asked him not to mention the teeth marks in opening, in case they weren't a match.

Wesley folded his hands in front of him and said, "There are considerations that I would like taken, Your Honor, in the introduction of that evidence and will object when it is so moved to be introduced. As Mr. Jeffries cannot anticipate my objections, he does not have concrete knowledge as to whether these items will be introduced."

Tim began arguing. Yardley knew an attorney should never argue the merits of an objection during opening or closing; they would lose momentum and concentration, and if they lost the objection, they would immediately create an impression of lack of knowledge with the jury.

"I'll allow it," Judge Aggbi finally said.

"Thank you, Your Honor," Tim said. He adjusted his suit coat and turned back to the jury, visibly annoyed, and continued with his statements, laying out the facts of the case. "Don't let this man's legal trickery fool you," he concluded. "Find him guilty of first-degree murder, and make sure he doesn't kill anyone else again."

Wesley stayed silent until Tim sat down. Then he rose and approached the jury. He stood in front of them, a warm smile on his face, his hands behind his back.

"Ladies and gentlemen, let's go back to that horrific day in February nearly two decades ago when this beautiful young lady's life tragically ended. That morning, Jordan Russo rose and had breakfast, she spoke with her friend Ann on the phone for twenty minutes, routine conversation of the young about the day's plans, and then she decided she would go to the gym where she was employed for a quick workout.

"She dressed in shorts and her Nike T-shirt, slipped on her sneakers, and kissed her mother goodbye as she headed out the door. And that would be the last time anyone saw her alive. The police, FBI, and prosecution have no knowledge of what happened to Ms. Russo from the moment her front door closed until they found her body twenty-two days later. How far did she make it to the gym? Did she meet anyone? Did she stop somewhere for water or a sports drink? Did she get into someone's car or walk down some deserted alley? Was she assaulted in the middle of the street, and someone saw but didn't report it? Did she die that day or later?" He took a step to the right, his face to the floor, before looking back to the jury.

"The government cannot answer these questions. And they cannot answer the questions about my involvement with Ms. Russo, which is none. I have no doubt that Ms. Russo's mother, Isabella Russo, will get up on that stand and tell the truth: that she saw *someone* at the restaurant where Jordan Russo was employed as a hostess. I have been to that restaurant multiple times over the years. To the dismay of my waistline, because they happen to have the best German chocolate cake in the state."

A few muted chuckles.

"But the fact is I did not know Jordan Russo. I did not know she was murdered until the day I was charged for her murder. And frankly, it shocked me to my core. I thought, *How can this be?* I know the innocent get accused of crimes, but I know it intellectually, almost as an exam question. To actually be on the receiving end of such injustice, I can tell you, ladies and gentlemen . . . well, it is the most horrific thing you can imagine. I feel as if the entire world has fallen on my head, and I'm frightened. I've been frightened since that first night after being charged. I didn't know what to think. Had I offended someone who went to the police and made up some half-baked story about me? Was it an innocent mistake?"

He held up a finger, casually strolling past the first row of jurors and looking each in the eye.

"Then, when I saw that the case had been taken up by the US Attorney's Office, and I saw Jessica Yardley's name on the indictment, I knew what it was. You see, Ms. Yardley and I were dating and lived together. I even had plans to propose soon."

Yardley sat still, staring forward.

"It was a beautiful relationship," he said with a smile. He lost the smile slowly, as good as any soap opera actor. "But it was one not destined to last."

He looked to Yardley.

"Ms. Yardley was once Jessica Cal. Her husband was the mass murderer Eddie Cal. He killed fourteen people, that we know of, and is currently sitting on Nevada's death row. Ms. Yardley told me on multiple occasions that she feels responsible because she was his wife, and she should have known she was married to a monster."

Yardley remained motionless. Looking forward and not meeting his eyes.

He turned back to the jury and said, "Ms. Yardley told me she would never let that happen again." Wesley inhaled and shook his head. "Unfortunately it began affecting our relationship. Her paranoia became uncontrollable. She began hallucinating things that were not there. She had been in therapy for quite some time, but I recommended that she ask the doctor to adjust her medications. She began—"

Yardley whispered, "Object, damn it."

"Um," Tim said, standing up, "objection."

"Sustained," Aggbi said quickly, seemingly waiting for the objection.

"Of course," Wesley said. "Forgive me. It is my life on the line, Your Honor, and my passion may get away from me occasionally." He turned back to the jury. "The point is she became unstable. So unstable that I informed her that I couldn't bring children into so unstable a relationship, and my goal has always been to have children. Lots of them."

He sighed, as though thinking about a painful memory. "When I told her this, she grew furious, throwing things, hitting me, destroying my possessions. She swore that she would get back at me somehow. And now here we are. I'm charged with killing a woman I didn't know, and the police happened to find a ring and hair that allegedly belong to her among possessions that Ms. Yardley had put into storage."

Both hands leaned on the banister in front of them. "I don't want to hurt Jessica; I really don't. I still care for her, and I can't imagine the trauma she went through being married to a mass murderer. But I also don't want to die in a cell for a crime I did not commit. She can't take revenge on Eddie Cal, so she is taking it out on me."

The sound of his fist hitting the banister made her flinch.

"I did *not* kill Jordan Russo," he said forcefully. "I have *never* met Jordan Russo. I am innocent. Please, *please*, do not let an innocent man suffer for the maliciousness of one unstable, damaged woman who happens to have the power to destroy people's lives. Please."

He looked each juror in the eyes and then sat down.

65

"Damn it!" Tim bellowed as he kicked over the wastebasket in Lieu's office.

He paced the room as Lieu sat in his chair and Yardley leaned against the wall with her arms folded.

"I told you not to let her anywhere near this case!" he shouted.

"Easy, Tim," Lieu said.

"If I lose this case, Roy, if I lose this, it will be in all the media. My name will be on the news as having lost my first case to that piece of shit representing himself."

She said, "They'll also mention the little fact that a serial murderer went free to kill again, if you care about that sort of thing."

"Screw you, you crazy bitch."

"Hey!" Lieu said. "That's crossing the line."

Tim sighed and shook his head, his hands on his hips. "I know," he said to Yardley. "Sorry." Then to Lieu: "Look, I'm just upset. We shouldn't have let her near this, and now she's going to tank the case. I want her off. Now."

"It'll be worse," Yardley said.

"How so?" Lieu asked.

"Wesley would've argued what he did regardless of whether I was on the case or not. I work in this office; you can't change that. The fact that I'm sitting there shows we have nothing to hide. It's better this way than if I hadn't been there. But if you were to take me off now, after he told them there's a conspiracy out to get him, the jury would believe him."

Lieu nodded. "She's right, Tim."

He shook his head and then pointed to her. "Fine. You stay. But keep your mouth shut and don't even look at that jury, you understand me?"

He stormed out of the office.

Yardley turned to the glass walls and looked out over the Strip. She heard Lieu tapping his pencil against the desk.

"Is what he said true? About the hallucinations?"

"No," she said dispassionately, "but I was emotionally broken after Eddie. I couldn't get out of bed most days. I stopped caring about things like eating and hygiene. The only thing that pulled me out of it was having to take care of a new daughter. She saved my life."

Lieu stayed silent a moment. "Are you better now?"

"I am. Therapy and pharmacology are arts, not sciences. It takes some testing with different strategies to find the right one." She turned to him. "Why did you let me second chair? You could've put me on paid leave while the trial resolved, and I wouldn't be anywhere near the case."

He inhaled through his nose and then said, "Agent Baldwin said if you weren't involved in the case, the next time we needed a favor from the Bureau, or if we needed him here for an emergency hearing on a case, his phone might just happen to be turned off."

She grinned. "Cason said that?"

"He did." Lieu leaned forward and dropped the pencil back in the holder. "I know you're right—it would appear terrible to the jury to take you off now—but you also can't do anything. Just let Tim handle it. We've got the evidence, and all Mr. Paul has is conjecture."

"The jury likes Wesley. They don't like Tim. Don't underestimate how powerful that is. You have to find a way to make him unlikable."

"How do we do that?"

"Let me use Cason to find something from his past. A man like this has a trail of broken bodies and hearts behind him. You have to make sure the jury sees that, or else they're going to let him go."

———

The next morning, Yardley spoke on the phone to Tara for twenty minutes. She had excitement in her voice, a sense of optimism Yardley hadn't heard in a long time. Tara had been learning to ride and could already jump a horse on the minor course they had at the ranch. She'd learned rifle, and today her grandfather would be introducing her to the bow.

It was a radical transformation from the moody teenager to a young woman sounding more and more like she was ready to stand on her own. And though Tara had always been brilliant, always had school and painting come easily to her, it sounded like she was being challenged with physical skills and was enjoying the change.

From the moment Tara was born, Yardley had worried about what would happen if she met her father. If she would fall under his spell. Or hate her mother more. Instead, it seemed to have freed her from whatever shadow had clung to her soul. The moment she and Steven had raised the possibility of Tara staying with her grandparents, she'd agreed.

"Forget Wesley, forget this whole shit place," Tara said to her now. "Just come here and let's live on the ranch. You're so smart—you could be a prosecutor here in a second."

Yardley grinned. "I'll join you soon, sweetheart. You listen to your grandparents and be good."

Steven came on the phone briefly. "Come out as soon as you can. There's always a place for you here. It's your home."

"Thank you. And thank you for watching her. If this case goes wrong . . . if Wesley gets out . . . I can't have Tara anywhere near here."

Steven said, "You do what you have to do. We'll be there when you need us."

They hung up, and Yardley showered and changed before going down to the courthouse.

Baldwin stood in the hallway waiting for her. A mob of paparazzi circled her, shouting questions and shoving digital recorders in her face. One man asked if she was a serial killer groupie, which got chuckles from a few others. She pushed her way through them without saying anything.

"You okay?" Baldwin said after they entered the first set of double doors to the courtroom.

"I'm fine."

"I almost jumped up and bashed Wesley in the face when he was saying that bullshit in opening."

She gently touched his hand, letting him know she appreciated him. "Don't waste energy worrying about it. Let's just do our jobs."

The first witness was retired detective Thomas Shelley with the LVPD. A bigger man in a suit that didn't fit well, he carried himself with a straight back and the air of a professional witness. As Tim questioned him, he laid out the circumstances of the discovery of Jordan Russo's body, from the coordinates to the state of the remains to the timeline of when Jordan had last been seen on the day she'd disappeared.

Occasionally, Yardley glanced over at Wesley without moving her head. Wesley had his fingers steepled in front of him as his eyes focused unblinkingly on the detective. He hadn't raised any objections to Tim's questions or the detective's responses, but he had a folder with loose papers in front of him on the table. Yardley had no doubt whatever was in there wouldn't be good for their case.

When Tim announced he had no more questions and sat down, Wesley rose. He went to the lectern and watched the detective a moment.

"Good morning," he said.

"Morning."

"Detective, you left out a little bit of your résumé, did you not? You did a stint with the Nevada Highway Patrol."

"Yes, just eight months before being hired by LVPD."

"Why did you quit the highway patrol?"

"I wanted career advancement. I have a degree in criminal justice and knew that I wanted to be a detective, and the NHP doesn't provide that type of advancement."

"Was it amicable? Your quitting?"

The detective swallowed. Yardley's eyes narrowed as she realized what was coming. Tim was taking notes on a legal pad, adding and taking away questions he was going to ask the next witness.

"Yes, it was amicable."

"Interesting," Wesley said, going to the folder on the defense table. "I have here a transcript from a case you handled while at the highway patrol, *State v. Myler*. Do you recall it?"

Shelley didn't say anything. Wesley put one copy of the transcript, less than ten pages, on the prosecution table. Tim put his pen down and flipped through it. Yardley tried to read over his shoulder.

"Myler was a suspected drunk driver you pulled over, correct?"

"Correct."

"You pulled him out of the car and had him perform field sobriety tests and a breath test, which provided evidence of impairment?"

"Correct."

"Your Honor, may I approach the witness?"

The judge hesitated and looked to the marshals, who, as casually as they could, stepped closer to the witness box.

"You may, Counsel."

Wesley put on his spectacles and took the portion of the transcript over to the detective. "During the trial, Mr. Myler's attorney filed a motion to suppress evidence based on lack of reasonable suspicion, correct?"

"Correct."

"Now you say, in your police reports and under oath at Mr. Myler's motion hearing, that the reason you pulled him over is a blinker that wasn't working. Correct?"

"Yes."

"Mr. Shelley, this transcript is only nine pages. Will you please explain to this jury why the transcript is so short?"

He glanced at Tim, clearly looking for help. "I, um . . . I was advised by the judge of my Fifth Amendment right to not incriminate myself under oath. I exercised that right and said nothing further."

"And the defense's motion was granted, correct?"

"Yes."

"Why?"

He wouldn't answer, so Wesley said, "Because unbeknownst to you, the defense had acquired a video that they did not hand over to the State, correct? Mr. Myler's sister was behind the two of you and began recording the incident on the family's camcorder when she noticed you following Mr. Myler's car, right?"

The detective stared at him.

"Your Honor, could you please instruct the witness to answer my questions?"

"Detective Shelley, answer the question, please."

"Yes," he said, his face turning red. "There was a video."

"And this video showed that his blinker was working just fine and he used it correctly when he changed lanes before you pulled him over, correct?" Silence again. "Your Honor?"

"Detective Shelley, I have asked you once to answer Counsel's questions. Please do not make me ask again."

"Yes, his blinker was working fine. I just missed it."

"Just missed it?" Wesley said mockingly. "How interesting. Now, in your time with the NHP, when you testified in court, you got paid time and a half, did you not, Detective? Overtime pay, since you still had to put in a full day on patrol."

"Yes, we did."

"So the more people you arrested for drunk driving and the more times you had to appear in court, the more money you made. Correct?"

"It's not like that. You—"

"Did you or did you not make more money if you testified in court more, Mr. Shelley? Please answer my question."

"Yes, I would."

"Now, you got fired after this, didn't you? As part of a deal you made with your superiors, you would be allowed to quit and find other employment, but they asked you to leave the NHP, correct?"

"It wasn't like that. You're making it sound much worse than—"

"Were you asked to leave the NHP or not?"

"Yes. I was asked to leave."

"You were fired."

He bit his lip. "Yes."

"Excellent, thank you." Wesley went back to the folder and took out a document. He placed a copy on the prosecution table. It was Detective Shelley's application to the LVPD.

"Did you know about this?" Tim whispered to Yardley.

"No. I'm not supposed to do anything, remember?"

Tim's face turned pink, and he looked away. She could just imagine the expletives flying at her in his mind.

Wesley said, "Mr. Shelley, please show where on your application to the Las Vegas Police Department you list your firing from the Nevada Highway Patrol."

Shelley's jaw moved to the side, and he was sweating. "I think at this point, Counsel, I have to stop talking."

"The judge already informed you—"

"I have to invoke my Fifth Amendment rights, Counsel."

Wesley lowered the application. "You lied on the application, didn't you?"

"I must invoke my Fifth Amendment right to remain silent."

"You lied when you were on the NHP under oath, and you lied on this application, and you just lied again about this case, didn't you?"

"I must invoke my Fifth Amendment right to remain silent."

Yardley could see he was panicking. Though retired, he must've had some other employment that would be at risk if he were charged with perjury.

Once invoked, the Fifth Amendment right against self-incrimination in federal court was all or nothing. He could not answer any other questions, or else he would have to answer all of them. Wesley could now say anything he wanted, and Shelley couldn't respond.

"Ms. Yardley came to you, didn't she, Mr. Shelley? Assistant US attorney is a powerful position. She asked you for a favor, didn't she? 'Get me some evidence in this homicide I can use.'"

"Again, I must invoke my Fifth Amendment right to remain silent."

"Did she threaten you to get her that ring and the hair on this case, or did you just hand it over to curry favor later?"

Tim finally rose and said, "Objection, Your Honor. Mr. Paul is mischaracterizing the evidence and the detective's testimony, and he's badgering the witness, along with five other objections."

Wesley took a step back. "The witness will not answer my questions, Your Honor. Under *Smith v. Gebell*, I'm allowed to ask each individual question and have him assert his Fifth Amendment rights on each question separately."

Wesley went back to the table, took out another document, and put a copy down on the prosecution table: a copy of the Ninth Circuit Court of Appeals case *Smith v. Gebell*. The relevant portions had been highlighted.

"May I approach the bench?" he said meekly.

"Certainly."

Wesley handed the judge a copy. Yardley had not actually read the case before. It looked to be an obscure case from 1977, but Wesley had included research that found it had not been overturned by any court and was still good law.

The highlighted portions made clear that he was allowed to ask his questions and that a witness asserting the Fifth Amendment had to invoke it on each individual question. Tim, she was certain, had never read the case either.

"Mr. Jeffries, anything to say?" Judge Aggbi said.

"I'd like a chance to brief this."

The judge, probably despite herself, grinned slightly. "To be frank, I've never heard of this case, so please allow me a moment."

The judge turned to her computer. Yardley watched Wesley, who was leaning against the lectern. Detective Shelley drank water from a plastic cup and kept dabbing at the sweat on his neck with tissues. Tim bit down on a pen so hard it was leaving grooves.

After about five minutes, Judge Aggbi said, "It does appear to be current law. I'm going to allow this line of questioning. You may continue with this witness, Mr. Paul."

Shelley looked white as a ghost. The sweat that had formed on his forehead in huge droplets now ran down his face and dappled his sport jacket with small circles. He pulled more tissues from a box on the witness stand and patted his neck.

"What did you get for giving Ms. Yardley evidence to plant among my things?"

"I must invoke my Fifth Amendment right to remain silent, Counselor."

"Did she threaten you?"

"I must invoke my Fifth Amendment right to remain silent."

"Did she have something over you? Have you lied in other cases, and she's found out?"

"I must invoke my Fifth Amendment right to remain silent."

Wesley went on like that for ten minutes. Yardley glanced at the jury; they eventually stopped paying attention. They'd made up their minds about something: they either believed Wesley that Shelley was a liar who'd worked with her to railroad him, or they believed they should just disregard everything the detective said but that he hadn't gone so far as to engage in a conspiracy. The only thing she knew for certain about juries was that you could never be sure what they were thinking.

66

By the time court ended that day, Wesley had made a fool of every witness Tim had put up. A homicide detective couldn't explain what a false positive was or why eyewitness testimony was flawed, so Wesley explained it to him in painstaking detail in a way Tim couldn't object to, essentially giving a lesson on the defects of eyewitness testimony to the jury.

A DNA evidence expert had to admit that the DNA testing used on hair could only identify with 100 percent certainty what species the hair came from. As far as matching found hair to the hair of a defendant or victim, the laboratory had a 16 percent false positive rate and a 14 percent false negative rate, in response to which Wesley looked to the jury and said, "Innocent people going to prison and guilty people walking free. We have to wonder what clown college the FBI learned this witchcraft from."

The medical examiner's testimony was better, as he was accustomed to plenty of court time and being cross-examined by defense counsel. Since Wesley wasn't disputing anything he said, his testimony only took an hour, and the judge decided to call it a day afterward.

They rose for the jury to file out, and Tim said, "Make sure to clean up all the exhibits and have the marshals lock them up in the jury room. And you might as well toss the garbage." He said it in a way that suggested it was her job to clean up after him.

One thing Yardley's prior boss had told her before retiring was to never clean up or fetch anything or make copies or answer phones for any of the men in the office. They would see her as a secretary from then on and treat her as such.

Yardley stood rigidly a moment, anger coursing through her. She had to brace herself against the table and close her eyes, picturing a cool stream in a lush forest. The smell of pine in her nostrils and a blue sky overhead. After half a minute, she opened her eyes and removed the exhibits, then threw away the water cups and scraps of paper left behind.

———

The main balcony was the part of the house Yardley spent the most time in. It was wide and deep and could've held much more furniture than she had placed there. The mountains were the main draw. She could look at them and think about how ancient the land was, how even though humanity somehow claimed it as its own, it had been there for two billion years and would be there another two billion. Long after humanity had gone extinct.

There was a knock at the door. Yardley shouted, "Come in."

Baldwin joined her on the balcony a few seconds later. He tossed a file on the table in front of her and sat down. They watched the moonlight over the desert a moment before he said, "You sure you want to look? It's not pretty."

Yardley opened the file. It was the background investigation for Wesley Paul.

"Wesley's his real name," Baldwin said, "but his surname is Deakins. He changed it to Paul in his twenties. Also, the degree he claims to have from Harvard Law? Doesn't exist. It's a forgery, along with his grades and law journal memberships that he used to get academic positions. I can't find any real academic record for him anywhere. You think it's actually possible for someone not to go to college or law school and be a professor and lawyer of his caliber?"

Yardley stared at a photograph of Wesley in the file: a DMV photo from at least twenty years ago. "He earned a perfect score on the Nevada Bar Exam. If he could do that without attending law school, I have no doubt he could fake being a member of any profession."

Wesley Deakins had a file with the Department of Child and Family Services. Yardley skimmed the story of a tragic life that had no chance of ending in anything other than horror. Somehow, she had never asked much about his background, and she knew exactly what Wesley would say to her about it now: *You didn't want to know.*

Was he right? She had convinced herself that she could never have a partner in her life after Eddie Cal, but when Wesley had come along, it had felt so . . . good. In her most private thoughts, the ones she never admitted to anyone else, she knew she had realized her relationship with Wesley would somehow be ruined one day, but she'd wanted it to last for as long as possible.

Wesley had been born in Los Angeles on the date he'd told her, but instead of the generic middle-class parents he'd conjured, he'd been raised by Elaine and Larry Deakins. The Deakinses' criminal histories started when they were juveniles with shoplifting and expanded to robbery and various drug crimes.

"Hardcore addicts and dealers," Baldwin said. "Methamphetamine. They got in right during the craze, when it was really taking off out here. Cheap and easy to make, don't need a chemistry degree. Looks like they were cooking it in their basement with little Wesley asleep upstairs."

"Where are they now?"

"They're dead. Sold an extremely toxic batch to some biker gang, who weren't very happy when some of them ended up hospitalized or dead, so they made an example of the Deakinses. Can you guess how they were killed?"

Yardley stared at him. "In their bed with their throats slit," she said softly.

He nodded. "Wesley came out of his room and found them while they were dying. The sons of bitches made him help clean up the blood and bodies." He shook his head. "Can you imagine helping to clean up the dead bodies of your parents?"

"That's why he became fascinated with Eddie. Eddie killed his victims in the same way Wesley's parents were killed."

Baldwin nodded. "Probably his way of trying to gain control over it. Why start now, though? Why when he's over forty?"

"There's two possibilities. Either he's been doing it awhile and we don't know about the other couples, like we didn't know about Jordan Russo. Or"—she met his gaze—"he started now at Eddie's request."

Baldwin looked shocked. "Why would Eddie want that?"

"His last appeal is almost decided. He's running out of time. You've seen the fun he's had inserting himself into this. Maybe it was his way to see me and Tara. Or maybe he has bigger ambitions. He could be hoping to file an appeal based on new evidence, arguing that we convicted the wrong man and the Dark Casanova has always been Wesley."

"No way that works."

"Probably not, but it'd buy him some more time at least."

Baldwin got a text and checked it quickly. He gestured at the DCFS file and said, "Well, anyway, after all that, he bounced around from foster family to foster family. There were some allegations of sexual abuse against one foster father, a Roxley Hayes. Looks like Hayes disappeared about fifteen years ago. No trace of him ever found. I have a pretty good guess what happened to him."

Yardley read in silence awhile before closing the file and setting it down. "His life never had a chance."

"You sound sorry for him."

"I'm sorry for the child that had to watch his parents die. I'm not sorry for the man who's now inflicted that on other children." She stared at the closed file. "I should've looked into his past before."

"Hey, no one does deep background checks on their boyfriends. It'd be weird if you did." He was quiet a long while and then said, "If you don't want to be alone right now, I can stay."

She looked at him and smiled sadly. "If you were to stay . . . I think that would be bad for both of us."

"Are you sure?"

She nodded. "One day. But not today."

He rose and approached her. Gently, he kissed her cheek, then left. When she heard the door close, she opened Wesley's file and read it again.

67

At eleven, Yardley knew sleep wouldn't be coming. She had Ambien in her medicine cabinet, but there was something she had to do first.

This time, instead of guards, the warden herself was at the prison gates waiting for her.

"You didn't have to come yourself," Yardley said.

"I was here anyway. Taking off for a few days tomorrow and just needed to finish up a few things."

Gledhill led her inside, and they walked the corridors, their footsteps echoing in the silence.

"How you holding up?"

"As good as can be expected, I guess."

Gledhill was silent a moment as she scanned her key card on a door. "Jessica, I'm going to be honest with you. As your friend, I don't think this is healthy for you. Coming to see him all the time. He plays games with people. I've had more guards transfer out of his unit than anywhere else, because he knows exactly what to say to hurt people. Just little comments here and there that stick with you." She held the door open for her. "When my boy was in the hospital for those few days and his fever just wouldn't go down, everyone here found out. Eddie asked me how much cheaper smaller coffins were compared to full size. I ignored him, but I kept thinking about it all day. By the end of the day, I was sitting at my desk crying."

Yardley kept her eyes forward. "I don't have a choice."

Yardley arrived in the room first. She waited until Cal was brought in to tell the guard to turn the cameras off. Cal watched her with a mischievous grin until the camera was off and the guard left.

"Thank you for letting her come see me," he said.

"It was her choice."

"She's . . . astonishing. She has your strength. I think it would be amazing to get to watch her grow up . . . but I'll likely have a needle in my arm by the end of the year."

Yardley took him in, trying to remember the man she had fallen in love with, and couldn't. Like a portion of her memories had been destroyed by her consciousness in order to protect her mind from the pain it wasn't sure she could handle.

"What did you say to her?"

"She asked me for something, and I gave it to her. I owed her as much."

"What did she ask for?"

"That's between me and her." He grinned. "Does it bother you that she and I have secrets?"

She leaned back and folded her arms. "Tara told me about Jordan Russo. Is that what she asked for? Something else we could prosecute Wesley for so he doesn't get out?"

He said nothing.

"We've filed charges against Wesley and are in trial. But he's doing well. Even with what we have, I'm not sure we can get a conviction."

"Are you prosecuting him yourself?"

She shook her head. "They won't let me because they think it's too much of a conflict."

"There's no way around it?"

"There is. If he signs a full conflict waiver saying that he agrees to let me do it and he won't appeal anything that comes about because of the conflict. But even if he were willing, my office wouldn't allow it. I think they're nervous that if I lost, people would think I did it on purpose."

"If you were a man, you'd already be prosecuting this case. You know that, right? They think you're too emotional. They don't see in you what I see. That fierceness. The ability to take pain others would find unbearable and still keep fighting. It has to be you that prosecutes him, or he will get away with it."

Yardley felt the air from a vent in the ceiling turn on; it was cool and smelled slightly sour, like the recycled air in the cabin of a commercial plane. "What else did he tell you about Russo?"

He shrugged. "What will you give me if I tell you?"

"I don't have anything else to give you, Eddie. I already let you see her. I can't do anything about getting your execution stayed. The only motivation I can offer is that I think Wesley might kill me and Tara if he's released from custody. I don't know if you care about that or not."

He reached out, his shackles rattling lightly, and touched the glass barrier between them. "Do you understand him yet? His psychology? What type of stalker is he?"

She crossed her legs and placed her hands on her knee. "There's five categories of stalkers. I think he falls into what's called the intimacy-seeking stalker. They're typically extremely isolated, with accompanying delusions of nonexistent relationships with their victims. In a very real sense, I'm not the target of his behavior. You are. He's formed what he thinks is a close bond with you, and he believes you reciprocate that bond. That's why he's willing to kill for you. Many members of death cults that murder or commit suicide at the request of their cult leader are actually intimacy-seeking stalkers."

He nodded. "You haven't given me any of Jordan Russo's reports. How did she disappear?"

"She was jogging to a local gym. We think Wesley picked her up in his car on the way. It's a busy road from her home to the gym, no real alleyways or anything like that. So it's unlikely she was grabbed in the middle of the street with witnesses everywhere. She got into a car willingly."

"Hmm. That'd be rather reckless for him to risk being seen with her on the day she disappears, don't you think? I would describe Wesley as a lot of things, but reckless wouldn't be one of them, would it?"

Yardley's heart began to race. "No, it wouldn't."

The grin returned to Cal's face. "Wesley told me he's only had one friend his entire life, Dominic Hill. A neighbor that grew up with him in Los Angeles. They moved out here together. Dominic helped him with Jordan Russo. Personally, I would've killed Dominic after. Why take the chance of leaving someone with that kind of information out there? But I think Wesley was in love with him. Or at least thought he was."

Yardley rose to leave, and Cal said, "I'd hurry. Since you're prosecuting him for Russo, Dominic's suddenly become a liability, and Wesley doesn't do well with liabilities."

———

By the time she arrived home, every muscle in her body screamed with fatigue. A deep fatigue that seemed to weigh her down like an anchor around her neck. She made some coffee and quickly drank down a cup.

She sat in her chair in the home office, pulled up the criminal records database, and searched for Dominic Hill.

She found three that had lived in Las Vegas for at least twenty years. One was nearly eighty and one deceased. The third man was younger than Wesley by two years and had done a stint in prison for sexual assault. His criminal history before that was mostly voyeurism charges, stemming from going into women's locker rooms and filming them from shower stalls or hiding in changing rooms at clothing stores and filming women from underneath the doors. He had nearly thirty arrests on his record, going back decades.

Cal was right: Wesley Paul wouldn't have picked up Jordan Russo on the day she'd disappeared. That would be sloppy, and all it would take was one witness to identify him. He would, if at all possible, have someone else pick her up, and he would be somewhere with a lot of other people that could testify they'd seen him there at the time Jordan Russo had disappeared.

A photo of Hill came up in the database. Thick neck, short hair, powerful jaw, and large eyes. Yardley checked the clock on the computer. It was nearly two in the morning. She decided to have more coffee and stay up rather than attempt sleep. She wanted to catch Dominic Hill early in the morning, when he would be unprepared.

68

The trial resumed at nine in the morning. When Yardley arrived at court late and took her seat, Tim didn't look at her. He kept his eyes forward, his thumbs underneath his chin as he stared at the judge's bench.

"I expected you here early to set everything up," he said without looking at her.

Yardley said nothing.

The first witness Tim called was a psychologist who had evaluated Wesley before the trial had begun.

"So what you're saying," Tim said after an hour of testimony describing Wesley's likely mental stability, "is that Mr. Paul is of sound mind and understands exactly the repercussions of his actions."

"Correct," the psychologist, Dr. Jarvis, an elderly man with a long face and glasses, said. "He's of perfectly sound mind with no noticeable mental disorders, at least not the Axis Two disorders I previously discussed. I didn't even find noticeable anxiety or depressive disorders, which is rare considering how much of the general population suffers from these."

"In other words, he's normal."

"There is no real definition of normal, Counselor, but I understand your meaning. And yes, he does not have any acute mental disorders that make him incapable of understanding his actions."

"Thank you, Dr. Jarvis."

Wesley rose and said, "Dr. Jarvis, you are being paid three hundred dollars an hour to testify today, correct?"

"Correct."

"You make over two hundred thousand dollars per year flying around the country testifying in high-profile criminal cases?"

"That's about right."

"You're here because you're paid to be here?"

"Well, not the only reason, but yes, I'm paid to be here."

"You ever testified for a defendant?"

"No."

"You've been retained by Mr. Jeffries and Ms. Yardley's office on dozens of cases, correct?"

"Yes."

"In fact, I believe you and Mr. Jeffries went golfing before."

"We did, yes."

"He's your friend."

"I suppose so."

"If you started losing cases, if you came in here and your testimony started leading to acquittals, Mr. Jeffries, despite being your friend, would be less likely to use you, correct? Just common sense, wouldn't you say?"

"Well, I don't know."

"If you came in and started screwing up his cases, you think he'd continue to hire you? Is that what you're telling this jury?"

"No, no, I suppose not."

"So you'd, naturally, again just common sense, *like* the prosecution to prevail in the cases you testify in."

"I have no incentive one way or the other."

"Dr. Jarvis," Wesley said with a smile, "I would like you to read something from your website." Wesley stepped from the lectern to the defense table and pulled out a page with Jarvis's face on it. He held the paper in front of Jarvis and said, "Please read the highlighted quote."

Jarvis cleared his throat. "It says, 'I will help you win your case. Don't delay, call today.'"

"'Don't delay, call today,'" Wesley said, looking at the jury with a grin. "Catchy little ditty. Frankly I thought it a better slogan for an enema health clinic or escort agency rather than an allegedly respected member of the medical community, but what do I know?"

Jarvis pursed his lips but didn't say anything.

"Now, Dr. Jarvis, are you aware there are sixteen different errors in your report?"

Jarvis sighed. "No, Counselor, I am not. Though I'm sure you're about to explain them to me."

69

In the evening after court, Baldwin, Tim, Yardley, and Lieu decided to have dinner. It was well past eight, and they had missed dinner with their families. This would be the first time Yardley had ever eaten a meal with her boss.

The Italian restaurant was nearly empty, and they sat at a booth in the corner. They chatted a bit about inconsequential matters, Yardley remaining quiet while they discussed some college football game. After the breadsticks but before the meals came, Lieu said, "It's not going well."

"It's about what we expected," Tim said.

"No, it's not. He's making your witnesses look like idiots, Tim." He paused. "It may have been a mistake to let you first chair this."

"How can you say that? I have more convictions than anyone—"

"Cut the bullshit. We both know you take the easy cases to trial and decline or deal on everything else." Lieu leaned back in his seat. "He didn't dispute a single thing Dr. Jarvis said, but he made him look like a money-hungry, biased liar who doesn't know when there's mistakes in his own reports. He did that specifically to make you look bad, not Dr. Jarvis." Lieu looked at Yardley and Baldwin. "Do you agree?"

"Yes," Baldwin said. "We're losing."

Tim, anger rising in his voice, said, "Hey, I'm not going to sit here and be attacked for a case that I didn't want and that was thrown in my lap at the last minute, that Jessica didn't prep properly and didn't fully brief me on. I can only go to war with what I have, and I didn't have squat."

"There's no use assigning blame," Yardley said. "The point is to fix it." She looked to Baldwin. "When do we know about the bite marks?"

"Dentist is flying out day after tomorrow for the comparison. He says he can have a report ready a few hours after that."

"See," Tim said. "The teeth are the primary evidence. Doesn't matter how incompetent the witnesses look up there. He has no explanation for his teeth marks being in the victim's bone."

"I think—" Lieu stopped suddenly as his phone buzzed. A moment later, Tim's rang. Yardley glanced at the number on his screen: it was the court clerk.

———

Judge Aggbi had called an emergency meeting at the courthouse. Marshals were brought in to open the building and provide security. When Yardley, Lieu, Tim, and Baldwin arrived, a marshal informed them that Wesley was already there and waiting for them outside the judge's chambers.

"You ever had this happen?" Baldwin asked Lieu.

"Never. Whatever it is, even an emergency, can usually wait until morning."

Outside the judge's chambers, Wesley sat on a wooden bench next to an obese man in a slick pinstripe suit with bright rings on several fingers. His silver beard was neatly trimmed, and his dark eyes followed the four of them with disdain. A marshal stood on either side of the two men.

One marshal poked his head into the judge's chambers and said, "Everyone's here, Judge."

They filed into the large room. Lieu and Tim sat in the two chairs across from the judge. Wesley sat in the corner, and a chair was brought in for the large man and pushed up to the side of the judge's desk. Yardley and Baldwin stood in the back of the room.

Judge Aggbi wore a suit but no robe. She folded her arms, and Yardley could see anger clearly written on her face.

"Your Honor," Lieu said, "I hope that everything—"

"Quiet, Mr. Lieu." She looked to Wesley and said, "Would you please introduce your associate, Mr. Paul?"

"Certainly," he said, his hands shackled and lying limply in his lap. "This is Mr. Wehr Parker. He is and has been my private investigator for years, and I work with him extensively at the Guardian ad Litem's Office. Mr. Parker, would you please inform them why we're here?"

The large man tossed some papers on the desk. "Those are phone records for a Mr. Dominic Hill," he said in a deep voice. "You'll notice the circled call was during the lunch break today to Mr. Jeffries here."

Tim's face had gone completely white. Yardley could see his fingers dig into the armrests of the chair. Lieu didn't notice and said, "I still don't see why this couldn't wait until morning."

The judge said loudly, "Please bring him in, Marshal."

The door behind the judge opened, and the marshal led in Dominic Hill. He stood there calmly and looked at everyone in the room.

"Please tell them why we're here, Mr. Hill," Aggbi said.

He looked at Tim. "I called Mr. Jeffries today and told him I had important information about Wesley Paul and this trial. He agreed to meet with me today at a coffee shop. He didn't want to meet at his office."

Judge Aggbi could barely contain herself. She alternated her gaze between Tim and Yardley and said, "And so you met with him alone?"

"Yes."

"Your Honor," Tim said, trying to smile, "I am currently drafting a motion on this very issue and planned on handing over the information to the defendant as soon as—"

"Mr. Hill?" the judge said.

"I told him I knew Jordan and had information on the case but that I was a registered sex offender and needed to keep my name out of it. Then I told him what I knew."

"And what was his response?"

"He said that it was my lucky day and to go away and not tell anyone. That I should consider moving out of state. I called a buddy that used to be a cop, and he said to tell the court and the defense. Your clerk told me that Mr. Paul had an investigator listed as a contact, so I called him."

Judge Aggbi leaned forward on the desk and stared Tim in the pupils. "Did you advise this witness to abscond?"

"Judge," he said, his face red, his hands shaking as if he'd downed ten cups of coffee. "He's a damn sex offender and an ex-con. You really going to believe him?"

"I recorded our conversation," Hill said. "Just in case. I don't have it here, but I'll get you a copy, Judge."

Aggbi's gaze didn't move from Tim. "Do you want to hear it, Mr. Jeffries?"

Tim was silent a long time. "No," he said quietly.

Aggbi exhaled forcefully. "Ms. Yardley, did you know about this?"

"I learned about Mr. Hill this morning, Your Honor," Yardley said, choosing her words carefully, "and advised him to call Mr. Jeffries. But I had no idea that they'd met. I wasn't informed."

"Were you going to turn his information over to the defense?" Aggbi asked Yardley.

"I was instructed that I was not allowed to have any interaction with the evidence or witnesses in this case unless specifically ordered to do so. Whether any evidence was introduced or handed to the defense wasn't discussed with me."

The judge nodded. "Mr. Jeffries, you are off this case immediately. I am filing an ethical complaint with the Nevada Bar tomorrow. I am also dismissing this case in the interests of justice for gross misconduct by the prosecution."

Lieu had turned red and stared at Tim like he was about to strangle him.

"Thank you, Judge," Wesley said with a wide smile.

"Wait," Yardley jumped in. "I agree Mr. Jeffries should be taken off this case. I won't object to any of this evidence being admitted to the jury, and in fact I'll admit it myself. But a full dismissal is unwarranted. There's precedent that precludes a dismissal with prejudice in circumstances of ethical misconduct by the prosecution, which means we would just refile on this case at a later date. We're nearly done with the government's case. There's no reason to throw all of that away. I can continue the case myself."

"Your Honor," Wesley said, "what just happened here is about the worst violation I've ever seen by any prosecution agency in my nearly twenty years of practicing law. Why would Mr. Hill contact the prosecution unless he had exculpatory information about the crime I'm on trial for? For that matter, he's admitted to knowing the victim and may be a suspect himself. And the government told him to leave the state. If this isn't grounds for a dismissal, I don't know what is."

Judge Aggbi tapped her fingers against the desk. "Ms. Yardley's right. I'm going to remove Mr. Jeffries from the case but allow the trial to go forward."

"Your Honor—"

"Mr. Paul, I understand your anger and frustration with this, but the caselaw is clear that I have discretion in how I dismiss the case. This is my decision, and I've made it. Please note it on the record tomorrow for purposes of appeal, and you can argue it in the Ninth Circuit."

"I will," he said sternly.

"You and your investigator can arrange an opportunity to question Mr. Hill about the information he shared with the prosecution. You're all excused."

"Outside," Lieu said through clenched teeth to Tim.

Yardley was the last to leave, and Aggbi said, "Jessica, sit down." She sat. "Did you know what he was going to do?"

"Absolutely not. I met with Hill and got his information and told him to call the lead prosecutor on the case. I had no knowledge of what occurred after. I assumed Mr. Jeffries would inform the defense of the witness and ask for a continuance of the trial." She hesitated. "They've tied my hands on this case, Judge. I was instructed to not touch the evidence, to not gather any more evidence, to not interact with the witnesses unless specifically asked to do so and only in a limited capacity."

A moment of anger rose in her, and she had to remain quiet to swallow it back down.

"When they told me to second chair, I was informed that my job would be to hand Mr. Jeffries things during the trial, and Mr. Jeffries made clear that part of my duties were to . . . clean up the courtroom afterward."

Judge Aggbi's anger faded, and a sad gentleness came over her. She leaned back in her high-backed chair and said, "My first time in court, the judge yelled at me for wearing pants. He said that women had been given enough rights already and he'd be damned if they looked like men in his court, too." She sighed. "Well, you wanted responsibility. You have it now. I hope you know what you're doing."

70

As Yardley left the judge's chambers, she saw Wesley and two marshals waiting by the attorney-client room. Wesley said, "Just a quick word?"

She hesitated and then went inside the attorney-client room. The marshals leaned against the wall behind Wesley, and he said, "Marshals, I'd like to talk to her in private."

"Can't do it," one of them said.

"It's fine," Yardley said. "I take full responsibility. Just wait outside the door, please."

They glanced at each other but did what she asked. When they were alone, Wesley grinned.

"That was fortuitous, wasn't it? Someone who happens to know Jordan Russo and is a registered sex offender wants to talk about the case, and little Timmy tells him to leave the state."

"Lapse in judgment."

"Seems like it." He cocked his head to the side. "You knew he would tell that witness to abscond, didn't you? Tim isn't one to be humiliated as badly as he would be if he lost this case, and he just figured no one needed to know about Mr. Hill. That's why you told Hill to call him instead of just telling Tim about him, isn't it?"

Yardley folded her arms but said nothing. Wesley chuckled.

"Why, Ms. Yardley, that is downright devious of you. I cannot wait to hear what it is Mr. Hill has to say about the death of Jordan Russo. It must be quite juicy. My investigator will be interviewing him tomorrow after court. I wouldn't mind if you gave me a little preview of what he's going to say, though."

Yardley looked out the windows. "I want you to sign a conflict waiver to allow me to prosecute you."

He laughed. "Why? Do you want to spend more time with me? I knew you still had a thing for me, even after all this."

She turned to him as a slight look of amusement came over her face. "Don't you want to see if you can beat me, Wesley? Impress me with your legal acumen? Or will losing to a girl destroy that fragile little ego of yours?"

"No need to get rude. I would happily sign a waiver. I think this will be downright fun for both of us, don't you?"

71

Yardley didn't have to do much convincing to get Lieu to step aside and give her the case. It was a win-win for him now that Tim's unethical behavior would get media attention. If she got a conviction, he could say he'd known she was the best person for the job. If she lost, she would get the blame and be called either incompetent or complicit and still in love with Wesley.

The bite mark analysis would be done by the next afternoon, and Yardley worried she'd have to delay the trial, but Tim had so many witnesses listed that the trial could go another three weeks before running out. She cut 90 percent of them and only kept two on the schedule for today, mostly as a placeholder until the report on the bite marks came back.

As she sat in court, waiting for the judge to come out, she thought she should at least feel a slight pang of guilt for what she had done to Tim, but she felt nothing. She'd asked Hill to call him and not mention that they had spoken, that it would be better for him if it seemed like he was coming forward on his own.

She'd understood Tim would do nearly anything to win this case. He wanted to be attorney general one day, or governor like his grandfather, and a loss on this case would never be erased from people's minds. Hill's information wasn't exactly the exculpatory evidence Wesley hoped, but Hill was a sex offender with similar crimes in his past who knew Jordan Russo. No matter what he said on that stand, Wesley would blame him for the killing, and that might be enough to create reasonable doubt for the jury. With Tim thinking he was the only person that knew about Hill, she'd guessed he would ignore him and never tell anyone. Then Yardley planned on turning over everything she had found on Hill; Lieu would surmise that Tim had kept a potentially exculpatory witness from the defense, they would have to let the judge know, and Tim would be removed from the case. Lieu would have no choice but to let Yardley prosecute it.

Yardley had not expected Tim to tell Hill to run. She had underestimated how much he cared about public perception. He would no doubt be sanctioned by the Bar and suspended by Lieu if not fired.

It didn't matter, she told herself. The only thing that mattered was protecting her daughter, and she'd done what she had to do to ensure that.

The judge came out and gave a few preliminary instructions and read into the record the waiver of conflict signed by Wesley. When the judge was through, she asked Yardley to call her first witness.

The first witness of the day was a nervous intern with the crime scene investigation section who took photographs and made drawings of the bodies. Yardley took longer than necessary with him because she'd noticed while he was testifying that the jury found the background of crime scene cataloging interesting.

The next witness, who she put on after lunch, was Isabella Russo.

"You're Jordan Russo's mother?"

"Yes," she said timidly.

"Please tell us what you remember about your daughter's death, Ms. Russo."

She swallowed and glanced at the jury but couldn't face them. "Jordan was gorgeous. Just athletic and with a beautiful face and brunette hair that came down past her shoulders. She'd been getting the attention of men since thirteen. It always frightened me. I always told her father that we had to be extra careful with her. I knew men paid a lot of attention to her. She graduated high school early by one year, so she was going to start college in the spring, studying anthropology. Don't know why—she just said she liked it."

"What was her interaction with the defendant?"

"I'd seen them together twice. One time I went to pick up Jordan at the restaurant where she worked as a hostess, Telly's over there on Bluff. She was standing outside the doors talking to him."

"To who?"

She pointed to Wesley. "That man there."

Yardley felt the same faint hesitation she'd felt when Isabella had identified Wesley so quickly at the lineup, but she pushed past it. "Let the record reflect that Ms. Russo has identified the defendant, Wesley Paul."

"So reflected," the judge said.

"Did anything happen while you watched them, Ms. Russo?"

"No. They were just talking and laughing. But then she walked away to come to my car, and I saw him, Wesley Paul, stare at her backside. Stare all the way to the car. And so when Jordan got in, I said, 'Sweetie, he's no good.' She didn't think anything of it. I never thought her boyfriends were good enough."

"When was that?"

"Back in January of that year sometime. Maybe middle of January."

"When was the next time you saw them together?"

"About a week before she was taken." She had to stop a moment and sit quietly. "She, um, she was getting off her shift, and I told her I'd pick her up, and she said she was getting a ride with someone, but she wouldn't tell me who. She just said it was a friend. So I went down there to make sure. You know, mother's worry. So I went down, and I saw the two of them pulling out of the restaurant in his car. She was gone for about four hours and then came home. Wouldn't talk about what they did or anything."

Yardley lifted Jordan's journal. "Ms. Russo, do you recognize this?"

"Yes. It's Jordan's journal."

"How do you know?"

"Her aunt, my sister, gave it to her for her birthday one year."

"Do you know your daughter's handwriting?"

"Yes, of course."

"Is it her handwriting in these journal entries?"

"Yes, it is."

"Did you give the journal to the police?"

"No. I couldn't find it. We looked everywhere for it and it just wasn't in the house. It makes sense he took it, I guess. I don't know why I didn't think of it at the time."

Yardley felt a stab of sympathy for her, that she would now have to imagine Wesley Paul searching Jordan's room. "Move for admission into evidence as prosecution exhibit fifty-four."

"Any objection?"

Wesley rose. "Your Honor, sidebar."

They approached. Yardley put her arm on the judge's bench as Wesley did the same. She could smell his scent, and it sickened her, so she took a step back.

"Your Honor, this journal was found by Ms. Yardley recently without anyone else to verify that's what occurred. Its veracity is deeply in question. I would object to its entry on hearsay grounds."

"It falls under the then-existing mental-and-emotional-state hearsay exceptions, Your Honor. You have Ms. Russo confessing her deepest emotions toward the defendant, expressing her mental state at the time around her death, which is what the exception was carved out for. I'm not introducing these journal entries as verification for truth of the matter asserted, just to get a sense of how she felt toward Mr. Paul at the time of the relationship."

Wesley said, "Ignoring the fact that not only didn't we have a relationship, I don't know who she was."

"Not knowing them never stopped you from killing someone before."

Wesley stared at her with venom, his mouth twisting in an ugly frown as the judge said, "I do find they fall under the then-existing mental state exception and will allow them into evidence. Please step back now."

They returned to their positions. Once the journal had been admitted, Yardley gave it to Isabella and said, "Will you please read the entry for January tenth of the year she was killed?"

Isabella opened the journal, flipped to the page, and began reading. "I'm so lucky to have met Wes. He's older than me and I first didn't like that 'cause he has wrinkles on his forehead. But now I think they're adorable. Funny how that changes when you get to know someone, huh? He's from Tennessee and I love his accent. He's got this smile that just warms my heart and he knows how to make me laugh and he's super smart. Probably the smartest person I've ever met. He teaches me so many things about the world and how it works. I just hope he doesn't get bored with me. I feel so stupid around him, like I don't know anything. I hope he knows that I have a lot of love to give and a lot of other good things besides being smart.

"We had—" Isabella had to stop for a moment. "We had sex the other night for the first time. He likes it more rough than I do but I didn't mind. It was different. I had a lot of bruises after and he choked me really hard and I had to wear a scarf for a few days at work. I told him I don't like it that rough and he apologized and said he would . . .'"

Isabella put the journal down.

"I'm sorry, Ms. Yardley. I can't keep reading this."

"It's okay," Yardley said, taking the journal. "The jury will be able to take it back and read it themselves." Yardley put her hand on Isabella's arm and said, "It's okay; you did great. Thank you."

Yardley took a transparent evidence bag off the table and brought it over to Isabella. "What is this, Ms. Russo?"

"It's Jordan's ring."

"Are you certain?"

"Yes," she said, taking the bag and examining the ring. "It has the inscription 'To My Bumblebee,' which was what her father called her."

Yardley introduced the ring and handed it to the jury to examine.

"Was she wearing it the day she disappeared?"

"She was. I saw it on her when she gave me a kiss before leaving."

"And it was found among Wesley Paul's belongings, correct?"

"Objection!"

"Withdrawn," Yardley said. "Thank you, Isabella."

Yardley sat down. She'd known that last question would be objected to, but she wanted the jury to hear where the ring had been found before putting Baldwin on the stand to explain about the lockbox.

Wesley stared at the woman on the stand, running his finger over his lower lip. Isabella sat with sunken shoulders, staring at the floor: a broken, defeated woman. Wesley had to be careful how he approached her.

"You wear glasses, Ms. Russo?" he said, rising.

"I do."

"Nearsighted or farsighted?"

"Near."

"So you have trouble seeing things from far away?"

"Objection, Counsel is testifying."

"Overruled."

"You may answer," Wesley said.

"Yes, some trouble."

"How far away was the person you claim to be me standing from you that first time you saw them?"

"Objection, calls for expert testimony."

"She knows how far things are, Your Honor."

"Overruled."

Wesley, with a hint of annoyance, said, "Go ahead, Ms. Russo. Answer the question."

"Oh . . . about twenty feet maybe. I was pulled close to the door."

"What was the weather like?"

"Objection, relevance."

Wesley sighed. "It's relevant to how clearly she could see, obviously."

"The objection is overruled."

"The weather, Ms. Russo," Wesley said.

"Sunny."

"Anything obstructing your view?"

"No."

"Do you have a history of mental—"

"Objection," Yardley said. "Relevance."

"Haven't asked it yet, Judge."

"Agreed. Overruled."

"Do you have a history of mental illness, Ms. Russo?"

"Objection, relevance," Yardley said.

"It's clearly relevant, Your Honor, in how Ms. Russo interprets what she sees. What if she has a history of hallucinations or delusions? Certainly I'm allowed to explore that."

"I'll allow it."

"You may answer," Wesley said. "Any mental illness?"

"No, not really."

"By 'not really' you mean—"

"Objection, calls for speculation."

"Overruled."

Wesley glanced back at Yardley and then continued, "I think what you meant to say was—"

"Objection, Counsel is testifying."

"Overruled."

Wesley hesitated a second and then said, "You meant you have some mental illness, correct?"

"It's not really a mental illness."

"What is it?"

"Depression."

"Chronic depression is a—"

"Objection, mischaracterizes the evidence. She never said 'chronic depression,' just depression."

"Sustained."

Wesley sighed and said, "How long have you had depress—"

"Objection, Counsel lacks personal or professional knowledge to ask about the duration of depression."

"Overruled."

Wesley glared at her a moment and then turned back to Isabella and said, "How severe is your depression?"

"It comes and goes. Sometimes not too bad and sometimes bad."

"By 'bad' do you mean—"

"Objection, vagueness."

"Overruled."

"Ms. Russo, by 'bad' do you mean—"

"Objection, beyond the scope of direct."

Wesley chuckled with just a hint of anger. "That is not an objection in the federal system, Your Honor. Ms. Yardley should've learned that in law school."

"The objection is overruled, Ms. Yardley."

Wesley adjusted the sleeve of his sports coat. His face had flushed a slight pink. "You have more than depression, don't you, Ms. Russo? Isn't it true—"

"Objection, compound question."

"Sustained."

"Ms. Russo, you have—"

"Objection, speculation."

"Overruled."

"Ms. Russo," he said calmly, "please tell this jury what other mental illnesses—"

"Objection, improper characterization."

"It wouldn't be improper if you'd let me finish a damn question!"

Wesley had raised his voice, his face red as he snapped at her. His brow furrowed with anger as he glared at Yardley. He had turned exactly in the direction of the jury, and they could get a good look at his face. When the anger faded enough for him to realize what he had done, he cleared his throat, swallowed, and said, "Judge, will you please instruct Ms. Yardley to only make relevant objections?"

"I cannot tell if they're relevant or not until the objection is made, Mr. Paul, but I'm happy to instruct on the importance of relevant objections if you like."

Wesley scowled at Yardley. She stared right back at him. Wesley sneered, away from the jury, and said, "That won't be necessary. No further questions for this witness."

72

The day ended at four, and before Yardley left, Wesley said, "That was particularly well played. She was a grieving mother, so even though the jury saw you were purposely interfering with my questioning, they thought it was to protect her and sided with you. I'm proud of you. Very clever."

She hung the strap of her satchel over her shoulder. "I couldn't care less what you think about anything, Wesley."

Baldwin waited for her near the doors, a grin on his face. When they got out into the hall, she said, "What?"

"What?"

"You have a mischievous grin on your face. Like a ten-year-old boy caught doing something bad."

"I just enjoyed that a lot more than I thought I would. He seemed completely in control until that moment."

"He has a temper, always has. I didn't notice it before because he attempted to control it around me, but looking back, I can remember glimpses of his real personality slipping out. I just wish I'd been paying more attention."

"We're not built to think the unthinkable about people. You did nothing wrong."

He walked her down to the parking garage and to her car. As she put her satchel in the back seat, he said, "Did you want to grab dinner?"

She paused and looked at him. "Cason . . . I'm not really at a spot in my life—"

"Whoa, whoa, before you finish that sentence and insult me, let me just tell you that I like you as a friend. And if all you want to be is friends, that's cool with me. But I don't even want to have that conversation right now. I can't imagine what you're going through with all this, and I'm sure *that* is the last thing you want to talk about, and it should be. Right now, I just want to make sure I'm here for you."

She smiled and squeezed his hand. "Thank you. I know you're here for me. But I need to prepare for tomorrow."

As she pulled away, she saw him watching her car leave the parking garage.

It was six in the evening when Yardley got the text she was waiting for: the forensic odontologist would be landing on a red-eye flight. In the morning, he'd go directly to the coroner's and perform the comparison to see if the teeth marks on Jordan Russo's right foot were a match to the retainer made from Wesley Paul's teeth.

Yardley nibbled a salad standing next to the sink. A pair of Tara's shoes sat by the front door. She still remembered the tiny boots she had bought as her first pair of shoes. Little gray moccasins for her chubby feet. It seemed so recent. Like she could reach out and touch the memory.

Money had been tight then, and Yardley had to choose between the boots and buying dinner for herself the next few days. She'd chosen the boots and eaten some peanut butter with a spoon until her next paycheck. She had never told Tara that story. Tara would never know the choice she'd had to make and how easy it had been for her to decide to not eat so that her daughter could have nicer shoes than the ones from the thrift store.

She washed the plate and put it away before going out to check the mail. The sun was still out, the sky light pink with a few scattered clouds like cotton. A neighbor of hers, an elderly woman, was out and stared at her. When Yardley waved to her, she turned away.

A few bills, a few advertisements, and a notice from the federal district court addressed to her. She opened it. It was a motion and order from Eddie Cal's attorney asking for a stay of his execution. The document exceeded fifty pages, but Yardley scanned enough to get the point: That there was new evidence exonerating Cal for the crimes he'd been convicted of. That Wesley Paul was the actual Dark Casanova, and evidence showed he had manipulated Cal into a position where a conviction against him and not Wesley was favored. Yardley's office had sent her a copy of the motion since she was prosecuting Wesley.

Nice try, Yardley thought.

At first it gave her a small satisfaction at how ridiculous the motion was. It stank of desperation. The hopelessness of an animal that knew it was going to die. But Yardley understood that in his spot, she would file the same motion. A sliver of hope to live was better than none at all.

It also confirmed to her the question of why Wesley had started the killings now. This motion was Cal's lifeline, and he needed new murders and a new Dark Casanova for it to have a chance at working. She had no doubt he had told Wesley he only needed a suspect, but in reality what he needed was a conviction.

She folded the motion, walked to the blue recycling bin in the driveway, and threw it in. She didn't have the energy to waste feeling bad for a monster.

Now the elderly woman had strolled over to her mailbox, which wasn't far from where Yardley stood. Despite the earlier discourtesy, Yardley said, "How are you?"

"Better than you." She input a code into the keypad on the mailbox and took out several envelopes. "You bring strange men into your bed, depraved things are bound to happen after. Sleep with dogs, you're bound to get fleas."

Yardley stared at her, then said, "Have a good night, Rochelle," before going into her house and shutting the door.

73

Yardley and Baldwin met the forensic odontologist in the lobby lounge of his hotel early the next morning to go over the exam and what would be happening in court if the bite marks matched Wesley Paul's retainer. He was a tall man, slim, with deep-set dark eyes and a poofy fluff of salt-and-pepper hair. The thin glasses on his nose kept slipping down.

Dr. Griffin Johnson had done this for over thirty years and needed little preparation for a trial. But Tim had been right about one thing: this was the primary piece of evidence in this case. It was the only direct evidence they had that Wesley had attacked Jordan Russo before her death. If the bite marks came back a match, Wesley would fight it with everything he had.

Yardley said, "I'd like you to testify today, but the judge may want to give Wesley time to go through your report. We can fly you out and then have you back on whatever day the judge schedules for your testimony, but I'd like to get you in today if at all possible."

He nodded. "What should I expect?"

"He's going to attack you with things you may have forgotten about."

He shrugged and pushed up his glasses. "I've had tough cross-examinations before. Nothing new."

Yardley glanced at Baldwin, who looked at her silently. "Is there anything in your past that an investigator might have turned up if he dug deep enough? Maybe criminal charges that were never filed? Past inaccuracies in testimony, drug addiction, mental illness, stays in mental health facilities, anything like that?"

Johnson interlaced his fingers on the table. "Not that I can think of, no."

Baldwin said, "He'll say that you're paid to be here and only testify for the prosecution. He's done that for every expert in this case."

"That's a simple rebuttal. I don't testify just for the prosecution. It's predominantly prosecution, merely because you have more work, but I have testified in dozens of trials for the defense."

"That's good," Yardley said. "We should probably mention that right as I'm introducing you."

"I think that's a good idea. We should likely discuss the recent advancements and criticisms of forensic odontology as well."

"Like what?" Baldwin said.

"There've been numerous recent studies calling into question the accuracy of the field. The problem is that skin is highly elastic, so bite marks can shift and display alterations due to the skin's movement. One study suggested that to be accurate, the bite mark must be analyzed in exactly the position the victim was in when the bite mark was made. Add to that the irregularities in the skin before the bite occurs at all, and you have good doubt as to the veracity of bite marks. What's different about this case is that the bite mark is in bone, something fixed and generally immutable. Far more accurate than a bite in skin. I should explain all that to the jury first thing."

Yardley looked to Baldwin, who raised his eyebrows, impressed.

She checked her phone. "The medical examiner is meeting you in an hour to take you to the morgue. Call me as soon as you're finished."

By the time Yardley sat at the prosecution table, a surge of confidence had swelled inside her. Wesley had adeptly attacked every witness, but the fact remained that the jury believed Isabella that she had seen Wesley and Jordan together. They believed Jordan's journal, ring, and hair had been found among his possessions, they understood that Jordan was sleeping with an older man named Wes from Tennessee who had a southern accent, and if Dr. Johnson was able to match Wesley's teeth to the marks embedded into Jordan's bone, they would have everything they needed for a conviction. Even with only an inconclusive finding for the teeth marks, explaining to the jury that she'd likely kicked him trying to crawl away and he'd bit her would add a bit of gruesome detail that would stick with the jury in the deliberation room.

Yardley glanced behind her. Baldwin wasn't there. The judge would be out in about five minutes. She should have received a text or a call an hour ago that the comparison had been completed. Yardley texted Baldwin and asked where he was.

She got a brief response:

Tell the court you need a delay. Johnson won't be testifying.

74

Yardley parked across the street from the hotel. She didn't get out right away. While she sat in here, it wasn't real. Not yet. Once she left the car, it would be real, and the feelings would barrel into her. Guilt most of all.

Police cruisers lined the curb, along with an ambulance and fire truck. Baldwin's car was there as well. Yardley went inside the hotel. Paramedics and EMTs hovered over a body in the lobby.

Baldwin spotted her and came over.

"What happened?" she said.

"They think it was cardiac arrest."

Yardley stared at the corpse. Corpses always looked smaller than the person had been in life. As if death immediately shrank the body, something lost when that last beat of the heart came and went.

"He was on his way to meet the ME," Baldwin said. "No one saw anything, no one heard anything. Wesley certainly is thorough."

"He has someone out here," Yardley said. She thought a moment. "The investigator."

Baldwin took out his phone and put in a call.

Without the bite mark evidence, was there enough to convict Wesley Paul? She couldn't be certain, and she needed to be certain.

"I'll have my cell on if you need me," she said to Baldwin before leaving.

"Where you going?"

"The jail."

———

Yardley watched as a guard led Wesley into the attorney-client meeting room and sat him down.

"Ms. Yardley," he said with a grin, "you are truly a sacred lotus among weeds. I cannot tell you how much it brightens my day to see you."

She looked to his cuffs and the chains that ran down to the shackles around his ankles, which were secured on a metal ring bolted to the floor. Yardley had purposely not brought in her purse. She lifted her blouse and ran her hands over her waistline and legs, showing him she had no recording device.

"Oh," he said, "so this is to be an intimate conversation? How tantalizing. Careful, though, everyone will think you still love me."

Watching him, the sneer on his face, the wrinkles by his eyes, the slope of his forehead, she realized that the veneer of charm he had built for her was no longer there. He had worn a suit of a human being, a human being she would relate to and love, and now the suit had come off, and only this *thing* remained.

"I have to hand it to you," she said. "The cold efficiency is just stunning. I thought you would want to prove how much smarter than me you are by beating me in trial on equal grounds, but I suppose it's much easier to kill a witness than cross-examine him. It was your investigator, right? Who is he really?"

He tilted his head slightly as he watched her. "How's Tara? Does she miss me? We had a bond, you know, she and I."

"She didn't have a bond with you. If you felt like she did, it was purely imagined, or she was pretending for my sake."

"And who are you pretending to be, Jessica? Fabricating this entire case against me doesn't seem like the Jessica Yardley I know."

A scar ran along his thumb, and she stared at it. It had happened in the kitchen at her home while he cut vegetables for a dinner they were hosting.

"You came here to see if I'd reveal anything about where Mr. Parker is. Surely you know me better than that, don't you?"

"I came here to tell you that your efforts were wasted. I'm going to convict you, Wesley. You killed Johnson to prevent him from testifying but also to scare me." She leaned forward. "You don't scare me. When I look at you, I see a frail little boy. A little boy who saw the death of his parents and then forced that pain on other children the rest of his life because he was too pitiful to overcome it. You couldn't even come up with your own method of killing. You had to steal Eddie's. You're pathetic."

His face went still as a statue, his eyes losing the shine they'd had upon first seeing her.

"You're weak, Wesley. You became exactly what those men that killed your parents wanted you to become. You're their offspring. It's them you honor with all this, not Eddie."

"You don't know shit about me and Eddie," he barked, the chains around his wrists rattling as his hands curled into fists and he brought them up to the table.

"Your parents were little more than trailer trash, wouldn't you say? Cooking methamphetamine in the basement while their child slept upstairs. Couldn't have been easy for you. I'm sure there were many days they forgot to feed or change you. Do you remember those days? The days you lay in your own waste, staring up at the ceiling, your stomach burning with hunger, just praying that your parents remembered you?

But you didn't exist to them, did you? Not until you had to mop up their blood."

He lunged for her. The chains held him back, but he grunted like an animal against them, and when he realized he couldn't reach her, he spit in her face.

She wiped the spit off with the back of her hand.

"Goodbye, Wesley. See you in court."

As she turned and left, she smiled.

75

Yardley, Wesley, and two marshals sat in Judge Aggbi's chambers. The judge slung her robe over a coatrack and retrieved a soda out of a minifridge before sitting down and putting her feet up on a footstool.

"I'd be happy to grant a short suspension of the trial, Ms. Yardley, in light of what's happened. But no more than a few days. You would need Mr. Paul's stipulation for any longer."

"That won't be necessary. The prosecution is prepared to continue without Dr. Johnson."

She nodded and looked to Wesley. "Mr. Paul?"

"Nothing's changed for me since the tragic death of Mr. Johnson. Health first, correct, Your Honor? When we don't have our health, we don't have anything. Sadly, a lesson many like Dr. Johnson learn too late."

Aggbi put the soda down, ignoring him, and said, "Then let's go ahead and resume. My understanding is you have two witnesses left before resting, Ms. Yardley?"

"Yes, Your Honor."

"Well, I think we can finish them today or tomorrow at the latest. Mr. Paul, how many witnesses will the defense be calling?"

"Just one, Your Honor. Dominic Hill. And I will not be testifying."

"Then I anticipate no more than three days before sending this to the jury. Thank you both. Let's head out there."

The marshals took Wesley out. Before Yardley could leave, Aggbi said, "Jessica?"

She turned. "Yes?"

"He's dangerous. And you might lose this."

"I know."

"What will you do?"

She looked out the only window in the judge's chambers. "Whatever I have to."

———

When the jury was recalled, Aggbi said, "Next witness, Ms. Yardley."

"Agent Cason Baldwin, please, Your Honor."

Baldwin strode to the stand. Yardley quickly went through his involvement in the case. The testimony was so quick he gave her a look several times that said, *What are you doing?* She wanted him off the stand as fast as possible.

Wesley cross-examined him much as he had done in the motion hearing, raising doubt as to his motives and suggesting he was simply doing a favor for Yardley, a former lover, in fabricating evidence for her. Maybe, she thought, that might've worked at the beginning of the trial, but now the jury had seen his rage. They would see his contorted face barking at her when they went back to that room to deliberate. Watching the jury, she didn't think they believed him anymore.

When Wesley was done, the judge said, "Ms. Yardley? Any redirect?"

"None, Your Honor. Agent Baldwin may be excused."

"Thank you, Agent Baldwin. Ms. Yardley, your next witness, please."

"The prosecution calls Mr. Dominic Hill to the stand."

Wesley's eyes widened, and he glanced back to the courtroom doors just as the marshal stepped out and called Hill's name. Wesley clearly hadn't expected her to call him.

Hill strolled through the doors in a suit and tie. He didn't look at anybody as he made his way to the stand. He was sworn in and sat down, glancing only once at Wesley. Yardley took the lectern.

"Name, please."

"Dominic James Hill."

"Mr. Hill, are you familiar with the defendant in this case, Mr. Wesley Paul?"

"I am, yes."

"Please tell us how."

He looked down and pulled lightly on his tie to straighten it before raising his eyes to hers again. "We met as kids in Santa Barbara. I think I was eleven and he was a few years older. I lived next door to a foster family he ended up living with."

"Describe your relationship to him."

"It was good. We became friends quickly, had a lot of mutual interests. Later we went to parties and played sports together, things like that. We moved out here after high school. We eventually lost touch, but we were close for a long time."

"Do you know what this case is about?"

"Yes. The murder of Jordan Russo about twenty years ago."

"Were you friends with Mr. Paul at that time?"

"I was."

"Ever have lunch at Telly's on Bluff Street around that time?"

"Multiple times."

"Anything of note ever happen there between you and the defendant?"

Hill inhaled deeply and then looked at Wesley. "Yes. Jordan Russo was our hostess there a few times. She and Wesley hit it off, and whenever we went back, he always asked for her by name and would spend some time up front talking to her. In fact, we began going there too much. The food wasn't bad, but I'm not one to enjoy eating the same things so often."

"Objection! This is ludicrous. I've never had lunch with this man in my life," Wesley snapped as he rose to his feet. "Sidebar, Your Honor."

"Of course."

Wesley was speaking before they were out of earshot of the jury.

"Your Honor, Mr. Parker interviewed Mr. Hill on my behalf just yesterday afternoon. This is absolutely *not* what Mr. Hill relayed to him. He was clear that he has never met me and has never seen me with Ms. Russo, and that it was his brother that murdered Jordan Russo and he feels guilty for the crime and is coming forward now to exonerate me."

"If he's lying," Yardley said, "Mr. Paul can cross-examine him on it. If the Court finds evidence of perjury afterward, our office would be happy to look into it."

"The objection is overruled," Aggbi said. "The proper time to discuss this is after your cross-examination, Mr. Paul."

Yardley saw the flush of pink in Wesley's face. He was getting too angry too quickly; he wouldn't be able to hold himself in check.

When she was back at the lectern, Yardley said, "Describe what you saw of their relationship."

Wesley's eyes never left Hill's. Absolute rage emanated from him now as he glared at Hill with a pure hatred that Yardley was certain the jury could see.

Hill said, "My understanding was that they began dating, or at least as close to dating as Wesley can get."

"What happened next?"

"He began having sex with her. I talked to him about it once, told him it was a bad idea. That she was too young for him. He said he had a lot of girls her age around—"

"Objection!" Wesley shouted, shooting to his feet. "Sidebar."

"You may approach."

Yardley stood close to the bench as Wesley stomped over. His face was red, his lips curling and uncurling as though tremors were going through them. He was losing control.

"Your Honor, he is perjuring himself at the behest of Ms. Yardley and making a mockery of the Court. I would ask that this witness's testimony be stricken and he be disqualified from testifying. This entire trial is an elaborate game put on by Ms. Yardley to convict me for a crime I did not commit."

"Ms. Yardley, have you influenced this witness to change his testimony today?"

"No, Your Honor. I simply told him to tell the truth. I've made a deal with Mr. Hill, and he will be granted immunity for his involvement with the death of Ms. Russo in exchange for his testimony today. Mr. Hill has never mentioned a brother in all of our conversations and informed me that he lied to the investigator to protect himself."

"Then I object on notice grounds. I received no notice that he would be testifying."

"He's your witness," Yardley said. "No notice required."

The two glared at each other, and Yardley didn't think it impossible that he would attack her right then. She took a step forward instead of back. The marshals would get to him in time before he did any real damage. The pain would be worth it to show the jury what he really was.

Wesley sensed what she was doing, took a deep breath, and said, "Your Honor?"

"I'm allowing his testimony, Mr. Paul. Please step back."

Yardley returned to the lectern and said, "Mr. Hill, what happened after Mr. Paul began sleeping with Ms. Russo?"

"He became . . . odd around her."

"Odd how?"

"Just began making inappropriate jokes, stuff like that. It's hard to remember because it was so long ago, but I remember a few things. Like he asked me once if I wanted to have sex with her. He said he would drug her and that I could come over at night and bring any friends if I wanted."

"Objection! He's lying under oath, Your Honor, because he and his brother killed this poor girl and have found a scapegoat. This is an absolute travesty of justice! You cannot allow this to go on."

"Mr. Paul, please refrain from objecting unless the objection deals with admissibility of evidence, not a witness's credibility. Credibility is for the jury to decide. Now do you have an evidentiary objection?"

His lip curled in a snarl, and he sat down.

"Did you have sex with her, Mr. Hill?" Yardley continued.

"No. I thought he was kidding. But looking back, he clearly wasn't."

"Objection, he could not know my state of mind."

"Sustained."

Yardley said, "So what happened as the relationship progressed?"

Hill shifted uncomfortably in his seat.

"I suppose," Yardley said, "this is a good time to mention this, Mr. Hill. I've offered you a deal in exchange for your testimony today, and we should get that on the record. What is that deal?"

"You said you would give me immunity in exchange for my testimony about what Wesley and I did to Jordan Russo."

She nodded. "And that deal is now on the record. Please continue. What happened?"

Hill inhaled through his nose and stared at Wesley, animosity bubbling between them. "He said he wanted something from her."

"What?"

"To see her die."

"Ridiculous!" Wesley said, jumping to his feet. The marshal behind him ran up. "You're lying, and she told you to lie!"

Aggbi said, "Mr. Paul, sit down immediately."

"I cannot just sit here and let this man make a mockery of this Court and the justice system I so love, Your Honor. He is lying through his teeth."

"And you will have your chance to ask him anything you like. Now please sit down."

Wesley glanced over at the jury and then sat.

Yardley continued, "He said he wanted to see her die?"

"Yeah. He said he has certain . . . needs. That there were things he needed in order to have a fulfilling sex life. And I should get this out there—I'm a convicted sex offender. I made mistakes, too. So I guess he thought we could commiserate or whatever."

"What did you do when he said he wanted to see her die?"

"I laughed. I thought he was joking. But then he didn't laugh with me, and I knew he was serious. He said he wanted my help."

"Help how?"

"He said he didn't want to be the one to pick her up. That it would be good if someone else picked her up, because if anybody saw, they'd be looking for that person, and that person could have a solid alibi when Wesley did the killing. Like, I pick her up and drop her off a block away where no one is around and then immediately go somewhere with cameras, a bank or whatever, so we can prove I didn't kill her."

"Why would you agree to help him, Mr. Hill?"

He cleared his throat. "I, um . . . I'd been sleeping with someone at that time. A younger girl. Sixteen. I have a long history of offenses— even back then I did. I have a certain psychological problem, and it's led me to a lot of trouble. Wesley didn't come right out and say it, but it was clearly implied that if I didn't help him, he would be placing a call to my probation officer at the time." He glared at Wesley. "We'd been friends since we were kids, and he was ready to sell me out in a second if I didn't do what he wanted."

"But you knew at this point he wanted to kill her, yet you still helped him."

"I just . . . I thought he wasn't serious about killing her. That I would pick her up and drop her off and they'd go have sex somewhere and laugh about it. I just didn't think he would go through with it."

"Now, Mr. Hill, you were supposed to have a solid alibi for the time of Ms. Russo's death, correct?"

"Yes."

"Do you?"

"Yes."

Yardley took out a few still photographs and approached him. "What are these?"

"These are pictures of me at the Vegas Downs Racetrack that I took."

"On what date?"

"February nineteenth of oh one, the day Ms. Russo disappeared. You can see I took the photos near the date-and-time ticker at the racetrack. I picked her up a little before eleven and then dropped her off at Wesley's car up the block before going to the racetrack. I spent half the day there."

"Move for introduction of exhibits sixty-six and sixty-seven, Your Honor."

"Objection!"

"On what grounds, Mr. Paul?"

Wesley stuttered. The anger had overwhelmed him and clouded his thinking. Yardley said, "Your Honor?"

"The exhibits are so admitted."

Yardley turned back to Hill. "What happened after you spent the day at the racetrack?"

"Wesley came down and met me outside in the evening. He seemed really happy, relaxed. I asked him what happened, and he said he'd done it."

"What did you take that to mean?"

"I took that to mean he'd killed her. I asked, too. He said she jumped out of his car when she realized what he was there to do, and he had to chase her down. When he got to her, he grabbed a rock and smashed in her head."

"How did he convince her to go out into a secluded section of desert with him in the first place?"

"She wasn't going to the gym—that's just what she told her mother. Wesley had told her he had a surprise for her out there, and she didn't fight at first." Hill glanced at Wesley. "He said the most enjoyable part was seeing her eyes when she realized why they were really there."

Wesley was on his feet. "This is a farce of everything our legal system stands for. You just vomited on every princ—"

"Mr. Paul," Aggbi said sternly. "I have given you several chances. Marshal, please remove Mr. Paul from the courtroom."

The marshals moved in. Wesley hurled his chair, and it slammed into a marshal's face. He lunged at Yardley. Her purse sat on the chair next to her, and her hand was already inside. She pulled out a canister of Mace and sprayed into his face. He shrieked as his eyes slammed shut, the room filling with the acrid stench of burning chemicals. Another marshal leapt over the defense table and tackled Wesley to the floor.

76

The Red Sun Motel consisted of two separate buildings that faced each other. The investigator, Parker, had rented a room in the farthest one from the street under a false name with another person's credit card. What he hadn't done was change the license plate on his rented car. A street-view camera at a toll station had snapped a photo of the plate, which they had a BOLO call out for, and they'd tracked down the motel he was staying at shortly after. Parker had a flight scheduled for three hours from now to Mexico.

Baldwin slipped on his Kevlar vest. Several officers were already at the motel and had circled the property. Two agents from the Bureau took point, and Baldwin stayed behind a moment until he was ready. He checked the magazine in his Glock.

The officers rounded the back, and Baldwin followed his two agents to Parker's door. He glanced into the window, but the curtains were drawn. They took their places by the side of the door, and an officer ran up with the battering ram.

Baldwin held up three fingers and counted down: three . . . two . . . one.

The door burst open as Baldwin shouted, "FBI!"

The first shot rang like a firecracker exploding in his eardrum. Parker sat on the bed with a rifle. One of the police officers standing next to Baldwin collapsed. Baldwin held his breath as Parker turned the rifle on him. Parker fired, and the shot went wide and blew into the wall.

Baldwin fired twice, both rounds entering Parker's head just above his right eye. He flew back onto the bed, the rifle flopping out of his hands. Baldwin kicked the rifle away. The blood flowed out of Parker like a stream and soaked the bed.

77

The next day the jury was recalled. Wesley had tried in vain to get a mistrial declared, but Yardley's arguments and case citations had confirmed what the judge already knew: the defendant couldn't simply ask for a mistrial because of their own misconduct; otherwise any defendant in any trial, sensing they were about to be convicted, could do something unexpected and trigger a mistrial.

Back in court, Hill finished his testimony, detailing how Wesley had shown him Jordan's ring and hair. Wesley attempted to cross-examine Hill, but he was now in cuffs and chains and had lost his composure. It was apparent to everyone in that courtroom that the jury was not listening to a thing he said.

Once Hill was excused, Aggbi turned to Wesley and said, "Any witnesses, Mr. Paul?"

"I guess not," he scoffed. "I suppose this is what justice is in this country now, right, Your Honor? Let a man get up there and lie through his teeth, let the government be complicit in it, and let an innocent man suffer for it. I assure you, Judge, this is not over, and the Ninth Circuit, not you or this jury, will be deciding my fate."

"So noted, Counselor. If there're no further witnesses, I'd like to take a break before we begin closing statements."

———

Deliberations varied in time. Yardley had one that had run eleven days, and she had one that had taken less than five minutes. As the jury was led away to the deliberation room after both sides gave their closing statements, she watched their faces. A female juror looked back to Wesley, and the disgust on her face couldn't have been clearer. Wesley noticed, too, and shouted, "What the hell are you looking at?"

Once the jury left, Yardley turned to him, a marshal there behind him, and said, "That wasn't good trial work, Wesley. That jury hates your guts."

"They're worthless tadpoles. This isn't over by a long shot. We'll battle this out in the appellate courts for years, and if there's even the slightest chance to do it, I will run this to the Supreme Court."

She slung her satchel over her shoulder. "Looking forward to it."

Baldwin waited for her outside of the courtroom. His hands were stuffed in his pockets, and his tie hung loosely around his throat. He looked tired.

"Rough day?" she said.

"You could say that. We found Parker. Not his real name, by the way. He was a former NYPD detective that served eight years in Sing Sing for attempted murder and racketeering. There were allegations he carried out a couple hits for the mob while still a cop. Looks like he was the guy you hired when you needed some dirt done." Baldwin glanced at his shoes. "He, um, didn't go quietly." He looked to the courtroom. "Wesley's really become unhinged."

"He knows he's going to be convicted. I also paid him a visit at the jail and brought up his parents and then told Hill to have a lot of eye contact with him during his testimony. He can control a lot about himself, but not his temper." She watched him as they walked. "Are you okay?"

He shrugged. "He shot first. I'll be all right. The Office of the Inspector General put me on paid leave until the shooting's cleared, so looks like I have some free time."

Yardley took his arm. "I think I'll take you up on that dinner, then."

78

The meal had finished, and Yardley and Baldwin strolled casually through a quaint neighborhood tucked away near some parks and an elementary school. They stopped at a little shop selling spiritual trinkets, and Baldwin bought her a mala bracelet of yellow and gold that the owner said brought protection. He put it on her wrist, and his touch lingered longer on her skin than it had to.

By the time they left the store, Yardley had received the call: the jury had a verdict. It had taken less than two hours.

Back in the courtroom, Wesley didn't even attempt to hide his disdain. He watched the jury file in with the contempt of a man watching his executioners. When the judge said to rise, he remained seated and spit onto the tabletop. Yardley hoped the judge wouldn't make a point about decorum by removing him; it would be best to just get through this.

"Will the foreman please rise?" Aggbi said. A man in a button-up shirt with gray hair rose. "It's my understanding you've reached a verdict?"

"We have, Your Honor."

The verdict form was passed to the judge, who read it silently and handed it back to the marshal before saying, "What says the jury in this matter?"

The man read from the verdict form.

"In the matter of the United States versus Wesley John Paul, a.k.a. Wesley John Deakins, on the sole count of murder in the first degree—"

Yardley's heartbeat drowned out all other sounds, and everything slowed to a crawl in her vision. She didn't want to move, but she also knew this was the moment she wanted to remember: watching only one thing while that verdict was read. She looked over to Wesley, and they stared into each other's eyes.

"—we find the defendant guilty."

The judge thanked them for their time and gave them some instructions on gathering their belongings. Yardley and Wesley stayed still. The marshal moved between them as the judge waited for the jury to leave before informing Wesley how sentencing was going to work, who he was going to meet with to prepare a sentencing report, and when they would be back.

"Forty-five days enough time, Ms. Yardley?"

"Plenty, Your Honor. Thank you."

Wesley's gaze didn't shift from her until one of the marshals forced him to look away as they dragged him back into the holding cells to be transported to the jail.

Yardley saw Isabella Russo sitting in the pews. Yardley thanked the judge and then went and sat by Isabella.

"That's it, then?" Isabella said.

"He'll file appeals, but they likely won't have any merit. Eventually, he'll exhaust his appeals, and he'll live in a cell until the day he dies."

Isabella nodded and took her hand. "I'm glad you got what you wanted, Jessica."

"This isn't what I wanted. What I wanted was a normal life to raise my daughter in. To give her a childhood she can look back on fondly."

"We can't always protect our children from men like him." She had a photo up on her phone, which she looked at. Jordan Russo hugging her mother at some sports event. "But I'm glad there's people like you to fight people like him."

They hugged, and then Isabella left. Yardley stayed in the courtroom after everyone had gone. She strolled over to the jury box and touched the wood banister in front of the seats. A grin came to her, and she inhaled deeply, wanting to remember the scent of the courtroom at this moment, and then she left.

79

Yardley jogged through the canyons near her home, a dust storm whipping her face as she descended the mountain back toward civilization. Tara texted her and asked if she could sleep at a friend's house tonight.

Tara had come back from the ranch to take some placement exams for entrance into the UNLV mathematics program. She had tested at the doctoral level and was allowed into the PhD track, the youngest student ever admitted to a doctoral program in the state.

Yardley had asked for a hiatus from the US Attorney's Office, and Lieu had granted it. She would be leaving for the ranch tomorrow with her daughter.

What she remembered most about the Cals' ranch was a cold mist in the mornings that burned away quickly. The crisp air filled her lungs with an icy sting, and she liked the sensation of numbness in her face. She looked forward to leaving the neon and exhaust of Las Vegas.

Eddie's mother, Betty, had once told Yardley that her son had loved the cold morning mists as a child, and she would frequently find him wandering around the nearby forest by himself. She'd said it with a sad fondness, as though he'd been out there collecting flowers. Yardley imagined him doing much more sinister things, hidden by fog and trees like a camouflaged predator.

The Cals had a guesthouse, which they offered to Yardley and Tara. Yardley had accepted, but it would only be temporary—she knew she wouldn't leave Las Vegas behind. Not yet. But she'd let Tara decide for herself. It gave her a raw anguish to think of life without her, but the Cals were elderly, and she wanted Tara to have as much time with them as possible. Steven had informed her that they were leaving everything they had to Yardley, and she'd told them to leave it to Tara instead.

Yardley stopped her run and cooled down with a slow walk. She checked her phone and saw a photo had been sent to her by Oscar Ortiz. Emilia at her second birthday party, with a text that said, Sorry, but plan on getting pics all the time. It made Yardley smile.

Not long after Wesley Paul's trial, Yardley had pushed the US Attorney's Office and the FBI to go house to house again and put up flyers everywhere they could between Ortiz's home and Wesley's condo. She'd constantly harassed every reporter and news anchor she could to get Emilia more airtime and had even secured a half-hour special about her disappearance on a cable news network.

The FBI helped as much as they could, but resources were slim, and the search was a massive undertaking. On top of that, nobody but Yardley seemed to believe Emilia was still alive.

Yardley put together volunteers to help in the search in her spare time, and Tara began a social media campaign that provided more. Soon, they had over two hundred people knocking on doors and hanging flyers in the evenings and on weekends.

A woman living twenty minutes from Wesley's condo saw one of the flyers and called the police. She was a single mother who ran a home day care and told the police she had been paid $7,500 by a young girl's father to watch her for a couple of months. The father had stated he had an emergency trip to Europe for work. After two months and no word, she'd attempted to reach him. His phone number had no longer worked, and the home address he'd listed didn't exist. She'd been too scared to contact the police because she didn't have legal immigration status, something Wesley had no doubt counted on.

The woman said the father had contacted her a month before dropping the baby off and made the arrangements, telling her he could get the call to leave at any moment.

She hadn't known what else to do with the child, so she'd kept her, hoping the father would return.

The woman identified Wesley Paul in a lineup as the man that had dropped Emilia off. The US Attorney's Office had filed kidnapping charges against him, and the case was still pending.

Ortiz had been allowed to keep his badge. He'd been transferred to the bank fraud division, where he would be sitting behind a desk all day, and Baldwin had told her that Ortiz couldn't have been happier for it.

Wesley Paul's planning and attention to detail stunned the FBI. It didn't stun Yardley. She just wished he had put a mind like that to a different use.

Wesley was the last monster haunting her, but he was only there because of the first.

She showered after her run and drove to the prison.

When she got there, she sat quietly, staring at the building for a long while.

Yardley had gotten permission from Warden Gledhill to use the warden's office for this meeting. The warden's office had no recording devices and was soundproofed, so no one could hear what was said. But the reason she wanted it was that it had a lot of light coming from several windows, and Yardley didn't want to be in a dungeon again with Eddie Cal.

She stood at the window overlooking the parking lot, watching the way the sunlight danced off the windshields of the cars in the lot. Glinting like a secret wink. She heard the door open and the rattle of chains.

Eddie Cal sat in front of her. He seemed thinner and had let his scruff grow back. He grinned at her as she sat down across from him.

"How's Tara?" he said.

"She's well. We'll be leaving tomorrow to see your parents and staying there awhile."

"And you came here just to see me before you left? I'm flattered."

Yardley reached into her satchel and took out a digital recorder. She hit play, and Wesley's and Cal's voices came on, discussing the details of Cal's crimes.

"Wesley recorded the conversations you two had in here. I found several of these in his condominium in a little space he'd carved out in the floor of the kitchen. We found the DVDs of the Dean and Olsen murders there. It was really difficult to find, actually. The FBI had to use a probe because there was no indication the floor had been tampered with. We found a lot of photographs of me and Tara, as well. Some journals he'd filled with notes while he watched us through the years." She sighed. "So many lives ruined, Eddie, just to give you a slim chance at an appeal. Those families deserved better than to die for you to maybe have a little more life."

"His parents died in a very similar way. Perhaps in time he would have picked it up without me." He rested his forearms on his thighs as he leaned forward and glanced at some papers on the warden's desk. "I didn't tell him to do that to the children, though. I also said he was to protect you and Tara, never harm you."

"You knew he was unstable," she said, "but you still asked him to watch me. What if he decided to kill me and Tara? Would you have felt any remorse? Would you have felt anything?"

He blinked but said nothing.

"The only reason I'm here, Eddie, is to let you know that I'm going to do everything in my power to make sure your execution isn't stayed. I won't let you disgrace those families by using their deaths like this. You'll be dead by the end of the year, and there's nothing you can do about it."

She rose to leave, and he said, "You think he was the only one? I told you, I have a lot of fans."

She folded her arms, staring into his eyes, and thought that if there was any justice, Isaac Olsen would grow up in a world where Eddie Cal and Wesley Deakins were both dead.

"They can't help you now," she said.

He smiled. "There's one that can. She just doesn't know it yet."

She scoffed, "I wouldn't help you if my life depended on it, Eddie."

"I wasn't talking about you."

She held his gaze just a little longer and hoped it would be the last time she would see those eyes, the eyes she had so easily fallen in love with, that she only saw now in dreams that would wake her trembling in cold sweats.

"Goodbye, Eddie."

80

Yardley had some paperwork to submit to the court on a few ongoing cases before she could relax for the much-deserved hiatus going into effect tomorrow. In her years at the office, she had never taken a single vacation.

As she drove from the prison, she kept replaying what Cal had said. *There's one that can. She just doesn't know it yet.*

He'd said it with a smile, as though it was a secret shared between them. It had given her chills, a frigid unease that grew the more she thought about it.

It was the *she* that made Yardley uncomfortable.

She pulled over onto the side of the road and sat there with her hazard lights on. She could go to the ranch tomorrow and never think about this again, or she could follow through with the thought that wouldn't leave her alone.

Yardley pulled back onto the road and flipped a U-turn.

———

Isabella Russo worked as a schoolteacher in an elementary school near her home. It was a flat building surrounded by palm trees and a soccer field with fake grass. Yardley waited in her car in the parking lot for a long while, her stomach in knots, a lump in her throat that made it hard to breathe.

What are you doing here, Jessica?

It would take five minutes, and the unease would go away. It was worth five minutes to know for certain.

Inside the school, the ceilings were low and the walls plastered with announcement flyers, art projects, posters, and class photos. She asked the main office where Isabella's class was, and the receptionist directed her to the end of the hallway.

Yardley stood at the door and watched. The third graders were practicing multiplication tables. A sea of young faces with innocent, glimmering eyes. Isabella saw her and smiled.

"I'll be right back," she told the class, then asked her teaching assistant to take over. She came out into the hall and gave Yardley a hug.

"How are you?" Yardley said as they hugged.

"I'm doing good. I saw you on the news the other night. They had a story on about you and that missing little girl. I'm so glad she was found."

"Me too." She glanced to the classroom and saw that several children were watching them. She took a few steps back so no one could hear, and Isabella followed. Yardley folded her arms.

"I hate to even ask this, but I just want to get it out of the way, and you will never see me again."

A look of concern came over Isabella as she said, "What is it?"

"When you identified Wesley in the lineup . . . you were so certain. There was no doubt in your mind."

"You don't forget the face of your daughter's murderer."

"You didn't know he was her murderer when you saw him back then. And it's been twenty years, Isabella. No one can be that certain of a face they saw for a few seconds after twenty years."

Isabella looked away. "It's him. We both know it's him."

Yardley watched her in silence until she looked up again and their eyes met. "Did someone show you a picture of Wesley before the lineup?"

Isabella swallowed. She looked back toward her classroom. "I need to get back."

"Was it Agent Baldwin? Isabella, look at me . . . this is really important. Did Agent Baldwin show you a photograph of Wesley before the lineup and tell you he was the one that murdered your daughter?"

She shook her head. "No. It wasn't him."

"But someone did."

Isabella's eyes drifted to the floor. "I need to go."

Yardley lightly touched her wrist, getting her to look up again. "Who was it?"

"They helped me remember more quickly. That's all. I would've remembered him whether they showed me a picture or not."

"Who was it, Isabella?"

She debated in silence and then finally said, "If I tell you, you have to promise me it stays between us. They helped me lock away the man that killed Jordan. I won't let them come to any trouble."

Yardley glanced at the teaching assistant, who said something that made the class laugh. She turned back to Isabella, who held her gaze steadily now. She was serious: she wouldn't tell her who it was unless Yardley promised nothing would happen to them. It was possible she could find out on her own somehow, but it was also possible she would never know.

"I promise," Yardley finally said.

She nodded. "I don't know her name. She never said. But she came to my house and showed me a picture of Wesley Paul. She said this was the man that murdered Jordan. She said if I told anybody she had shown me the picture, I wouldn't be able to testify against him and he would get away with it, but she wanted me to know that this was for certain the man . . ." Isabella swallowed, and her eyes began to wet with tears. "That this was for certain the man that killed my little girl." She took a tissue from her pocket and dabbed at her eyes. "She said he's killed a lot of people and if I couldn't identify him, he was going to get out and kill a lot more. Maybe even my daughter, because he might think it would be amusing to kill Jordan's sister."

Yardley felt faint. Weakness in her knees made her aware she might not be able to stand anymore.

She could leave—say goodbye right now and never know. She could live with it. It would be something unsaid between them, but she could live with it.

"What did she look like?" Yardley nearly whispered.

"A teenager. Maybe fourteen or fifteen. She looked a lot like you, actually, but she had really blue eyes. The bluest eyes I think I've ever seen."

81

Tara was still six weeks away from having a driver's license, so she took an Uber to the courthouse. Tomorrow, she would be leaving with her mother for her grandparents' ranch, the place in the world she loved most. But today, she had something to do. Something she'd been looking forward to.

She hadn't wanted to look out of place in the courtroom, so she'd worn a pair of her mother's heels—they pained her with each step, and she wondered why women put themselves through it—and she'd bought a blouse and long skirt from a thrift store. She wore glasses and had her hair in a tight bun. Glancing into the rearview mirror before getting out of the car, she figured she looked at least nineteen.

She got through the metal detectors without setting them off and went up to Judge Milton Hartman's courtroom. The first case on the calendar was Wesley Deakins. A hearing to schedule his appeals.

Wesley sat at the defense table, waiting for the judge to come out. He appeared pale and had lost a lot of weight. He looked unhealthy. Like someone that had been ill for a long time.

Tara sat directly behind him in the pews, close enough that she could lean forward and whisper to him.

"How is prison treating you?"

Wesley turned around, then chuckled. "The younger Ms. Yardley. What are you doing here? Come to see the first hearing on my many appeals, or did you just miss me?"

"You're really pale, Wesley. I used to think you were handsome, but you look sick now."

"Prison can do that to you. Not much sleep. Though I'm fortunate to have a cell to myself. One small concession for my services. The guards need legal help from time to time."

"Sounds like you're right where you belong."

He grinned. "Did your mother send you? My first appellate brief hasn't been accepted by the higher court yet. Is she attempting to use you to garner information about it? I know she doesn't want me free, but using you is a bit excessive, don't you think?"

"She doesn't know I'm here."

His head tilted slightly. She could smell him, his body odor and the prison jumpsuit that had soaked up his sweat and hadn't been washed.

"Then why are you here?"

"I'm here because you have hope, Wesley. And you don't deserve hope."

"What does that mean?"

A bailiff glanced at her, and she stayed quiet until his attention went somewhere else.

"When my father sent me to Dominic Hill, convincing him to lie about you and Jordan Russo wasn't the hard part. He's just some crazy idiot obsessed with my father, like you. If Eddie told him to kill himself, he would ask if he wanted it done with pills or a gun."

She watched the realization dawn on his face. "The real tricky part, Wesley, was putting Jordan Russo's hair and ring with your stuff my mom put in storage. I didn't want anybody to see me in there, so I had to take my mom's keys while she was asleep and go down there. I didn't want the hair and ring just out anywhere, and then I remembered that cigar box that was on your desk. I had to open it without damaging it, so I was going to take it to a locksmith, but you wanna hear something crazy? The day before, I found a lockpick on my mom's desk. It was just sitting there. I don't even know why she had it. Opened the box in a second. It's like fate, really."

Wesley's face contorted into a grimace, his eyes fixed on her with a growing hatred. It delighted her.

"You're lying." He said it without his southern accent, and Tara could see why he had picked it up. His real voice reminded her of a weasel. It didn't match his face.

"Do I look like I'm making this up?"

He watched her awhile. "How did you get the ring and hair?"

"Jordan Russo was my father's first victim. They were going hiking the day she was killed, and my father had left a notebook out in the back seat. She reached back there to get something and saw the notebook. It had a lot of different drawings for torture rooms and what he would do with some of the body parts of the women he killed, addresses of potential victims, things like that. But the page it was open on was a drawing of her bedroom that showed her in bed with her throat cut. You know how amazing an illustrator my father is, so she knew it was her." She paused and looked out one of the windows. "He said Jordan looked at him, and without them saying a word, she just *knew*. She knew it with such certainty she actually jumped out of a moving car."

Someone came by and said something to an attorney, and Tara waited until they left before speaking again.

"He kept some of her hair and the ring. He was worried about the police finding out about their relationship, so he snuck into her house and stole her journal, which mentioned his name a bunch of times."

Wesley fully turned to her now. His eyes had narrowed to slits. She could smell his bad breath.

"Do you know how hard it is to copy an entire journal, Wesley? To have to mimic somebody else's handwriting for that long? I still feel the ache in my hands. Luckily she didn't write in it that much, and I'm ambidextrous and could switch it up. I think I did a pretty good job, don't you? All I did was change *Eddie* to *Wes* and add a few details about you, but I thought I should redo the entire journal so it all looked the same. Then I had to blot the ink with coffee and heat it in the sun a couple hours to fool lab tests into thinking it was much older than it was. You really should've had someone try to date the ink, though. That was just sloppy lawyering."

He was silent a long while and then burst out laughing. "Hilarious. What is this? Last little jab at me before you and your mother go riding off into the sunset? It won't work. Those appeals will be argued, and I'll subpoena Dominic Hill to—"

"Dominic Hill is halfway across the country. Actually, that's not even his name anymore. You will *never* find him. And without him, the only thing you have is his testimony at your trial saying you killed Jordan Russo." She glanced around and saw a young couple in the front row across the room, absently staring at the judge's bench. The woman had bloodshot eyes from recent crying.

"You know what I do feel a little bad about? Lying to Isabella Russo. She seemed like a nice lady, and now she thinks you killed her daughter. But the real killer is sitting on death row, so what's the difference, I guess, right?"

"No," he said in almost a whisper. "You couldn't do this."

"You have to hand it to Eddie, though. You're the perfect idiot for him to use. He said you didn't even hesitate. As soon as he asked you to start killing, you did."

"No. Eddie wouldn't do that to me. He loves me."

"He thinks you're pathetic. He used you. He needed you to start killing so he could argue on appeal that the Dark Casanova was still out there. He didn't care if you were convicted, but he owed me, and I wanted something to bury you with. He told me where he kept a lot of things the police never found."

He swallowed, and his eyes filled with fury as he said, "I will destroy you. I will bring all this out on appeal, and you and your mother are going to be the ones in a cell."

"Destroy me with what, Wesley? Hmm? Dominic Hill will never be found. Isabella Russo's not going to help you. When your investigator reaches out to her, she'll say she doesn't want anything to do with the case. You'll have to subpoena her, and my mom's office will quash that subpoena because of harassment."

She stared off at the judge's bench and at the seal of the state of Nevada that hung behind it.

"You did surprise me with the dentist, though. My father said they would exhume her body and find the bite marks they missed last time. I was worried about that, but he said it'd been so long that the comparison would come back inconclusive. I wonder, though, if he actually knew you would kill the dentist? I mean, if you knew the entire case was set up to convict you for something you didn't do, you had to expect that the dentist would testify that the bite marks were a match to you, right?"

Wesley said nothing, his eyes cold.

"I feel bad about that, but how could I predict you would kill him?" She took a deep breath. "All that death because of a pathetic rat like you."

The bailiff announced the judge, who came in a second later. Everyone rose except for Tara and Wesley.

Tara leaned close to him, staring into his pupils, and whispered, "Did you honestly believe I would ever let anyone hurt my mother again?"

He jumped at her, and she quickly leaned back. Wesley fell across the pew. The rattling of his shackles echoed in the courtroom as the bailiff lunged at him and slammed into his back. Another one sprinted over from the front entrance of the courtroom. They grabbed Wesley's arms and twisted them behind his back, causing him to howl in pain as they hauled him away. She thought he sounded like a frightened pig.

Tara casually walked out and left the courthouse. The grin never leaving her face.

ACKNOWLEDGMENTS

I wrote my first short story in fifth grade, and through the decades I have worked with a lot of different people in the book industry. None have been as cool to work with as everyone at Thomas & Mercer and Amazon Publishing. Special thanks to Megha for constantly pushing to make me a better writer, to Kjersti for taking a chance on me, and to Gracie and Sarah for always making me feel welcome and appreciated. I could never thank you guys enough.

And of course thank you to my readers; you can never know how truly grateful I am to you.

ABOUT THE AUTHOR

At the age of thirteen, when his best friend was interrogated by the police for over eight hours and confessed to a crime he didn't commit, Victor Methos knew he would one day become a lawyer.

After graduating from the University of Utah School of Law, Methos sharpened his teeth as a prosecutor for Salt Lake City before founding what would become the most successful criminal defense firm in Utah.

In ten years Methos conducted more than one hundred trials. One particular case stuck with him, and it eventually became the basis for his first major bestseller, *The Neon Lawyer*. Since that time, Methos has focused his work on legal thrillers and mysteries, earning a Best Novel Edgar nomination for his title *A Gambler's Jury*. He currently splits his time between Southern Utah and Las Vegas.